THE COURTING SEASONS

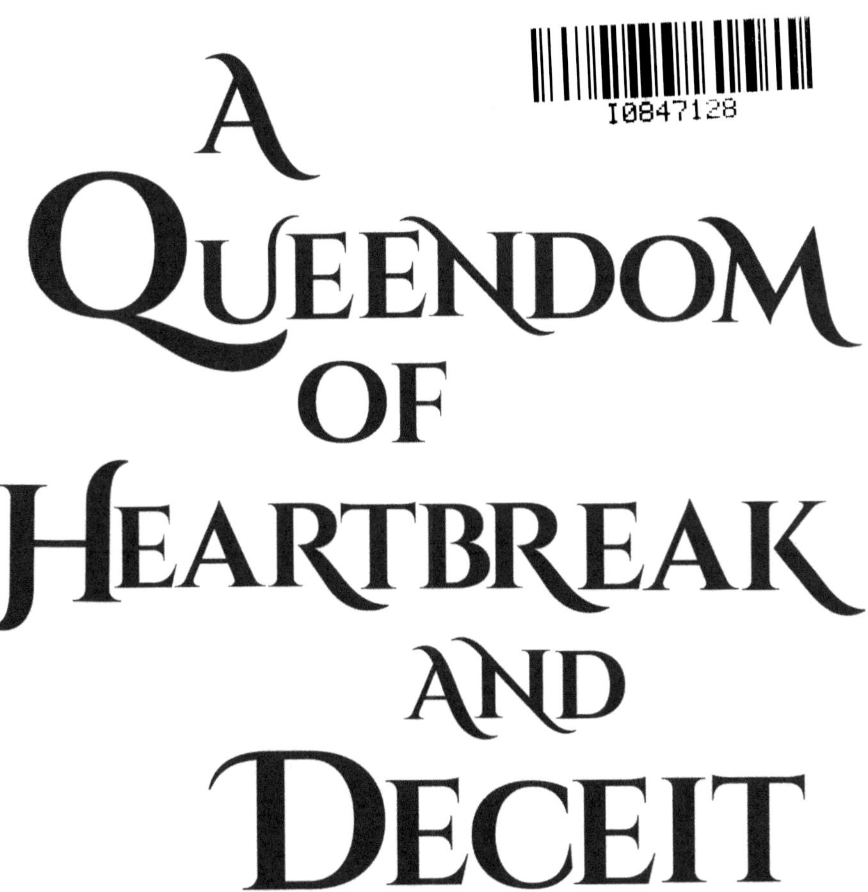

A Queendom of Heartbreak and Deceit

N. F. SCHMITT

Dedication

To my husband, Cody.

Books by N.F. Schmitt

The Courting Seasons

A Kingdom of Promises and Lies

A Queendom of Heartbreak and Deceit

A Queendom Book 3 – *To be Determined*

A Kingdom Book 4 – *To be Determined*

FaeVille

Kierian

Tennyson - *To be Determined*

Erilea - *To be Determined*

KINGDOM
SHEDIWARK
KINGDOM
T'CUDTER
KINGDO
THEORI
QUEEND
GREWT'

KINGDOM HAYVERTON
KINGDOM T'LOVONESS

PRONUNCIATION GUIDE
Monarchies:

Grewt'en: Groot-N

Hayverton: Hay-Ver-Ton (or) Have-Er-Ton*

Shediwark: Shed-E-Wark (or) Shed-Uh-Wark*

T'Cudter: Tu-Cud-Ter

Theorines: Theo - Rhines

T'Lovoness: Ta-Love-Oh-Ness

**Depends on monarchy of how they pronounce it*

CHARACTERS:

Amity Lovanna: A-muh-tee Luhv-ah-nuh

Deveroux Theox: Deh-Vr-Oo Th-Ox

Eloise: El-Oh-wheeze

Esame: Ez-Uh-May

Fairness: Fair-Ness

Finch Azrael: Finch Ahz-ree-uhl

Gideon Orion: Gi-Dee-Uhn Oh-rye-uhn

Grace Lily: Grace Lil-lee

Iryse Skyvien: Er-Reese Skiv-E-N

Killien Knox: Kill-E-N Knocks

Lydia: Li-Dee-Uh

Montgomery Victory: Mont-Gum-Er-Ree Vik-Tr-Ee

Myrese: Mehr-Reese

Olivia Jade: Oh-Liv-E-Uh Jade

Opal: Oh-Puhl

Percival Chivarly: Per-civ-val Chiv-Er-Lee

Persamina Rowena: Purse-A-Mean-A Rowe-N-A

Rachelle Mortese: Rah-Shell More-Teese

Rafael Baylor: Raf-A-L Bay-Lore

Regalius Baylor: Reh-Gale-E-Us Bay-Lore

Regina Isadora: Reh-Jean-Uh Iz-Uh-Door-Uh

Rohanna Mrycella: Roh-Ahn-Nuh Mer-Sell-Uh

Serenity Novena: Sir-Ren-Nit-Tee Nuh-vee-nuh

Stella: Stell-Uh

Tearani Ryver: Tear-Ron-Knee River

Tiviola: Tiv-E-Oh-La

Voltaire Edric: Vole-Tear Ed-Rick

NICKNAMES:

Irysey: Ers-See

Livvy: Liv-Vee

Mina: Mean-Nuh

Monty: Mont-Tee

Nitty: Knit-Tee

Reggie: Redg-Gee

PETS:

Pumpking: Pump-King

Sugarplum: Shu-gar-Plum

Chapter One

My giggles filled the horse stable rafters. It was late morning, and the promise of warm summer days lingered in the crisp spring air. We knew we should be quieter, but I couldn't help myself. Held in his arms, I felt happy. Yet, with the nagging fear of being caught, excitement zinged through me. Falling in love with the stable boy had never been my intention, but here I was, hopelessly and deliriously in love.

If my mother had been a maid, my secret romance wouldn't need to remain hidden. Instead, she had been born a Lady – and not just any Lady, but the heir to Wyndmeer Manor. While I was not the eldest daughter, my family's history still came with expectations to uphold.

For months, I had been researching through our library's archives, trying to build a rational argument as to why Theo and I belonged together. Every day, I spent countless hours reading, trying to find a moment in history when another lady married below her rank. Time, however, was not on my side. With each passing day, I feared I was another step closer to being caught.

"You have that far-off look again," Theo murmured, trailing kisses from my cheek to my neck. A soft moan escaped from my lips, and that was all it took to break the spell. I disentangled myself from his strong arms. Mornings were too active in the stables —had it been dusk, I would have chanced it longer.

Theo's hands grasped my hips, yanking me back to him. He kissed me deeply, and in a moment of weakness, I gave in. Wrapping my arms around his neck, I pulled him closer to me, needing more of him.

I never had noticed Theo much before. He had always been a scrawny boy covered in stable dust and dirt soiling his clothes. It wasn't until the year I turned seventeen that he caught my eye. I had recently been gifted Clover, my mare, as a birthday present. Normally, the main stablemaster prepared my family's horses, but he had been under the weather that day.

Instead of the appropriate stable hand attire of black pants, a white ruffled shirt with a red string tied in a bow around the neck, and hair neatly tied back, Theo had left little to the imagination. His muscular chest glistened with a layer of sweat, leading down to a pronounced v-dip that disappeared into the loose black pants that hung off his hips. He still wore the red string around his neck as if he were a present, waiting for me to unwrap.

Theo had given me a devilish, knowing smile as his honey-brown eyes roved over my body, and I couldn't stop thinking about him. I had been flustered the entire time I rode Clover, anticipation building as I neared the stables, eager to see him again. When had Theo gone from a mangy, stable boy always under everyone's feet to someone causing my heart to pitter-patter? How had I never noticed him changing?

Two days later, when I mounted Clover, he slipped the first flower in my hand, a single red rose. He winked when I looked at him, taken by surprise by the gift. It wasn't until I had ridden out of sight that I brought the flower to my nose. I lingered longer on my ride that day, spending more time smelling the flower and thinking of the handsome male waiting for me than I did focusing on the ride. I had kept the rose, drying the petals to stay preserved. It currently laid, protected, in my nightstand drawer.

A horse nickered outside, and once again, I was pushing him away. Theo was an intoxicating addiction, and I was the fool who kept tempting fate with all these dicey chances.

"We need to stop, or else we will be caught," I rushed out in explanation as he reached for me again. I put my hands up and walked backward to put distance between us. When I felt I was far enough away, I glanced to where my discarded book lay next to the chair I had been occupying before Theo distracted me. I bent down to retrieve it, dusting away the debris clinging to it.

"Everyone is out doing chores; we have a little while," Theo attempted to persuade me, but I shook my head.

I was about to reply when the alert horse neighed loudly—someone was coming. We didn't blink an eye; Theo grabbed a nearby pitchfork, and I flipped open my book to a random page. Seconds later, my Father strolled through the stable doors. His gaze landed on me, and I pretended to be completely immersed in my book.

"Ah, there you are, Serenity," he said by way of greeting. I feigned a startled jump as I looked up at him.

"Hello, Father," I replied with an innocent smile. My pulse raced with a mixture of exhilaration and fear from almost being caught. "How are you today?"

"Have you been here all morning?" He asked, ignoring my question as he eyed the book in my lap.

"Yes, Father," I coolly lied while uncrossing my legs to smooth out the minimal wrinkles from my dress.

"I will never understand why you choose to read in the stables when there is a perfectly good library and other places within the manor to read." He glanced over at Theo, who paid us no mind while mucking the horse stalls. I crinkled my nose from the fresh smell of horse dung that he scooped. I doubted Father suspected anything.

"It is the only place I can receive a moment of peace. My sisters know where to find me within the manor." This was not an outright lie. While my older sister wasn't afraid of horses, the younger two were. A fear I had not quite grasped, considering they each had their own horse and the beasts were quite docile. As a child, I had never wanted to be away from my horse.

"Speaking of sisters," Father began, "Amity has been looking for you."

"What does she want *this* time?" I huffed with a roll of my eyes. The mention of my older sister was the quickest way to damper my mood.

"That is between the two of you." He raised an eyebrow at me and then glanced at the book in my lap again. "What are you reading today?"

I rose from my seat, bringing the book with me. "History of the Six Monarchies by Ser Rylei Doaka of House Kalka. I only began it today." I crossed the space between us, anticipating to preen under his compliments.

"Ah, a dull read but the most accurate on the topic. Bit of a long read as well." He glanced at the book cradled to my chest. *The History of the Six Monarchies* was quite thick at over eight hundred pages. It was filled with in-depth knowledge along with beautifully penned illustrations for house banners, symbols, plants, and whatever else the artist desired to draw.

"I do not know if I would call it dull. It can be quite fascinating," I countered. After all, I was only three hundred and some odd pages deep in it.

"Fascinating?" He chuckled. "Only you would find it fascinating. Tell me, why are you interested in reading all the historical texts? Your sisters prefer their romance novels, and your brothers never read unless I was forced them."

I laughed, shaking my head and waving my hand, aware of how different I was from my siblings. We left Theo alone in the stables and walked together along the stone path to the manor's side entrance. The flowers along the way were beginning to bloom; a few butterflies and bumblebees flitted between them.

"I like comparing the texts; it helps me find similarities and where each author focuses their efforts. For example, Taurok focuses more on the way of living for the classes, while Blaisi takes an interest in trade. Kakda has a fascination with the death of each royal family and their houses. She even goes into a bit of detail about how to make the specific poisons."

"Should I bar you from the kitchens?" Father jested, cutting me off. "Will you be making your own poisons, Daughter?" He raised his eyebrow in amusement.

I laughed again. "No, no. As I was saying, Father, each historian has a predominant focus—some in-depth, others surface-level. I am collecting each reading to layer together. I want to understand the ultimate history of them all." I felt the passion bubbling up within me. What started as a simple task to find Ladies who had married below their rank had now molded itself into something that exhilarated me.

"And what do you plan to do with the knowledge of all this history that no one has done prior to you?" Father's eyes twinkled. He delighted in watching me be more than a simpleton.

"I want to write the most completed history book of all time with a combination of all of these texts, minus the fluff," I replied.

"Fluff?" He questioned, his expression amused to see where I was taking this.

"Blaisi goes on and on for paragraphs—sometimes pages—about what the trader's travels were like. I am not interested in the great details of storms that prevented sea travel or how broken wagon wheels came about. That, Father, is fluff."

"Ah, I see now. Yes, Blaisi can be quite extensive in his details, but what better way than to understand the issues that merchants, traders, and travelers deal with on a regular basis? You were fortunate enough to be born as a Lady's daughter and to never have to know these struggles."

I simply smiled and nodded at his admission. I knew these were one of those times that if I goaded Father, it would have turned into a lecture instead of a fun debate.

Instead of knocking, I barged into Amity's office. Father had left me at the foot of the stairs to go about his own business. Coward. That was a lie. Father wasn't a coward, but with Amity being the head of the family, his hands were tied on whatever she needed me for. Sometimes, I wondered how it had made my Father feel when his wife had passed away six years ago, and his eldest daughter took over all duties and responsibilities. Instead of the parents guiding the child, the child was making all decisions for the family as a whole.

My eyes landed on my elder sister as she sat at our late mother's desk. She wore a puzzled expression from the letter she was reading. The only acknowledgment she gave me was a flick of her eyes from the paper in her hands and then a nod of indication for me to sit in the chair across from her. Begrudgingly, I crossed the room and took my place. I was well aware that if Amity had not been born, I would be sitting where she was now. At nineteen, that idea made me too nervous. However, she'd been twenty-two when she became the head of our family.

Despite the seven-year age difference, Amity could pass for my twin in every way except for our style and personality. Her silver hair wove into intricate braids in an elaborate style, whereas mine was simply parted into two sections, braided at my ears, and tied back behind my head, leaving the rest to cascade down my back to my hips. While I wore a blue flowy dress, she wore a burnt orange dress that may have been a bit outdated.

I had always felt that a wall stood between us because of all my siblings; she was the one who had always been out of reach. Initially, I had blamed the age difference, but my eldest brother, Ace, was only two years younger than Amity, and we got along fine. The rest of my siblings delighted in Amity's company, and I sometimes wondered what I had done wrong for this barrier, but then I dismissed it when my focus turned to a new event in my reading.

Amity's cerulean-blue eyes blinked from the paper to me. I didn't miss the subtle glare she cast me before rearranging her facial features into a friendlier one. I was uncertain why she even bothered; it was no secret how she felt about me. I sat there waiting for her to speak first as I arched an eyebrow, unamused by her summoning. She delicately placed the letter on the desk and smoothed it out.

"In two day's time, I will be heading to Kingdom Theorines to meet with their ruler, King Ashborn. During this trip, Father will be accompanying me and considering—" she drawled the last word out while looking me up and down. "—your enjoyment of *historical literature*... you will also be accompanying us."

"What?" I leaned forward, gripping the edge of the chair's handles, not certain I had heard her correctly.

"I suggest you begin packing for the trip," she replied coolly, ignoring my outburst.

"What is the meaning of this trip?" I asked, narrowing my eyes. Amity had never hidden her disdain for my research, and now she offered me an opportunity on a silver platter. There had to be a catch. I knew I was a fool for even questioning what she was offering me, but it was peculiar for a house from Queendom Grewt'en to travel to another monarchy's lands.

"Some simple negotiations, nothing more," she replied flippantly, her voice rising slightly in pitch. She gathered various pieces of paper on her desk and began shuffling them together.

"What sort of *negotiations*?"

Amity rose from her seat, discarding the stack of papers. Walking around to the back of the chair, she looked out the window at the manor's grounds below.

"With all your research, I am sure you are aware that the majority of trade goes through the Kingdom of Theorines due to its location along key trade routes."

I nodded, even though it was futile with her back to me.

"With our manor being close enough to Kingdom Theorine's border, I have been in the process of working out a deal to help benefit our people."

"Is that not the *Queen's job*?" I tried to argue.

"If you were the eldest daughter, you would understand the position I am in. However, since you are the second-born daughter, you need not worry." Amity let out a sigh of annoyance. "That is all. I will be making the announcement tonight at dinner with everyone in attendance. I once again suggest you begin packing for the trip."

"How long will we be staying?"

"At a minimum, a month, but anticipate packing for upwards of three or more months."

I opened my mouth and slammed it shut. There was no point in arguing with her; as head of the house, she could do as she pleased. Promptly, I rose from my seat and did not hide my annoyance as I slammed the door to our late mother's office louder than necessary.

While meticulously folding one of my dresses before dinner, I absently gazed at all the dried flowers I had placed around my room. Each one brought a new memory of Theo, and I smiled warmly. He had gifted me every single one, and I had kept them all; some had held up fine, while others had seen better days. Discarding the task at hand, I surveyed all the dried flowers, trying to find the perfect one.

Smiling, I chose the recent red-to-yellow tulip. I had been walking along the path that weaved behind the stables when Theo secretly handed me the flower. I often took afternoon strolls through my family's lands to get away from everyone. In turn, it offered Theo and me more opportunities to see one another without causing any suspicion. I took it upon myself to chat with various servants to ensure Theo was never signaled out.

The tulip had yet to fully dry, and I knew it would be a perfect contender for what I was about to do. Plucking it from the vase where it resided with the other dying flowers, I went to my nightstand and, opening the drawer, withdrew my favorite romance novel. The one I would never let Quiet read, for fear she would accidentally wreck the book. Opening it, I flipped to the back and, with careful ease, separated the petals, laying them flat on the paper. With equal care, I closed it slowly, pressing the tulip within the pages. Then, no matter where I was, I could take a piece of Theo with me.

Chapter Two

The room held a heavy silence at dinner while I swirled the spoon in my soup. Normally, my siblings were loud and boisterous; however, tonight, the only sound that echoed off the walls was from the silverware against porcelain dishes. Amity had yet to make the announcement, and I had been packing the entire day, unable to inform my siblings of the upcoming departure, but solemness still hung in the air.

Earlier, while I packed, I tried to rationalize how I would find time to be with Theo before I left on this extended trip. The only logical solution I could devise was sneaking out when everyone was asleep. I glanced at Amity and rolled my eyes as she ate, completely unphased.

I had never been away from Theo and the thought made me queasy. I wondered how he would react. I presumed the staff was unaware otherwise he would have said something. I tried to rationalize with myself that maybe Kingdom Theorines's royal library would give me the answers I had been desperately seeking.

"Everyone, I have an important announcement to make," Amity said, clearing her throat as six heads turned to her. Father and I were the only two who did not eye her curiously. My two older brothers and two younger sisters were glancing between each other and Amity. Every time their eyes met mine, I would flick my gaze to Amity and wait on bated breath, letting go of the spoon and calmly resting my hands on my lap. If I had thought the room was quiet before, the lack of silverware clanking against porcelain made it deafeningly silent.

"In two days' time, I will be traveling to Kingdom Theorines to meet with King Ashborn. On this trip, I will be taking Father and Serenity."

The room broke into a cacophony of noises as my sisters groaned in response, while my brothers protested loudly. Everyone began to argue about why they should be allowed to attend as well. Amity raised her hands in an attempt to silence them, but it went unnoticed by everyone except me. When her eyes met mine, I gave a simple shrug. It must have irritated her because she slammed her hands down on the table, causing the dinnerware to shake near her.

"Silence!" she yelled, causing everyone to obey. We rarely witnessed her lose control of her emotions. I chanced a glance at Father who wore a bemused expression while he watched the head of the house try to maintain order.

"This discussion is non-negotiable. Serenity will be attending, and the rest of you will stay here and behave yourselves like the good little Lord and Ladies you have been raised to be." Amity's eyes lingered on each of her younger siblings for a moment, even me. I glared back at her in contempt as if she assumed I would not behave on this trip. If I had it my way, I would not leave their library, nor partake in any social events. Then, there would be minimal ways for me to embarrass her or the family.

"Why are you going, big sister?" Pulchra's quiet voice spoke up. I glanced at the youngest child of House Wyndmeer. Pulchra was unlike the rest of our parent's children. While we had all been born with silver hair and cerulean-blue eyes, she had come out with midnight-black hair and almost jet-black eyes. She had been an unexpected pregnancy for our mother, being born thirteen years after our sister, Quiet.

Initially, I had hated Pulchra. After all, her birth had taken my mother's life. At fifteen, I had blamed her every day for the first two years of her existence. Slowly, my hatred melted into disdain, and when I had become her favorite person in the manor, my feelings changed to adoration for my youngest sister. She had slowly mended a crack that I had never realized formed within my heart. Now, I could not help but bend to the four-year-old's ways; she had become the perfect little Lady's daughter.

"Well, Pulchra-Darling," Amity began as she took her place back in her seat. "When a royal requests your presence, you are expected to follow their orders.

"But this is another monarchy's royal requesting it," piped in Quiet.

"Yeah, why are we taking orders from a *Kingdom*?" The eldest brother, Ace, asked.

Amity pinched the bridge of her nose, and I could tell from here that she wanted to tell them all to stop pestering her about the topic.

"Because we are. Now, please stop asking. Finish your dinner; some of us still need to pack before our trip." Amity's gaze landed on me, and I pursed my lips. Maybe if I had been given additional time to pack, I wouldn't be the bane to Amity's existence. My apologies for being the last to know about attending this trip. The lingering thought of sneaking out to tell Theo continued to nag at me.

"How long will you all be gone?" Loyal, my other brother asked.

"At minimum, a month, but it could be over three months." Amity's voice gave a warning for everyone to rethink asking any more questions. Earlier, she had told me it would be up to three months, but now she was telling them it could be more than three months. How long was this trip going to last?

After dinner had concluded, my siblings made snippet comments under their breath about how they wanted to attend this trip. I kept my mouth shut and hurried to my rooms, waiting on pins and needles for them all to retire for the evening. I couldn't risk going to Theo too early and being caught. I paced in my room, my eyes bouncing between my trunks, still needing to be packed, the window, and the doorway to leave my rooms. When I believed I had waited long enough, I made myself wait another ten minutes before departing.

Slowly opening my door, I listened. Upon hearing no one else, I crept down the silent hallways of the manor toward the stables. Fear shot through me when I pushed open the backdoor and it creaked, but I heard no movement from anyone checking on the noise. Glancing outside, luck had been on my side. The new moon gave me additional coverage that I had not been anticipating. If anyone looked out a window tonight, they would be hard-pressed to notice me sneaking along the shadows, and it was highly unlikely they would be able to identify me.

My elation from the new moon coverage quickly diminished when my own sight failed me. My footing became uneven, causing me to stumble. My hands barely caught me in time, preventing me from eating dirt and rocks. Every time I tripped over something, my irritation spiked. When I cracked my right shin on a boulder, I had to withhold the string of curses from frustration. My dress caught on more bushes than I had been aware of on the path to my destination.

When my hand finally pressed on the wood of the stable doors, I found relief. I refused to think about the trek I needed to make back. Inhaling a deep breath for courage, I breathed in the smell of horses, hay, and leather inside. To avoid another door making a ruckus, I opened the stable doors slowly and slid inside, silently closing it behind me.

The darkness outside was nothing compared to the pitch-blackness within the stables. Every hesitant step I took was based off memory. Tentatively, my left fingertips found the first wooden post of an empty horse stall. I trailed my hand along the smooth wood, using it to navigate my way. I hoped I didn't run into anything else;

my body was already battle-worn from the outside. I jolted when the warm breath of my Father's steed brushed against my neck. I moved quickly along.

It was at the ninth stall that I rammed my left shin into a stray pail or stool, causing me to trip and slam into the back wall of the stables. I let out an "oof!" from impact.

"Well, that hurt," I complained to myself, pushing off the wall. I rubbed my right cheek, trying to ease the pain. In the darkness, I glared at the loft I knew was above me. While I had not meant to be loud, Theo must have heard me. Why had he not responded? Gingerly, I let my hands trace along the wooden wall until I found the ladder leading up to his loft. Miraculously, my shins avoided any further collisions.

"Theo!" I whispered as loudly as I could manage. I had never been in his loft before; it would have been too risky to explain my reasoning if we were caught. It never deterred me from being curious about what his sleeping area looked like. Multiple times, instead of reading in the stables, I fantasized about what his bed would smell like as I lay curled next to his still-sleeping form. I smiled, temporarily lost in the thought.

"Theo!" I called again, a smidge louder, but I was met only with silence. Could he have already been asleep?

"Theo!" I tried once more. Crestfallen, I couldn't shake the looming thought—maybe he wasn't here. Wrapping both hands around the ladder's sides, I hauled my first foot onto a rung as fear coursed through me. I found it difficult to breathe; I had never climbed a ladder before—it was unladylike. Spots danced across my vision even in the darkness as dizziness took hold, my head spinning. Quickly, I climbed back down. When both feet hit the wooden floor, I hunched over, gasping for air. I would not be doing that again.

Slowly, I rose and brushed the escaped wisps of hair back behind my ears. I turned around to face the stables' entrance and leaned my back against the ladder. A shiver ran through me in response to the feeling the ladder had given me. Edging off the uncomfortable rungs,

I rested my weight on the cold wooden wall beside to it. The conundrum weighed heavily on my mind: should I wait for Theo to return? The issue was, I hadn't the faintest idea how long he would be away.

Pushing off the wall, I paced a small distance back and forth, careful not to knock into anything. My mind raced, trying to figure out all the possible places he could be. Maybe he was down at the river bathing, but if not, where else could he be? I tried to push the thought from my mind, but it forced its way to the forefront; what if he had taken a stroll to Crog's Hallow? What if he had gone to that dingy tavern?

I knew I could spend all night waiting for him to return, but by morning, I would have more questions to answer if I were caught sneaking back into my rooms. Sighing, I reached out, shuffling my feet until my hands found the stable railing again. I hissed to muffle my shriek when one of the horses nipped my shoulder. I didn't think it would cause a bruise, but it soured my mood all the same. Tonight had been a waste, and I directed my anger at Theo. If I got ahold of him tomorrow, I would not hold back my frustrations.

My hands finally found the stable doors. I wish I could give myself a moment to sigh in relief, but now I had to make the dreaded trek back. Bracing myself, especially my shins, I opened the stable doors and silently crept back to the manor.

Chapter Three

"Alright, you two. Here is what is going to happen while I am gone," I stated firmly the next day, my gaze snapping back and forth between my two younger sisters. They lounged on my bed, choosing to keep me company as they watched me pack. Neither of them responded to my firm tone, I pursed my lips and narrowed my eyes at them. Amity ought to be the one giving them this lecture, but instead, here I was, doing so.

"You are going to behave. You are not going to cause any of the house staff problems." My eyes cut to the youngest. "Pulchra, you *will* listen to your older sister, Quiet."

Quiet perked up at this new responsibility she was being laden with, her face turning smug. An evil glimmer entered Quiet's eyes as she smiled at our younger sister. *Could these two survive weeks together without me?*

"And Quiet, you will not abuse that power. You will help your baby sister with her needs. She is still learning and growing. Not to mention Ace and Loyal will still be on the premise to boss you both around."

"*Ugh*! You are such a mom!" Quiet complained.

16

"You are just mad that you can't be bossy!" Pulchra sassed back.

"Cannot," I corrected.

"Sorry-" Pulchra looked down at her lap. "-Quiet, you are mad that you cannot be bossy to me." The youngest retorted.

"Better," I praised as I continued folding dresses into my trunk. I had dismissed the handmaidens from helping me pack. Having people fret about annoyed me when I was perfectly capable of doing things myself.

"Do you think you will fall in love with one of the princes?" Quiet asked, changing topics. She flopped onto her stomach, propping herself up on her elbows, and rested her head in her hands. Lazily, she kicked her legs back and forth. I was not a fan that her feet were mere inches away from where my head slept at night.

"You have been listening to one too many bedtime stories," I chided.

"I have not! You are going to live temporarily where not one but *two* eligible prince brothers live. Do you think that is *not romantic*?" Quiet huffed. She rolled onto her back, letting her arms splay out as she took up most of my bed. "I am so jealous of you!"

"Only you would believe that. Riddle me why a prince would even consider marrying someone like me?" I laughed at the ridiculous notion. Quiet looked at me upside down from her position.

"Because you are pretty like a faerie," Pulchra answered in wonder, staring at me in a dreamlike state. I could only fathom how far her imagination was running.

"You have also been hearing one too many bedtime stories, but thank you, Pulchra." I tapped the tip of her nose with my finger. "You are very pretty as well."

She giggled, covering her nose with both hands.

"I would flirt with the princes if given the chance," Quiet grumbled, more to herself than anyone else.

"Well, maybe next time you can go and do exactly that. I, on the other hand, will be researching."

"Serenity," Quiet groaned. "You are going to die a spinster. You cannot live with your nose in a book. You need to find a husband. What better way than to flirt with eligible royals?" It wasn't been the first time someone informed me I would die a spinster due to my bookish ways. Yet, I seemed to be the only one unconcerned. I had my Theoadorable and only needed to find the loophole for us to be together.

"Oddly enough, there are three siblings older than me who are all unwed. I am not too concerned about the spinster life. Besides, not everyone is interested in romance and happily ever afters with royalty, Quiet." I packed a pair of shoes.

"If I had the opportunity, I would marry a prince and have my happily ever after." Quiet sighed, staring up at my ceiling.

"I would marry a faerie." Giggled Pulchra.

"Only you would want to marry a creature of stories," Quiet groaned again. She probably believed she was the only sensible sister in the family. Amity was too busy running the manor and our lands to notice anything else, I always had a book in my hand, and the youngest sister still held the world in wonder. I knew someday Quiet and Pulchra would face hardships, and they would think back to these days when life was simpler. While I found some of these conversations quite comical, I still treasured them all the same, wishing things would never have to change.

"Pulchra, if you ever encounter a faerie, do not tell them your name. Do not make a deal with them. Do not trust them," I instructed without pause from my packing.

"Seriously, Serenity." Quiet rolled over and sat up on alert. "You will give in to her whims but will not take the chance when opportunity knocks at your door to go after not one, but two princely brothers. . . I don't know Nitty. Sounds like you are not as smart as you think you are." She shrugged nonchalantly. It had been some time since she had last called me Nitty. Quiet had started the habit when she was still a toddler herself. Back when she could not fully say my name, it had always come out as 'Nitty.'

"And I think you spend your days staring at the clouds too much, fantasizing that you are the princess from all those stories the nursemaids read to Pulchra at night." I looked over at Pulchra and winked as I tapped her nose again, causing another fit of giggles from the youngest.

"*Yeeaaahhhh,* Quiet," Pulchra chimed in, full of giggles.

Our middle sister huffed.

I hoped one day she would receive an opportunity like this. I wish she would be swept off her feet by someone worthy of her. Whomever she marries already has my sympathies because never once has Quiet lived up to her name's meaning.

"Alright, my packing is complete. Can I please have a moment of peace?" I asked of my sisters. They glanced at one another and promptly left my room while I sealed my trunks. I turned and surveyed everything I was bringing with me, then sighed and flopped onto my bed, closing my eyes.

This trip made me nervous. I had never been away from home. The texts I had read about Theorines informed me that the lands were filled with lush green grass and trees. Their kingdom had fertile land to grow crops and a climate in whichmany pasture animals thrived in. The flip side was that they experienced all four seasons. I had never experienced snow and was curious what it would be like.

Queendom Grewt'en only experienced heat that fluctuated with the seasons. We were a tropical climate filled with sand dunes. Father's estate was close to the border of Kingdom T'Lovoness, where we could see their mountains in the distance. Our lands were filled with sandy grass with some sparse timber woods. We were far enough south that our villages and towns often received sea travelers, some bold enough to come to the estate seeking Amity for investments in some grand adventure they had schemed up. They never left with anything more than a full belly of food.

One of my siblings had thwarted my every attempt to seek out Theo today. There was no doubt in my mind that he had been informed of tomorrow's trip. He had most likely been ordered to prepare for our departure. I would need to sneak out again, my only hope being that I could see him this time. I wanted to be alone with him one last time.

When darkness settled on the lands, and everyone retired to their rooms, I once again slipped out into the night. I wish I could say I was less clumsy, but that would be a lie. I stumbled and bumped into more things; by the time I reached the stable doors, my shins were crying in protest. They had yet to recover from the previous night, and now they throbbed even worse.

I quickly slipped inside. The door closed quietly behind me, but my attention was drawn to the dimly lit candle burning at the far end of the stable. Hope rose within me, and I navigated towards it. It didn't provide much light, but it was better than stumbling through the stables blind as I had the night prior.

Quietly, I called up to the loft, "Theo," but was met with silence. It would have been a careless mistake to leave the candle burning unattended in the stables. My sister had dismissed staff for lesser offenses than this. When I reached the bottom of the ladder rungs, I quietly called his name again. He could not have gone far, but I worried about his absence.

"Serenity," Theo's low voice was filled with surprise. I turned to find him standing at the stable doors. His wet hair dripped onto the floor and my mouth went dry. Water glistened and ran down his muscular chest. My eyes trailed the droplets to the v-dip of his hips, where they disappeared beneath the waistband of his low-hanging pants. I gulped.

"Theo," I began and had to clear my throat when my voice came out raspy. "You should not have left your candle burning unoccupied." Of all the things I could have said, that was what I chose first? I mentally kicked myself for the idiocy.

"I only went down to the creek to wash up . . ." His eyes lingered on me a second before he closed the distance between us. ". . . I did not mean to cause turmoil for you." He smirked as he halted before me, his fingers gently tucking a stray lock behind my ear. My pulse spiked, and I had to remember to breathe as my heart raced.

"If Amity or one of my siblings happened to stop by and find it burning, you could be fired and then where would that leave us?" I argued, attempting to keep my wits about me.

"I will be more conscious next time." He teased, tilting his head. Theo's arms wrapped around my waist, bringing me close to him and leaving little space between us. "Why are you here, Serenity?"

"I-I came to see you." I wet my bottom lip with my tongue, briefly sucking it into my mouth before releasing it again. He tracked the movement, his eyes lingering on my lips, causing me to swallow as I rushed out, "I am sure you have already heard about tomorrow's trip to Kingdom Theorines. . ."

"I heard you would be gone for quite some time." The statement dropped between us, laced with sadness. He shifted his weight onto his other foot, and I felt the ladder rungs press into my back. The candlelight cast flickering shadows across his face, making his features appear almost haunting.

"Y-Y-Yes," I stuttered. "It may, it may be more than three months."

His gaze flicked to the candle and back to me, his eyebrow slowly raising in question.

"I wanted to see you one last time before my trip," I whispered while my arousal continued to build.

"You are making it sound like you are not coming back." He smiled warily, his eyes searching mine to ensure that wasn't my intent.

"That is silly talk," I laughed, shaking my head. Some of my nervousness ebbed away.

"So, then did you come just to see me one last time or. . ." He trailed off, his eyes becoming suggestive as lips curved into a knowing smile, and he waggled his eyebrows.

"I did not want to leave without a proper goodbye."

"And what is your definition of a proper goodbye?"

Instead of answering, I rose onto my toes to press a soft kiss against Theo's lips.

As I snuck through the manor past midnight, no one else had been awake or roaming the halls. I slipped quietly inside my bedroom and clicking the door softly shut. I rested my back against it, closing my eyes and tilting my head upwards. I smiled, my stomach clenching from the thrill. Warmth rushed through me, but was quickly followed by the cold, sadness. I had to remind myself the days would pass and soon I would be back here and with Theo again. What were a few months compared to having a lifetime with him. If Kingdom Theorines's royal library held the answers I were seeking, it would be worth it.

"How was Theo?" Quiet's voice broke the silence. I jumped, searching the room, until I found her sitting in a chair by the window. How had I not noticed her?

"Quiet, what are you doing here?" I was still processing that she knew about Theo and me.

"I watched you leave and decided to wait for you to come back, or I would come get you if you had taken too long," she replied nonchalantly, staring at me before tacking on, "which you did, by the way. Take too long, that is."

I watched her cautiously. "How do you know I was with Theo?" I weighed my words carefully, hoping I was focusing on the right way to divert this conversation.

"Serenity, you make it pretty obvious what is going on between you and Theo. I'm not dumb." She twirled her hair flippantly, her lips pursing.

"How long have you known?" I asked slowly, the door supported my weight, and I was too afraid to move away from it.

"Quite some time." She paused her hair twirling, her eyes flicking to the lock between her fingers. "I also walked in on the two of you kissing in the stables, confirming my suspicions."

"Why did you not say anything?" I asked exasperated.

"Because –" Her gaze flicked back to mine as she aggressively flipped the lock. "-I figured there would come a day when I could blackmail you with the information."

"You would not *dare*." My eyes widened as my heart sank.

"No, not tonight. I will cash in when it is a more opportune time with Amity." She eyed me.

"When did you become like this?" I asked, pushing off the wall. A slight sense of relief washed over me as anger bubbled its way to the top.

"When my older sister is perfect, it becomes quite interesting to see her gallivanting around with a lowly stable boy." She dropped her hair, changing over to pick at her nails. "And you should know, you're the biggest cliché in a historic romance book." Quiet rolled her eyes. She dropped her hands to the chair's armrests and pushed herself up to stand. My younger sister crossed the distance between us. "I love you Nitty, but do not throw your life away over a stable boy. You do not see it, but the potential within you could lead to so much more in life than what you are trying to force yourself to settle with."

She held my gaze until I nodded slowly in confirmation. With a curt nod, she brushed past me and left my rooms without another word. I blinked rapidly, looking at the floor, trying to make sense of how my younger sister had gone from bemoaning princes yesterday to blackmailing me tonight.

Quiet didn't let on how long she had known about Theo and me. I had kissed him plenty of times in the stables, which certainly didn't help narrow it down. One word from her and she could ruin everything I had been working towards. I lingered for a second on what she had said. *Was I trying to force myself to settle?* I shook my head at the notion. No, I had feelings for Theo. Feelings that had grown after our parting goodbye tonight.

Within a day's time, Father had made his suspicions apparent, Quiet knew, then who else was aware in my family? I'd never thought my sister was dumb, but I had never credited her with how observational she could be. I believed I had been discreet with Theo, but perhaps I had grown careless without realizing it. If Quiet had walked in on us kissing, then maybe others had as well. However, if Father truly knew the truth, he would have already informed Amity, and she would have had Theo banished.

How many staff members kept secrets from Amity? I'd been under the impression the staff were loyal to her, but if certain members of my family knew, then surely the servants did as well. I shook the notion from my head. The servants my late mother had once employed now held their loyalty to the new head of the house—Amity. If it ever came down to choosing between her and the second eldest daughter, their allegiance had always been clear, or was it?

I knew eventually I would be wedded to another Lord's son or a potential prince. Those were my only options as a Lady's daughter. There were neighboring Lords with eligible sons, but none had ever stirred anything within me. They were polite, well-bred, and perfectly suited for marriage—yet not one of them had ever made my heart race the way Theo did.

I dismissed the thoughts aside. Tomorrow would mark the beginning of long, grueling days of travel, and I would have plenty of time to fret then. For now, I needed to cleanse the lingering tension from my body and find solace in sleep.

The next morning, I awoke with a headache. I had tossed and turned all night, and when my mind had finally drifted off, the handmaids were barging in, ushering me to wake up and be ready for breakfast. Through my grogginess, my eyes burned as I squinted at the sunlight now streaming through the opened curtains. Irritated, I stumbled out of bed. I bit my tongue to keep from snapping at the girls fluttering around me, as they stripped off my nightgown and replaced it with a morning dress. Meanwhile, another brushed out my hair, weaving it into the braid I preferred.

When they finished making me prim and proper, I trudged along to the breakfast hall. I was the last one to arrive. My petite heels clicked loudly against the cold marble flooring, creating an echo from the silence. Pulchra and my brothers were too busy eating their breakfast to take notice of their surroundings. Quiet raised an eyebrow at me with a smirk on her lips. I wanted to tell her where she could send that smirk. Meanwhile, Amity casually sipped her morning tea while reading a document in front of her; Father mirrored her actions, engrossed in his own document.

Father's attention turned to me when I pulled out the chair next to him. Amity shook her head in disappointment at my delayed arrival.

"Not like you to be late, Serenity. Everything alright?" Father asked, concern washing over his face as he looked me over. I forced my emotions into check, determined not to reveal the turmoil left behind from last night. Keeping my gaze carefully averted from Quiet, I offered a neutral expression.

"I did not sleep well last night—too excited for the trip today, Father," I replied calmly with a weak smile. Picking up my fork, I focused on the meal before me, sunny-side-up eggs and hashbrowns mixed with cheese and peppers—letting the familiar act of eating ground me.

"You ought to be excited; this will be a big adventure for you," Father replied, his voice warm as he reached over to cover my hand, giving it a small squeeze. His touch was comforting, but I couldn't help feeling detached, as if the excitement he spoke of was not entirely my own. I tried to force my smile to appear more genuine, but it felt like a strained mask. Out of the corner of my eye, I caught Amity staring at our father, and for a fleeting moment, I wondered what she wasn't saying. Quiet sat across from me, and I caught her rolling her eyes, her subtle gesture adding another to the unspoken tension hanging in the air.

"A new adventure with two eligible princes," Quiet commented. She gave Father a wide, innocent smile as she winked at me. My hand was trapped in his hand as he gave me another small, reassuring squeeze.

"That there is." He chuckled. I sideways glanced at him, my eyebrows furrowing at his response.

"A new adventure with a new library," I offered, attempting to redirect the conversation. Quiet let out a disgusted sound, before flopping back in her chair. Father released my hand with a pat and resumed his attention to the parchment in his grasp.

"Yes, of course. The books." Amity interjected quickly, her voice tight. My confusion shifted to her now—why was she acting so differently today?

Chapter Four

The carriage halted; we had arrived. The weeks of travel had been strenuous. While I enjoyed my father's company, Amity's presence caused me stress. She repeatedly drilled into my head the etiquette I would need to follow while we stayed with the royal family. Despite my multiple attempts to remind her of my research on royal history, Amity would not let up. Father, on the other hand, barely jumped in to referee between the two of us.

I reminded Amity multiple times a day that I would spend most of my time in the library—a place I assumed would be void of royals. She chided me, claiming I would need to attend all meals and any other social events required. The more she let slip, the more nervous I became about what this stay had in store for me. I refocused my attention back to Kingdom Theorines's library. I could not wait to get my hands on their historical pieces, ones I would not be able to find anywhere else.

"Serenity," Father's voice admonished, breaking my thoughts. "I can already see you calculating. Please wait until you have free time to peruse the library." He chuckled.

"I am not quite certain what you are talking about, Father," I smarted back.

"Right, and I am supposed to believe that?" He quirked an eyebrow, and I tried to withhold my smile. "You are my daughter through and through."

While growing up, I tried to shake the notion of how different I was from my siblings. Every time that thought bubbled to the surface, I popped it and buried it beneath my wealth of historical knowledge. Sitting here in the carriage with Father and Amity, those bubbles of thought surfaced rather quickly. Maybe my days with my head in the clouds were coming to an end. I knew I wasn't the perfect Lady like my older sister or late mother. I didn't openly swoon over the princes; instead of needlework, I took notes from dusty scrolls. When it came to dresses, I let the dressmaker do as she pleased, as long as it didn't interrupt my reading. I was running out of time to find a historical moment where a romance similar to Theo and mine occurred. I had never anticipated that the beginning of my research would bring me this much enjoyment. However, the pleasure it brought was starting to distract me from my original mission.

"Enough, you two," scolded Amity with a huff. "You are *both* to be the representation of our house. Behave yourselves."

I rolled my eyes in annoyance as Father leaned back in his seat. Sometimes, I mused on how it must rankle him to have his child boss him around. Then again, he probably was accustomed to it from growing up in a Queendom and having a Lady for a wife.

The carriage door opened, and we were greeted by a servant. Looking past the servant, I caught my first glimpse of Theorines's castle. The exterior was quite charming, the light grey walls were surrounded by hydrangea bushes of every color. Everything about the castle was charming, designed as if it had been created from a fairytale.

Aside from the servant in front of us and a few gardeners, no one was else in sight. I wondered when we would be introduced to the royals. Equally, my thoughts floated to the library. How quickly would I be able to step into it and have a plethora of research at my fingertips?

Amity accepted the servant's hand first. She gave us one final warning glare before departing the carriage. Father winked at me and then followed Amity out. I glanced around the carriage with a sigh of relief, who knows how long it would be until I would be heading back home. The reprieve of leaving the cramped quarters was a warm welcome.

The servant offered me his hand, and upon accepting it, he helped me out of the carriage. I stood next to my family, breathing in the fresh air as we all took in the full view of Castle Theorines. Above the hydrangea bushes, lovely flowering vines climbed up the gray slate stone, adding a touch of beauty. There were more gardeners than I had initially noticed, pruning and tending to the various plants around the perimeter. Several trees surrounded our carriage on both sides. Despite their age, they were full of life with their leaves and tiny blooming flowers. Butterflies lazily floated around the gardens, and in the distance, peacocks decorated the grounds with their full plumage. It was a shame that Quiet and Pulchra were not here, they would have been entirely in love.

"The King and Queen are awaiting your arrival," the servant spoke. There was a slight tone of annoyance in his voice, as if our arrival had inconvenienced him.

"Let us not keep them waiting a moment longer than," Father replied in good humor, and we began following the servant toward the castle's front entrance.

Amity flicked him a warning glance, which Father ignored.

"Who knew castles could be so big?" he continued on lightly instead.

"You have been to Castle Grewt'en before," I countered, confused as to why he would state that.

"Yes, but neither of you have been to a castle. I am only commenting on what you are currently thinking. . . If I had a guess, that is."

"We have all read stories about their size," snipped Amity. She most likely was becoming annoyed with our incessant chatter in front of the servant. Somehow, in her mind, we were ruining the perfect, well-behaved image she had planned for our arrival. I suppose we ought to be mindless, quiet puppets at her disposal as she controlled our strings.

I bristled at her tone and chose to come to Father's defense. "Reading and seeing are two very different things, Amity."

Amity's body jerked as her head whipped to me.

I raised my right eyebrow slowly at her, knowing I was putting her in a bind—whether to react or stay quiet and avoid causing a scene. She pursed her lips and narrowed her eyes.

"I am quite aware," she snarled, "I can read about small farming villages or Mother and Father can take us to the local ones to truly experience the celebrations."

Memories of past festivities flashed through my mind. The heartache from Mother's smile as we celebrate with the local villagers still stung. We would dance and eat cherry pies, while my brothers caused the local girls to blush from their flirting. It was one of the rare moments that Amity and I would get along. We would tease each other about which villager boy we found cute. Back when Theo had been nothing more than a scrawny stable boy, always covered in dirt and straw—a servant I had barely paid attention to.

"Precisely," Father praised. Amity straightened her shoulders and quickened her steps to walk ahead of us. I looked at Father, and his eyes crinkled as he smiled, conveying the unsaid apology for his eldest child. With Father close to me, I felt safe even when there was no danger. Something about his presence had always lulled me into a sense of safety. Maybe it was because he, like most Lords, always carried a sword, or perhaps because I had witnessed him in more than one fistfight when someone had been disrespectful to our family. Either way, I knew that nothing would go wrong with Father by my side. He would never betray me.

The servant leading us didn't even reach for the door handle; the light-stained double oak doors opened simultaneously. Amity faltered in her step from surprise, and I could not help but gawk upwards at the height of the doors. It was there, I spotted two boys entering their teenage years, looking down at us with bored expressions. I caught one of the boys' eyes, and he quickly looked away. Both of them held ropes that were hooked to a mechanism that caused the doors to open.

My attention was brought back to the threshold as the smell of freshly baked cinnamon bread wafted toward me. In the center of the foyer lay a circular pink area rug, and surrounding the walls were various tall vases filled to the brim with flowers. Instead of gray stone walls, decorative tapestries were hanging from the walls, brightening the area in various colors and designs. If I had the chance, I would come back here to study the tapestries. Multiple scenes were stitched into them; if I had to guess, they told a story. I expected a grand staircase in the foyer, like the ones described in fairytales, but instead, it was a vast entrance filled with multiple archways and doors.

The servant led us through one of the archways into the talking parlor without pause. He informed us that refreshments had already been provided before departing promptly. My gaze settled on the array of pastries and various pitchers filled with different beverages. The royal family had spared no expense in ensuring we were well provided for. However, my nerves kept me from indulging. Instead, I chose to take my seat beside Amity while Father perused the assortment.

Now that we were alone, I made no effort to conceal my gawking as I took in every detail of the room. Instead of tapestries, the walls were painted with bright, airy scenery that led up to a domed ceiling. A golden chandelier hung at the center where all the images converged. I couldn't tell if the wall murals were meant to tell a story or simply serve as decoration. Bringing my attention back down to the floor, I found a mosaic of tiles in colors of cerulean-blue, violet, emerald-green, and citrine-yellow spiraling inward to all meet at the center, where the most extensive tile was a striking sky-blue stone.

Light lilac area rugs were placed only beneath the furniture, which was adorned with pastel crushed velvet cushions. Amity and I sat upon a pale pink settee.

We hadn't waited long before the doors glided open, revealing the King and Queen of Theorines, followed closely by their two sons. We stood as Amity and I dropped into a deep curtsey while Father bowed. We waited on bated breath for them to release us; I kept my head low and eyes downcast out of respect.

"Rise," crooned King Ashborn, his single word commanding the respect of the entire room. I rose slowly from my curtsy, a flutter of unexpected awe stirring within me as I faced The King. The weight of his presence left me momentarily breathless, caught off guard by the surge of emotions I hadn't anticipated. We waited as the King's eyes trailed over us, lingering on me the longest. Instead of meeting his stare, I focused on King Ashborn's long brown hair styled in a single braid down the front of his chest, the tip grazing the floor. My mind wandered back to the passage I had recently studied about the people of Theorines.

The Theorines Culture:

Theorinians are easily identifiable by their long, uncut hair. Theorines have the belief system that to cut one's hair is to severe one's memories, knowledge, and experiences. Theorinians take great pride with their hair and often have the most elaborate of designs that still show off the length of their hair. If a Theorinian commits a crime, depending on the severity, it can depict how long of hair length may be cut off from them.

Theorines is generally a peaceful civilization that does not condone violence, even in punishment. However, if a Theorinian sees another Theorinian with cut hair in any variation of length, avoidance, disdain, and right-out feigning acknowledgement of the shorn Theorinian is common practice. The shorn Theorinian may not leave Theorines for a period of time depending on the length severed from their head. Only a Theorines is allowed to cut another Theorines hair for punishment.

If another Monarchy attempts to punish a Theorinian in the same attempt it can create a disruption in the trade route system as Theorine's will shut down their trade route to the Monarchy that shorned a Theorinian. A Theorinian may be punished the same way as the rest of the people in that country as long as it does not involve hair since the Theorinians are the only country that will cut hair as punishment. If a foreigner visits Theorines and requires punishment, Theorines will send the foreigner back to their rightful country to receive their punishment. Thus far, it has kept Theorines a peaceful place. The people are quite friendly.

King Ashborn's long, braided hair reflected his Kingdom's practice. I had anticipated him to have more elaborate braids and designs in his hair than the simple one he wore, especially upon greeting us. I had been under the distinct impression that royals would do anything to flaunt their nobility, yet, the royals of Theorines all adorned simple braids. The simplicity was striking, a stark contrast to the grandeur I had imagined, and it spoke volumes about the values of this Kingdom—humility, history, and the preservation of the identity rather than the outward display of wealth.

Though I hadn't come across any mention of it, a nagging question lingered in my mind: could his hair ever be cut? Would he still be able to claim the throne if even the slightest portion of it was severed for a broken law? Or were the royals, like so many other rules, exempt from such a punishment? When it came to my research, there had been little to no information regarding punishments for the royal family. It made me wonder—if the royals were truly above the law, then what would happen if they broke it? How would they atone? My hand fidgeted at my side, the urge to reach up and touch my silver locks nearly overwhelmed me.

I noted that their laws must not apply to facial hair, as King Ashborn was completely clean-shaven. His strong jaw and high cheekbones only heightened his striking features. He was breathtakingly handsome, and something stirred deep within me that I couldn't quite place. I startled a bit, quickly pushing those feelings down. I was here for one purpose—to find a way to be with Theo. Besides, I never stood a chance with a married king. Not that I wanted that. I was merely confused by The King's presence. Shaking off the unwanted feelings, I continued my assessment of the king before me, who, in turn, continued to assess me.

King Ashborn wore Theorine's colors—a navy-blue jacket paired with smoky lavender pants. Throughout, the attire was accented with various shades of smoky gray, giving the outfit an air of sophistication and subtle elegance that complemented the royal regality of his presence. Despite the elegant clothing, it did little to conceal the muscular build hidden underneath the fabric. A flush crept up my cheeks, the heat pooling in my belly at the thought. *Stop it, Serenity.*

Shifting my focus from The King, I turned my attention to his wife, Queen Izralda. She stood slightly behind him, to the left. Unlike her husband's assessing stare, she was fighting back a smile. Her dimples peeked out from her cheeks, and the harder she fought to suppress her smile, the deeper they became. Surprisingly, her braided black hair was looped halfway upwards into a ring. I'd been under the impression that her hair was longer than her husband's. It was then that I noticed within the single large braid, smaller braids were woven in, adorned with silver trinkets and spirals throughout her hair. Queen Izralda tilted her head to the side, and the little bells chimed in various peaceful and melodic sounds.

Her eyes met mine, and they were the most unusual color I had ever seen—a deep violet with flecks of red that glinted at the center. She tilted her head to the other side, sending another chime of bells. Light caught her eyes, shifting their hue to lilac while the red flecks deepened into a striking magenta-pink. Her attention flicked to her husband before returning to me, a knowing smile played on her lips.

I wanted to tell her she was wrong in her thought process, that I was only having a reaction to being in the presence of royalty. That I harbored no lust-filled feelings for her husband. The regal aura she carried was only enhanced by her attire—a simple, yet elegant, smoky lavender dress with a plunging V-neckline, revealing a tasteful amount of cleavage. A smoky gray sash cinched her waist, accentuating her figure.

Shifting my focus, I studied the two prince brothers standing beside their parents. I couldn't yet distinguish which one was Prince Gideon Orion or Prince Finch Azrael. Each bore a striking resemblance to one of their parents, their inherited features unmistakable. Both were taller than me, their presence just as commanding as their father's.

The shorter of the two bore a strong resemblance to their father, with rich brown hair and deep brown eyes. There was an innocence to his features, a softness that set him apart from the imposing presence of King Ashborn. His hair was styled into two long braids that extended just past the middle of his back. If I had to guess, he was most likely Prince Finch Azrael, the younger of the two brothers. The moment he caught me looking at him, his face flushed.

The other prince looked bored to be in attendance, but when his violet eyes met mine, he smiled. Unlike the Queen's, his eyes lacked the red flecks. His long black hair was loosely braided, the ends left untied at his hip. Dressed entirely in black, he wore an unbuttoned shirt that exposed his bare chest. His ease was almost unsettling. Before I could linger on it, King Ashborn spoke again, drawing my focus back to him.

"Lady Amity Lovanna, I would like to thank you for accepting my initiation to visit my kingdom. May I inquire who your additional guests are today?" King Ashborn's gaze lingered on me once again. His eyes slowly trailing down my body and then back up, catching my eye. I shifted my gaze to the floor, my face flushing.

"Thank you for the invite." Amity dropped into a polite curtsey, dipping her head. "King Ashborn, allow me to present my Father,

Lord Lambert, and my sister, Lady Serenity Novena." Father bowed as I dropped into another curtsey as a sign of respect.

"Welcome to my home," King Ashborn greeted. "Your sister is far lovelier than we had heard. The silver is quite an interesting hair color," he mused. Tingles raced through my body as I caught the glances of his sons, who appeared more interested in me than before. The shorter prince's eyes were wide, barely blinking. It seemed that I wasn't just of interest to The King. How, amidst all the formalities, do these royals from another monarchy know about me? The only logical conclusion I could come to was that Amity must have mentioned me in her letters to The King.

"Yes," Queen Izralda spoke, her voice full of warmth. "The silver is quite unique, very lovely indeed."

"Thank you," my sister and I answered in unison. Amity stiffened slightly, not expecting me to speak. Though she couldn't react now, I knew she was silently keeping a tally of everything she would scold me for later.

"Wherever did it come from?" Queen Izralda pushed, while continuing to admire our unique hair color.

"Our late mother had silver hair," Amity answered.

"Aside from that, are there any other unique qualities about Lady Serenity Novena?" King Ashborn asked. I struggled to maintain a pleasant expression, despite the urge to furrow my brows at his unexpected interest in me.

"She has a deep love for reading, especially when it comes to history," Amity interjected with a smile. I glanced at her, puzzled by her sudden pride in this fact. Amity had never shown any interest in my hobbies, yet now she beamed like a proud parent while our father remained silent.

"Then she must see our history collection in the library," Queen Izralda responded gleefully with a gleam in her eyes.

"Yes, it is quite extensive—though not as vast as T'Lovoness's, but we are quite proud of it." King Ashborn remarked, stroking his chin thoughtfully. The confusion I felt for my sister's response was replaced with excitement at the mention of the library. Unsure if it would be improper to speak to the King and Queen, I settled on a smile, hoping it would suffice.

"My sons can escort you to the library," King Ashborn offered, volunteering the princes. "Lady Amity Lovanna, we will head to the study to discuss the matters we had written about. You are welcome to join us, Lord Lambert.

Without hesitation, I rose to my feet, already preparing to follow King Ashborn's directive. I nodded politely to the princes, trying to mask my nerves at the thought of being left alone with them. I glanced at my sister, who gave me a brief, reassuring nod, and then Father, who had already started to follow the King and Queen, bowing slightly as he went. The princes exchanged a look before the taller one spoke, his voice calm. "Shall we, Lady Serenity Novena?"

I swallowed, trying to keep my composure. "Lead the way," I replied, offering a small, controlled smile.

"I, too, will join you three in the library," Queen Izralda commented, her voice light and welcoming.

The Queen walked alongside me, not minding that her sons walked in front of us. None of us spoke, and I took the silence as an opportunity to admire my surroundings. Similar to the little bit of the castle I had already seen, decorative tapestries hung on the gray slate slab walls from floor to ceiling. Without the tapestries, I assumed the walls would feel quite drab and oppressive. The vibrant colors and intricate designs of the woven tapestries seemed to breathe life into the stone. I tried to translate the stories stitched into the fabric, but the imagery was complex, and I couldn't quite make out the full narrative. Still, the scenes appeared to tell of great battles and peaceful victories, of monarchs and mythical creatures. It made me wonder how much of Theorines's history was hidden in these textiles, waiting for someone to unravel their meaning.

"It is our history," Queen Izralda said, breaking my thoughts, as though she could read my mind when I struggled to make sense of them.

"Beg pardon, Your Highness?" I asked, startled.

"You have a lovely voice; it matches your beauty." She brushed aside my question.

"Thank you." I had not expected the compliment, nor had anyone ever remarked on my voice in the past.

"Do you sing?" She pressed.

"Not really. My younger sister has a very captivating voice and is almost always singing." I thought of Quiet and her constant singing sessions. She should have been gifted a name like Melody, Siren, or Singer, but instead, my parents named her Quiet. She was anything but quiet. Her voice could fill a room, and her songs could linger in the air long after she had finished singing.

"Someday, I would like to hear your sister sing since you speak this highly of her," Queen Izralda remarked with a gentle smile.

"I am sure the honor would be hers. When I return home, I will relay the message. I am certain she will be quite flattered." I knew Quiet would probably talk nonstop about it. She would be difficult to live with afterward, and I was thankful I did not have to share a room with her. Pulchra, on the other hand, just may go mad from the excessive chatter.

"How did you come to enjoy history?" Queen Izralda asked, her gaze intense with curiosity. I hadn't expected to be bombarded with so many questions. Everything I had read about royals painted them as distant and uninterested in those of lower rank, but Queen Izralda was anything but that. In fact, I had an inkling she was itching to loop her arm into mine.

"Oh, one day, I was looking for something in the historical texts, and before I knew it, I found myself reading through every history text and scroll we had on hand. I started requesting more to be brought to me on various topics. My goal is to create an ultimate historical text, combining the important details from everything I have found." I stopped myself, realizing I'd been rambling.

"Sounds like quite the cumbersome task. Did you ever find what you were initially searching for?" I believed it was Prince Finch Azrael who asked. If they had not been leading the way, I likely would have forgotten they were walking with us.

"Unfortunately, not yet," I replied, disappointed. I tried to remind myself why I was here and where we were headed.

"What are you looking for then? Maybe we can help?" The prince continued.

"Oh, it is a trivial matter." I giggled nervously. "No worries, at this point, it is the least of my focus in my historical research." I hoped my reply would deter them from asking further. If they pressed, I would not be able to outright lie to the royals.

"Nonetheless, we hope you find what you are looking for in our library," Queen Izralda remarked. "Well, here we are." The library's double doors were simple wood, with no indication that they led to a room of significance. Had I been looking for it on my own, I likely would've walked right past. The Prince brothers opened the doors and stepped aside, allowing their mother and me to pass enter. It struck me as unusual—royalty performing such trivial tasks for someone like me. But before I could dwell on it, my thoughts were swallowed by the sight before me. couldn't help but gasp in awe.

The library was three times the size of my family's. From the entrance, I could take in the entire room—endless rows of books stretching toward the high ceiling, interspersed with oversized seating areas designed for comfort and long hours of reading. Large windows allowed an abundance of natural light to flood the room, illuminating the countless shelves and casting a warm glow over the inviting reading spaces. If we were to stay for months and I had the luxury of spending each day here, I would be utterly content. A sharp pang of regret pierced my heart; the thrill of exploring this library outweighed my eagerness to return home to Theo. Yet, if I uncovered what I needed for us to be together, would the unknown months spent here not be worth it? Maybe distance wasn't a curse but a test—a way to prove what truly mattered.

I followed Queen Izralda through the library until we stood

before a towering wall of three bookcases, each packed from floor to ceiling with books.

"This here is the history section," she stated casually.

"All of this?" I breathed, unable to mask my awe at the sheer expanse of the collection. If King Ashborn insisted this was nothing compared to T'Lovoness's library, I could only imagine the grandeur of their collection. My entire collection from home would likely fit on a single shelf here.

"Yes, and you are welcome to read or borrow anything to your room. All we ask is that you return it to its rightful home when you are finished." Queen Izralda smiled warmly, her deep dimples making an appearance.

"Thank you, that is most gracious of you, Your Highness." I dropped into a curtsy, hoping my gesture conveyed my sincere gratitude for the opportuntity to access the library.

"Oh, stand up, Lady Serenity Novena. No need to curtsy on my behalf," Queen Izralda replied in an amused tone.

I awkwardly rose from my curtsy, feeling slightly off balance. Her unexpected statement had left me confused. Upon noticing the expression I'd failed to hide, she let out a soft laugh, the sound light and melodic.

"I have not always been royalty, as you probably are aware." Queen Izrala continued with a soft chuckle. "While I may be queen now, that was not always the case. I still find it odd to have someone curtsying and calling me by a title." Queen Izralda looked over at her sons. "I try to teach my sons to be humble as well." It had slipped my mind that King Ashborn had married his mistress after his first wife had passed away.

"I apologize, Queen Izralda, if I have made you uncomfortable." I felt a flush creep up my neck, unsure of how to proceed. The simplest solution seemed to be apologizing, but beyond that, I was at a loss for words. I wondered if someone like her would have sympathy for my situation and the reasons behind my research. Would she understand why someone like me, someone of lesser standing, would dare to dream of marrying a stable boy?

"Oh, not at all." She waved her hand dismissively. "It is a bit refreshing, actually, that not everyone has it at the forefront of their mind. When we first married, I had some difficulties with those who did not approve, but over time, it is not much of an issue anymore." She paused, her eyebrows furrowing as though questioning her own words. "I am not certain why I just told you that?"

"Do not fret; it is a common occurrence in my life. People tend to tell me their life stories," I surmised, brushing it off with a small smile. I attributed it to the quiet power my name held—serene, calm, and an easy listener.

"I bet you hear a lot of interesting things then," the black-haired prince, who had remained silent up until now, finally interjected into the conversation.

"Sometimes, yes." There were a few names I could ruin if I chose to spill their stories, but on the other hand, I could just as easily play matchmaker with a select few as well. I found it far more amusing—and less troublesome—not to meddle, simply observing as a bystander while events unfolded on their own.

"Maybe someday you will know a few of my secrets." The black-haired Prince winked at me, and despite my best efforts, a nervous giggle escaped. I felt the heat creeping up my neck, betraying me. Aside from Theo, very few had ever flirted with me; I had never imagined a royal would. My giggle faltered when I found the prince smiling warmly at me, amusement dancing in his eyes—I had assumed I would barely be in the company of the royal family.

"I will leave you to our history section. I must attend to queenly duties," Queen Izralda said, dismissing herself. I didn't even have a chance to respond before she glided out of the library. I stood there, blinking at her retreating figure as the doors closed, blocking her from view.

"You will get used to it. Mother does it quite often," commented the prince who had flirted with me.

"Good to know," I replied, trying to mask my nervousness. "Not to be inconsiderate, but I was not properly introduced to either of you. I am not entirely sure which brother is which." I hoped my bold question wouldn't come off as disrespectful. The two brothers exchanged a glance, smirking before turning their attention back to me.

"Who do you think I am?" Questioned the flirtatious brother.

"I would like to think you are the eldest, Prince Gideon Orion," I replied calmly as I calculated my odds against my reasoning.

"Why do you think *he* is Prince Gideon Orion?" The other brother chimed in. They both glanced at each other, neither giving any indication of whether I was right or wrong.

"Based on your hair length, his is longer than yours." It was the only distinguishing factor I could use to tell them apart. I knew the two brothers had been born two years apart and the taller one had longer hair.

They both looked at each other with raised eyebrows and then turned back to look at me.

"You would be the first foreigner to guess based on our hair length," commented the one I believed to be Prince Finch Azrael.

"Did I guess correctly?" I asked, pressing a bit. The two brothers exchanged a look again, silently communicating, before nodding and turning their attention back to me.

"Maybe you did. Maybe you did not. But I suppose only time will tell," Prince Gideon Orion replied, though I couldn't be sure, his tone playful and teasing, accompanied by a sly grin.

"Guess so." I shrugged, pretending to be unfazed as I turned my attention back to browsing the bookshelves. I held myself back from grabbing every text I had never read. My eyes immediately caught sight of five on the first row, each one tempting me. I had to remind myself that I would have weeks at my disposal to peruse these shelves. The question was, should I read in order on each shelf, or organize my list by what I deemed most important to least important, just in case the trip ended sooner than planned?

Definitely the last option. I could not take any chances of leaving here today and never seeing some of these texts again. I would need a quill, ink, and paper to jot down the titles I wanted to read, along with the scrolls that caught my attention. Then, I would need to arrange them from most important to least important. I only hoped that my decision on what was most important wouldn't turn out to be a mistake later, when time here is so precious.

"Ahem, are we interrupting you?" Prince Finch Azrael asked, though it might have been Prince Gideon Orion—his voice laced with curiosity and a hint of mischief.

"What?" I snapped out of the rabbit hole I had been spiraling down in. I turned to look at them, realizing I had not been paying attention to my surroundings again. "Oh, sorry." I flushed. "Beg my ill manners, I did not hear what you were saying. . . is there paper and writing materials in here?" I glanced around the room. hoping to find the answer to my question, before my gaze landed back on the princes. One prince looked at me confused, while the other wore an amused expression.

"There are writing materials over on that desk," the shorter prince said, jerking his thumb at a table behind him. I made my way to where he indicated, grabbing paper and a quill, but couldn't find any ink. *How odd.* I continued searching the desk, hoping to spot an ink pot somewhere.

"It is self-inking," he said from behind me. I turned around to face him.

"Self-inking?" I had never heard of such a thing. I looked at the ink quill, its golden design intricately elaborated with inlaid black patterns in the crevices.

"Yes, all the ink you will need is contained within it. When it runs out, it is refilled at the top. It is quite handy and typically prevents ink blots since it controls how much ink is dispensed." His fingers brushed against mine as he took the ink quill from my hand. He studied it before smiling and placing it back in my palm, his fingers folding over mine. A blush crept across his cheeks as he smiled at me, struggling to maintain eye contact.

"That is quite handy. I will need to find one of these for myself," I commented, wondering where I would even find one to purchase.

"They currently cannot be found in shops. Our inventor created them last year, so we have a few scattered around the palace," he explained. His hand squeezed against mine when he noticed my shoulders sag a bit from discouragement. He quickly added, "Just think—you will get to try a future invention before anyone else can, likely for years to come."

"Yes, I guess that is true." I still felt a bit crestfallen, but I would take what little gains I could. I walked back to the bookcases and began with the first shelf. Uncapping the ink quill, I studied the metal tip carefully. It was a curious thing, and I couldn't help but feel both nervous and excited to try it out. I started with shelf one, carefully writing down the first text title. The ink quill flowed across the paper with ease. *Oh, this I could definitely get used to.*

I continued to scribble titles down, lost in my own world as the quill danced across the paper. The two brothers remained silent, watching me curiously, until they each grabbed a book and began reading. I, however, continued recording titles, planning to rank them later when I was alone.

Some time had passed, and I finally finished the first bookcase; it held far more titles than I had anticipated. At this rate, I'd already calculated that I would need to spend most of my waking moments reading to even hope to finish everything within two full months. The promise of three gave me slightly better odds. I felt a spark of giddiness at the thought of choosing which text to deem important. I already knew it would be one on Theorines's history—surely the most detailed and authentic in its recordkeeping. I could already feel the ache forming in my hand just thinking about copying down every word I read.

I was so lost in thought, I didn't notice the library door open or the servant announcing that dinner was ready. One of the princes gave me a gentle nudge. I glanced up from my writing to find the servant patiently waiting for us to follow him.

"Serenity, it's time to eat," answered the one who had nudged me. The other black-haired prince lounged on the couch, a book open in his lap. His eyes met mine.

"You are going to need a break from your writing. You need food to replenish your strength." He stood up from the couch, and I placed the ink quill next to the paper I had been writing on. The brown-haired prince offered me his hand, and I took it. He didn't ask as he looped his arm in mine, startling me. I didn't have time to recover as his brother looped my other free arm. We walked in silence while they led me to the banquet hall.

"Do you both enjoy reading?" I asked, breaking the silence. After all, they had been reading the entire time we'd been in the library. The likelihood of spending more time with them in the coming months meant I should probably get to know them better.

"Our parents instilled the importance of reading at a young age," the prince replied. I still couldn't quite tell if it was Prince Finch Azrael or Prince Gideon Orion. "What about you?"

"Well –" I began before being cut off.

"Not your story of building the best historical text there could possibly be, but do you enjoy reading in general?" he interrupted me.

"I really did not enjoy reading until I began researching. . . I find enjoyment in it now, but never in the past." How peculiar—I had never really thought about reading prior in my life, and it wasn't until being asked now that I realized that.

"What did you enjoy before your research?" The other prince inquired.

"Well, to be honest, horseback riding and archery were my two favorites—anything outdoors, really." Both brothers slowed down to look at me curiously. I knew my response was not particularly ladylike, and to the princes, it was probably about as foreign-sounding as I was to their Kingdom.

"I would like to see you shoot a bow, if it is not too bold to ask." The shorter prince commented.

"No, it is not too bold to ask. If you have an archery setup. I would be more than happy to practice with you." I smiled. I tried to practice my archery at least once a week to stay skilled.

"We should ride horses together as well. I know some places with views that rival your beauty," flirted the taller one. I giggled again from his flirtation as a blush crept to my cheeks. It was hard to deny that I could easily become accustomed to this kind of attention.

"You are positively a flirt, but I will take you up on that offer." I winked. Two could play this game.

"Been told that a time or two. You will learn to enjoy it."

"Who said I did not enjoy it already?" I threw back saucily. If the bantering continued to stay like this, I had no doubt it would get the three of us into trouble. I admitted to myself that it was nice to feel seen. Their flirting seemed to draw out a confidence in me I didn't realize I had.

Chapter Five

When we arrived, the servants opened the banquet doors for the three of us. Similar to the rest of the castle, the banquet hall might have felt rather dreary if not for the vibrant, colorful wall hangings that brightened the cold, stone walls. I questioned how old this castle had been and why whoever had built it did not cover the slate walls like ours at home? Surely, a fresh coat of paint could breathe life into the room—though carpets and heavy fabrics, while cozy, were notorious for trapping dust. I suppose swapping out the wall hangings was a far simpler trade than repainting an entire castle room.

We were the last to arrive. The King and Queen were already seated at the table, as were my sister and father. I grew self-conscious as three pairs of eyes landed on us. It did not seem to faze Prince Gideon Orion or Prince Finch Azrael as they continued to stroll to their respective chairs. The table was round and designed to seat exactly seven—perfect for our small gathering. The last remaining open spot was between Amity and Father. To my sister's right sat the brown-haired prince, followed by his brother, the King, and then the Queen, who was seated next to my father. This confirmed my suspicions that the black-haired prince was the eldest of the two brothers, thus being Prince Gideon Orion.

"We like sitting next to our guests; it is too stuffy to use the long banquet table when we could sit at a smaller table," said Queen Izralda with a smile. Her humble roots were evident, likely from a childhood spent as a servant where families lived closely and valued togetherness. I had a sneaking suspicion she had nurtured that characteristic with her husband, who hummed in agreement. Their sons did not blink in response. They had never known another environment than this one while growing up, I supposed. Then again, maybe their parents had sent them off on travels to become more cultured and diversified in their knowledge of other monarchy customs. I swallowed down the envy I had for them, even if it was a made-up scenario in my head.

"This intimate setting is far more welcoming. I could see how it would make conversation amongst guests far easier than needing to yell across the table to one another." Amity jested. It was unlike my elder sister to attempt humor in a conversation. Rarely did she find amusement in joking with our family, yet here she was, trying to make our hosts laugh.

"Quite so," King Ashborn commented dryly. His gaze fell upon me, lingering a bit, and a tingling zipped through my body again. It was not like I had never been around other males before, but maybe royalty had a different effect on me.

"Did you find the library satisfactory, Lady Serenity Novena?" King Ashborn asked, breaking my train of thought.

"Yes, your library is splendidly amazing. I only hope I have enough time to read everything," I complimented, feeling excitement bubble within me at the thought of my future task.

"Father, you should see her," Prince Finch Azrael chimed in, full of pride and delight. "For the last hour, she has been documenting all the texts she needs to read. Later, she plans to rank them from top priority to least priority. It is quite something."

My eyes widened at the younger prince, who beamed at me. I had thought I was boring them, but it appeared I had made the younger prince enthusiastic about my task at hand. Maybe I had misjudged the royals completely.

The King looked at his son before returning his attention to me. "Is that so?" King Ashborn inquired.

"Yes." I flushed, trying not to squirm in my seat.

"Hmm, I quite like hearing about a Lady showing an interest in reading, and on top of that, history. It shows character and quality in their stature," King Ashborn complimented. I preened under his compliments as Amity sat up straighter. I refrained from looking at her, wondering why she seemed to bask in a compliment that was meant for me.

"My daughter will only leave your library when it is required. If you let her, she would probably sleep in there," Father supplied with a slight chuckle.

Amity faked a laugh, attempting to join.

"In that case, we will try not to require your time elsewhere," King Ashborn replied with a playful smile in amusement. "We would not want to hinder your reading." His eyes twinkled with delight, and I fought the urge to shiver at the intensity of his gaze.

"Thank you, King Ashborn. I truly appreciate it. I have only managed to document the texts from the first bookcase so far. There are two more to go, and then I can properly rank them and begin reading immediately after." I didn't mean to be so informal with the King, but the excitement of his interest made me lose my usual restraint.

"Finch, please make certain she eats when meals are not required," King Ashborn said, turning to the son seated next to Amity—further confirming my suspicions about which prince he was.

"Yes, Father." Prince Finch Azrael nodded in agreement.

"No worries, Father. I, too, will help. We have a date to go horseback riding tomorrow," added Prince Gideon Orion. I wanted to argue with him about calling it a date, but thought better of it—it was semantics, after all.

"Good." King Ashborn turned his attention back to me. "You like to ride horses?"

"She is excellent on a horse, King Ashborn." Amity jumped in before I could respond. "We even brought her mare along for the journey." I could not help but question why Amity was so eager to jump to my defense. I took offense to it—it wasn't as if I'd been ill-mannered or rude when speaking with royalty. Did she truly think I'd slip up and disgrace the family? If that were her fear, then why bother bringing me at all?

"Serenity also claims to be excellent at archery," tacked on Prince Finch Azrael. He hadn't used my title or full name, and I wasn't about to correct him for being informal. "We plan to practice together. I want to see if she is a better shot than me." Out of the corner of my eye, I noticed Amity and Father flinch ever so slightly, as if they couldn't help it. I wondered what that was about. Amity's flinch didn't surprise me—but Father's did. He used to praise my archery. When had that changed?

"I would like to be in attendance when this occurs," commented King Ashborn. Father relaxed a bit in his seat, but Amity stayed stiff.

"Most certainly," Father replied. "She would be honored for you to observe."

If I could have gotten away with it, I would have shot my father a bewildered, annoyed glance. But, instead, I forced myself to sit there, a pleasant smile fixed tightly on my face. The idea of the king watching this competition hardly felt like an honor. If anything, it made me nervous. When it came to archery, there would be nothing serene about me.

"Excellent, then it is settled. I will have the servants ready the archery field after dinner." With two sharp clasps of his hands, King Ashborn summoned a servant, who appeared almost instantly. He instructed the servant to prepare the archery field after the meal. My hunger faded away. I knew I was an adequate shot, but I could only hope I was not as rusty as I feared. I did not want to look a fool in front of these royals, lest I disappoint my family. If I performed horribly, I would be an embarrassment. Amity would never let me hear the end of it.

"Well, guess there will not be much time for practicing," jested Prince Finch Azrael. I gave him a watery smile, feeling the nervous tension crawl under my skin.

"I think I will join as well," jumped in Prince Gideon Orion.

"All the children competing. This will be fun!" Queen Izralda clapped her hands giddily. Her dimples deepened as she smiled, excitement contagious. It lifted my spirits slightly, though it did little to ease the knot of nervousness tightening in my stomach.

The servants brought out the first course, each dish covered with a gleaming silver lid. It smelled delicious, rosemary potatoes with filet mignon and seasoned carrots. My senses told me it was savory, but I barely tasted it. Food was an afterthought as I ate, my mind occupied with recalling every muscle I would need to engage for the best aim and accuracy. I needed to calm my mind. I tuned out the dinner conversations, searching for the headspace I needed to occupy to keep myself from failing. I questioned if it would be considered an insult to beat both princes at archery, or if they would take the competition in stride. I would find out the answer shortly.

The seven of us walked to the archery field. The King and Queen led the way, their two sons trailing behind, with my family bringing up the rear. Sweat trickled down my back, my palms clammy with each step I took. The jitters raced through me like a live current. I needed to steady myself; I'd found that calm during dinner, but it vanished somewhere along the walk here. I'd always trusted my archery skills. I was a decent shot with a bow, but I didn't have the faintest inkling of how my skills would hold up against the prince brothers. Never in all my years of practice did I have an audience outside of my family and the servants who worked for us. Now, I would be performing in front of royals and the royal servants.

When we arrived on the field, the servants were placing the final touches on the targets. While King Ashborn, Queen Izralda, Amity, and my father veered left toward the seating area to watch, the princes guided me toward the staging area. There were intricately carved recurve bows next to a quiver filled with arrows.

"How shall we start?" Prince Finch Azrael asked, his eyes scanning the bows and arrows before returning to us.

"Ladies first, of course," The elder prince replied, giving his brother an incredulous look, as if questioning whether there was any other option in the matter.

"I personally think the oldest should go first. I need to know what I am up against," I challenged, knowing I would end up going last if they agreed.

"Or, we could go youngest to oldest, give the baby a chance." Prince Finch Azrael winked at me. I could not stop the eye roll that happened, and gasped, covering my mouth the moment I realized what I had done.

"Ahhhhh," Prince Gideon Orion began, pointing at me. "Did you see that? She is finally showing her true personality."

"About time. It is quite boring when people are stuffy around royals. We are just normal people." Prince Finch Azrael shoved his hands in his pockets, shrugging as he rocked on his feet.

"Apologies for boring you, your royal highnesses." I gave an exaggerated curtsy that had left us all in giggles.

"I believe children," King Ashborn interrupted us, "we all gathered here to see who the most skilled archer is, or did you all forget?"

I flushed, sobering up to find King Ashborn attempting to hide his smile. I smiled back; his efforts failed as he broke into a full grin.

"Father," Prince Gideon Orion began, "we were trying to figure out who would go first."

"And who did you decide on?" King Ashborn asked.

"Still deciding." Prince Finch Azrael called out. "Lady Serenity

Novena, I do not think, wants to go first, despite being a *Lady*." Prince Finch Azrael could not help but to tack that last bit on.

"Then you go first, followed by your older brother. Let Lady Serenity Novena go last—maybe she will show you both up," King Ashborn ordered. With that, it was settled.

Prince Finch Azrael picked up his bow and readied the first arrow. I watched him draw the arrow back, preparing, as he eyed up the target. I took in a breath when he did, and when the youngest prince breathed out, he let loose the arrow. It made a thunk into the target. I continued to watch Prince Finch Azrael for his reaction, but he gave no indication of how he did. Closing my eyes, I took a deep breath, and turned my focus to the targets. When I opened my eyes, I was relieved to see it had not been a bullseye. It was close, if he had aimed three inches to the right, it would have been dead center. My competition was steep. I clapped politely along with everyone else. Prince Finch Azrael smiled broadly.

"Not bad, little brother, not bad at all." Prince Gideon Orion ruffled his younger brother's hair while he took the bow for his turn. Prince Gideon Orion looked over at me, and with a wink, added, "And now it is my turn to show you how it is truly done."

I did not withhold my eye roll, which caused both brothers to laugh. I may have become a bit too cheeky; it would be my turn next, and depending on how Prince Gideon Orion performed determined how much I would need to focus on hitting that bullseye.

I watched as the older brother drew his arrow and took aim. Prince Gideon Orion did it with a flair that his younger brother lacked. My focus remained on his face as the arrow was released, and when it thunked into the target, our audience gasped. Prince Gideon Orion's eyes widened a fraction momentarily, before giving me a cocky smile. I took another deep breath, steadying myself before looking at the target and seeing that he had hit a perfect bullseye. My confidence sank at the thought of beating that.

"If you wanted to forfeit now, I would understand, Lady Serenity Novena," Prince Gideon Orion offered. With that single sentence, I was determined not to allow these princes to find any meekness within me. I strolled toward him and, before he could hand the bow to me, took it.

"Lady Serenity Novena, are you certain you want to do this?" Prince Finch Azrael asked. I could tell he was trying to offer me a polite way out. However, the way Prince Gideon Orion spoke to me in that cocky manner made me want to at least attempt to put him in his place. Those were bold thoughts for someone who did not fully believe in herself.

"No, it is alright, Prince Finch Azrael," I replied, drawing an arrow from the quiver. I stood before the target, bringing the bow and arrow up. I pulled the arrow back, feeling the weight of the string wanting to snap. *Concentrate, Serenity. Be serene like your name.*

I breathed in through my mouth and closed my eyes to concentrate. Opening my eyes, I exhaled slowly and let the arrow go, feeling the light breeze it caused against my cheek. I closed my eyes again, not wanting to know the results. I was too rusty; I was probably even further from the bullseye than Prince Finch Azrael had been. The arrow made a cracking sound before it thunked, leaving the air thick with silence. It had to be bad. Reluctantly, I peeked one eye open at the target, my brain struggling to process what I was seeing. My arrow had split Prince Gideon Orion's right in half. I didn't know that was even possible.

"Did she. . . Did she just do what I think she did?" Prince Finch Azrael was the first to speak. His voice sounded incredulous.

"What did I do?" I whipped my head, looking at him, desperate to know if this was a thing. Did splitting an arrow in half have a name? I needed to know.

"You split my arrow in half!" Prince Gideon Orion stood there with his mouth hanging open in astonishment. I looked back and forth between the two princes before turning toward the audience behind us. Amazement was reflected on their faces.

King Ashborn stood up and began to clap. "Well done, my girl, well done, Lady Serenity Novena!" He shouted. Father and Queen Izralda joined in on the clapping as they, too, stood up.

Father strolled toward me and immediately wrapped me in an embrace. He murmured quietly for only me to hear, "You have made your Father very proud today."

I hugged him tighter, savoring the moment. Over his shoulder, I caught sight of Amity still standing next to the King and Queen; she gave me a nod of approval. It was likely the only compliment I would be receiving from her today.

"You have quite a daughter there, Lord Lambert," King Ashborn complimented. Then, turning to my sister, he added, "She is far more exceptional than your letters ever led me on to believe." *Letters*? What did King Ashborn mean by letters? How long had Amity been writing to the King of Theorines?

"Aye, she is quite marvelous." Amity smiled. The others wouldn't notice it, but I knew from years of living with her that the slight tilt in her voice carried another meaning. Her mind was clearly mulling something over, but she would never reveal her hand until the timing suited her best.

Father placed his hand on my waist, holding me gently but firmly in place. I wanted to take a step back, to piece together what Amity might be planning and how it connected to King Ashborn's remark. I kept my smile steady, refusing to let my face betray the swirl of emotions bubbling beneath the surface. I pretended to relish their compliments while my mind raced with what those letters could have possibly entailed.

"I will say," Queen Izralda began, "I have never seen an arrow split in half. This is quite splendid!" She bounced on her feet, clapping her hands. The motion caused her crown to slip, forcing her to pause her clapping to catch it before it tumbled to the ground.

"Your Highnesses, are you claiming it has never been witnessed or recorded until today?" I asked hesitantly. King Ashborn looked at his wife, my father, his sons and then settled his gaze on me.

"Not that I am aware of. . ." He paused, "Do you think you could do it again?"

"I am not certain, Your Highness." I lowered my gaze to the ground, searching for the answer I sought. "I have never done it prior to today, and if it truly has not been recorded or witnessed before, it might prove a difficult feat to repeat." I kept my gaze fixed on the ground, knowing it was not the answer King Ashborn wanted to hear, but I could not lie to a royal.

"Very well, you have made a valid point. To commemorate tonight, we will leave the two arrows as they are to future guests." King Ashborn did not seem upset by my response. I looked up to see warmth and understanding in his smile.

"I am humbled to hear your plans, Your Highness." I curtsied, emphasizing my respect.

"Boys, how about you entertain Lady Serenity Novena? I have much to discuss with Lady Amity Lovanna," King Ashborn ordered his sons while giving a speculative look. He turned his attention back to my sister, and together they walked toward the castle, Queen Izralda on King Ashborn's arm. I glanced between my father and the princes. Father merely shrugged and headed in a different direction, leaving me alone with the princes.

"Well, that was fun," Prince Finch Azrael said, his arms behind his back, rocking back and forth, as he kicked some rocks on the ground.

"Do you know something?" I asked suspiciously, glancing toward the backs of his parents and my sister. When my gaze returned to the brothers, neither of them would meet my eye. "You do know something. What is it? Tell me," I demanded.

"Quite bold of you to order a prince around," Prince Gideon Orion challenged, finally looking up at me.

"I apologize, Your Highnesses," I dropped into a curtsy quickly.

"Oh, stop curtseying." The heir grabbed my arm, yanking me up to him, my chest pressed against his.

"Oh!" I squeaked, pulling back and stumbling until my back

collided against Prince Finch Azrael's chest. He caught me with ease and held me in his arms. I tried to pull away, but he wouldn't let go.

"She is cute when flustered, is she not, brother?" Prince Finch Azrael teased.

"Quite. You probably should not play with her too much, or she may faint." Prince Gideon Orion jested. When the younger prince released his hold on me, I shoved away from him and straightened my dress, smoothing out the wrinkles.

"I will have you both know, I have never fainted a day in my life," I huffed.

"Good, we do not like swooners." Prince Gideon Orion smiled. "And you did not seem like the swooning type from the start. . . Well, unless it involves historical texts," he joked.

"Alright, you had fun with your jabs. With that being said, the sun is beginning to set, I plan to head to my room and retire for the evening." I tried to walk past Prince Finch Azrael, but he grabbed my arm, halting me in my path.

"Wait, I want to gaze at the stars with you," he blurted out sheepishly. He was not looking at me. Instead, his focus was diverted to the ground. Oh no, no, no. I did not need a Prince falling for me. We only knew each other for a day, how can one catch feelings this quickly?

"I want to join too," announced Prince Gideon Orion.

"Would it not be indecent for the three of us to be out after hours without a chaperone?" I questioned, raising an eyebrow. I needed to get out of this situation and fast.

"We can arrange for a chaperone to be in attendance if you wish," Prince Finch Azrael replied begrudgingly.

"How about on another night? It has been a long day and a long trip. I would like to rest for the evening," I countered.

"Brother, we are being quite rude to Lady Serenity Novena," Prince Gideon Orion casually stated, coming to my defense. "Let her rest for the evening. She will be around for quite some time to gaze at the stars."

I tried to convey my gratitude and he smiled with a small dip of his head.

"I guess you are right, brother. Come, Lady Serenity Novena, we will walk you to your chambers." Prince Finch Azrael offered me his arm, and I was a tad nervous about accepting if my hunch was correct about him forming a crush on me, but to deny a prince would be insulting. I looped my arm through his, we took one step before my free arm was once again claimed by the other brother.

"Better get used to us," Prince Gideon Orion warned with a wink. "We will be spending a lot of time together."

"Somehow, I have a feeling you are both trouble." I could not contain my laugh.

"We are the very definition of trouble," they replied in unison.

"Now you tell me." I tried to bend over as my laughter increased, but their arms kept me upright.

"Happy to humor you, Lady Serenity Novena," Theorines's heir continued on with his charm while they escorted me to my rooms.

"I can already tell you two will keep me on my toes," I surmised looking back and forth between the two.

"You have no idea," Prince Gideon Orion replied in a low voice, causing me to shiver at the sudden change of energy around us. When we arrived at my rooms, I quietly thanked them and shut the door, separating myself from them. I leaned heavily against the wood.

I was not certain what had happened between myself and the two princes, but I was sure it would not be good for my heart. Quiet would be ecstatic if she were in my position. Honestly, she would be screaming in delight if she heard it was happening to me. If only I could trust to tell her the truth. I rested the back of my head against the wood and looked up at the ceiling searching for an answer to a question I didn't even have. I would need to tread very lightly with these royals and their flirtatious behaviors.

Chapter Six

HELD TRUE TO THEIR WORD, AFTER BREAKFAST, I WAS LED out to the stables, where three horses were saddled for us. It came to no surprise to me that Gideon rode a black Friesian, perfectly groomed, while Finch sat mounted on top of a palomino thoroughbred. Clover, my Bay Quarter horse, must have been groomed since our arrival. I had never seen her shined the way she shone now. My girl was receiving the royal treatment. I politely accepted the stable hands' help climbing into my saddle. At home, I never needed help, but in front of the royals, I felt it best to be the serene picture of a lady.

Gideon led us at a walking pace, and I took the time to enjoy the lovely scenery as we rode. The brothers were silent until we were out of range of the castle.

"If you enjoy riding, we should take the horses out often together," Finch spoke up.

"Clover and I would like that very much." I smiled while patting my mare's neck. I had anticipated a feisty mare with an attitude, but this sweet girl was a complete lovebug. Thoughts of Clover often interlaced with memories of Theo, especially the memory of my first kiss. I flushed thinking about it.

I often rode my horse alone, not needing an escort on my family's lands. However, that day, I chose to be brave in my request. Nervousness filled my stomach as I requested for Theo to attend the ride with me. My excuse was flimsy that I planned to ride further out than usual and wanted someone there as a precaution. None of the other stable hands had batted an eye at my request, but Theo had given me a knowing smirk.

I waited while he saddled up a spare horse, watching how his muscles moved with every movement. He caught me more than watching him, and I flushed, averting my attention every time. When he was close to finishing up, I hauled myself onto Clover's saddle, never needing help. I found it silly when capable beings requested help. I was perfectly fine doing it myself.

Theo mounted his horse, and we casually walked out to the pasture, both of us remaining quiet initially. When we were out of earshot, I realized he was probably waiting for me to say something first. I considered all the things I could possibly say to start the conversation between us. However, it was Theo who broke the silence first.

"The weather is nice today," he commented. I kicked myself for how simple of a sentence it was. I could have easily stated the obvious like that.

"It is." I offered a shy smile, withholding the nervous giggle that threatened to erupt from me.

"But it is not as beautiful as you are." His honey-brown eyes pierced into me, and my heart stuttered a beat as I swallowed. Everything in my mind had completely disappeared with his full attention on me. Immediately, I felt like I was overheating and my skin was too tight as I bit my lip. The nervous giggle bubbled out of me.

"Th-Thank you," I stuttered out, stumbling over my words. I had never been called beautiful before, so how did I proceed from here? "You

too, I mean not beautiful, you are very sexy. I mean, oh no." While still holding the reins, I covered my face because of how badly I blushed.

Theo's rich chuckle caused me to peek at him through my fingers. The sun shining off his dirty-blonde hair with his dark tan skin made something stir within me.

"Come on," he flirted with a nod of his head. His horse took off in a gallop, and I urged Clover to follow in pursuit. We raced further away from the manor, the exhilaration of the speed making me feel like I was fully alive as I inhaled the air from the breeze.

He didn't slow until we were nearing the woods, our horses both breathing heavily, and I could only imagine what state my hair was in from the way the wind whipped through it. When his horse came to a stop, he dismounted and tied the reins on a low branch. I was dismounting when he took Clover's reins to repeat the process.

I turned my back to him; the wind caused the grass to move in waves on the hills. We were quite secluded in this location of the lands, and I highly doubted anyone was close by. My excitement and nervousness grew. I had not thought about what would come next when I got him alone, but yet here we were.

I hadn't heard him come up behind me, whirling when I felt his hand on my hip. He kissed me, and my eyes widened in shock. It was my first kiss, and I stood there, not knowing what to do. He broke our kiss, pulling back slightly while looking down at me.

"I didn't misread the signs, did I? You like me, right?" He asked, a little guarded while giving me a confused expression. There was minimal space between us. Theo's hands lingered on my hips, and I could feel the warmth of his body. His naked chest distracted me.

I nodded, swallowing while biting the bottom lip that he had just kissed.

"Do you want me to do it again?" He pushed, tracking the movement.

I nodded quickly.

His hands slid behind my back as his arms wrapped around my

waist, pulling me tightly to him. He looked down, smiling at me, and lowered his head until his lips gently brushed against mine again. Slowly, I kissed him back, relishing the feeling. My hands slid up between us, feeling the muscles of his abs. I fanned my hands over his abs, loving the way they flexed beneath my palms. He took another step closer to me, and I slid my hands to his back, holding him closer.

He broke the kiss again, pulled back and smiled down at me.

I smiled timidly back up at him.

Coming back to the present, I thought about how we had repeated many outings similar to the first time, slowly, the intimacy increased, and then one day, we made love under a pine tree. The outings became less kissing and more sex over time. When he wasn't escorting me, I was spending every waking moment that I could in the stables with him.

"Enny for your thought?" Gideon asked, flicking the enny coin my way. I missed catching it and it fell into the weeds, lost to the world. It was only worth one cent, not much to make a fuss over.

"Nothing, just thinking about home and all the horse rides I would take." It wasn't an outright lie by any means.

"With anyone *special*?" Finch pushed; eagerness and nervousness filled his voice.

"No, I often rode alone or, if I went further distances, a stable hand joined in case of an emergency." Another truth while omitting the depth of details.

"I would suggest until you become familiar with the terrain to always have an escort with you if you choose to ride on our lands," Finch replied.

Gideon volunteered himself and Finch to be the escorts over a stable hand. He claimed he would give me a far more excitable outing than a stuff royal stable hand would. At the walking pace we kept, I questioned if it would be more excitable than this. We stayed out in the open of the wildflower meadow, birds flying overhead as the beginning of butterflies and bees fitted between the flowers.

Gideon stopped his horse and dismounted without warning, Finch following suit. I looked between the two, confused as to why we were dismounting. Finch offered me his hand and helped me down, but I wound up in his arms. Clover pressed into my back, leaving me trapped in the middle.

"Um?" I smiled nervously, and taking the hint, he took a step back. I dismissed the interaction, smoothing down my dress. Straightening, I looked around the meadow; we were in plants that were to my knees, with some grown to the height of my hips. If I tried to move far, my dress would snag on everything in sight, which didn't bother me, but it would be a hassle to maneuver.

Gideon withdrew a blanket from a saddle bag, and flapping it out, let it fall onto the top of a tall grassy area. He didn't bat an eye as he and Finch laid down on it. There was an empty space between them that the grass beneath the fabric strained to push through, causing a mound.

"Come lay with us." Finch patted his hand on the mound between them. Not wanting to disobey a royal, I struggled through the grass, yanking at my dress as it kept catching. When I was able to lower my body to lay next to them, I was panting heavily from the mini-workout the terrain had given me.

"Didn't mean to make you out of breath so quickly," flirted Gideon.

"Could have picked a better spot," I grumbled. The awareness of how close their bodies were to mine stayed at the forefront of my mind. If I rolled one way or another, I would be curled up into their side. I chose to stay ramrod straight on the blanket in my location, looking up as we watched the clouds pass by.

"But what better place to relax than to be lost in nature," replied Gideon.

"Do you like being outside?" Finch asked.

"I do. I actually spend a lot of time reading outside," I answered.

"Good, then we will need to spend a lot of time together." I could hear the smile in his voice.

We stayed like that until the wind shifted and the smell of rain was in the air. Gideon quickly packed us up, and still at a walking pace, we headed back to the castle.

Chapter Seven

I FELL INTO A ROUTINE WITHIN A COUPLE OF DAYS OF being at Kingdom Theorines. Each morning, I would rise, eat breakfast in bed, and then spend majority of my day in the library. I took precarious notes often, sometimes deeming it unnecessary, but I would rather be safe than sorry later.

More often than naught, the princely brothers joined me. They were a distraction, hindering my progress at every waking moment. Queen Izralda was another distraction; her constant pestering of why I found certain texts more important to copy than others was incessant. I knew the royal family meant well, but if I could, I would lock the library doors and bar them from entering. The nagging thought of taking books back to my rooms to read in silence became more appealing with each passing day.

It was on day three that the princes requested that we address each other informally. My assessment of Finch having a crush on me continued to prove true. I had difficulty gauging if Gideon was overly flirty or if he, too, was developing feelings for me. I found it peculiar that I had not spotted another female around our age in the castle.

Due to this, I reasoned with myself that it was the only reason they showed any interest in me and spending time in my company.

After the initial day, King Ashborn did not stir as many butterflies within me. I chalked it up to nerves of being introduced to my first royal and nothing more. However, an interesting tidbit I heard from Queen Izralda is they were not completely exclusive. I knew Queendom Grewt'en did not practice monogamy, but I was not aware that Kingdom Theorines did not as well. Queen Izralda had corrected me that it was something that the two of them had decided. It eased my guilt that King Ashborn had an unabashed wandering eye upon our first meeting.

I rarely saw my sister; Amity continued to have long, private meetings with King Ashborn. When I tried questioning her, she would dismiss me. When I attempted to pester Father on it, he feigned a lack of knowledge. I pointed out he had sat in the first meeting, but he genuflected, claiming it was a simple meet and greet. My family's secrecy infuriated me.

Two weeks later, the brothers had yet to become bored with me. They continued to hang around the library. While taking written notes, I simultaneously was taking mental notes on each brother. I cataloged every detail I could about them, already deciding to dedicate a chapter to each prince in my book.

Gideon hid his nervousness to inherit the throne by chuckling and then flirting; responding with the correct words that would be expected from him. I caught onto the specific hitch of his chuckle that the heir would only use when he was nervous. The same chuckle came out when regarding his parents displaying their open relationship. Considering he had grown up around it, it surprised me he was uncomfortable with it. From the way he talked, I had pieced together that his teachers preached monogamy, and probably never had a royal who did not practice it in Kingdom Theorines.

Finch, on the other hand, was carefree. The lack of weight of ruling a kingdom on his shoulders caused him to goof off and generally get away with it. His curiosity about my research was rampant regarding the aspect of the ocean and traveling. Those two topics were his favorite conversational pieces. I felt I disappointed him by my lack of experience. I could only converse about what I had read about. Finch's enthusiasm burst when he tried to describe to me the feeling of a boat rocking beneath his feet while the ocean's salty air blew through his hair. I listened, nodding and smiling to encourage him to continue. He promised he would take me on a trip to his favorite island so that I could understand the feeling he loved.

"What would you want to be if you were not a prince?" I asked Finch one day when only the two of us were residing in the library. I had taken a break from my research and was lounging on the couch across from him.

"A sea captain," he answered without missing a beat. He placed the book he was reading on his chest, and even from here, I could see it was a fictional tale that involved the ocean.

"Does any of your books ever involve the romance of a sea captain and a princess?" I nodded at his book.

"No, never." He laughed.

"Any romance in general?" I pushed, enjoying teasing him. When it was only us, he was more relaxed and able to converse. While Gideon's company was nice, he often dominated the conversation, causing Finch to remain quiet.

"Sometimes." He gave me a pointed look. I sat up on the couch, leaning forward.

"I bet those are your favorites to read," I teased further.

"Where else would I find all my suave wooing tips." He rolled his eyes, and I laughed. Aside from a few times of him flushing when he was a bit too nice to me or when I caught him staring, Finch has never flirted with me. He has always been respectable, and I cherished the friendship blooming between us. We were able to talk on an intellectual level, which evaded Gideon at times.

"Ah yes, very suave."

"What about you? All I see is constant romance research in your historical texts." Finch raised an eyebrow, daring me to deny it. I swallowed, sobering up.

"Your library has some promising information in my research." I tried to deflect with a shrug.

"Right, do you actually read romance novels or only historical things?" He pushed, sitting up, we were almost knee to knee.

"I do read romance books that do not involve any history at all." I smirked with a shake of my head.

"What is your favorite?" He pushed. My mind thinking of the book currently packed away in my trunk with the pressed flower in it.

"It's called 'A Romance Unlike Ours,' and it's about –" Finch cut me off.

"– How about I read it? No spoiling it, okay?"

"There are no ocean travels in it," I challenged.

"I may not survive." He placed the back of his hand on his head and pretended to faint back onto the couch, causing me to laugh at his melodramatic ways. He leaned up, joining in on my laughter. He promised once it was in his possession he would read it right away, so we could compare thoughts on the book. I was excited to have someone new to hopefully gush with me over the book. I would have lent him my copy, but I didn't want to risk the pressed tulip in the back being ruined by accident.

The princes studied me just as much as I studied them. When I began to run low on parchment paper, they would silently place a fresh stack on the desk I used. If I was unable to reach a book or scroll, I didn't need to ask, they would fetch it for me. Finch would flush and become nervous, his words jumbling when our bodies became pressed together from his reaching above me. Gideon, though, would place his hand on my hip when he retrieved the literature out of my reach. Sometimes, his fingers would squeeze slightly, pulling me closer to him. Upon receiving the book, I would detangle myself from him and find Finch trying to hide a sour face.

They, like their mother, would inquire why I considered a

passage important enough to be copied. Some days, I copied whole books down for my notes, fearing I would never have an opportunity to read them again. The work was tedious, and my hands cramped often. I felt the pain from it every day, but at two weeks, here I was not even a quarter of the way through. The distraction from the brothers did not help, but my hand was grateful for the breaks.

We had yet to go horseback riding again since my second day here. The weather had put a damper on that. Which was the same for Finch's need to stargaze with me. It had not rained in the last couple of days, and I knew it would only be a matter of time until Finch asked me.

Similar to her sons, Queen Izralda had also requested to drop the formal title and to call her Izzy. The only one that remained with a title firmly attached to his name was King Ashborn. In the short time of living here, I had become comfortable with these royals. However, I feared too much familiarity may cause troubles later on in my life. It was at that moment that I was pondering the implications when King Ashborn strolled into the library. In the entirety of my time of being here, he had never visited before. I quickly rose from my seat to respectfully greet him in a curtsey.

"King Ashborn," I murmured with my head tilted to the ground.

"Rise Lady Serenity Novena," he ordered. I rose, and it was only when I was standing upright that he crossed the distance to me. He stopped before me, and I silently waited for what would happen next. My nervousness caused my heart to race from the thrill of the unknown.

"Are you finding my library to your satisfaction?" He asked. I found the way he worded the question peculiar; it was almost as if he was asking for my approval. Aside from the initial day when we arrived, King Ashborn had not shown any more interest in my love for reading and researching. I assumed his wife had been spying on me and filling him with information.

"Yes, Your Highness." I gazed back longingly to the filled bookshelves. "I fear I may not have the time to finish my research before our departure." It had been a personal bubble of mine that continued to grow each day. King Ashborn looked past me to my workstation. I wondered what he was thinking; the room felt warmer than before. His eyes roved over the notes I had been copiously copying. I restrained myself from wanting to block his view. Instead my hand rested on the desk beside me. His gaze tracked the movement and slid from my hand up my arm and landed on my face.

"That would be an unfortunate matter." He looked over to his sons, his eyebrows furrowing, before looking back to me. "Walk with me, Lady Serenity Novena," he ordered turning on his heel to begin walking toward the front of the library. My gaze flicked over to the brothers who were watching us with intent interest, and back to the king. I hesitated for a brief second and then scrambled to catch up to King Ashborn. When I was halfway to the king, my mind caught up to the facial expressions the brothers had been wearing. Gideon's face had been uneasy; he wasn't smiling, and his eyes showed fear. Meanwhile, Finch wore a crossed expression, clearly disgruntled. Did they know something? This did not help ease my nerves about what this conversation may have ensured.

I walked a step behind King Ashborn's side, keeping up with his pace.

"Lady Serenity Novena, you have adjusted rather well into our home, would you not agree?" King Ashborn questioned, breaking the silence.

"Yes, Your Highness, I would agree." I could not say it was much of a change from being at home. I was still in a library, researching regardless of the location. It had been an easy adjustment for me. Instead of siblings bothering me, I had two brothers interrupting my concentration.

"That is excellent to hear. You are nineteen, if I recall. Am I correct?"

"Yes, Your Highness. I recently turned nineteen in the spring." Why did my age matter? Where was this going?

"My eldest son, Prince Gideon Orion, is twenty as you may know."

"I was unaware of his age, but I knew he was older than me, Your Highness."

"There comes a point in every heir's life when they need to start considering marriage. I will not be King forever, and my son needs to start looking forward to his future." King Ashborn sounded certain in his statement.

I nodded in agreement, but I was not certain why this would involve me; I was a Lady's daughter, not a princess. "That makes sense, Your Highness," I replied pathetically.

"Have you heard of The Courting Seasons, Lady Serenity Novena?"

"Very little, Your Highness, only what I have read or heard from a passing traveler." My mind recalled a text I had read in passing about the yearly events.

The Courting Seasons were created by Queen Opal of T'Lovoness, to bring peace and prosperity amongst the six Monarchies. They were established to help mingle the next generations with each other and establish relationships amongst the Monarchies. The Courting Seasons allow the free will to find a marriage partner without parental or any other influence involved. Arranged marriage couples are encouraged to participate as well to establish relationships with the others.

The Courting Seasons helps broaden a young individual's perception of various Monarchie's societal views as they live amongst their peers at the hosting Monarchies castle. Currently, only Royals host The Courting Season, with Kingdom T'Lovoness hosting the biggest one every year during summer. Kingdom Hayverton hosts a smaller one in the fall, followed by Queendom Grewt'en in winter.

To participate in The Courting Seasons, the individual must be no younger than eighteen and no older than thirty. Individuals may participate in as many Courting Seasons as necessary and may continue to participate with their partner even afterward. Once a couple is wedded, it is expected that the couple will not interject themselves into The Courting Seasons. They may attend some balls but should instead focus on their new life as newlyweds. This does not include royal heirs; they should still attend The Courting Seasons with their new spouse for one to two years to encourage additional relations with other monarchies.

The Courting Seasons have been around for roughly twenty years. Queen Opal began the tradition after reading about The Courting Games, which were put into practice hundreds of years ago. History is uncertain as to what caused The Courting Games to cease in existence.

"I see." King Ashborn continued walking before saying his next words. "I plan to send Prince Gideon Orion and Prince Finch Azrael to participate in Queen Opal's courting season in a month." I could not decipher why King Ashborn would be divulging these details to me. I held no sway over his decision-making when it came to his sons and their future spouses.

"I could understand how that would be a beneficial decision." I tried to reply in a sophisticated, scholarly way. "The Courting Seasons bring favorable relationships and friendships amongst the six monarchies due to the large attendance." The travelers who passed through my family's manor during their travels, mentioned that sometimes hundreds of eligible bachelors and bachelorettes attended. The sheer volume did not surprise me, considering how many children the monarchs had, then coupled with how many lords and ladies there were per monarchy, sometimes up to sixty to eighty. Queendom Grewt'en had fifty-four lords alone. Top this information off with respectable merchant children being allowed to attend, and the number of attendees continued to rise.

"Indeed, your sister voiced a similar opinion," King Ashborn replied thoughtfully.

"I beg pardon, King Ashborn, but may I inquire as to why you have summoned my family here?" I knew it was not my place to ask;

it was a bold question and caused him to pause in his footsteps. He turned to look at me.

"You are a very brilliant-minded child, Lady Serenity Novena," he complimented, and the heat crept up my neck and into my cheeks.

"Thank you, Your Highness." I dropped into a quick curtsy.

"However, if that brilliant mind has yet to figure it out. . . Then maybe it is not as brilliant as I had thought." He looked at me speculating. "Regardless, my decision has been made and you will be sure to find out soon enough." The King dismissed me, leaving me to stand there to watch his receding back. I tried to grasp the backhanded compliment he had given me. I tilted my head to the side, trying to puzzle through it. Turning, I slowly walked back to the library, trying to figure out what he meant. What was I missing? What had I not figured out yet?

I opened the library door to walk back to my work desk. Scratching my arm, I continued to puzzle over the king's words. What had he meant that maybe I was not as brilliant as he had thought? Rounding the corner, both brothers sat upright and to attention quickly. I gave them a half-hearted smile, rubbing my arm where I had scratched it. Maybe I shouldn't have come back here.

"What did Father want with you?" Gideon asked first.

"He talked with me about The Courting Seasons," I answered him cautiously. I took my seat at the desk, looking over the notes I had been mid-copying before King Ashborn had come to collect me. I felt numb and couldn't even focus on the words I had scrawled on the parchment.

"What about?" Finch pushed.

I did not let my eyes stray from my notes as I replied, "he asked if I knew much about them and that he planned to send the two of you there in a month." I looked up to gauge their reaction. It may not have been my news to tell them if they were not already aware.

"Is that all?" Gideon asked. Why did it feel we were all tip-toeing around on broken glass? The energy in the room suddenly felt thick. I swallowed.

"More or less yes, why? Is there something the two of you know?" Both brothers looked at each other. I knew they were having a silent conversation similar to what Quiet and myself would have at times. Gideon was the first to turn to look back at me.

"We are not at liberty to say. You will know when it is time," Gideon replied.

"But surely you could give me a hint if you know?" I pushed.

"Father swore us to secrecy, and we cannot go against Father's wishes. You will know soon enough." Gideon said firmly.

I huffed in annoyance. Amity would not tell me, Father would not tell me, King Ashborn would not tell me, and now the prince brothers would not tell me. Initially, all I had wanted to do was come here and read their historical texts, but now, to find out I am being kept in the dark on something everyone else was cued in on did not bring me joy. Maybe if I stayed home, I could have just daydreamed about the library and not feel this sense of betrayal for the unknown.

Gideon rose from his place on the couch and came toward me. When he stood in front of me, he placed both of his hands on my shoulder and looked down at my face. I found sorrow in his eyes while he silently begged for me to trust him.

"Serenity," he softly said. "Please understand if I could, I would tell you right now . . . but until your sister or my father makes a decision, I am not at liberty to say a word." He stopped himself, his eyes searching mine. Trying to seek if I understood that I needed to be patient. The sorrow in his eyes did not go away, and I was not even certain what was causing him to be mournful about the situation.

"I think I can respect that, but can you answer me one question?" I decided to see if I could push this a little further. His warm hands slightly squeezed on my shoulders.

"Depending on the question, maybe." His expression became guarded.

"Why do your eyes hold so much sadness over this?" It was as if I had slapped him, he took a small step back as if to catch himself. His hands slid to only his fingertips, touching my shoulders. I watched as he processed what I had asked, emotions flashing over his face. He settled on an answer, his hands coming back to firmly rest on my shoulders.

"Serenity, I hope you will still be my friend when everything is out in the open." He squeezed my shoulders with that sorrowful expression and turned to walk away to the entrance of the library.

"Gideon!" I called out, halting him in his tracks. He looked over his shoulder, awaiting my reply. "I have a feeling whatever this secret is, you do not have a say in the matter, meaning I should not punish our friendship for it. When the dust falls, I will still be your friend." I knew I was blindly agreeing to something that I may come to regret, but I had to remind myself that a prince could not go against a king's decision.

Prince Gideon Orion looked at the wall, mulling over my words before he replied, "I hope that your promise will stay true. I would be greatly remorseful to lose you as a friend." He then continued to walk to the entrance of the library. When he was out of sight, and I heard the door open and click shut behind him, I looked over to Finch, who was still sitting in his chair.

"Well?" I asked with an arched eyebrow to the youngest brother. I really was not certain what my question to him was, but I would take whatever response I received. Sometimes, asking the vaguest of questions received the most detailed responses.

"Just go easy on Gideon, he has a lot to deal with in the upcoming months." Finch got up from the chair, and passing me, he too left, leaving me all alone in this library. Somehow, I knew I was going to witness history in the making. I just was not certain if I would enjoy it, though.

After that, I had a difficult time focusing on my research. It should not have been this difficult to copy words on parchment, but I kept spacing off my mind wandering on what this huge secret could be and how did it involve me?

I had been walking leisurely down the corridor with no particular place in mind. The castle was peaceful when everyone was settling in for the evening. It was during these moments that I enjoyed the silence the most. I could explore without being required to make polite small talk; the hallways were empty, not even a servant on a mission to complete a task. I admired the artistically done tapestries, sometimes slowing to take in additional details on one and then barely glancing at the next one.

Queen Izralda had sent a scholar to recite in depth the history of Theorines and how the tapestries depicted it if you knew what you were looking for from the story. I quickly dismissed the scholar, feeling they had been too much of a know-it-all. I did not care for the way they looked down their nose at me, tsking when Queen Izralda informed him of my historical quest, as she had put it.

Finch came around the corner and was startled to find me. I smiled, acknowledging him. He gave a small wave as we met in the middle.

"Serenity, what are you doing at this hour?" He asked.

"This is when the castle is quiet and I can take the time to enjoy it the most," I answered. "One could inquire as to what you are doing at this hour as well?"

"I had trouble sleeping." His lips quirked to the side. "Would you care for company?"

I raised my arm, smiling, and he took it. We walked in silence back the way he had come from.

"Do you have trouble sleeping often?" I inquired, finally breaking the quietness.

"Sometimes, yeah." He tilted his head to the side. "Would you humor me by following me somewhere?"

"Sure, why not." I had nothing better to do, and my curiosity was piqued by where he was taking me. He didn't say much as he led us further within the castle until he opened very elaborate double doors. Following him in, I realized we were in his royal chambers.

"Finch, am I allowed in here?" I asked, trying to take a step back, but he held my arm fast.

"Yes, you are fine. Besides your present is here," he rushed out pulling me forward and then dropping my arm while he went to a desk and started rummaging through the drawers.

"Present?" He had made no mention of a gift the entire way here.

I glanced around the entertaining portion of his rooms; knotted wood floors were covered with blue and gray area rugs. The walls were painted in various colors that melted into each other, and as I turned in a circle, I realized they resembled the sky at various times of the day, complete with a sunset in bruised pinks and purples, that followed a sunrise in pinks and reds. I tilted my head to the side, and the more I put the pieces together, the more it became apparent his entertaining room was designed to be like a ship.

"You really enjoy being on a ship?" I asked.

"Yeah, it took some time to get the walls the correct shade of color as the sky," he replied over his shoulder. I heard an 'aha' and then he was striding back to me.

I watched him with amusement and curiosity.

"Close your eyes and open your hand," he instructed, and I obeyed.

I felt something light being placed in my waiting hands, and opening my eyes, I found a darling blue box, wrapped with a matching bow. He watched me eagerly as I undid the bow and removed the lid. Inside, I found a gorgeous metal self-inking quill. Silver swirls played on the exterior with blackness laying underneath.

"Hold it up to the candlelight," he urged, and as I did so, the silver metallic shifted to shades of blue, purple, and hints of pink.

"Oh, Finch, it is beautiful," I gushed.

"I am glad you like it. I had our inventor make one specifically for you." He took the quill from my hand, and turning it slightly, I found my name intertwined in the swirls on the quill.

"Oh, Finch." I didn't think I had ever received a more lovely gift than this in my life. I continued turning the quill in the light, admiring the colors that danced a crossed the decorative surface.

"I figured you would appreciate it." His voice was warm, and I looked up at him smiling. He was watching me and not even looking at the quill.

"I do, I cannot wait to begin using it tomorrow," I gushed, already excited from the thought. He chuckled from at enthusiasm.

"I am glad. Come on, it is getting late. Let me walk you to your rooms."

The entire walk back, I twirled the quill, watching it shift colors and smiling every time my name on the quill came into sight.

Chapter Eight

A FEW DAYS LATER, MY VIEW BECAME BLOCKED BY A bouquet of flowers, and I leaned back in my chair, startled. Gideon's rich laugh came from my reaction, and I found it was him holding the bouquet.

"What is the meaning of this?" I smiled, taking the bouquet and inhaling the flower scents. It was a mixture of daffodils and tulips and reminded me of all the flowers Theo had gifted me these past couple of years.

"I thought a pretty girl like you deserved a pretty bouquet of flowers," he flirted.

"Oh really?" I sniffed the flowers again, relishing in their floral scent.

"Yes, really. Figured this desk could use some brightening up." He procured a vase he had kept hidden from sight behind his back. It was a deep blue with realistic clouds painted upon it. He placed the vase on the desk, and I put the flowers in it, smiling at the new decoration.

"I will bring you flowers every week," he promised.

"Sounds a bit cumbersome," I teased with a shake of my head. Silently, enjoying the thought of having something to brighten my day when I looked at them.

"For you, I am willing to make sacrifices," he deepened his voice going down on one knee, and I couldn't contain my laughter.

"Ah yes, please go slay the beasts who prohibit you from collecting these rare flowers," I played into his dramatics.

"I shall My Lady." He took my hand and planted a kiss on the back of it. I laughed harder until tears formed; he cracked a smile, joining in with me. That was how the servant found us to announce it was time for dinner.

We were still laughing and lightly nudging each other as we walked to the banquet room. When the doors opened, all heads turned to us, and I realized they probably had heard us the entire walk here. I quickly wiped a tear away as Gideon straightened, trying to compose himself. We took our seats and tried to avoid looking at each other, to prevent our giggles.

"Do I even want to know what has you both in a laughing hysteria?" King Ashborn stated with a raised eyebrow. I quickly looked away from him, my shoulders shuddering, and found Amity giving me a crossed look. Changing my direction of focus, I met Gideon's eyes, and we both broke out in laughter, unable to contain it. Father attempted to clear his throat, but it did not help to any avail.

"Glad to see the two getting along," Queen Izralda chirped in.

"I suppose." King Ashborn rolled his eyes and began eating while our laughter subsided. If I allowed the thought of Gideon and slaying imaginary beasts to enter my mind, I had to fight my smile from turning into another fit of laughter. He had been overly dramatic in his responses, and there was something about it that made me unable to contain my emotions.

The King cleared his throat, and everyone gave him our undivided attention. Gideon shifted in his seat while Amity sat ramrod straight.

"Lady Amity Lovanna and family, you have been our honored guests for nearly three weeks. I have greatly enjoyed getting to know you all better." King Ashborn's gaze passed over us.

"Thank you, King Ashborn, for allowing us to be your humbled guests," Amity began, "We are grateful for this hospitality, even with my sister, Lady Serenity Novena, being an unexpected guest from our original exchanges."

My muscles tightened as everyone turned their attention to me. I gave a weak smile, trying to not appear uncomfortable.

"Indeed," King Ashborn claimed the attention back to him. "But if she had not arrived, my mind would not have been as secure as it is now on my decision."

"I thank you, King Ashborn, for your kind words. I am glad you can see why my sister is a special Lady." Amity placed her hand over my right, giving me a small squeeze of affection. I reframed from looking at her incredulous.

"Yes, I can see why. Which is why I am pleased to announce that if your sister, Lady Serenity Novena, or my son, Prince Gideon Orion, does not find someone to marry at the upcoming Courting Seasons at Kingdom T'Lovoness, we will announce their arranged marriage." King Ashborn raised his glass in a toast. Amity, Father, and The Queen followed suit, raising their glasses in unison.

The room closed in on me; I dropped the roll I had been holding in my left hand. The food in my mouth tasted like ash as I looked at Gideon, who was smiling at me apologetically. I looked to my father who was sitting on my left. He also was smiling and gave my left hand a squeeze. My head turned to Finch sitting across from me; his mouth was scrunched up as his eyes betrayed him, turning red from trying to hold back the tears forming.

I turned my attention back to the King and gave him a meek smile to show my gratitude. "I thank you for this opportunity, Your Highness. I can only hope to continue to please you and Prince Gideon Orion." I was not certain how I managed to pull that sentence off without my voice shaking, but I sat there with a watery smile plastered on my face as I felt myself suffocating.

"I am certain you will," Queen Izralda spoke up. "We mentioned just forgoing The Courting Season and having you marry our Gideon outright, but everyone should experience The Courting Season once. How fun it will be to mingle with other peers around your age." Queen Izralda clapped her hands giddily. "I mean, you are both practically arranged already, but why not have the opportunity to explore before settling down, right, Dear?" She turned to look at her husband.

Of course, in an open relationship, these two would see it that way. I saw it as I was trapped regardless of my choice. No matter the results, I will be married by the end of summer, and it wouldn't be to Theo. My gaze flicked to my future betrothed, either I would become his wife or someone else's. Dread slammed into me; I would become Queen.

I was not royal material, let alone queen material. I looked to Amity, who was chatting animatedly with Queen Izralda about wedding planning. *How had she done it?* How had my sister convinced them I would be the perfect match for Theorines's heir? My sister was cunning, but this was a whole new level I had never witnessed.

Turning my attention to Queen Izralda, I wondered how she had done it? She, after all, had started as The King's mistress. She had never been raised to be a royal, yet here she was ruling next to His Majesty's side. How difficult of a time did she have to transition over from being a hidden lover to being in the center of attention. Did she have anyone nurturing her along the way? I suppose she most likely would guide me along on this new path. When she noticed me staring, she smiled, and I gave her a weak smile in return. Taking my focus off her, I stared down at my full dinner plate in front of me. The food barely touched. I finally knew the secret they had all been keeping from me, and King Ashborn was right; maybe I was not as bright as was believed. All the signs had been presented to me; I had been too daft to recognize them.

When dinner ended, I hurried back to my rooms alone, where I could fall apart. No one had attempted to engage me in conversation after the announcement, and I feared my voice would have cracked if I had to talk. I barely glanced at any passing servants, trying to fight the tears that blurred my vision from falling.

Yanking the door to my rooms open, I escaped inside, where I shattered. My future had been ripped away from me. The historical scrolls on my desk caught my attention, and my legs gave out from beneath me. I crumpled to the ground, digging my palms into my eyes. All my time researching had been for naught. There was never going to be a future with Theo. My sister had been arranging a marriage for me, and my father knew about it.

I stayed wallowing at my stolen future until I didn't have any more tears to give. Begrudgingly, I pulled myself up and went to my desk. Tenderly, I touched the scrolls as if they were fragile and could break. It was silly, the scrolls didn't even contain anything that could have helped Theo and me. They contained information on Theorines's agriculture and prosperity.

Wiping away a tear running down my cheek, I pulled a blank sheet from the stack and a self-inking quill I had borrowed without permission. I needed Quiet to pass along the information to Theo. I twiddled with the words I would need to use to convey the message. I scratched out and ruined various sheets of paper until I finally settled on the simple sentences.

I am in a secretive, tentative betrothal to Prince Gideon Orion of Theorines. Please inform those who need to know of the engagement. Prior to our wedding, Prince Gideon Orion and I will be attending Kingdom T'Lovoness's courting season with the chance to find love in another before an arranged marriage announcement occurs.

I included information on what living in the castle and two Prince brothers were like. Even if Quiet had minimal interest in my research, I still included a few tidbits of history that I believe she would have found interesting. I folded the letter, sealed it, and leaned back in my chair, staring down at the envelope. The impact hit me. No matter if I found the answer now, it wouldn't matter. I was never returning home.

Chapter Nine

THE FOLLOWING MORNING, I WAS AWAKENED ABRUPTLY AS a flurry of maids came barging into my room. The Queen's personal dressmaking team followed them, claiming they would prepare the dresses I was expected to wear during my attendance at The Courting Season. All curtesy paid by The King and Queen. They did not want their potential future daughter-in-law to be ill-dressed at this event.

From the gossip I gathered from eavesdropping in on the servants and dressmakers, King Ashborn wanted to sour The Queen of T'Lovoness a bit. Supposedly, Queen Opal did not care for anyone who was not a royal, and with the future queen for Theorines being me, King Ashborn wanted to ensure the other monarchy's royals respected his future daughter-in-law. I was conflicted between feeling gratitude for the protection and the daunting sense of having vicious wolves snapping at my heels every step of the way.

I had minimal opinion about the dress style, color, or the need for breaks. I had become their personal mannequin and dress-up doll all in one. They compared dresses to my complexion and how extravagant they needed to be or not. I could not decipher their way of thinking. One dress would be filled with ruffles with barely any skin revealed and the next would be a simple strapless, satin dress with a slip up the leg. However, no matter the material, it always felt like butter against my skin; nothing was irritating.

It was mid-afternoon and I could barely stand as my head nodded, trying to stay awake. A maid instructed me to raise my arms, and when I was too tired to comply, she nudged me, causing me to jerk awake. I groggily obliged; through blurry eyes, my room was a cacophony of fabric colors and patterns. I pitied the servants who would clean up after The Queen's dressmakers left.

Clap. Clap. The sharp sound of hands clapping jerked me upright. I must have dozed off while standing. I glanced around the room and found the head dressmaker frowning at me. I never caught her name, nor did she care to call me by anything other than 'girl.' She clapped her hands twice again.

"We are done for today," she announced. She didn't wait for anyone to respond as she turned on her heel and departed. I wondered if tomorrow I would be receiving the same treatment. The maids closest to me started yanking the dress they had been working on off me. They didn't bother to dress me in any of my personal attire, leaving me to stand on the wooden podium in only my slip. The room stayed a mess of colorful fabrics, and I was too tired to bother with anything else. I stepped off the podium and staggered to my bed. I didn't care if I missed dinner tonight. Lunch contained of fruits and some pieces of bread. I would deal with my hunger in the morning when I woke up.

"Come, Serenity, we are going to ride horses today," announced Gideon gallantly. I had not seen hide nor tail of either brother the last three days. I barely was allowed to leave my rooms, all my meals being delivered while the dressmakers worked. My days of being pricked, poked, and prodded came to an end last night when the head dressmaker stated they had no more use for my body and all the dresses would be delivered in a week.

My rooms were cleaned, and I could once again freely walk

around the area without tripping over fabric or accessories. By my calculation, the number of dresses thrown on me during those three days was more than my entire life's wardrobe. I doubted I would ever have need for that many dresses in the duration they were being made for, but no one could claim I wouldn't have style.

"Come on, Serenity," Gideon repeated.

"I need to get this text copied down," I replied without looking up. Three days of being someone's personal dress-up doll put me behind. During those three days, I had an infinite amount of time to think of my next steps. I needed to keep my mind going and the only way I knew how was through my research. I still could write my book.

"Your Prince commands you to ride horses with him," Gideon countered. I raised my eyebrow, amused, while my focus did not stray.

"Last I knew, you were not my Prince, as my monarchy is Queendom Grewt'en, and this is Kingdom Theorines."

"Hmm," he mused, and I felt the warmth of his body on my back as he placed both of his hands on either side of me on the desk. "Are you or are you not in Kingdom Theorines, on our soil?"

"I am." I bristled slightly. Gideon had done nothing wrong; his hand was forced into this secretive and tentative arranged marriage, the same as mine. This, though, felt more intimate than all the times he would place a hand on my hip while helping me reach a book too high on the shelf.

"And are you or are you not betrothed to the future king of Theorines?" Teasing entered his voice as he leaned in closer, his chest pressed against my back while his breath tickled my ear.

"I-," I began and had to clear my throat, shaking my head slightly. "I am."

"Then, we are going horseback riding. Let me show you your future country. I already have your horse readied." He grabbed my hand, and as I protested, he gave me a wink. He dragged me to the doors, Finch, who had been quietly lounging on the couch behind me, zeroed in on my hand within Gideon's. I looked over my shoulder, longingly back to my writing desk.

Leaving the library, Queen Izralda walked toward us. She wore an amused expression as she witnessed her eldest son dragging a poor innocent victim toward the stables. I pleaded with my eyes for her to save me.

"And where are you both headed off to on this beautiful day?" She mused.

"We are going horseback riding out to the fields and will have lunch at the lake." Gideon did not pause to talk to his mother.

"More like against my will," I grumbled as I looked back over my shoulder while we passed her, hoping she would save me. Queen Izralda laughed instead.

"Well, have fun, please make sure Serenity has a good time as your prisoner." The nerve of this Queen, she was condoning her child's behavior. I was not going to win this battle and had no choice but to go along with Gideon's schematics.

Upon reaching the stables, I found my horse Clover saddled beside his Friesian. The stable boys held the reigns to the horses awaiting our arrival. I dug my heels into the ground, and the image flashed through my mind of Theo standing while holding Clovers reigns for me.

"Serenity?" Gideon asked, confused by my silent protest as I brought us to a sudden halt.

"Where is the chaperone?" I uttered, my voice cracking barely above a whisper, licking my lips. A silly notion, considering we never had one prior, but Finch had always been with us as well.

"We do not need one. We are betrothed, after all." Gideon attempted to drag me forward, but I stayed in place. It had minimal to do with a chaperone and everything to do with the countless rendezvous Theo and I had from taking the horses out.

"Please?" He begged.

I left the memory and gave the faintest nod. Untangling myself from Gideon's hold, I closed the distance until I was petting my mare.

"Need help?" Gideon asked.

Glancing over at him, I shook my head and hauled myself up and into the saddle. I looked back down at him from my seat, and his expression changed to amusement.

"Never witness a Lady do it herself?" I mused.

"Most would prefer a prince to help them," he replied with a chuckle as he hauled himself into the saddle on the horse next to mine. "But then again, you are not like most girls."

"Not sure if I should take that as a compliment or an insult."

"Take it as a compliment, Serenity." He smiled and then made a clicking noise, causing his horse to walk forward.

"Ever do more than walk your horse?" Gideon asked over his shoulder to me. I urged Clover to pick up the pace until we walked alongside him.

"Everything but jumps."

He clicked his tongue again, and his horse picked up speed and went into a canter before going into a full gallop. I instructed Clover to follow suit. The two of us raced over the grassy terrain. Clover followed Gideon's horse with every turn along the way. In the midst of taking in the scenery around us, I had not been tracking which way we had come from. I suppose if I became lost, I could try to follow back the bent grass blades from the horse's bodies.

Gideon's horse slowed when a lake came into view. I could see a blanket and picnic baskets had already been laid out. He had been planning this before he had come to retrieve me. We cantered to a stop, Gideon dismounted and coming around to my horse, he offered me his hand. I refused, swinging my leg over Clover and lowered myself to the ground. He chuckled, shaking his head.

I surveyed the lake with the timber butted up against it. For a moment, I pretended Theo was here with me. That we had ridden our horses out to a secluded location like this, away from everything. That he had planned a picnic by a lake, and we fed each other food and drank wine together. I smiled to myself, knowing he would jump into the lake, trying to convince me to join him. The two of us would be laughing and smiling at one another. I would tell him I loved him, and he would kiss me and recite the words back. We would stay out here all day and then watch the moon rise as the stars came out. The ache in my heart formed when I thought of all the times we had made love under the open sky. Shaking my head, I turned my attention back to Gideon, who I realized had been watching me.

"Enny for your thoughts?" He flipped a coin my way. I fumbled to catch it in my right hand.

"Oh. I was just thinking how everything changes from here on out." I flicked the enny back to him.

"Do you- Do you think you could become accustomed to this lifestyle?" While the nervous laugh hadn't presented itself, he still shifted on his feet.

"I suppose I really do not have a choice in the matter." I shrugged lamely, while watching the calm lake that had small ripples cascading on it from the light breeze. I knew it probably was not the answer he would want to hear from his future bride, but I was too tired to exchange pleasantries.

"We will make the best of it," his voice quiet as he wrapped his arms from behind me, hugging me slightly.

"Did you know you would be placed in an arranged marriage?" I found his warmth comforting as we slightly rocked back and forth, taking in the scenery. While I never had considered my sister deciding my future, as an heir he probably had known since childhood. What would it have been like growing up, knowing that marriage was less about love and more about political connections? What part about me made me the most desirable candidate to marry a prince?

He sighed and held me tighter. "My parents received countless offers my entire life. I was the one that championed for a chance at the courting seasons, playing on my mother's emotions for love."

I turned my head to look at him, and found sadness lingering in his eyes. Our faces close enough that I could feel the warmth of his breath. We were two souls trying to navigate and make the best out of the circumstances that life had dealt us.

"You will have freewill living as a royal and the funds to buy any book you require," he offered, as if it were an apology for what our families had done.

I tried to give him a smile, but knew it fell flat.

"Come, let us stroll around the lake, because I have a feeling neither of us is hungry." Gideon let go of me and I felt the absence of his body warmth as his arm slipped into mine.

"It is quite a nice day compared to all the previous dreary rainy ones we have had," I commented trying to make small talk.

"Yes, I will agree. I was beginning to worry I would not be able to bring you out here." He chuckled in his telltale sign that he was nervous. He guided us to walk around the pond.

"Well, it is very pretty out here. I am glad the weather lightened up for me to be able to see it." We were both trying to make the best of this situation.

"Yeah?" His voice raised in hope.

"Yeah, however, I have only been here for three weeks. I am certain there would have been many opportunities for us to have taken this stroll." I challenged, humor entering my voice.

"Only to an extent Serenity. The courting season will begin in a month, and we will be departing soon." Gideon's grip on my arm tightened.

"Does the Courting Season make you nervous?" I knew I was walking into uncertain territory with this question.

"Yes and no. I know, regardless, I will have a wife by the end of this season," he commented, followed by another nervous chuckle. I looked up at his face to find him clenching his jaw.

"Would you prefer it to be by choice or . . ." I trailed off, tightness forming in my chest. Did I want him to be honest in his answer?

"If I had a choice, I would wish for you to pick me freely."

His raw honesty caused me to stop, he faced me.

"Gideon," I breathed.

"I do not want to be the one to take your freedom away." He swallowed. "We could find someone else to love during The Courting Seasons. I only hoped the person I am to rule the rest of my life with will choose me as well."

"She would be a daft fool to not like you," I tried to lighten the mood. We were already halfway around the lake and the picnic basket was a small dot in the distance.

"Why because I am a prince?" He tried to give me his dashing smile but just as his laugh, it fell flat from the somber mood.

"Well, there is more to it than just being a prince. You are a good man Gideon anyone would be lucky to have you," I encouraged him, even as I knew what I was saying.

"I feel sorry for the person who ends up with you, Serenity," he joked as if giving himself a pity-party.

My eyes widened in shock. "And why is that Gideon?"

"Because the poor fool will not know if their wife is filling their head with lies or truths." He barked out, laughing.

I slipped my arm from his and, playfully, made an attempt to shove him into the lake. He dodged out of the way, and I had no time to catch my balance as I fell face-first into the cold lake. Water surrounded me; we had been on a bank, and it was not shallow here. I came up to the surface, and clearing the water from my face, I saw Gideon diving in towards me. I squealed as I moved out of the way before his body crashed into mine. My body shook as I coughed water from my lungs.

He went under before his head popped up next to mine. Gideons hands came up on my waist, and I instinctively wrapped my arms around his neck for balance as our legs kicked in the water. Parts of my dress floated on the surface around us from all the air trapped under the fabric.

"Are you okay, Serenity? I tried to catch you, but I missed. I am sorry!" Gideon rushed out, looking me over, to ensure I was not injured anywhere.

"Yeah, I am okay." I looked at the steep bank and could already estimate we were not getting out of the lake from here. We were going to have to swim to a shallow area. "But we have a problem," I commented feeling my dress becoming heavier, trying to pull me down from the water soaking the material.

"What is that?" He asked concern filling his voice, his eyebrows furrowing as his eyes searched me over again.

"My dress is going to take me under. I need to get out of it." I panicked. Fear coursed through me from the thought of dying, but I knew I couldn't cling onto him or he would drowned with me.

"Turn around, I will undo the laces," Gideon ordered quickly.

I was afraid to let go of his neck but did as he instructed. We were close enough to the bank that I was able to grab a couple of measly small roots that I hoped would keep me afloat if I was pulled under. With deft fingers, the laces started loosening quickly. He pulled the straps off my shoulders, and the two of us shimmied the dress down my body, letting the lake claim it. I was thankful for three things at that moment; one was that I had a light slip on that I wore under my dress. Two we were still in the water because I was certain my slip would be a bit transparent and leave nothing to the imagination. Three that Gideon worked fast enough to save me.

"I liked that dress," Gideon commented.

"I think the lake liked it more." I laughed. He rich laugh joined with mine. When we stopped laughing, we looked up at the bank again and came to a silent agreement that neither of us would be able to climb out that way.

"Well come on, we are going to have to swim a bit to find a way out," I said as I tried to move to swim. I figured there had to be another shallow area along the lake aside from where the picnic basket and our horses were. It would be quite a long swim if we had to swim across the lake.

"Wait, Serenity." Gideon grabbed my arm as I was passing him in the water. I felt his other arm wrap around my waist as he pulled me to him. I barely turned my head to look at him in questioning when his lips crashed against mine. He yanked me even closer to his warm body as best as possible while our legs kicked beneath the water.

The hand that had grabbed my arm let go as he brought it out of the water and cradled my head while he deepened the kiss. My eyes were wide open in surprise, finding his closed as he kissed me hungrily. Confliction coursed through me on what to do. He was a prince and my betrothed; I did not think I could deny him. Making a rash decision, I chose to kiss him back and wrapped my arms once again around his neck.

Feeling me return his affection, Gideon's grip on my head tightened as I felt him nip my bottom lip, pulling it into his mouth. I opened my mouth in response to the kiss and let my tongue explore his. We formed a rhythm of nipping and sucking each other's bottom lips and then caressing each other's tongues. I felt something sparking with him that I never had felt with Theo's kisses. It was not until he released my head to grip a root along the bank that I realized I had stopped kicking entirely. My legs were wrapped around his waist, and his other arm was still securely holding me to him.

We laughed against each other's lips at the predicament we were in. I leaned forward, wanting to keep kissing him. I wanted to chase this feeling I had never felt before. I had never anticipated to be in a predicament like this one. The little voice that nagged me to stop, I shoved to the back of my mind where I could not hear it.

Between the water and the lazy kicking of his legs to keep us afloat I felt his cock begin to harden as it pressed through his pants against my bare bottom. Oh. My slip had ridden up high on my waist, exposing my bottom and legs beneath the water. One of the few days I decided to not don panties, and I was naked in the water straddling a prince. Gideon broke the kiss.

"If you. . . if you want to undo my pants, I can uh," he tried to hint towards what he was getting at.

I bit my lip, looking back and forth between his eyes. At the moment I wanted to say yes; I knew what I was doing was indecent, but who would ever know? We were in the water; he would never know I am not a virgin. Would I ever have an opportunity like this again? Did I want to be known as the boring historian lady who preferred books to boys? Regardless of how I tried to re-write my fate, in the end I would still end up a wife to the man in front of me.

Hesitantly, I released my right hand from behind his neck and trailed it down between our bodies. A smile graced Gideon's lips. Our bodies pulled apart a bit as my hand went between where my body was flushed against his. I started to undo the buttons of his pants, one-handed and clumsily. There just had to be six of them there, he didn't wear simple pants like I was accustomed to.

With the last one undone, I slowly reached into his pants to grasp his hard cock. It was thicker than Theo's, causing me alarm. Biting my bottom lip, I stroked him a few times, eliciting a moan. I held his half-lidded, lust-filled eyes as I guided him to my entrance. The tip rested there a moment with my hand holding it in place. Gideon's eyes searched mine, asking permission, and I gave him a small nod.

He pushed inside me while the arm wrapped around me, guided me down onto him. I sucked in cold air, gritting my teeth to lessen the feeling from the stretch of his girth.

"Shh, shh, it's okay, Serenity. It's okay," Gideon comforted as he continued to push into me. When my hand still wrapped around his cock touched my skin, I let go to allow him full access. I tried to relax as he pushed further within me. He withdrew, and I squeaked, not prepared, as he thrusted all the way in.

"I'm in, I'm in. The worst is over," Gideon tried to soothe, He kissed me, diverting my attention away from the slight pain I still felt. I relaxed my body as I rolled my hips. He sucked in air, pulling out slightly and then thrusting back in.

"Can you move against me? It is a bit difficult for me in this position." He gave me an apologetic smile. I leaned in to kiss him as I rolled my hips again. His arms on my waist gave an indication to pick up the speed and how he wanted me to ride him. I breathed heavily as I grinded on his cock, his moans grew louder until he was cumming in me. We panted as he showered my neck with kisses while his length slipped out of me.

"Tonight, Serenity. Tonight, I will come to your room and repay the favor," he promised. I was unsure what favor he was referring to, but I nodded as I kissed him back.

"We probably should get back to shore," he joked, his hand shook while holding the root to keep us afloat. "Would you be able to rebutton my pants?" He asked, embarrassed.

My face heated, but I nodded, and reached down between us with both hands, my fingers lightly held his soft member. He moaned, and I tucked it back into his pants. Making quick work, I righted the six buttons, and when finished, I bit my lip.

"Are you okay to free float?" He asked, and I nodded.

I felt giddy as I unwrapped my legs from his waist. My arms moving back and forth while I kicked in the water. "Is there any place close by we could get out of the water?" I asked, looking around at the high riverbank in which we were currently nestled.

"If we swim a bit to the right, there should be a way to get out, and if swimming becomes too much, at least we'll have the bank roots to keep us above water." Gideon led the way, with me following. It was not long before my feet began to squish in the mud below. I had not realized my shoes had also been lost to the lake. This was going to be one fascinating story to tell when we got back to the castle.

The water became shallower as we waded back onto land with my hand in Gideon's helping me keep my balance. My slip was clinging to me. Thankfully, it only went to my knees and did not make walking difficult. Gideon turned around to look at me and stopped abruptly.

"What?" I asked my head whipping to look behind me at what he was looking at. There was nothing there, and I looked back at him to find his eyes glued on the lower half of my body. I looked down and instinctively tried to cover up. I had forgotten the slip would be see through with the water clinging to me. My trying to be modest snapped him out of his trance as he began yanking his wet shirt over his head and handed it to me. I looked at it curiously, uncertain.

"Put it on, it should help cover things a bit better." He stood there looking away to give me some privacy. I accepted it and admired his muscular body as I put his wet shirt on over my slip. Looking down, I could see it had helped cover more than my slip had.

"Thank you," I said, giving indication that he could look again.

"You are welcome. We will wrap the picnic blanket around you for the ride back," he replied, thinking ahead to the situation.

"This will be a fun story to tell our families," I commented.

"I am sure it will be." He laughed, and we began to make our way back to the other side of the lake to where the picnic and our horses were.

The ride back to the castle was chilly in wet clothing. Even with the picnic blanket shielding me from the wind, it wasn't enough as I shivered the entire ride back. Unfortunately, when we arrived, I did not receive the luxury of a warm bath or changing out of these soiled clothes. We were immediately ushered into The King's office where, his wife, Amity, and Father sat waiting to hear our story. We recounted the accidental playful shove that had put us in the state we were in, conveniently leaving out about us having sex. No one looked too pleased at my overly exposed predicament or how I lost all the articles of clothing I had worn to the lake. Despite my state of undressed, we were not offered additional clothing or blankets as we stood there shivering.

The only one showing sympathy was Queen Izralda. She fretted like a mother to make certain we were okay. She had ordered the servants to have warm baths waiting in our rooms for us. There was a small inkling that the smell of lake clinging to us did not appeal to anyone either as they crinkled their noses. King Ashborn's expression changed from disappointment in his son putting us in a dangerous situation to amusement.

When we were finally dismissed, I headed straight to my rooms, where three maids had readied the bath for me. The Queen ordered that I was to be pampered after the traumatic experience. I had not considered it traumatic, but who was I to tell someone to stop massaging shampoo into my hair while another maid rubbed soap over the rest of my body. They scrubbed, massaged, and moisturized me with scented oils to clear all lake water. I could not pinpoint the scent they rubbed into my skin while they brushed my wet hair to prevent snarling.

When my hair was dry, they helped me into a simple pullover dress. I had never received pampering like this before, and I could become accustomed to it. If I became Gideon's bride, could this be a daily thing for myself? Upon finishing, the maids dismissed themselves when a knock came to my door. I found Gideon on the other side, coming to escort me to dinner. He offered me his arm, and we walked towards the banquet room.

"You smell delicious," he murmured for only me to hear in the hall and I flushed.

"You do, too," I murmured, catching whiffs of him as well. A yearning for him stirred within me. I wrote it off as my body responding to what we had done earlier. Something passed between us, because his bicep squeezed against my mine. I returned the gesture to let him know I had the same thoughts. We shared a private smile.

Upon entering the banquet room, everyone else had been awaiting our arrival. The first thing I noted was our seating arrangements had changed. I would now be placed between Gideon and my father. I welcomed the change, not wanting to sit between my family and the way they current looked at me.

Amity and Father's disappointment reflected on their face. I mentally braced myself, knowing Amity would be giving me an earful at some point. Father, on the other hand, it may be a while before he forgives me for the situation earlier. It was not like Gideon, and I had done it on purpose, but to argue that to my family, the point would be moot. King Ashborn assessed us with approval as

Queen Izralda clapped her hands, happy to see our arrival. The only one not looking at us was Finch as he glowered at his empty plate.

Gideon quietly let go of my arm to pull out the chair for me. I found it odd; he did it instead of a servant. I sat down as he pushed it under me and took his place beside me. The King clapped his hands so signal the servants. They brought platters full of food out and started filling our empty plates. Gideon's face reflected nothing as his leg intertwined with mine under the table. He slowly moved, rubbing it up and down.

"Well, after a very eventful afternoon, it is nice to sit here together on an uneventful evening, is it not?" King Ashborn began. We all murmured our agreements.

"Where did you learn to swim Lady Serenity Novena?" King Ashborn asked. My Father stiffened beside me. Either the King chose not to notice how upset my family was at this situation, or did it intentionally to rile them up more. I was not certain which was the case.

"Well, Your Highness, we have a pond back home, and my older brothers would often take me swimming in it." I was treading dangerously but did not want to lie to The King.

"It is a good thing you knew how to swim, or we would be remorse to not have you at the table with us tonight. Is that not right, Lady Amity Lovnanna and Lord Lambert?" King Ashborn drew his attention to my family. Father perked up at being drawn into the conversation while Amity's soured face smoothed into a pleasant and grateful smile.

"You are correct, King Ashborn. While I had been against my sister being unlady-like, trailing after our brothers on their adventures, it is something that we can all be grateful for today." Amity gave me a leveled gaze as she finished the words. Father nodded in agreement. I turned back to my food, focusing my attention there as I ate. My stomach growled in protest. I had not eaten anything since breakfast. We had never touched the food in the picnic basket.

"Yes, yes, very fortunate indeed. I will say the castle has not been this lively in quite some time. It does us all some good," King Ashborn commented.

We all nodded in agreement.

Gideon's leg, slightly moving against mine, continued to distract me. My cheeks flamed from the thought of my legs wrapped around his waist with no clothing separating us. Anticipation built within me from his promise to visit tonight. Would he arrive after Amity gave me a tongue lashing or during the middle of it? A knot formed in my stomach.

I glanced over to the heir, giving him a shy smile.

Chapter Ten

After dessert, we were fortunate to be released to spend the rest of the evening to our preferences. Part of it may have been due to Queen Izralda mentioning to her husband that Gideon and I were probably exhausted after experiencing the traumas of the day. She tacked on that as a family, Amity and Father probably wanted to spend time with me after almost losing me to the lake. I felt she was being a tad melodramatic with her wording. Aside from the weight of my dress pulling me down, there was never another time I feared for my life.

The doors to the banquet room barely closed behind my family when Amity grasped my arm, digging her nails in. I look at her, startled.

"My room, now." She growled all pretenses of being a respectful lady dropped from her face. The woman who stood before me was my older, pissed-off sister, a stranger to most but someone I was familiar with. I glanced at Father and was met with his disappointment. Queasiness slid through me as Amity marched us to her rooms.

She didn't wait as she ushered us all in and closed the door behind her. I couldn't even get a word out in time as she whirled on me.

"What you did today was a stupid and irresponsible thing. What were you thinking?" She seethed.

"I-," I began, but she cut me off.

"I don't want to hear your excuses."

I considered correcting her improper use of language but decided otherwise. I stood there with my hands balled into fists at my sides while she scolded me. Father did not come to my rescue; I had not made him angry since I was a child. Disappointing him was not something I was accustomed to in life.

"How do you think you looked to your future-in-laws?" She threw her hands up in the air and started pacing. "A few days ago, your engagement to the heir was announced, and how do you show your appreciation?" She didn't wait for me to answer. "By throwing yourself in a lake and arriving back to the castle, exposing your body to all—"

"—I was wearing clothes!" I interrupted hastily.

"Ah, right, clothes that showed everything. I could see your nipples through the sheer cloth, Serenity, and so could every servant and staff here. Future Queen of Theorines and everyone has already saw her naked. No modesty." She pinched the bridge of her nose, exasperated.

Father shifted uncomfortably and coughed.

"I cannot help that. However, I am going to correct you. I am not engaged until after The Courting Seasons," I argued.

"You could have ruined your entire reputation with that stunt today. You are lucky The King did not call off your potential engagement right then in there." She warned.

"It is not like I had a choice in the matter," I spat and pursed my lips while glaring at my family. "And furthermore, for that matter, we are from Grewt'en. The question of my reputation is laughable considering the promotion of sex and polygamy." I darkly laughed while they gasped at my indecent language.

"In Grewt'en maybe, but in other places, it is different." Amity's words shook from the anger vibrating off her. "You are nineteen. You cannot remain unwed forever." Her blue eyes pierced through me.

"How long have you been arranging my future behind my back?" I hissed. The secret, the half-truths, the surprise arranged marriage was all coming to a head now.

"Ever since I saw you being sweet on that stable boy."

I staggered back a step, my eyes going wide.

"I was not going to let you ruin your life," she continued, "by shackling yourself to him. I could have accepted quite a few proposals for your hand, but I held out for the right one. And it is a good thing I held out. Marrying a prince is definitely the right one. I am just grateful that stable boy did not get you knocked up."

I couldn't even look at Father; I was still stunned. Amity had known.

"How long?" I repeated again.

"Over a year now," she answered, and I shook my head, stunned. "Stop acting like a child and start acting like a Lady of society."

"Amity," I began, but she cut me off once again.

"The stable boy has been fired and removed from the manor. You will never see him again. Your future is to marry Prince Gideon Orion, not some lowly servant."

Amity dismissed me after that, and on shaking legs, I walked back to my rooms. All the anger had left me, only hollowness remained. Who could I have ended up with if Amity accepted the first offer? Would I have been married to a complete stranger or someone many years my senior? What if it was from a family in Grewt'en that I did not care for? None of it mattered, because Theo was gone. Even if I returned home, he wouldn't be there.

Opening my room's door, I slipped within the room, and let it click quietly behind me. Slowly, the hollowness filled with anger again. I had always acted like the perfect lady in society. I never acted out or did anything to embarrass the family. The lethal rage lacing through me made me cross the area to my bedroom. I Yanked my simple slip dress off, tossing it haphazardly over a chair, not caring. I grabbed a short, light-blue silk robe that barely went to my mid-thighs, tying the belt into a bow at the hip. I looked in the mirror and opened the top of the robe to reveal more cleavage. I would start acting like a Lady of society another night, but tonight I would be anything but. My family stole my future freedom because of my unlady-likeness. Maybe it was time to show them how unlady-like I could truly be.

I did not have to wait long for the knock to come on my door. I welcomed Gideon in and locked the door behind us. I wouldn't allow anyone to interrupt us unexpectedly, especially if my sister chose to give me another tongue lashing. His eyes roved over my barely covered skin, lingering on the ample amount of cleavage and high hemline of the robe on my thighs.

Wrapping my arms around his neck and pulling his body close to mine, I greeted him with a deep kiss. His hands gripped my hips tightly and wasted no time hauling me up. I wrapped my legs around his waist like earlier and he walked us to my bedroom. He laid me down on my back on the bed with him on top. Breaking the kiss, he pulled his shirt over his head, and I scooted my body further into the bed until my head nestled on the pillows. My legs crossed as I curled my toes in anticipation.

I watched, unashamedly, as he removed his shoes and undid the six silver buttons on his gray pants. Letting them drop to the floor, he kicked them off to the side, and stood naked with his cock completely erect. I swallowed but hid the nervousness of his size by biting my bottom lip. I uncrossed and recrossed my legs. Leisurely, I trailed my fingers up the middle of my chest, letting him track the movement.

He crawled onto the bed, and lifting my top ankle, uncrossed my legs to situate himself to kneel between my thighs. "Let me unwrap you."

I nodded, and he leaned forward, his fingers pinching the sash on my robe. He pulled the bow apart, and dropping the sash, he reached forward with both hands and opened the robe, exposing my naked body to him. His eyes darkened from the sight as he drank me in.

"Do you approve?" I murmured. I tried to be coy like the heroines I had read in the romance novels my sister enjoyed.

"Yes," he breathed; leaning down, he pressed his lips to my neck. His chest barely grazed my nipples. Gideon trailed kisses down my neck and captured one of the hard peaks in his mouth, sucking on it possessively while his hand rolled the other hardening nipple. I ran my fingers through his hair, loving the feel of its silkiness. His hard cock pressed into my belly, and nervousness tangled with the butterflies that filled me.

His mouth left my nipple and he trailed kisses down my belly, settling his head between my thighs. I jerked when his tongue slid between my folds.

"Relax," he murmured. I melted into the bed, my hands leaving his hair to dig into the sheets when he did it again.

He repeated another long, slow lick before settling on the sensitive bud, sending pleasure through me. His left hand continued to play with my breast, molding it and lightly pinching my nipple. I felt the fingers of his free hand pushing into my entrance while he sucked. I pushed my hips up into his face, feeling pleasure build within me. He licked around my clit, teasing me with the sensation it was creating while his fingers continued to move in and out of me.

"Gideon," I gasped as his tongue flicked against my clit. My right hand left its grasp on the blankets to grip his hair once again. I moved my hips against his mouth as I instructed him with my hand what I wanted. The pleasure continued to build within me; he sucked my sensitive bud in, and with a soft nip of his teeth, waves of pleasure crashed through me. I bucked against his mouth and he followed my every move, prolonging my orgasm as I gasped his name.

Gideon's mouth left my clit at the same time he withdrew his fingers. Pulling his body up above me, he thrust his hard length into me. I was still pulsating around him when he moved within me. He wiped his mouth on the back of his hand before claiming my mouth with his own. I could taste myself on his lips and tongue. His right hand hooked under my left leg, yanking it up high on his waist, giving him deeper access. I moved with him, reveling from his length. He grinded against my clit with each thrust eliciting moans into his mouth from the after waves of pleasure it caused.

His thrusts picked up speed, the grinding building another orgasm. "Gideon, please keep that up," I gasped. "I am going to cum again."

He growled, keeping with the rhythm. I felt the build coming close to me cresting over.

"Serenity, I do not think I can last much longer," he panted, thrusting into me, hitting a sweet spot. Between the friction against my clit, and knowing he was withholding for me to feel pleasure, the orgasm came crashing over me. I yanked his head down, moaning as I kissed him deeply. He yanked my left leg even higher, and I instinctively brought my right leg up slightly. The angle gave him better access, each thrust going deeper and harder until I felt warmth spreading within me from his cum. Gideon's thrusts became a little less controlled until he was collapsing on top of me, panting into my neck.

My arms wrapped around him; hugging Gideon close to me. We lay there enjoying the after pleasure with his length still within me. I allowed myself to enjoy this moment and not think of anything else but being here with him. Gideon began to move within me, initiating another round. Kissing him, I fell into a rhythm with his thrusts.

I awoke alone to light streaming through my curtains. Gideon must have left sometime in the night after I fell asleep in his arms. I knew it was for the best, but it did not ease the small bit of disappointment I felt. He wasn't aware that I was using him as a distraction to all the emotions I was feeling after this week. I threw an arm over my face to block out the world. I wanted to silence my mind, but it was futile.

I wondered if my letter to Quiet had been delivered yet? Had she let Theo down for me? A crack formed in me at the thought of his broken heart and then finding another to spend the rest of his life with. Somewhere along the lines, we had not been careful enough, causing me to be placed in an arranged marriage. That wasn't even the proper terms. Gideon and I would only be wedded if we did not choose anyone else when The Courting Seasons ended.

The Courting Seasons, an event to be surrounded by eligible bachelors looking for a match. Did I even have the mental capacity to attempt being courted by a stranger? A small part of me considered putting off the inevitable, but if that meant additional months of freedom... My mind trailed off to the royal library of T'Lovoness's. King Ashborn had made the comment Kingdom Theorines's was not as vast as T'Lovoness's. I could spend those that time perusing their history and not participating.

Amity's statement of gratitude that I hadn't ended up pregnant lingered in the back of my mind. Little did she know I had been taking a tonic for years to prevent an occurrence. To not break the habit, I had brought the tonic on the trip. One less stress I needed to fret about during everything that had occurred these past few days.

Chapter Eleven

It was as if a spell had broken. Three weeks passed by and the three of us were being loaded into separate traveling carriages to T'Lovoness. Only last week that I had received Quiet's reply to my letter. She was quite giddily happy about my attendance to The Courting Seasons and demanded regular letters updating the whole experience. She was hopeful that my secret pre-arranged engagement would mean she could attend The Courting Seasons in three years when she turned eighteen. I rolled my eyes, knowing I would most likely be disappointing her. My plans of occupying T'Lovoness's library hadn't changed.

We were informed the trip would take two weeks. The travel plans mapped out inn's we would be staying at, in our own respective rooms, of course. That didn't dissuade Gideon from crossing the hall to my room each night. He was the most attentive and by the end I found myself waking up still in his arms. While I became flustered, Gideon remained unruffled by the idea of being caught. When I challenged him on this, he countered with Finch, and the servants already aware of our pre-engagement, so why did it matter?

Somedays, I was too exhausted from our daily travels to argue with him.

It was into the second week that Finch cornered me one night while Gideon washed up in the bathhouse. Finch had been rather solemn since his father announced my engagement to his brother. The silence continued on this trip with him barely talking to either of us.

"Why do you let my brother trapeze into your room every night? You should be more respected than that," he accused. I had not expected this to be where the conversation to go.

"Finch, I really do not have a say in the matter. Our families have already decided our future fates." I couldn't tell him that every time I lay with his brother, I used it as a balm to nurse my heartbreak. Nor could I tell him that despite me bickering with Gideon over being caught, secretly, I hoped that we would be. Maybe if my reputation became tarnished, then I could seek out Theo. If I ruined myself enough, maybe then Amity wouldn't be able to salvage the damage.

"That does not mean you have to condone his behavior, Serenity," Finch argued.

"I do not know what to tell you, Finch." I was at a loss for words.

"I wish you could look at me the way you look at him." Finch glared at the inn's worn floorboards. It had crossed my mind that Finch was pouting over the engagement announcement. I reached with my right hand under his chin, bringing it to look up at my face. He continued to glower.

"I do not look at him any differently. We are simply both stuck in the same destiny that was set for us. I am sorry, Finch, if this hurts you." I tried to convey my sympathy through my eyes. He looked back down at the ground with his shoulders sagging.

"I just wish it could have been me." He turned and walked away down the hall back to his room. I returned to my room and half an hour later Gideon showed up.

On our final night together, Gideon managed to give me five orgasms, knowing it would be difficult to achieve alone time in the upcoming weeks. He claimed there would be too many other guests mingling about. I did not object to a single one of those orgasms. I woke up to the sixth orgasm with his mouth still on my clit. I may be upset by the lack of choice in my future, but at least I knew my bedroom would be filled with pleasure from this man.

The final morning of our trip, it was decided that I would need to travel in my carriage alone again out of modesty. I rolled my eyes at the absurdity of it all. By this point, everyone on the trip was aware of Gideon and my nightly endeavors. However, to keep our engagement a secret, the King's captain, Rolph, deemed it necessary we kept up the pretenses of not being arranged. I wondered when Rolph and his soldiers returned to Kingdom Theorines how much of this trip would they inform King Ashborn about.

I was positive Rolph would give a full report. He came off as a no-nonsense captain of the guard. The next question I had gave me both delight and caused my stomach to knot slightly. Would my family still be in attendance to hear the full report? To my knowledge, no one had caught Gideon and me sneaking around the castle. Furthermore, it could instill in my sister just how unladylike I truly could be. I crossed my legs, smiling to myself. Debating how much embarrassment I could bring my sister.

The carriage wheels and horseshoes melody changed from dirt to cobblestone roads. I had a minimal desire to peer out the window as we entered the city of T'lovoness. I could hear the shouting and whooping of villagers upon seeing Kingdom Theorines royal carriages. I rolled my eyes, slumping back into the seat, and crossed my arms over my chest. I pursed my lips, wishing I could block out the cacophonous noise they were creating. It was deafening. Were they this loud with every monarchy that arrived? How loud were they when they saw their own royals?

I had brought three historical texts with me, but they were all packed away, not that it would do me much good. I became quite carriage sick trying to read. Without Gideon sharing the space to keep me entertained, all I could do was stare at the four wooden walls or keep my eyes closed. I furrowed my brows annoyed as we continued our way to the castle.

Rolph started shouting at the castle guards, and I heard the creaking of what I supposed were wooden gates opening to let us in. The sooner I was locked in the castle, the sooner the days could pass for me to be done with this whole ordeal. Thankfully, Theorines did not host their own courting seasons. This would be a one and done participation. I questioned how much my absence would be noticed if I stayed cooped up in the library. Any non-mandatory events I would be skipping completely.

The carriage came to a halting stop, and I barely had time to sit up straight as the door was being opened by a T'Lovoness servant, he was dressed in very frilly white attire. There were rumors that Queen Opal was a bit over the top. If this servant attire was any indication, I could only brace myself for the next three months. Withholding my apparent annoyance, I accepted his hand as he helped me out of the carriage. I glanced over to the brothers, who were hiding smirks behind their hands. I had been independent, not accepting help, the entire time they have known me. It must have been a sight to witness me accepting it now. They ought to know it was only because society deemed it so. Then again, I could sour Amity more by not following societal rules. I'm sure it would get back to her. I dismissed the thoughts, I was in a conundrum of not wanting to ruin my little sister's future while not caring if I was being spiteful to our older sister.

I glanced up at the pearlescent castle with green vines climbing up the pillars. It was pretty in its own ornate way. Quiet would be in awe over how much it looked like something out of a fairytale. The lawn, however, was quite plain; there were shrubs styled into various animal shapes and spirals. It was a bit of a letdown on how plain the grounds were compared to the castle itself. It didn't matter; I would be spending the majority of my time with dusty books, away from it all anyway.

We walked up the castle stairs together, and I found it rather odd not to be near Gideon; normally, my arm would be tucked into his. Even Finch stood a further distance away from me than usual. The castle doors opened, and we were separated. I was handed off to another servant dressed in frilly attire, who led me up a grand double staircase to the left while the brothers were taken up the one on the right. I watched them across the balcony as I followed the frilly servant. Gideon gave me a reassuring smile up until the hallway wall blocked us from view. The servant remained silent, leading me down the corridor. We passed along other guest doors, and I caught glimpses of ladies settling in with their servants. I did not have any servants, and it was peculiar that I hadn't been sent with any to help with this event. I would assume servants would be a social status indicator, but I was fine with getting ready myself.

"Lady Serenity Novena." The servant stated, positioned himself outside a door, and continued in a bored voice. "This is your room. Please be advised your things will be unpacked shortly once the princesses have settled in. On behalf of their royal majesties, they suggest taking a bath and preparing oneself for the introduction ball. A meal will be brought up prior." From how monotoned he sounded, he must have already given the speech a few hundred times today.

"Thank you," I replied curtly. Opening the door, I let myself into my temporary new living arrangements. The main room was done in deep sapphire-blue curtains that matched the carpet beneath my shoes. The sitting furniture was a mixture of emerald-greens with magenta throw cushions on them. There was a writing desk alongside the big bay window, and walking over to it, I looked out the window. It was a nice, albeit boring, view of grass and trees with a small pathway leading up to a very elaborate fountain with a few benches around it. This side of the castle mirrored the aesthetic of the entrance. Both lacked any form of decoration or true beauty, the grounds being rather plain compared to the castle itself.

Leaving the writing desk, I walked toward the door that led to my bedroom. Opening it, I was greeted with a modest four-poster bed with a cream bedspread. In here, the carpet had ended and transitioned to wood floors with a large peach area rug under the bed; which matched the long hanging curtains. Somehow, I had a feeling the white bedding was there for purity reasons. It was a little too late for me. I also found it rather insulting, given I was a lady from Queendom Grewt'en.

Leaving my bedroom, I walked across the short hallway to the opposite room. It was smaller than mine and not as elaborate. A room made for any attending servants that I have brought with me. The room would go unused during my time here. Leaving the servant's room, I entered the final room at the end of the tiny hall and found the bathing chambers. A beautiful, gilded bathtub sat in the middle of the room with pillars on all four sides of it. There was a vanity with a large wall on the far side and an ornate toilet in the corner. My gaze lingered back on the bathtub.

Looking down at my travel clothes, I deigned I probably should bathe. There was a light knock at my door, and I didn't even have time to respond as a group of servants came in with my trunks. They all curtsied and entered my room to put my clothes away.

"We will be, but a moment. Please take your time relaxing in the tub." One female servant stated. I nodded and closed the bathroom door behind me for some privacy. I pulled the travel dress over my head, not wasting a moment. The bathtub had already been pre-filled with warm water, and pink flower petals rested on the surface. I wonder if, in every room, they prepared the water for their guests. I supposed it would be more convenient with the introductory ball tonight.

Slipping my foot into the tub, it was a perfect temperature, and I lowered into the tub, allowing the heat to seep into my skin, soothing my aching muscles. If dinner was being served here prior to the ball, I calculated I had enough time to wash my hair. It would be nice to have a fresh, clean start here.

When I was pruny, I left the bathing room with a fluffy towel wrapped around me, heading into my bedroom. The servants had unpacked, organized, and disappeared during the time I soaked. Opening the closet door, I flipped through the dresses. The servants had arranged them from simplest to elaborate. I rifled through the dresses, never having the opportunity to see the final results until now. They were stunning, even the plain ones. I settled upon a metallic green dress that was positioned in the middle. I could not recollect being fitted for the dress, like many I perused, but I did enjoy the color of this one.

I admired the dress on the hanger. Instead of having a corset in the back, it had sixteen golden buttons running up the front in two rows of eight. I quickly undid the buttons, thankful it would not be challenging to re-button once on me. With the buttons undone, the whole top part area opened up. I pulled the dress over my head, and standing in front of the gilded mirror, folded the bottom right fabric flap over my chest and stomach as I began to rethread the buttons through the top left fabric eyelets.

The dress had short, puffed sleeves, and the bottom part of the skirt flowed loosely out and lightly pooled at the bottom of my feet. I had hoped putting the dress on would have dredged up some form of memory of it being made, but alas, it did not. I probably would have this feeling with many of the dresses in my closet, all of them becoming a surprise to me.

Glancing in the mirror, I would need to do something with my damp hair. I grabbed a section from each side of my head by the ears and brought it to the back. Grabbing a random hairpin, I twisted it into place. It was simple but good enough for me. This was not an elegant occasion tonight, just a simple meet and greet. I did not have any reason to stand out, lest the other girls find me as competition. I preferred to avoid that drama.

I finished my hair when a knock came to the door. I heard the door click open despite my not informing them I was ready. I glanced out my bedroom door to the main entertaining area and found a servant bringing in food hidden beneath a silver platter. I watched as they placed it on a table along the wall, noticing me they informed that I had one hour to eat and then my presence was required in the grand ballroom to be properly introduced to the royals of T'Lovoness.

I nodded, confirming that I had understood. The servant dismissed themselves, and I crossed the room to where the food sat waiting for me. It smelled delicious, and lifting the lid, I found there was roasted chicken, corn, and seasoned rice. Under another lid, I found the dessert was strawberry pudding. Yum.

Chapter Twelve

When an hour passed, I deigned it was time to make my entrance at the grand ballroom. I had minimal sense of direction as to which way to go, however, deciding the wisest course of action was to follow the other girls wearing equally confused expressions. I followed a few paces behind three of them, not feeling overly ambitious to be dragged into their conversation. They were giggling over how handsome the princes were, and I withheld rolling my eyes. I noted their lack of tiaras, wondering what monarchies they hailed from. Their dresses gave no indication either, not that they would be able to tell from my metallic green dress that I was a Lady of Grewt'en.

The further we walked, the more others crowded in alongside us, soon we were all heading down the grand staircase to the main level. Watching others file through a set of double doors on the left indicated that must be our destination. We shuffled through, and the grand ballroom room was quite vast. Pillars lined the edges, with three elaborate chandeliers hanging from the ceiling. Everything was donned in gold and blood red with navy blue accent colors.

I noted how the room was separated. Princes and princesses were on the right side while everyone else that did not wear a tiara or crown were crowded on the left. The non-royals outweighed the royals in attendance, and I wondered why we were seperated. This was The Courting Seasons; we were all supposed to have an equal chance despite the societal hierarchy.

I surveyed the lesser crowded side of the ballroom and hadn't been able to spot Gideon or Finch in the throng of royals. Maybe they hadn't arrived yet. My gaze trailed to the front of the room. King Lucien stood at the top of the stairs with his wife, Queen Opal, and their son, Prince Regalius Baylor. Their focus on the royal children being introduced to them. I wondered, if after the royal children were introduced, would the rest of us be introduced as well? We were quite a large group, and I could foresee introductions taking well into the night.

"Oh, hello." Smiled a fawn-haired girl. She had a splash of light freckles across her nose and cheeks. I could tell she was uncertain about herself, and her dress of cheap green and yellow fabric probably did not do her any favors in this entourage.

"Hello," I replied kindly. I did not know why she signaled me out amongst the crowd of non-royals, but here we were.

"My name is Lydia of Grewt'en. You are from Grewt'en, too, are you not?" She continued, and I noted her lack of title. She must be a merchants child then.

"I am." I wanted to keep this conversation short but with the swarm of bodies surrounding us, I had no where I could escape to.

"Oh, good! I guessed correctly." She smiled hesitantly. "I was hoping to find a friendly face from home."

"It is a pleasure to meet you, Lydia of Grewt'en." I dipped my head in acknowledgement, wishing she would go away.

"Where are you from in Grewt'en?" She either chose not to receive the hint or was daft.

"I am Lady Serenity Novena, sister to High Lady Amity Lovanna of Manor Wyndmere." I hoped my title would make her back a way a bit.

"Your father is Lord Honorable Lambert?" Lydia practically shouted.

I flinched, side stepping away, and bumped into another guest. I murmured my apologies as other guests looked our way from her outburst. I did not want to be associated with her. She, instead, took a step forward, following me as she continued to prattle on, gushing over my father.

"Your father is the most kindest man I have ever met! He buys my father's wares all the time; he is actually the reason I could attend this courting season. He supplied the funds for me to be able to afford dresses and accessories." She slightly blushed.

My gaze perused over her again. I was a bit curious how much funding *my sister* had given her to attend, considering the dress was a bit shabby. I knew I should not be too judgmental, considering my wardrobe had been funded by King Ashborn of Theorines, but she did not need to know that. I needed to be like my name, serene, but right now, I wish my name was Priscella. Then, at least, it wouldn't be weird if I were prissy with this merchant's daughter.

"My Father is a very generous, benevolent, and kind man; however," I paused to compose myself and gave her as serene of smile as I could muster. "My sister is the head of the house and the one who is charge of the manor's money. After all, we are from Grewt'en, where women rule."

Lydia's smile widened as she nodded and apologized for her mistake. Internally, I rolled my eyes. I gave her a tepid smile, returning my attention to the royals in search of The Theorines Princes.

"I wonder when it will be our turn to be introduced to the royals," Lydia commented. "I want to capture Prince Regalius Baylor's attention."

"I am not certain. I have never attended one of these," I commented, dryly ignoring her comment on T'Lovoness's heir.

"Me neither! This is my first." She squealed.

I took another step back, trying to create distance between us.

She followed again. A banging noise sounded through the room, sparring me from needing to respond. Everyone shifted their attention to the front of the room, where a male servant in the same frilly attire as the others stood on a dais.

"Will the Lord and Ladies please step forward to begin being introduced to King Lucien, Queen Opal, and their son Prince Regalius Baylor." He pounded his wooden staff again on the marble flooring, concluding he was done speaking, and resumed his spot back at the base of the stairs in front of the royal family.

I gave Lydia a dismissing smile, hoping she would understand I had no choice in the matter. I escaped her by walking into the throng of other Lordlings and Ladies to stand in a line for my introduction. My gaze finally found Gideon and Finch surrounded by other princes. They were too focused on talking to not even noticed me.

I was fifth in line for introduction, and the moment I curtsied for The Royal Family, I planned to leave and find the library. I assumed they would be recording everyone in attendance tonight, and I did not need it to be reported back to King Ashborn the lack of my name on the list. I could easily come up with a lie about why my name had been missing, but then I would need to begin keeping track of every lie I told. It was more work than it was worth while I stood idly by, waiting my turn.

I observed Queen Opal had little interest in us non-royals. Her steel gray hair was curled and styled in an elaborate beehive on her head. Her brown eyes lacked warmth, while she pursed her red-stained lips. She wore the biggest, frilliest dress I had ever witnessed in the colors of Kingdom T'Lovoness.

King Lucien, on the other hand, smiled friendly. His jet-black hair was streaked with white strands, as was his medium-length beard. His blue eyes twinkled as he took in the guests being presented to him. Despite him being the ruler, he did not command as much power as his wife did.

Their son, Prince Regalius Baylor, was quite chatty, especially regarding a lady. He had black hair like his father, but unlike either of his parents, he had deep jade eyes. A single dimple on his right cheek appeared when he smiled. He was quite handsome to look at. However, from where I stood, I could hear he was an outrageous flirt, maybe worse than another prince I knew.

"Name," the servant with the wood staff asked, bored. Did any of these servants have personality or were they all completely lacking in emotions?

"Lady Serenity Novena, daughter of the late Lady Verity Melody of Queendom Grewt'en," I responded. A servant sitting behind the one holding the wooden staff, scribbled my name onto the scroll. I had been correct in assuming they were keeping track.

The lordling in front of me walked away after his introduction and exchange of words. The bored servant presented my name to the royals. Taking a step forward, into the empty space, I curtsied low, and when I rose, King Lucien greeted me with a warm smile. Queen Opal was fanning herself, not even paying any attention to me. Her gaze was looking out to the prince and princess. Prince Regalius Baylor smiled at me, and I meekly smiled in return.

"You are far lovely to look upon, Lady Serenity Novena," he flirted.

"The same can be said about yourself, Prince Regalius Baylor." I decided to entertain his flirting.

"Oh, you will be a fun one. Yes, you will." He laughed. His eyes sparked with amusement.

I furrowed my brows at him, uncertain how to respond.

"My son," interrupted King Lucien. "Believes he is humorous. Please ignore his whims and enjoy the rest of your stay here." King Lucien waved his hand to dismiss me.

I curtsied again, and glancing back at Prince Regalius Baylor, he gave me a wink. I did not react as I turned away from him. Time to find the library. I was three-fourths of the way to leaving the ballroom when my arm was looped into another's.

"Where are you headed?" Lydia's voice came from my side. I

glanced at her and weighed my options heavily here. If I told her the truth, she would have an inkling of where to find me during our time here. If I lied and told her I was going to my room, I would need to make certain that when I doubled back, I did not run into her on the way.

Then again, my worst-case scenario would be going to the library, grabbing a stack of texts, and holing myself back up in my room. I would lock the door and not make a peep if Lydia figured out my room location and came looking for me.

"I planned to return to my rooms and retire for the evening." I let the cool lie roll off my tongue. If she followed, I would dismiss her at my door and then wait for a bit before attempting to find the library. Lydia's face fell, and her shoulders slumped.

"Oh, I was hoping you would stay here and hang with me for the dance," she pouted. I had been unaware of there being a dance after introductions.

"Well, it has been a pretty tiring day. I just arrived after two weeks of travel," I offered as a reason without thinking.

"Two weeks? Where did you travel from?" Lydia pounced on it. From my father's manor to here should have only taken a week.

"I was visiting family friends prior to making the trip here." This was not an outright lie, and I did not need to justify my answer to this simple merchant's daughter. At some point, I would need to write to Quiet about my adventures these last few weeks, leaving out my adultery behaviors. I knew Quiet would be prancing about the manor, excitedly telling anyone who would listen to what I was up to.

"I suppose two weeks of travel would be pretty tiring. I arrived yesterday." She forced a smile.

"Yes, quite an eventful and tiring day," I replied quickly, maybe a bit too brightly. I dared not pick up speed to my room while giddiness coursed through me. Even though she had not unlooped our arms, each step brought me closer to ridding myself of her and then finding the library.

We stood at the bottom of the staircase, and I glanced at her with a raised eyebrow.

"Where are you headed?" I finally asked, curiosity getting the better of me. I was hoping this would make her unloop her arm from mine. I need to put distance from her and her garish dress.

"Oh, I decided I, too, would go to my rooms," she dully replied with a half-smile.

"Why not stay and enjoy the ball? Maybe you will find another Lady to spend time with," I offered. Secretly, I was hoping she would find someone else to cling to.

"No, it is okay."

"Where are your rooms?" I inquired while we climbed the grand staircase. I had a sinking feeling I would have to go all the way to my rooms.

"Umm, to the left, then the right, and then another right." I was following her directions in my mind, and my heart sank. She was staying in the same corridor as me.

"Do you enjoy your rooms?" I settled on to ask her.

Her smile brightened a bit. "I have never had rooms as deluxe as these or as big. Well, technically, I have a room back home, and that's it."

"For being here a day, are you enjoying your time?" I decided to continue the conversation; it was better than the awkward silence. We were at the top of the stairs and taking a left.

"Absolutely! I also really like the prince; he is quite a looker, if you know what I mean." She nudged my ribs with her elbow a few times to get her point across.

"I suppose so, if that is your type." I kept the eyeroll to myself. Prince Regalius Baylor was nice to look at, but it was apparent with the way he reacted to me he was cocky and a flirt. A thought came to my mind, and I needed to ask her. "Why did you not stay to be introduced?"

"Oh, they won't be introducing merchant children. Queen Opal does not care about us." A little bit of her happiness left her voice.

That seemed a bit hypocritical, but I chose not to voice my opinion out loud.

The other hypocritical thing I noted about this kingdom is despite neither King Lucien nor Queen Opal being from Queendom Grewt'en, they had chosen to give their son a Grewt'en name. He was not regal now, but maybe eventually, if he matured, he could be one day.

The lull in conversation must have bothered Lydia as we took our first right. She spoke up with a teasing voice. "You don't find Prince Regalius Baylor dreamy?"

"I have been around a few princes before; they are all the same." I shrugged nonchalantly. Her arm squeezed against mine.

"It must be wonderful being a Lady's child! All the people you meet and all the places you see," she gushed. I was not about to let on that the only traveling I have truly done was to Kingdom Theorines, and the only people I met were the ones who came to the manor and stayed.

"It has its merits, I suppose." I shrugged.

"Have you ever kissed a prince?" She pushed as we rounded a second corner, and my serene mask fell.

My face completely blanching in bewilderment. Lydia caught sight of my slip-up.

"Aha!" She gave me a devious smile. "I knew you were faking your personality." My stomach dropped as fear flashed through me; this little wench had tricked me with her outrageous question. I was not certain how to even respond to mend the situation. First, I had slipped up with Gideon and Finch, and now I did again with her. I had practiced my masking for years; why was I failing miserably at it now. I slowed my steps, her arm tightening on mine to continue dragging me forward. We had one more corner to turn, and we would be in our corridor, and then I could be rid of her.

"We are going to get along just fine, you and me. I can already tell." The confidence exuded from Lydia. I watched as the meek merchant's daughter vanished completely. Lydia's head swayed back and forth with a big grin.

"I beg your pardon?" I sputtered.

"You're not as serene as you want others to believe you to be." She called me out. I took immediate offense to it. "Ut-ut," she tutted, silencing me. "You believed me to be a pathetic, door mouse merchant's daughter. I am a merchant's daughter. Your sister did supply funding for me to be here, but I am definitely no door mouse. Between your status and my acting, we will be a formidable foe amongst these non-royals."

I furrowed my eyebrows at her. This girl was not normal. She was quite unusual. I did not know how I was going to escape her. "It was lovely meeting you . . ." I knew her name but chose to play dumb to shake her, potentially.

"Lydia," she did not miss a beat or appear offended.

"Lydia, but this is my room." I gestured toward a door I believed to be mine, hoping to lose her.

"No, it is not." She gave me an amused look.

"Yes, it is." I smiled sweetly, trying to get her to drop my arm. She would not budge.

"Miss Serenity is a liar." She called me out.

"I am not." I was appalled by her mannerisms while also admiring her boldness.

"Yes, you are."

"How do you know I am lying?" I challenged.

"Because that door leads to my room. Your room is two down from mine," she replied matter-of-factly.

I blushed hotly. This little merchant wench called me out on my lies and my mistakes. Glancing around, I was very grateful for this hallway being empty.

"No worries, we are going to get along just great."

My gaze perused this bold merchant's daughter. She smirked at me; her eyes glinted with a knowing mischievousness. "You are trouble," tumbled from my mouth. It was the first thought that popped into my head. She threw back her head, laughing at my statement.

"You are going to learn to love it," she promised. At the very least, I supposed she would make enduring this season bearable. Maybe even entertaining.

"Perhaps," I shrugged.

"Now, where do you really plan to go?" She pushed. Her arm squeezed mine tighter, preventing my escape route.

"I was going to find the library. I like to read." I decided I would find this library and then never spend time in there. I would just need to borrow texts and scrolls to copy either in my room or another desolate location to escape her.

"Reading is so boring, though," she almost whined.

"You do not have to attend with me," I countered.

"Hmm, it would be boring otherwise." She began dragging me the opposite way that we had come from. I was getting the feeling I was just some sort of entertainment for this merchant's daughter.

We wandered aimlessly, trying to find the library; it was not until we came to some elaborate doors that we finally found it. At this point, I could not remember the path we had taken to arrive here and hoped the trek back would not be too cumbersome. The library was completely empty, probably because everyone was with the royals currently and still preparing for this courting season.

"Sure are a lot of books," Lydia looked around with disdain. Out of my peripheral vision, I could see her nose scrunched up. She seriously did not need to have followed me here if she was going to disrespect books this much. I shook myself out of her arms and began to walk the shelves, looking for the history section. There were rows upon rows of texts and scrolls.

The walls, with books stuffed in shelves to the ceiling, had ladders on wheels that reached to the top. I was never going to leave this library, could I bring a bed in here and call it good? Unless something unprecedented happened, I would be married to Gideon in the end.

Either way, I really did not need to ever leave this room other than to eat and go to the bathroom.

I continued to peruse titles on the spines of the books, having not found the history section until I reached the back corner of the room. The history texts stretched all the way up to the top of the ceiling, and there were smaller bookcases surrounding with scrolls stuffed into them.

Lydia pinched one of the history books between her fingers, her nose still scrunched in disgust. "History? This is what you like to read? What are you, some old war general?" She tried to joke.

"Maybe in a past life," I replied, not giving her the time of day to believe she was getting under my skin with her remarks. I continued to browse all the titles at eye level. This library probably would have enough information in it to help me complete my ultimate historian book. I pulled a book off the shelf that was about T'Lovoness's history. Taking it over to an overstuffed armchair, I sat down and began to read. Lydia let out the biggest and loudest sigh I had ever heard in my life. *Melodramatic much?*

T'Lovoness obtained its name when the first King and Queen founded it. They were very fond of the words "Two Lovelies" as they were often referred to. This eventually came to their Kingdom being deemed "T'Lovoness".

pronounced Ta-Love-oh-ness

The names of the first King and Queen have since been lost in history over the course of centuries. There are some who believe in older historical texts that the King's name was actually T'Lovoness, but majority of texts support it was the play of words off the King and Queen's love for each other.

T'Lovoness Kingdom was started after the wars came to an end, and most of the land was a desolate wasteland after years of bloodshed. T'Lovoness was a new budding Kingdom in the aftermath and needed to find a way to forge on its own while still creating allegiances and connections with other monarchies. They had begun with the courting games. Eligible bachelors and bachelorettes of all pedigrees would come to participate in the games to find their love matches. Not much is known about the games other than there had been death casualities documented among participants.

At some point in history, the courting games had come to an end. They resumed when Queen Opal began her reign alongside King Lucien. Queen Opal changed the name from Courting Games to The Courting Seasons with a less violent approach.

Today's Courting Seasons today allow Royals, High Lord and Lady's children, and Highly Respected Merchant children, to participate. Queen Opal has changed it so that peasants may not participate, and not all merchant children can either without an endorsement. This is the most updated and accurate historical text on The Courting Seasons within T'Lovoness.

I tucked the book under my arm, unsure if it was allowed to remove books from the library, but it never hurt to try. Wordlessly, I left to return to my rooms. Lydia followed in tow without complaint. She didn't even make a comment on the book I was taking with me.

After a few wrong turns we were finally down our corridor. How many trips would it take until I had the way memorized. I had thought for certain someone would stop us, but it seemed without a tiara or crown upon our heads we were nobodies. While this apparently bothered Lydia, I did not mind it one bit. It would grant me the freedom I needed to move about the castle as I pleased. We were approaching the doors to our rooms, and I was ever so happy to rid myself temporarily of the fawn-haired girl.

"What do you plan to wear at the ball tomorrow night?" Lydia asked. I knew she was trying to prolong this conversation, and I wanted to escape her.

"Not certain," I replied briskly. Only a few more steps, and I was resting my hand on the doorknob.

"I was thinking of wearing a mint green dress, maybe with some cream, little pops of pink as well."

"That sounds nice," I replied distantly as I opened my bedroom door. Lydia tried to follow me in, but I blocked her way. "Look, Lydia, it was nice meeting you. It has been a very long day, and I would like to be left alone for the evening." I had never been this sharp with someone, but I did not know how else I would shake this girl.

"Oh, uh yeah, I understand." She took a step back and I closed the door on her face. *Finally, a moment alone.*

Chapter Thirteen

The next morning, I finished dressing in a simple yellow dress when there was a knock on my door. I assumed it would be the servants barging in, but when no one came fluttering in, I went to see who was on the other side. Unfortunately, it was Lydia, and my eyes were assaulted by her dress. I didn't know where it was safe to look at. It was more than my brain could process. The abomination was a bright neon yellow mixed with purple polka dots and had random green pinstripes running down the sides with the polka dots. It was atrocious. Her eyes skimmed up and down my body, her lips tightly pinching before she eased a smile onto her face.

"Oh, good, you are ready! Let us go together." Lydia's fake smile remained plastered on her face. If she wasn't happy to see me then why did she come to get me?

I could not even protest. I blamed my senses for being too overwhelmed to even respond. Her perfume smelled cheap and heavily slathered on, like a poor alcoholic version of honeysuckles. I had to hold my gag as she pressed close to me, looping her arm through mine. Blindly, I allowed her to lead us toward the stairs. I glanced at the abomination she wore. Had my sister been aware of what the family's money was endorsing? Prior to meeting Lydia, I did not even know Amity had any involvement in The Courting Seasons. She never talked about it much, and now magically, I am here with this atrocity. At least I did not have a true stake; otherwise, my reputation by association with this merchant's daughter would be ruined.

We arrived at the banquet hall for breakfast with the other attendees. A migraine was growing. Many guests gave us a wide birth, and if I was not attached to the thing assaulting their vision, I too would be giving it distance. We were instructed to sit at the side tables in the back of the room while the royals sat at the main banquet table with The King, Queen, and their Princely son.

I led Lydia and myself to a table where I recognized three sisters, who were the daughters of the neighboring Lady next to my family's property. Lady Malevolent in Grewt'en had six children and it appeared three of her daughters were attending this year.

"Is that Serenity?" The middle sister, Greta, asked as we approached. Greta could be highly distinguished from her two sisters. She had flaming-red hair that was stick straight and soft brown eyes. I had come to learn her voice had a lot more bite in it than she ever intended when she cared about something.

"Never thought I would see you here," Ivy, the oldest sister, commented. Ivy had straight blond hair and green eyes. Her face was all angles with sharp cheekbones and a straight nose leading into light pink lips that always appeared pinched. I always had the distinct feeling she was trying to portray perfection at any given time.

"Is Quiet here too?" Mimzy, the youngest sister, asked, looking behind me for my younger sister. Mimzy had mousy brown hair that was curled with bows on each side of her head. She still had chubby cheeks like a kid and an innocence about her that needed protecting. She and Quiet were stuck together like glue when we were all together. I had the feeling Mimzy was not ready to grow up despite being eighteen.

"Why would Quiet be here? She is too young to attend." Greta ridiculed her younger sister, causing Mimzy to slouch lower in her seat.

"Greetings Ivy, Greta, and Mimzy," I said ,dipping my head at each sister before looking at Mimzy. "Quiet is not here. Like Greta said, she is too young yet. She may possibly attend when she turns eighteen in three years. I am sure she would love to see you before then." I smiled, giving encouragement and hope to the youngest sister. Mimzy gave me a shy smile back.

"Who is your friend?" Ivy raised her eyebrow with a nod at the hideous thing beside me. I felt Lydia's arm tighten against mine slightly at being noticed. I glanced at her.

"Ivy, this is Lydia. She is a respectable merchant's daughter that my sister endorsed to be able to attend." I watched as all three sisters assess to what my sister had purchased. Only Greta and Ivy gave my dress another once over, the older sister's lips pursing more. I knew they were trying to decipher where my dress had come from. None of the local dressmakers worked in this style. They probably were also curious as to why I was attached to the abomination dress next to me, without waiting for permission to join their table. I withdrew my arm from Lydia's and, pulled out a chair to take my seat. Lydia followed suit. I knew the sisters were fine with me sitting at their table, but the apparent disdain they didn't bother to hide for Lydia spoke volumes of their thoughts on her.

"Did you two know each other growing up?" Greta inquired, looking between Lydia and myself.

"No, we met yesterday." I responded. I wanted to disassociate myself and Lydia as much as possible. The less I was attached in association with her, the better.

"Well, that is true, but I have seen Serenity from a distance whenever my father was selling wares to her family. We live quite close to her manor." Lydia spoke up.

I looked at Lydia, my face scrutinizing why she chose to drop this random bit of information without my knowledge. She could have told me this anytime yesterday or on our walk here; why drop it now in front of my friends?

"We were not expecting to see you here, though, Serenity." Ivy redirected the conversation back to me, dismissing what Lydia's statement.

"Have you been attending the previous years with no luck?" I replied casually, popping a grape into my mouth from the fruit platter in front of us while we waited to be served breakfast. Ivy was three years older than me. I knew I had hit the mark with the way her face flashed with shock momentarily.

"It is not *so* easy to catch a spouse even with this many eligible singles about." She sniffed, pinpointing me with a look. More like Ivy did not know how to flirt and was having a difficulty. Out of the three sisters, Mimzy would probably have the easiest time becoming engaged, followed by Greta and then Ivy. Greta may have a sharp tongue, but I have witnessed her flirting. I was surprised Greta had not found someone if this was her third year attending.

"Well, I thank you for forewarning us," I responded, not giving much thought to what she said in the matter. I was not here to court anyway, but they didn't know that. I ate another grape, watching the sisters. I'm sure their mouths would water to know I was already pre-arranged to the heir of Theorines, that they were sitting before a future queen. I smiled to myself, feeling a bit smug even if I didn't care for how the circumstances came about.

We did not receive our food until after the royal's table had been served. While we waited, my eyes lingered on the royal's table, and I could not find Gideon or Finch in the group. I did not know why I was a little discouraged by that; maybe it was because I wanted to see someone friendly. The three sisters were great, but sometimes it was like weaving through the conversation to avoid being verbally injured. They were not my favorite of neighboring Lady children, but they would have to do.

"Does Lady Trustworthy's children attend The Courting

seasons?" I asked the sisters. I gazed around the room for any recognition of her horde of children.

"I had heard they would be arriving late this year," Greta informed.

"Any idea of how many will be coming?" I inquired.

"Last I heard, the whole litter, aside from the baby, who is only seventeen," Greta was quick to reply again.

"Twelve of her kids are coming?" I asked incredulously.

"We visited them last fall, and that is what Lady Trusty stated. She said she was going to send the whole eligible litter this year, and whomever did not find a spouse she would begin sending out letters to arrange it. She wants them all out of her manor," Greta leaned in, gossiping, using Lady Trustworthy's preferred nickname of being called 'Trusty.'

"Just means competition will be more difficult this year with a litter of twelve new bloods coming into the array to fight for a spouse." Snipped Ivy.

Lydia squirmed in her seat a bit.

"Does she not have more sons than daughters?" I was trying to recall through my memory of her children.

"She does, but there will still be more people to compete against," Ivy said sharply.

"Could you not pick one of the sons?" I inquired a bit further. The two older sisters both looked at me and began to laugh. I was not certain what I had said that was so funny.

"Please, and live on Lady Trusty's land? I beg not." Greta laughed.

"I would prefer to leave Grewt'en if possible," Ivy commented looking at the other guests.

"Why?" This surprised me. Grewt'en was a lovely place to live; granted I had not traveled to experience other places, but I had no ill-will intent to leave the Queendom.

"The further I can be from Grewt'en, the better." Was all Ivy replied with as the servants set down our meals in front of us. The rest of the meal was with Greta spilling small gossip here and there and Mimzy asking about Quiet. Lydia would attempt to jump in, but the two older sisters ignored her outright. Honestly, I did not want to tie myself in association to anyone at this table other than Mimzy, but I knew I would probably be shackled to them all and then some more when Lady Trustyworthy's horde arrived.

W hen we were dismissed from breakfast, I chose this as my opportune time to head back to the library. I did not make it far when a hand caught my arm. I was pulled back around to come chest-to-chest with Gideon. Finch was standing slightly behind him.

"I had wondered when I would see you." He smiled, so much for subtleness.

"Gid—Prince Gideon Orion. Prince Finch Azrael." I dipped my head in respect to them. I could not quite curtsy with Gideon's grip still on my arm. He released it, realizing his mistake. All the girls behind me gasped and dropped into their curtsies, murmuring their respects to The Princes' of Theorines. Finch knocked Gideon out of the way, in an unprincely-like manner, to stand before me.

"Lady Serenity Novena, may I have the first dance with you at tonight's ball?" He asked. I took a step back, completely surprised by the abruptness. Gideon pushed him a bit out of the way.

"I think it is only right she dances with the *eldest* brother first, do you not think so as well, younger brother." Gideon gave Finch a pointed look, trying to communicate that he had more of a stake over me for the future than his younger brother ever would.

"How about whoever finds me first will get the first dance?" I challenged, flirting a bit. The girls behind me were quiet, hanging onto our every word.

"The dance is *mandatory* Serenity. You need to be in attendance," Gideon commented, forgetting to address me by my proper title. The girls gasped, noticing the informality or maybe it was because I had two princes fighting over me in a very public location. Gideon knew if I had the opportunity, I would not even show at the ball.

"Yes, yes, I am well aware. I will be there." I did not conceal my eye-roll from him. I hadn't been aware that the ball was mandatory, but I was not going to reveal that to him. Our familiarity with each other would cause me problems with how thirsty these single ladies were that stood behind me. I knew any of them would claw their way to move above their rank by marrying a royal. They wouldn't have any issue tearing me to shreds to make it happen.

Gideon gave me a lazy smile before he dipped his head and walked away toward the other royals. Finch scowled, dipping his head, and followed his brother. Taking a deep breath, I braced myself before turning back around to face the females. They all wore a mixture of shock, confusion, and envy on their faces.

"You know the Princes' of Theorines?" Ivy asked, her voice rising almost into a shrill.

"Yes, their father, King Ashborn, had business with my sister this past spring. I accompanied my sister and father on the trip and became acquainted with Prince Gideon Orion and Prince Finch Azrael during my stay at their castle." No sense in hiding the truth now. I was certain if I did not tell them, somehow it would come out, and I did not need that extra headache later.

"So," Greta pushed forward, "you would say you are on friendly terms with the prince brothers then?" I could see the wheels in her mind beginning to turn just as fast as Ivy's and Lydia's were. Mimzy was the only one not calculating amongst the mix.

"Yes," I took a step back, becoming guarded. "We became friends during my stay."

"You can introduce us to the princes next time," Ivy ordered. "Tonight, at the ball, to be specific." It was not a request. However, Ivy did not outrank me by any means. If anything, my family's property was far vaster than her Mother's, and our lands held more villages. If we wanted to become technical in matters, I outranked her in that alone.

"Introductions will only be made if the princes want them." I gave Ivy a leveled gaze. "I have no reasons otherwise to do so." She stared back at me, but I refused to look away first. When she realized she would not win this battle she finally diverted her attention to say something to Greta.

Dismissing myself, I decided to head back to my room. There were currently no mandatory events for ladies until tonight's ball. I would take advantage of continuing my research during this time.

It took mere seconds, and Lydia was walking by my side.

"Do you and those sisters get along?" She asked. She was a nosey one.

I gave her a sidelong glance and continued walking forward without responding.

"I just got the feeling there was a bit of a power struggle back there. Do you get along with Lady Trusty's children?"

I ignored her questions and kept walking. People we passed by had momentarily vision loss from Lydia's dress as they bumped into things. Or at least that is what I imagined.

"I like Lady Trusty's children," she continued, not the least bit ruffled that I remained silent. "They have always been kind to me, especially the oldest Pierce. He has always been nice to me." I could hear the awe in her voice; it was evident she had a crush on Pierce. He was not a bad guy, always friendly to everyone around him. I was surprised he had not been wedded yet at twenty-nine.

"Do you like Pierce?" Lydia pushed.

"*Lord* Pierce is nice to everyone," I commented, emphasizing his title. Maybe I was being harsh, but I wanted to be left alone. I also did not want to have these conversations where everyone could hear and then begin to gossip.

"I suppose he is. What about his brother Thoughtful? Do you like him?" Lydia kept pushing, once again not including his title. I stopped walking and grabbed her arm. She looked at me, shocked by my grip. We were far enough out of earshot of the others for me to say under my breath.

"Listen, you do not have conversations like this in earshot of all these gossip mongers. I do not want to be a part of it. These are private conversations. *Do you understand?*" I hissed at her.

Her eyes wide from shock, she gave a couple of small nods.

"Good." I released her arm and continued to my destination with her trailing behind me. I opened and shut my door, not allowing her the opportunity to come in. The rest of the day would be my time to read and copy the important details I found in the historical text I had found.

I sighed, glancing down at all the parchment that held my most recent copied notes. I had made a second trip to the library before lunch, returning the borrowed books, and obtaining a larger stack to return with to my room. My door remained locked, and I ignored every single knock that came upon it. The only exceptions were the servants bringing lunch and dinner.

The handle jiggle once, which made me a bit crossed about whomever was trying to come into my room. I had a sneaking suspicion it was Lydia, but the person on the other side of the door never announced themself.

Unfortunately for me, the hour was becoming late, and I needed to prepare for the first mandatory ball of the season. The royals never announced how many of the balls would be required and I hoped it would be minimal. I understood the first one, but thereafter, it sounded exhausting.

Leaving my writing desk behind, I went to the armoire in my bedroom to sort through the dresses. It would be expected of me to choose a dress from the extravagant side of the wardrobe. I found a gorgeous silvery two-piece dress that shifted blue from the fabric movement. It was a nice mix of the color of my hair and eyes. I noted the back was a corset, and I would need to use a doorknob to help cinch up the laces by myself before I could begin tightening them by hand.

I grabbed the silvery-blue corset top portion of the dress, pulling it over my head. I took one end of the corset laces and looped it on the doorknob. Methodically, I pulled, working it back forth until I could tighten the stays by hand.

When I deemed it tight enough that I could still breathe comfortably, I glanced at the top portion in the mirror. It was simple, no ruffles, eyelets or lace, just a glittery silvery blue that sparkled. I reached for the hoop skirt off the bed and stepped into it. Once it was situated the way I liked over the corset top, I tightened the laces. Lastly, was pulling the behemoth of a bottom over my head. The bottom portion of the dress was heavy, I questioned if the seamstress found the heaviest material in her shop and said, 'Yep, this will be perfect to break the poor lady's hips.'

I was thankful I had not readied my hair yet; tugging it over my head was a chore. I felt like I was wrestling a losing battle, but when it finally slipped down over my body, I was heavily breathing and caught a glimpse in the mirror of the redness in my face. The worst part is I knew I would have to remove it again later. I only hoped this was the heaviest of my dresses.

Looking in the mirror and then down at the dress from right to left and back to the mirror, I gauged I had a decent two feet on each side of the dress at the bottom portion. I had never worn a dress this big in my life, and I would need to be extra cautious to not draw attention to myself by bumping into anyone or anything. The bottom was almost as simple as the top portion; however, the fabric here billowed and layered over one another, which was probably the reason the material was heavy.

Looking at my red face and messed up hair, I did not have the faintest idea of how I could create an elaborate hairstyle. I undid the simple up-do twist and running a finger through my silver locks, I chose to put it in a simple bun high on my head. I could tell by how warm I was feeling standing here that it would become worse in a crowded area. Especially if I had to dance with those two brothers. I chose a simple black velvet choke to wear on my neck and nothing else for jewelry.

Lydia banged her fist on the door, which I ignored. She wanted us to walk together, but I refused to be summoned like a dog. She shouted, which mortified me. Eventually, Lydia gave up and left, but only after she had jiggled the handle, testing it.

I waited a few minutes for my departure to the ballroom, and when I arrived, it was already in full swing. People were coupled up dancing to the music the band played. I stood near the entrance, browsing the room for any recognition of anyone I may know. I noted many guests were wearing dresses in pinks and greens, how unfortunate for them to all be wearing dresses in the same color. Even a few of the males were in pink or green tuxes. It made me think of Lydia's atrocious dress from earlier.

As my eyes fell upon guests, taking them in. Many sets met mine as well. Some of the royals looked me up and down, sneered, and then returned to their conversation. The non-royals, upon seeing I did not wear a tiara, continued with what their conversations, not deeming me interesting enough. There were a few that gave me a questioning eyebrow, I returned a small smile and nod, before moving on to look at the next person. I left the doorway and headed to a wall to hide behind some pillars. I wanted to keep to the secluded shadows for as long as possible. I had not caught sight of Lydia or Lady Malevolent's daughters yet, and I would rather find them first before they spotted me.

"I believe you owe me the first dance," Gideon's voice carried to me. I looked to my left, not finding him. Glancing to the right I found him walking toward me. The pillars hid him in shadow; only in between, when the ball light cascaded on him, could I see him clearly. The closer he came, the harder it was to hold back my smile. He stopped before me, and I matched his grin.

"I suppose I do." I smirked.

"I did not think you were going to make it."

"It is *mandatory* is it not?" I countered.

"You are late."

"Perfection takes time."

"Do you really care about perfection, Serenity?" He raised an eyebrow. Gideon knew me well enough by now to know the answer.

"No, I suppose I do not." I held out my arm to him. "Come along, let us get this dreadful dance done and out of the way."

"Please act a little happy to be dancing with a prince," Gideon tried to make his voice sound wounded.

"I have done more than dance with this prince in particular; a dance is simply nothing special at this point," I replied under my breath.

"You have a point there, Serenity." Gideon laughed.

We lined up on the dance floor next to the other couples. I noted a few craning their necks, trying to figure out who I was, and most likely, what right did I have to dance with a prince. I chose to ignore them; their jaws would drop later when our engagement was announced. Maybe my smugness was putting the carriage in front of the horse. For all I knew Gideon, could end up finding someone else to fall in love with during the season. Then where would that leave me? There was no one back home for me now.

Earlier, I had read an interesting small snippet about the original Courting Games. It nagged in the back of my mind. If peasants had been able to attend, I could have announced my engagement to Theo on the first day of the games, and this would have all been done and over. The mention of reported deaths made me both nervous and curious. What had all occurred during the games to make them that violent? None of it mattered since I didn't even know where Theo was now.

My heart conflicted for a bit as I found Gideon smiling at me. I felt a stab of betrayal; I was not being true to myself or to Theo, and a part of me felt remorse to admit that Gideon was a far better and more tentative lover than Theo had ever been. The other hard truth I always dismissed from my mind was that a life with Theo would give up my well-built home of luxury in a manor. Theo did not have property, and I most likely would need to begin working in a kitchen or laundress to help us survive. I pursed my lips from the thoughts. I believed I loved Theo, but being away from him made me realize what he could never offer me.

"If I had an enny," Gideon began, bringing my attention back to the present and to someone who could provide for me in more ways than I had ever imagined in life. "I would pay for your thoughts right now." The band sounded, and we took our first steps in the dance.

"Oh, I was just thinking how about the season. A lot of things could happen between now and the end. I only hope I can put a good dent in the historical section." None of it was a lie. I had been thinking about it at the start, but my thoughts drifted further into the reaches of my mind that I avoided during my research.

"I happen to be friends with Prince Regalius Baylor. I am sure after the courting season, I could pull some favors for you to finish your research here." Gideon threw this tidbit out there with his charismatic smile.

"I may be reaching on assumptions, but I am becoming under the distinct impression, that The Queen does not favor anyone who is not a royal," I countered. I wanted to know if my observations that endorsed the gossip were correct, even if I did smile from the favor he would be willing to ask for me.

"By then, though, you will be married to a royal. Will you not be?" He countered my comment.

"I guess you are right there." I giggled. "How about the other monarchy's historical sections? Have strings there, too?" I pushed.

"Whatever your heart desires, I am sure we can make some negotiations," he promised. My heart tore again. Gideon would give me the world easily on a platter, but yet, I was thinking about a past love. After all, that was all Theo could be to me, a past love.

The dance came to an end, and I barely could take a step before Finch grasped my hand to claim the next dance. He was full of smiles. I had not found him this happy since before our departure from Kingdom Theorines.

"Lady Serenity Novena, I apologize for not being able to secure your first dance, but please allow me to have your second dance." He bowed, kissing the back of my hand; I curtsied.

"I would be honored for you to steal my second dance." A few couples rotated out around us on the floor, and we prepared for the next dance. I could hear a few whispers from the surrounding people of not one but two princes dancing with me. I heard someone loudly hiss, 'She's not even a royal.' I glanced past Finch and caught sight of Ivy narrowing her eyes on me, curiously enough, I had not spotted Lydia yet.

"Are you having a good time, Serenity?" Finch asked me, bringing my attention back to him.

"I would not say balls are really my thing; takes away from my research," I answered honestly, "but it is alright. How about you?"

"Yeah, you are more of an archery kind of Lady." He winked with a laughed, and I joined him. I suppose, though, if I wedded Gideon, there could potentially be more archery and other adventures with the two brothers. That is until Finch found a wife.

"We never did have the opportunity to lay under the stars." Finch's voice became saddened.

"I know." I tried to give him an encouraging smile. "But hopefully, we can remedy that after the courting season has come to pass." My words caused the opposite effect I had hoped for. His shoulders lowered a bit.

"Yeah, I suppose," dryly, he commented.

"Finch," I tried to argue with reason, "you know I have no more say in the matter than Gideon does." The song was coming to an end.

"No, Serenity, you were the only one who did not have a say in the matter." The dance ended with Finch bowing. He stood up and briskly walked away from me, leaving me to ponder those words in the middle of the dance floor. It was not until I was being yanked off the floor that I snapped out of my thoughts. The next dance was beginning to start, and I had been standing there like a daft fool. I looked at the hand wrapped around my wrist dragging me, and I found myself blinded by Lydia's flashy reflecting dress. She had tiny mirrors sewn over every inch of it, and as the lighting and other people's attire captured into the mirrors, it shown it's way into my eyes. I blinked multiple times, shaking my head to regain my sight.

"You danced with both Princes of Theorines!" She squealed. "I knew it yesterday that you were close with them, but I did not realize how close!" She was far too excited by this revelation.

"As I mentioned, I had stayed with them the month prior to this courting season with my sister and father. We were all the same age and became friends fast enough." I commented distantly. My mind continued mulling over Finch's words and what they had meant. What did he mean by saying that I was the only one who never had a say in the matter? Did Gideon have a hand in the matter of us being engaged? I believed the only deceit had been my sister arranging an engagement to Gideon. Was there more to the story that I needed to solve?

"You need to introduce me to them!" Lydia continued to prattle on. "I have seen them both talking to Prince Regalius Baylor." She, like Ivy, had it in her mind that I would introduce her to the prince brothers. Despite how Finch had left me confused, I still would not subject them to Lydia or Ivy.

"As I stated this morning to Lady Ivy, I will not be doing any introductions unless they request them." I picked up my dress to make walking easier. "If you want to talk to them, you will need to do it yourself without me." I left Lydia, maneuvering through the crowd toward Gideon. He was standing in a circle with other males; I recognized Finch, Prince Regalius Baylor, and a few sons from Grewt'en, but then there was a prince and a few other males that I could not place.

Gideon noticed my approach and gave me a warm, welcoming smile. Finch, noticing his brother's diverted attention, followed his gaze to me. He looked back at Gideon and then turned his attention to Regalius. I stopped in front of the group and, out of my peripheral vision, noticed Queen Opal's eyes on me. The group stood close enough to the front of the ballroom where she and her husband sat. I wished she would focus her gaze elsewhere, but I had a sinking feeling she would keep her focus on us.

"Lady Serenity Novena," Gideon greeted, "have you come for another dance?" His attention never left me as he spoke.

"No. I need to talk to you." I flicked my gaze from him to the other boys and back to him. "Privately." The boys oohed and ahhed like a bunch of girls. Gideon did not drop his smile, he offered me his arm that I graciously accepted. We walked away from his circle of friends until we were along the wall in the shadows of the pillars, far enough away that another guest could not eavesdrop on us.

"What is it, Serenity?" Gideon gave me a lazy smile.

"I need to know." I swallowed. "Did you have a choice in the matter on being engaged to me by the end of the season?" I searched his eyes, waiting for his answer. His eyes widened a fraction.

"Serenity, where is this coming from?" He reflectively took a step back; I followed him, not allowing distance to be put between us. I feared he would try to avoid answering my question.

"I need to know," I stated again. He looked back over to his brother.

"I am going to kill that brother of mine," he muttered.

"It is true then," I commented. I stepped to the side and rested my body against the wall. The hoop of my dress, pushing the whole bottom forward, and looking down, I found it absurd. Gideon stepped forward and grabbed my hand. I glanced at his hand connected to mine and followed it up his arm to his face. My lips twisted, not certain how I should feel other than the sadness creeping in.

"Not to the extent you are thinking, Serenity." His eyes pleading for me to believe him.

"Then to what extent?" I removed my hand from his to cross my arms. "Explain it to me." His eyes searched mine, before he dropped his head, sighing to look at the ground.

"My parents told me if I did not find someone to marry by the end of The Courting Season, I would be in an arranged marriage not of my choosing." He swallowed and took a deep breath. "Then you showed up; we had not been expecting you. I asked my father to talk to your sister and arrange it for us to be engaged." He looked up from the floor, his eyes pleading. "I am sorry, Serenity. I just did not want to be forced to marry a stranger." My mind started connecting the dots to what he had admitted and all the secrets everyone in the castle of Theorines had been keeping. I cleared my throat.

"Now tell me the complete truth. I know you are hiding something else," I challenged, holding Gideon's eye. If he had not included my arrival being the reason, I would have believed him, but the whole point of the trip was to arrange my hand in marriage.

"Your sister initially was traveling to my kingdom to negotiate your hand in marriage to Finch. I changed my father's mind." He gulped, not breaking eye contact. Sweat formed at his temples. While it was warm, I knew he was beginning to fear losing me. His eyes frantically searched mine. A coolness settled over me as bitterness filled me.

"So, that is why Finch has been in a foul mood this whole time." I snarled, filling my voice with as much venom as I could without raising it to draw attention. "You stole me from him?" This whole time, Amity had been making deals to sell me off to the younger prince and I had been the daft fool to never notice. Running through my memories, the evidence had all been there, but I was too blinded by a room filled with books to even remotely believe my father would allow Amity to do such a thing to me. How could I have allowed myself to ignore the signs, that in the end, my initial betrothal had been to the other prince, but the one standing before me had been just as guilty. I looked to where Finch stood; he and I were the only two who had never had a say in the matter.

"Serenity." Gideon took my hand, forcing me to uncross my arms. I pursed my lips at him. "I did not mean for it to happen; Finch is young, and he will find someone new to love. I just did not want to be wedded to a stranger," he begged me to understand.

"But yet –" I pushed off the wall "-you thought it would be okay to force my hand into marriage without my consent or my knowledge. You *played* along as if you did not have a choice in the matter either," I accused.

"I had planned to tell you, Serenity," he rushed out. I could hear the desperation in his voice, his eyes widening as the sweat rolled down his face.

"When?" I demanded. A laugh from anger threatened to bubble from my throat at how daft I had been to everything happening to me.

"I didn't think that far ahead, but I promise you that I would have told you eventually." *Eventually*. Even though he was taller than me, I looked down my nose at him, yanking my hand from his.

"Now, I am stuck at this stupid Courting Seasons because of you and our families. I am the one who will be forced into a marriage that had been kept secret from me." I seethed. I wanted to leave. I did not need him or any of these people. I tried to shove past him, but he blocked my way.

"Serenity, Serenity. Please do not look at it that way."

"Then how am I supposed to look at it, Gideon?" I glared up at him, his shoulders falling slightly as his face became crestfallen.

"I am a first-born prince, heir to my throne. . . I know I could probably easily find someone to marry me here, but I met you." He grabbed both of my hands within his. I tried to yank them away, but his grip held firm. "I found a friendship and an ease of a relationship with you. You went from a stranger to a friend within two weeks, and after what happened in the pond, I just knew . . . Serenity, I just knew." His eyes held unfallen tears with pleading for me to understand.

"We had been engaged before the pond," I stated calmly.

"Yes, but I just knew," he repeated.

"Knew what?" I asked softer, with less venom in my voice.

"That I would be happy ruling with you by my side. I am sorry I hurt you. I am sorry if you felt like I robbed you of your freedom. I saw an opportunity to be happy, and I took it. I would do anything to make you happy," he pleaded.

I mulled over his words. Did he truly believe that I could make him happy? While his apologies sounded sincere, I was not certain I could forgive him for tricking me. I supposed, regardless of this season, I would be marrying one of the Theorines's princes if everything he had said was true. The answer to my earlier question was answered. If Gideon found someone, I still would be marrying a prince of Theorines. I felt something crack within me.

"Serenity?" Gideon brought my attention back to him. "Do you forgive me?" I stared at him as I felt the light within me begin to extinguish. We were all pieces on the same board, thinking we had a say in where we moved next, but all along, there was a guiding hand rigging the game.

"Answer me one thing," I stated coldly.

"Anything."

"How long had my sister been negotiating my hand in marriage to your brother?" I wanted to know if his answer aligned with Amity's or if she, too, had been lying.

"A little over a year." I could no longer hear the ballroom music or the guests talking and laughing. Gideon was standing directly in front of me, but he might as well have been miles away. My back hit the wall, and I felt my legs slowly begin to give out as I slid down it. I numbly felt my arms being yanked back up as I fell against Gideon's chest. He was saying something, but it felt like my head was underwater, I could not understand the words.

I rested my hands on his shoulders, helping me to steady my balance as I stood, putting some space between our bodies. I couldn't breathe. No matter how much I gasped in the air, I felt it wasn't enough. I looked quickly to the left of the room, trying to understand why I couldn't breathe. Whipping my head to the right, I still didn't understand as I gasped more.

Gideon's hands rested on my face, forcing me to look at him. I tried to escape his grip, but my attempts were futile. I kept gasping, trying to force air down my lungs, but it was to no avail. Gideon kept yelling something, but I couldn't hear him. Tears blurred my vision.

Gideon was shoved out of my sight, his hands ripped from my face. I felt my body being jerked and pulled along. A sob escaped my throat, my tears making the male to my right blurred. I couldn't focus on him if I tried. He opened a door and slammed it shut behind us. I numbly felt the cool air that replaced the warm, cloistered ball room. A hand was on my back. Bringing my fists up to my face, I choked on my sobs.

My dress loosened, and I felt more air entering my lungs. The male shoved me into a chair, and I tried to protest, but then they pushed my head between my legs. The dress of my fabric pushed up into my face, and distantly, I heard cursing as the stranger's free hand pushed my dress down for me to breathe.

"Deep, steady breaths," he ordered. "Breathe." I listened; slowly, my lungs felt the burn as air made it down them. My gasps brought lungfuls of air. I gulped them down greedily as spots blinded my vision with the tears. The silent sobs became audible as they racked my body.

The hand that had been pushing my back down to keep my head in place began to make circular, soothing rubbing motions. I was uncertain how long we stayed like that, but when my vision cleared, and I could breathe again, I slowly sat up, feeling conscious of the state I was in. Hesitantly, I looked to my right to see who my male rescuer was. I gasped, almost falling out of my chair backwards. He caught me before I fell, pulling me back into a sitting position.

"Easy, easy," he comforted. Uneasily, I tried to relax in the chair with him sitting next to me.

"Prince Regalius Baylor, why . . . what are you doing here?" I realized he had been the one to push Gideon away from me. How long had he been watching? His jade eyes assessed me while I regarded him warily. The silence between us stretched.

"Prince –"

"Don't." He cut me off.

"What?" My brows furrowed as I wiped away my tears.

"You are not formal with Gideon. Call me Regalius."

"Regalius." I tested his name out slowly on my lips.

"Good, now are you okay?" He asked.

I felt exposed, with his full attention on me. Shakily, I mentally checked my body, feeling the soreness in my lungs and jaw, the numbness in my face, and dried tear tracks on my cheek. I nodded.

"How did you know?" I whispered. He leaned back in his chair, crossing his arms and contemplating my question.

"I am heir prince to the largest and wealthiest kingdom; if I told you I have never experienced what you just went through, I would be lying," Regalius answered matter-of-factly, and I believed he was telling me the truth.

"Do you have episodes like this often?" I pushed, trying to bring myself on more stable ground.

"They're called panic attacks, and sometimes yes." He looked up at the ceiling. I tucked away this new information that I would include in my research for later.

"But how did you know? From where we stood, you would not have been able to see us." Regalius scratched the back of his head.

"After you had retrieved Gideon, Finch mumbled under his breath, 'I hope he gets what he deserves.' It made me curious as to what Gideon had done to you, I decided to pass by to have a better view, and that was when I witnessed Gideon boxing you in." I could not say I was happy to know he chose to spy on the conversation, but I had to admit to myself if he had not, who knows what state I could have ended up in. How badly would I have embarrassed myself if he had not stepped in?

"I suppose a thank you would be in order," I said slowly. Uncertainty laced through me. He had been spying, but he had also rescued me, and as a higher rank, it complicated matters as well.

"It is okay if you are not okay with me stepping in, but may I ask what Gideon had done to you?"

"Maybe another time." I rose from my chair and felt how loose my dress was on me. "Um, would you maybe tighten the laces so I can make it back to my room with modesty?" I asked, embarrassed.

"Follow me." He stood and headed to a door in the back of the room. Not having much choice in the matter, I followed him. When he opened it, it led to a dimly lit hallway.

"Servant hallways?" I inquired a bit surprised.

"Are you opposed to using them?" He asked over his shoulder.

"No, I just had not expected this." It seemed there were a lot of things about the T'Lovoness heir that I hadn't anticipated. Showing his side of vulnerability was one of them, using the hidden paths in the walls was another.

"It is beneficial for a royal to learn to use them to escape on a moment's notice." He continued to lead us down the servant's hallway, weaving corners and acknowledging any servants as we passed them. They all appeared unruffled to see the prince. He opened a door, and we entered a room laid out in a fashion similar to mine. He did not pause, leading me to the next door, and then we stood in the corridor hallway.

"I would assume, as a lady, you were put in this area of the castle." He answered before I could even form the question in my mind. I took in our location and realized my room was two down from this very door.

"Yes, thank you, Regalius." I curtsied and immediately slapped a hand to the top of my bodice to prevent it from falling down. He chuckled as my face flamed.

"You are welcome. Take the rest of the evening easy, Serenity." He nodded to me and turned back into the room, disappearing from sight when the door closed behind him. I did not dwell on where he would be off to now, I quickly hurried to my room. Yanking open my door and locking it shut. I hurried to the bathroom, I needed to know what kind of state I looked after crying so hard in front of the prince, and who knows who else had witnessed my panic attack, as Regalius had named it.

Peering into the mirror, I watched as the tears welled in my eyes again. My face was blotchy, my hair a complete bird nest, and my eyes were blacked from the smudged mascara and eyeliner. How badly had I disgraced myself with the way I looked? Numbly I loosened the rest of my dress corset and stepped out of it, discarding the silvery-blue dress over a chair. I scrubbed my face of all traces for reminders of what had happened tonight. Lastly, I combed my hair out, disgruntled at the snarls that had formed. When I found myself acceptable, I headed to the bedroom. I decided attempting sleep would help put tonight behind me. Tomorrow, I will deal with everything when I have a clearer mind.

Chapter Fourteen

The sunlight streamed through my bedroom windows. It, annoyingly, woke me. I still felt like crap and numb from the previous night's events. The last year of my life had been a lie with Amity. Coupled with Gideon, who I had come to think of as a friend, had been a part of that betrayal and lies.

King Ashborn and Queen Izralda knew my fate from the moment I walked through their doors. Finch's instant crush on me made more sense. It was not instant love or anything; he already knew I was to be his wife. Finch had been preparing his future with me until his elder brother swept in and stole his bride away. A sadness washed over me for the younger prince; who would he end up with now? As a prince here, I suppose he would have his pick of the ton, unless he held out in hopes Gideon found someone else. Then Finch would have his chance with me again. Covering my face, I didn't know how I felt about the idea of being traded back to the younger brother.

I could take the same opportunity while I was here. The future I had envisioned with Theo was over, and Amity made sure to seal my fate to royalty. All while my feelings had been blossoming for Theo.

Queen Izralda's words slipped into my mind as she excitedly clapped at the prospect of giving Gideon and I the opportunity to still find love here. I could spite Amity and the Theorines royals by choosing a different person to become engaged to. Maybe even a merchant's son, but then, I would be only entrapping myself in another loveless marriage.

I crawled out of bed and went to sit at the writing desk in my room; grabbing some blank parchment, I set my hand to writing a letter. I addressed it to Quiet, telling her what T'Lovoness castle looked like and how Mimzy was quite sad Quiet could not be here with her. I informed her that Lady Trustworthy's children would be arriving soon, knowing she would have some thoughts on the matter.

I decided to ask how home life was going without me there. I wondered if she was being kind to Pulchra and vice-versa. I ended the letter by inquiring if there had been any decent gossip. I sent her my love and folded the letter up. Pouring the melted wax on top of the envelope, I sealed it with my wax stamp emblem.

Sighing, I sat back in my chair and stared at the ceiling. I highly doubted Quiet had any inkling of the dealings Amity had been doing behind my back. The thought crossed my mind that Amity would also be arranging a marriage for Quiet. I had believed myself to be smart, but yet I had never foreseen this path being laid out before me. Despite Gideon keeping me in the dark, I found him to be a kind man, great in bed, and his connections would help me obtain access to most likely every single thing I needed.

Feelings had been growing for him, and I was sure they would continue to grow with time. For now, though, I wanted to be disgusted by the whole matter, and I felt chaffed by everything. If I could avoid him for a bit to get my bearings straight, it would be for the best.

I heard the door open; a servant must be checking to see if I would prefer to have breakfast served in my room. I grabbed my letter, planning to hand it to them to mail off to my sister. Shrugging a robe on, I went out to the main area but had not anticipated to find Lydia snooping.

"Can I help you?" I raised a brow at her. She straightened up turning to look at me. Her eyes scanned me up and down and while she was wearing a hideous fuchsia ruffled dress, I was still in a robe.

"I came, but . . ." she let the sentence fall flat between us.

"I could have sworn I locked that door," I stated blandly. Her gaze flicked to mine and she shrugged.

"It was unlocked. I heard you moving in your room, so I figured I would wait out here for you."

"I have no intention of attending breakfast this morning," I replied briskly. I wanted her to leave. She cocked her head to the side, her brows furrowing.

"You missed breakfast. I was collecting you for needlework," Lydia informed me. Now I stood there confused. Had I really slept that long? I mulled over my next decision and let out a sigh.

"I have no intentions of attending," I replied blandly.

"How could you not want to go?" She whined.

"I have more important matters to attend to today." Why she needed me to attend with her made little sense? Lydia was perfectly capable of doing things without me. We barely ecen knew one another.

"Like what?" She eyed me.

I held her stare, not allowing her to have the upper hand. My important matters would be staying away from everyone. She relented with a sigh when a minute passed, and I still had not given in.

"*Fine.*" She groaned. "I will just go by myself." She huffed, turning to leave. She looked over her shoulder to double-check that I had not changed my mind. I crossed my arms, raising my brows to indicate she needed to go. Her shoulders slumped, and she left. I did not hesitate to cross the room and lock the door behind her. This time making good and certain that it was indeed locked.

Turning around to face my room, I pressed my back against the door. I knew I did not have enough reading material in here to last me for the whole day. If I wanted to leave to trade out books, I would need to put on a dress. I looked down at my silken olive robe. I glanced back to the door leading to my room. I would copy what I had, and then sneak to the library to swap out for new books. If I timed it right, I could do it during either lunch or dinner when everyone else would be busy.

Three hours later, I wore a similar shade of olive-green. It was a simple dress that I could easily slip on and off. Once I swapped out my books, I would come back and continue to wear the comfy robe.

With the books in hand, I unlocked the door and peeked my head into the corridor. It was lunchtime, and thankfully, the corridor was empty. I ducked out and closed the door silently behind me. I walked as briskly as I could toward the library. I only passed servants on my way and was turned around once.

Opening the library door, it was deathly silent. The stack of books I carried, were becoming heavy in my arms, and I could not wait to swap them out and get my hands on the next stack. No one was in the library, and as I stood before the historical section, I started reshelving the ones I had back to their respective places.

I started grabbing the next set of five and was ready to grab an additional two for good measure. I didn't feel like making another trip here today or tomorrow. A hand settled on my right shoulder, and I jumped, whirling around to find myself face-to-face with the heir of Theorines.

"Gideon," I gasped, nearly dropping the five texts in my arms. He made an attempt to help keep them from falling.

"Shit. Sorry, Serenity, I did not mean to startle you." He rushed out. I clutched the books clumsily to my chest and took a step back, trying to put distance between us. I became guarded by his closeness to me. He noticed, and his face fell. "Serenity, please do not be like this."

"You kept me in the dark for months and expect me to not be hurt?" I hissed, the anger kindling within me from last night.

"I had no choice; I could not go against my father's wishes." He begged; both his hands came up to grip my arms, and once again, I felt him trapping me. My breathing picked up.

"Please release your hands from me." I gritted out. He searched my eyes, which burned from the tears forming. Feeling defeated, he dropped his hands back to his side. I stepped to the side and walked around him; I did not want to be trapped against the bookcases with him.

"Serenity, I never meant for you to feel hurt like this." He tried again. I clenched my jaw and took a deep breath; closing my eyes, I braced myself as I turned back to face him.

"You may not have meant to, but you still did," I calmly accused.

"Please forgive me. Can we please start over?" He begged. "Think of how good we are together." My body warming to the memory of his touch and the orgasms it could elicit. My resolve was beginning to dissipate, and I hated it. I flicked my gaze to the book behind him, not wanting to meet his eyes. He took a few steps toward me, and when I did not step back, he came all the way, wrapping his arms loosely around my waist.

"Serenity, I care about you. I promise I will never lie or hide anything from you again. I want a true chance at our future together." His voice sounded earnest. I flicked my attention back to him.

"Fine." I agreed, flicking my attention to him. "I am still not happy with what had occurred, but you need to prove to me you mean what you say." I challenged him.

"You got it." He nodded eagerly.

"So why did Amity arrange my hand to Finch, initially?" I wanted to know if he would be true to his word. He groaned, not releasing me from his arms. "Gideon?" I waited patiently.

"From the letters I read, your sister wrote your selling points to be married to a prince. Your historical knowledge and diplomacy would be an excellent contender for the royal family. The more letters she and my father exchanged, the more I realized there must have been an underlying issue she was not mentioning, so do you mind telling me what it is?" He challenged back.

I had not anticipated him turning the tables back on me. I wanted to escape, but with his arms locking me in place I could not. He promised to be truthful to me, but I had never agreed. Then again if I was going to have a future with him, maybe honesty on my part would be for the best.

"There was a boy back home that I had feelings for." I paused. "Amity knew about him."

"May I ask who it was?" Gideon interrupted. Snapping me out of my thoughts.

"It is a stableboy," I replied, guarded, knowing he would judge me.

"Do you still have feelings for him?" He asked hesitantly.

"I do." I watched as sadness filled Gideon's eyes. "But, I only found out a month ago that a future with him was not possible. No one can mend a broken heart that quickly. I do realize I never really had a future with him, no matter how much I had hoped for it. Amity informed me before we left for here that she fired him from the manor." I felt the surge of emotions wanting to make an appearance. I dared not utter Theo's name out loud to Gideon. There was a small, selfish part of me, that wanted to keep my first love's name a secret. My future husband didn't need to know everything. I debated for half a second and chose to add on, "I have been conflicted on my feelings since meeting you."

"You like me?" He asked quietly. Hope replacing the sadness.

I nodded my head. "But I am still not happy with you." I tacked on.

"Where does this leave us then?" He smiled sheepishly.

"I suppose still pre-engaged?" I shrugged.

"May I kiss you, future fiancé?"

"No, I am still not ready to forgive you fully yet." I untangled myself from his arms, and walked briskly back to the bookcase. I grabbed three additional books to take for extra measure, and left with a departing word to Gideon.

My hurt and anger from the previous night may have eased, but it did not mean he deserved easy access to me. The nervousness of running into him in the future dissipated. I didn't know how long it would be until I fully forgave him. I had not enjoyed him trapping me in the library, but it was done and over with. Now, the next thing my heart had to come to terms with was officially letting Theo go.

Chapter Fifteen

Queen Opal mandated another ball a few nights later. I had spent the last few days tucked away in the library. Gideon had attempted to butter me up with bouquets of flowers and slowly my anger dissolved. I still didn't entirely forgive him, but I also did not want to deal with the strained relationship. More likely than not, I would be leaving here in a few weeks to be engaged to Gideon. I didn't see the point of starting our marriage off in negativity.

I had not waited for Lydia to come collect me tonight. Instead, I enjoyed the solitude of watching the ball without someone chattering my ear off. Tonight, I donned a golden silken dress. The top fabric was angled, all gathering on my left hip in a giant golden bow. The bottom of the dress was simple, allowing the golden folds to fall naturally. I put a small hoop underneath to give it some shape. My long silver hair was done in a simple half up style, assuming it wouldn't become too warm in the room. I picked simple citrine stones for the earrings and the pendant.

Walking into the ball, I strayed away from Ivy and her sisters, instead choosing a high-top table on the opposite side of the room. It was the beginning of the night, and the guests dancing were putting on all the flares in their steps. It made me think of birds doing some elaborate mating ritual, which caused me to giggle before I could contain it.

"What did you find funny?" Gideon asked coming to stand next to me. I glanced around to see who else was near us and quite a few quests were watching.

"Oh, I was thinking how the dancers, with their extravagant moves, reminded me of some birds in a mating ritual." I smiled, withholding the laugh this time.

Gideon followed my line of sight as we watched the dance, witnessing certain individuals adding additional steps to show off.

"How about we join the mating ritual?" He flirted, nudging me with his shoulder. I offered him my hand to take.

"If you start making peacock noises, I am out," I forewarned.

"I would not dream of it," he promised, but neither of us fully believed it.

The music to the next dance began, and he started putting additional spins in, forcing me to think quickly on how to react and fall back into the correct step needed. I barely had time to chastise him, before he would send me into another spin. Most of my focus was spent making sure I didn't make a fool of myself, but he caught me and corrected me each time without it being noticeable. When the dance ended, I was breathing heavy, trying to convey my annoyance with him. He gave me a devilish smile, knowing exactly what he was doing.

"Mind if I cut in?" We found Regalius standing next to us, offering me his hand. I dropped into a curtsy.

"Not at all," Gideon replied, moving off to the side.

I graciously accepted Regalius's extended hand. He smiled at me; this was the first time we had spoken since the night he rescued me from my panic attack. I didn't know what to say; instead, choosing silence.

"You look lovely tonight," he complimented.

"Thank you, you look handsome yourself," I replied. He wore

the traditional blood-red jacket with dark blue pants. Gold threaded weaved in patterns along his cuffs and throughout the rest of the coat. Gold buttons threaded through the front of his clothing. He wore a simple gold crown with dark rubies and sapphires encrusted in the metal. His jade-green eyes reflected an understanding of how I was feeling.

The music once again began, and Regalius led us without adding any additional flares for me to keep up with. I relaxed into the dance, enjoying the way we maneuvered around the couples.

"If you ever need to escape like that again, come find me," he murmured quietly for only me to hear, and I regarded him, my heart stilling.

"If you are having another panic attack, that is, I will get you to safety."

"Why are you being nice to me?" I asked suspiciously. I ought to kick myself for my boldness, but the words had already escaped, and I was not about to apologize.

"Because sometimes it becomes lonely with all these people here, especially when you don't fit in."

I blinked, stunned by his words. I ought to be offended by what he was implying. I opened my mouth to speak but Regalius let go of me to bow. The dance had come to an end. He didn't give me a chance to respond as he went one way and I hurried back to my high top table. Grabbing a glass of wine, I took a sip, looking at Regalius over the rim. He wasn't looking at me, but his words continued to linger.

I could barely mull his words over as Lydia yanked on my arm. "You danced with Regalius! How was it? Think you could introduce us?"

I partially choked on my wine, trying to maintain my composure and coughing slightly to clear my throat. "You would have a better chance breaking into that circle and asking him yourself than me introducing you. We are not acquainted like that."

"But you danced together," she pouted.

"He only asked me when I had already been on the floor," I countered.

Lydia hmphed. I half-expected for her to continue pushing the topic.

"He is *so dreamy*," she sighed. *Ah, that was why.* Her focus was completely on Regalius and the princes he surrounded himself with. Polishing off my wine, I grabbed another glass, and soon after, I was left standing alone. Lydia had not become brave enough to ask Regalius for a dance, but she did nab another unsuspecting fellow.

Chapter Sixteen

Three weeks later, Lydia and I sat outside in the far corner, away from the guests, during teatime. I had brought a book with me, not wanting to participate but being forced to be present at the host's demands. Queen Opal was seated by the tearoom doors surrounded by the princesses, who were all being lazily fanned by pink and green dyed ostrich feathers. I realized the majority of their attire was similar to the feather color. As I gazed around, I took in that many other guests were in the same pink, green, and some black attire. I gazed down at my lilac-colored dress.

"Lydia, did I miss something on the color scheme?" I placed my book to the side. She looked over at me and rolled her eyes.

"This season is strawberry-themed," she replied matter-of-factly.

"Strawberry-themed?" I replied, confused.

She sighed, rolling her eyes again and propped her elbows on the table.

"Every year, Queen Opal picks a new theme based on usually fruit. She announces it after the season has started, and even the food is inspired by it. You're a lady, and we have been here for almost a month; how is it that you don't *know* this?" She asked exasperated. I bristled at the insult.

"Maybe because I found literature more fascinating than what society deems important." I sniffed.

"You barely attend any events; you will *never* catch a spouse with that attitude." She chirped back, patronizing me. Why had I even allowed her to drag me here today? I gazed out at the barren lawn, refusing to respond to her. All this wasted grass space that couldn't match the beauty of the exterior of the castle. Instead, it was green grass with sporadic bushes shaped like various animals.

"Isn't he just dreamy?" Lydia sighed, changing topics. Giving in, I knew who she was talking about as I turned my attention to where her focus was. I swallowed the nervousness hit me. Regalius wasn't looking our way, and I hurriedly picked up my book to distract myself. I did not need to draw attention to myself if he caught me staring. It had been three weeks, and we had not talked once since that evening. I clenched my jaw and focused on my breathing, not even reading the words on the pages before me.

"Serenity, don't you find him dreamy?" She pushed; there was a hint of a whine in her voice. I blinked rapidly, trying to calm my nerves and not look away from the pages.

"Yes, he is just the *dreamiest*," I replied hastily to quiet her. I tried to focus on the words before me, but it was as if I was reading a foreign language. I could not get my brain to understand their meaning.

"I just love his raven black hair, the way it has a slight wave to it," Lydia continued.

"You would love his hair even if it was straight and blonde or curled and red," I countered. I reread the sentence again.

"I suppose that is true . . . but he just looks all the more regal with his slightly wavy black hair." I heard the smile creeping in her voice. I slammed the book shut, giving up on trying to read. My gaze settled on her; she was practically draped on top of the table now, drooling over Regalius. It was not at all lady-like and if anyone noticed, she would definitely have whispers about her. I, unfortunately, probably would be attached to them.

"Did you really just use his name meaning to describe him?" I asked incredulously.

"Maybe," she drawled out. She did not even stop her longingly, eye fucking of the prince.

"Sit up straight. You are going to have whispers about yourself and your un-lady-like manner," I snapped at her. I did not mean for it to come out as harsh as it did, but it did make Lydia follow orders.

"What has you spitting nettles?" Lydia quirked her eyebrow at me.

"Some of us are trying to read as their friend pants over a prince out of their societal circles." I gave her a pointed look, hoping my meaning would sink in. She rolled her eyes with a huff. After weeks of her clinging to me, I somehow had become accustomed to her being around. She was the only female I truly talked to here and while I disdained the idea of being friends, it appeared to be what we were.

"It's *The Courting Seasons*; there are *no leagues,*" She argued. I laughed in response to Lydia, who scrunched up her face at me. I questioned how delusional this merchant's daughter could be. Even sitting here, it was evident the societal tiers placed amongst it. Queen Opal could say all her pretty words about her courting seasons, but the proof was in the pudding.

"Wherever did you hear such a silly thing?"

"It's what everyone says!" Lydia shouted, her face turning red. She covered her mouth quickly as pairs of eyes looked in our direction to see what the sudden outburst was about. Let alone the lazy sentence of words. Her cheeks pinkening from the extra attention, she gasped, and I thought I heard an 'oh no' from her. I surveyed the veranda, and my eyes collided with Regalius. He raised an eyebrow at me, and I gave a subtle shake of my head.

"I would not look now, but lover boy is heading this way," I commented blandly. Apparently my telling him no meant nothing.

Lydia squeaked in fear, dropping her hands immediately from her face. She started smoothing her dress down, trying to erase away any wrinkles. There were so many ruffles I did not think we could find a wrinkle in her lap. The top of her bodice was another matter, which in her case would be a near impossible task. I assumed, like me, she did not have a servant to do her bidding. However, the royal staff laundry servants should have been more careful with her clothes. Then again, they may have lost their sight of vision while attempting to look at it. In my time of being here, unfortunately for myself, I was beginning to become accustomed to Lydia's overly done dresses.

"Ladies," Prince Regalius Baylor's jovial voice almost sang in greeting.

"Prince Regalius Baylor." Lydia and I both dipped our heads in response. He eyed me momentarily, trying to communicate something, before turning his attention back to Lydia.

"Now, what is everyone saying?" Regalius did not beat around the bush. I admired that in a person, at least then, I knew what I was getting in a person instead of having to play a strategy game to get to the point.

"Oh, well, um. . ." Lydia fumbled. She had never spoken to Regalius before. It was quite adorable to witness her flustered for once in her life. Regalius must have been used to this kind of response because his face broke out in amusement, but his eyes reflected something different. Something that I could not quite put my finger on. It made me question how he planned to play his cards next? Would he be kind to her? Use pretty but empty words? Or would he toy with her like he was the cat and she the mouse?

"Come now, it cannot be that formidable to talk to a prince?" He jested.

"Lady Serenity Novena and I were having a disagreement about The Courting Seasons. Maybe a prince such as yourself could remedy this." Lydia must have grasped her wit to be able to finally respond. I did not miss a beat of her tacking on my title nor the compliment she paid the prince. It would not surprise me if she attempted to put myself in a bad light in front of Regalius. What she could not know is she would ultimately be making herself look the fool.

"And what was this disagreement?" Regalius's eyes caught mine again. He gave me a warm smile and turned his attention back to Lydia. He wanted her to tell him. I relaxed back into my chair. I had not noticed how stiffly I had been sitting.

"Well." Lydia faltered. I watched as her emotions played out on her face; it was evident she was still deciding how she wanted to weave this. "With The Courting Seasons, is it not for everyone to participate to have a fair chance with anyone else participating in the season?" She was going vague; she did not want Regalius to know which side her beliefs lay on.

"That is why The Courting Seasons were implemented, to begin with." Regalius replied simply. Lydia cut him off before he could continue.

"See, Prince Regalius Baylor, that is what I was telling Lady Serenity Novena. She believed that despite The Courting Season reasoning, that the leagues and societal circles still applied within." Lydia must have felt quite satisfied with herself because she shot me a told you so look. I rolled my eyes.

"Lady Serenity Novena is a very clever woman," Regalius complimented. Lydia whipped her head so fast I thought it would snap off her neck. I raised an eyebrow at him, wondering where he was going with his compliment. "I do not believe I have been introduced to you, Miss . . .?" He waited for her to supply the information. He knew she was not a lady, and this was a hit to her status.

"Lydia of Grewt'en," she supplied with a flush.

"Miss Lydia of Grewt'en, a pleasure to make your acquaintance." He took her hand before she could even offer it and kissed the air above it. I was not going to hear the end of this.

Lydia giggled, being rendered speechless. If I could, I would get up and leave right now. I would head to my rooms to continue my readings. I had to get through two more months of this bloody season and then have the rest of my life planned out for me with Gideon. I gritted my teeth, heat rising through my body at remembering last night when Gideon snucked into my room. This had become a regular occurrence for him in the last two weeks.

"Now, Miss Lydia," Regalius continued, and I could tell by the tone of his voice that it would not be good for her. "I happen to know Lady Serenity Novena quite adequately." *He does not*. Why was he filling her head with lies? Until the second night here, Regalius and I had never spoken before. The only other association I have had with him was during childhood when we had been in the same room together, but I barely even remember that instance. I wondered if he had been talking to Gideon or Finch to be able to make a bold statement like that.

"She is a brilliantly smart woman. Lady Serenity Novena knows how to see through things. Take her book as an example." He nodded at the one closed in my lap. "She reads the lines, but sometimes the story can be found in between the lines. That is what Lady Serenity Novena does." He smiled at me, and I smiled back, catching on to where he was going with this.

"I do not understand, My Prince?" Lydia asked, uncertain. Her smugness evaporated.

"Let me explain it in simpler terms, Miss Lydia. The lines will read The Courting Season is for an equal playing field, regardless of social status, family or connections. . . However, if you read between the lines, The Courting Season will never be able to fully erase that. The children of the high families who participate know they need to pick wisely who they court and spend their time with. This may seem like just an event for courting . . . But it is much more than that." Prince Regalius Baylor finished. He flicked his gaze over at his mother, surrounded by only princesses, and then back to us. I wanted to applaud him for his response; Lydia sat there floundering, trying to grasp the words to give him a reply. I knew nothing she said could even put a dent in response to his claim. How could one even begin to argue with someone whose own mother hosted and controlled the event? It was only a matter of if Lydia would take her head out of the clouds and admit it to herself.

"I will leave you both to it, Lady Serenity Novena. Miss Lydia." Regalius smiled at me with a wink, dipping his head. He did not even glance back over to Lydia before he returned to the group of princes waiting for him. I could not locate Gideon or Finch and wondered where they might be.

"Serenity, did you see that?" Lydia squealed with delight. "He spoke to me!" Apparently, the part of being completely insulted by the prince went over her head.

"I was a part of the conversation too, Lydia," I commented, annoyed with her idiocy.

"Oh, are you *jealous* that he showed me more attention than you?" She teased. Did this girl have her head kicked by a horse as a baby? I could care less about how much attention Regalius gave either of us, but her delusional mindset annoyed me enough to speak up.

"Last I knew, he complimented me as brilliant and claimed you were wrong with your beliefs." I stared her down. Daring her to argue with me. Of course, the nitwit was going to do it.

"See, there is that jealousy, had to point out he complimented you, and he never said I was wrong. We must be thinking of different conversations." Lydia smiled with a wink before getting up to stroll through the decorative hedges and mingle with the other ladies and merchant daughters. I stared at her backside, incredulous. I pitied the poor fool who married her.

"I do not know why you put up with that merchant's daughter." Ivy slid into the chair that Lydia had vacated.

"I have tried to shake her, but as you can see, I have been unsuccessful," I commented dryly.

"Yes, I suppose you are right. That girl is out there to make a name for herself." Ivy poured tea into a clean, empty teacup. Setting the teapot aside, she picked up her cup and sipped it. "Whether it is a good thing or not."

"She is delusional as well." It felt good to talk to someone else on my complaints about Lydia.

"I have noticed. She was telling Mimzy how she was going to marry a prince and had her eyes set on Prince Regalius Baylor. Can you believe the nerve of her?" Ivy took another sip.

"She has been claiming the same things to me." I rolled my eyes, watching as Lydia obnoxiously laughed amongst the girl group she had infiltrated. She continued to glance over to Prince Regalius Baylor, hoping to capture his attention.

"Someone should teach her a lesson." Ivy's gaze trailed from Lydia to give me a pointed look.

"I am not her keeper, Ivy."

"If it was not for your sister, she would not be here."

"I would suggest you remember your place." I briskly stated. I rose from my chair, tucked the book under my arm, and walked away to leave Ivy to stew over that.

I dipped back into the castle, away from everyone. I planned to head back to my rooms but didn't make it very far as both of my arms were linked by someone on each of my sides. I immediately went to grab my book, which was falling, but it was caught by Finch, who was on my left. I looked to my right, and there was Gideon.

"What do I owe the pleasure?" I asked the two brothers.

"Figured you needed an escape from all this stuffiness. Come on," Finch answered as they led me down the corridor. We took a turn down an empty hallway that I had not been to before or at least I believed I had never come here before. Even after all this time spent in the castle, I still became turned around in my directions.

"Where are we headed?" I inquired.

"That is for us to know and for you to find out," Gideon teased. I huffed but secretly was grateful that they were giving me a way to take my mind off things. We came to a set of white double doors, and Gideon, with his free hand, opened one of them.

"I would have got the other, but the book," Finch said as he raised it to emphasize his point.

"We are going to need to unloop arms to all fit," I commented. Even with both doors opened we wouldn't have been able to walk in all together at once.

"Or we walk through it sideways," Gideon offered, and before I could even protest, he was maneuvering us in an awkward sidestepping motion until we were all in the room. I couldn't contain my giggles from the silliness of it all. He rotated us again to reach out and shut the door behind us.

"Where are we?" I looked about the room. it was a simple, cozy room with violet walls. It had a bunch of overstuffed chairs in red and creams, and despite the summer heat, a fireplace flickered along the way. I found it odd to have it burning, but the room was not overly warmed by it.

"Just one of the many rooms offered to the royals to hang out away from the commoners," replied Finch.

"No, seriously, what is this room?" I laughed as I looked back and forth at each brother. Both brothers looked at each other, blinking before returning their attention to me.

"It is seriously a room for the royals to use," Gideon answered, this time a bit awkwardly.

"Oh," I commented a bit embarrassed, not realizing this was how far Queen Opal's segregation went. The royals received special rooms to avoid the commoners and hang out amongst each other. Currently, we were the only ones in attendance to this room. "Will I be in trouble for being in here?"

"Nah, we brought you. You are fine," Finch replied easily. They led me over to an area with multiple overstuffed chairs. Finally, they released my arms to allow each one of us to sit.

"Figured you needed an escape from all the clucking single females," Gideon offered. I raised an eyebrow at him, amused. I had been complaining to him about the females last night.

"I will not say no to that. I was just escaping both Ivy and Lydia," I replied matter-of-factly.

"That Lydia girl sure is attached to your side," Finch stated with a bit of a shudder.

"Yeah, she is a merchant's daughter from Grewt'en. Amity funded her wardrobe and attendance of being here." I held up a hand to silence their obvious question. "I have not the faintest idea why she did it either."

"I am glad we funded your wardrobe, some of the dresses she has worn . . ." Finch trailed off.

"I am aware since she is always around me." I looked over at Gideon, who sat in his chair, not saying a word. "I would toss you an enny for your thoughts, but I do not have one on me currently."

"I was thinking Lydia is not that bad. She is quite friendly, and it is nice of you to look after her. It is apparent she has not had much experience with royals and how to properly act. I will commend you, Serenity, for taking her under your wing when most would not," Gideon complimented me. It was nice to hear someone acknowledging what I was currently enduring, but I still did not want to be fully associated with Lydia.

"Lydia is fortunate that I am not one of the vipers wanting to sink their fangs into a poor, unsuspecting victim."

Both brothers laughed loudly at my comment.

"That is one way to put it, I suppose," a voice joined in on our laughter. I turned to find Regalius walking toward us. I immediately began to stand, but he raised a hand to stop me as he said, "In this room, you do not need to be formal." I sat back down in my spot.

"Regalius, figured you were too busy to come here today?" Gideon pried.

"Nah, I happened to see you hauling Serenity off, and I was curious as to where you both were taking her. Seems you three are all quite close." His gaze lingered between the three of us.

"That is what happens when you spend a month living together." Finch smiled.

I couldn't put my finger on it, but it felt as if Finch was staking some sort of unspoken claim on me. It seemed silly that being acquainted with one another a few more days could have some sort of stronger familiarity. We could have lived together and never spoken a word, but it wouldn't mean we knew one another better.

"So, I have heard from you two before," Prince Regalius Baylor turned his gaze upon me, "Is it true you split an arrow in half with your own?" *How much had these two bumbling idiots told Regalius?*

"Did they tell you it was Gideon's arrow I split?" I countered. I didn't enjoy not having the upper hand in the conversation, especially when it concerned me. How much did the T'Lovoness heir know about me, because of these two brothers?

"No, they did not. Think you could repeat it?" He asked, becoming increasingly intrigued.

"I will give you the same reply I gave King Ashborn. If it has not been documented within history or witnessed before, I could attempt to practice, but who is to say I would be able to duplicate the results again?" I did not want to ostracize myself with these princesses and ladies if they all watched me in an archery competition that Regalius commanded.

"Rightly so. You have a fair point. I hear you also enjoy horseback riding as well."

"Did they tell you the way I prefer my tea too?" I countered, shooting an annoyed look at the brothers.

"You do not like tea," Regalius stated.

"How do you know?" I gave him a puzzled look.

"You only drink it when it is required of you and, half the time, you pretend to drink it with imitation sips." My eyes widened at his accuracy of the truth.

"Wait, you do not like tea, Serenity?" Finch asked first.

"No, I do not. But how did you know?" I looked at Regalius, wondering how much he had been observing me in the last month. He was never close in proximity to me. How could he tell from the distance if I drank my tea or not?

"I have been watching you, Serenity; one begins to notice the little things if one watches carefully enough." He tapped his nose with a wink before settling into the chair next to us all. The room became a bit uncomfortable.

"I am surprised you have time to watch me when so many are always vying for your attention," I finally countered, even though I felt my statement did not have the strength behind it.

"A little delayed in a retort, but a good point nonetheless." Regalius laughed. "What did you call them? Vipers? I like that."

"Well, you are the juiciest prey they would love to sink their fangs into." I mused.

"Do you wish to sink your fangs into me?" He flirted, quirking an eyebrow. Gideon and Finch shifted uncomfortably in their chairs; Gideon let out his nervous chuckle. I leaned back in my chair, crossing my arms as I let my eyes trail over Regalius to make him wait for my answer.

"No, I do not. For you see, I am here for your historical section of the library and nothing more." I leveled my gaze at him. His move.

"My historical section? Why that?" He looked confused, not expecting that answer. I knew my response had come out of left field. Gideon jumped in at this point.

"She plans to write the ultimate historical book. She made a decent dent in our historical section at home but did not finish. She is collecting all the articles she can find to combine and have an easy reading material for someone who wants to learn a true guide to the past." I could hear the pride in Gideon's voice as he spoke of my goal. I blushed a bit. Aside from my Father, I had never had anyone speak this highly on my research.

"Not too many people take an interest in history. Is there a lot of holes that you have found in your research?" Regalius appeared unruffled at the change in conversation. I had thought for certain he would prefer for me to fawn all over him. However, instead of flirting and simpering away, he was inquiring about my findings.

"There are a few things that contradict each other, and there are some missing blips for which I am trying to fill gaps for. . . But every new piece I read adds another section to my notes, and thus ever growing the book I want to create."

"There is a private library within the castle that has exclusive historical documents in it. I could take you if you like?" Regalius offered.

I sat forward in my seat at the excitement of this offer. This could be a rare opportunity, and I did not want to pass it up. "Can we go now?" I asked, not wanting to wait a second. Regalius face changed to amusement from my excitement. He stood up, as did the rest of us.

"Come along then," Regalius chuckled as he motioned with his hand. We followed him out of the royal's private room and further down the corridor. We took a few different turns before we entered another set of double doors that led to the private royal library.

It was small and quaint, cozy even. The room was donned in deep reds and dark red mahogany wood. Overly plush chairs sat around a table. If the room had a fireplace, it would be complete, but I understood why fire would not be good thing in a room with such precious knowledge. I noted there was not a single window in the room either, it would be quite easy to become lost in time here.

"History scrolls are here. I am sure I do not have to advise you to be extra careful with them. Some are the last of their kind," Regalius cautioned as he gestured toward them. I nodded silently, walking up to the small bookcase. There was a total of twenty history books and fifteen scrolls. I was afraid if I touched any of them, they would fall apart.

Gently, I pulled a scroll from its slot, softly unrolling it, I began to read about the wars, about the Kingdom's prior to T'Lovoness's birth as a monarchy. My eyebrows rose. We had six monarchies present day. However, this was the first time I had read that during the wars, there had been a total of thirty-five battling each other for domination. The consensus was the Fae were to be blamed for this war; I had never heard the term before and cataloged it with the other things that had been lost throughout history.

I wondered if one of these documents held a map of where the original monarchy lines had been. I felt the land was not large enough for six at times. I questioned how cumbersome thirty-five had been. I had never been able to pinpoint where the wars had occurred either, but I supposed if all the monarchies had been fighting, it could have been the whole continent.

I knew the theory of how T'Lovoness obtained its name, but now I wondered if perhaps the other monarchies were either a monarchy that had won against all, a family name, or maybe a nonsense jumble of a bunch of monarchies combined.

I gently rolled the scroll back up and put it away to grab another. This one contained information on creatures that have long since been extinct for centuries. I continued to repeat this process as I made my way halfway through the scrolls. I became oblivious to everything else around me in the room.

I would need to either come back to copy these scrolls or attempt to remember everything and record it on parchment paper when I returned to my rooms. These scrolls held more documentation of the time before peace than anything else I had ever read. I could not let my memory falter on these details. These texts could hold hidden keys to bridge gaps I did not even know existed.

"Serenity. . . Serenity?" A hand waved in front of my face, causing me to jump. I looked up to Regalius's amused face. "We need to head to the evening meal." He commented.

"I do not need to eat. I am fine with continuing to read here," I replied, forgetting my manners. I continued reading the scroll, dismissing him with a wave of my hand.

"That is just the way she is when she starts reading. It is a good thing she does not have parchment paper and an inking quill to begin copying her notes," commented Gideon.

"Unfortunately, inking quills are not allowed in here to prevent documents ever befalling to an ink bottle being dumped on them and thus erasing our historical texts," Regalius informed.

"That is okay, I can memorize and record back in my room," I replied automatically without a thought. I sounded far more confident in that statement than I had felt in my mind.

"Serenity is a force to be reckoned with when she is reading history," Finch supplied.

"I can see that." I could feel the heat of Regalius's stare on the back of my neck. "Unfortunately, I cannot allow for you to stay in here without a royal family member at your side, and I am hungry. We can come back later, I promise." I looked longingly at the unread scrolls and then at the three princes waiting for me to get up for them all to be able to eat.

"Fine," I sighed. I pushed my chair back and got up from the desk where I had been reading. I had not even realized I had moved from standing in front of the bookcase to sitting at a desk. It had not been the first time I traveled unbeknownst to me while reading. I doubted the Royal family here had even the slightest idea of the importance of history they had within these scrolls. Yet here they were, tucked away in a personal private library, keeping the world ignorant of what it had been like before the time of peace. My eyes fell on Gideon's back. Did Theorines have a private royal library? I would need to ask when I had an opportunity, probably when he was sneaking into my room tonight.

I begrudgingly followed the princes back to the banquet hall. I tried to argue with them to let me go to my rooms, and I would reconvene with them after they ate, but they would not hear of it. When we entered the banquet hall, I knew I would have to break off from them and sit in my respected area. I could already tell I was going to be peppered with questions from Lady Malevolent's and Lady Trustyworthy's daughters, along with Lydia on top of that.

I began to excuse myself from following them and head to my empty seat when Gideon's hand captured mine. I looked at him, confused by the action.

"Sit with us," he offered.

"Sit at the royals table? I am pretty certain that would be frowned upon, Gideon." I replied, already knowing the kind of response I would potentially receive from everyone else in attendance. To my knowledge, no one else that was non-royal has ever sat with them.

"Not much can be said if I make you my honored guest, can it?" Regalius chimed in, joining Gideon's offer. I stared at him, knowing I could not turn him down under those circumstances. But he did not know what the aftermath would be when none of these princes were around to protect me.

"You will be upsetting the Vipers," I stated calmly. Prince Regalius Baylor's eyes twinkled with mischief.

"I like upsetting the nest." He laughed, grabbing my arm. The T'Lovoness heir forced me to walk arm-in-arm with him as Gideon and Finch took up our rear. I felt multiple pairs of eyes upon us, and I refused to look at them as we walked up to the head of the royal table next to his parents.

"Regalius what is the meaning of this?" Queen Opal tried to sound pleasant, but I could hear the warning in her tone. Her eyes quickly looked me up and down as her lips slightly pursed. She did not even attempt to hide her disdain at my presence entering her perfect little royal world.

"Mother, I have decided to have an honored guest sit by me this evening as we eat. Allow me to introduce Lady Serenity Novena of Grewt'en," Prince Regalius Baylor's introduction of me to his mother caused me to drop into a curtsy immediately. Nothing was said for a beat, and I waited with a bated breath. I could hear Queen Opal's disappointment as she responded.

"Very well. Rise, Lady Serenity Novena. Servants, bring an additional chair over here to be seated next to my son."

I rose slowly and looked up at Queen Opal. I responded, "Thank you for your kindness, Your Highness." She was unlike Queen Izralda. I found no trace of warmth in Queen Opal, only disdain as she continued to watch me through narrowed eyes. I withheld my shiver from her coldness. I was uneasy about how this meal would go.

A chair had been immediately procured, and with some shuffling, we were all seated. Gideon sat across from me with Finch on his right. I was seated on Regalius's left, and then there was some prince I did not recognize seated on my other side. I could feel multiple pairs of eyes on my back from every lady and merchant's daughter and then a pair of eyes on my right digging into me from Queen Opal. No one uttered a word. The deathly quietness at this end of the table was unnerving.

Each course came, and no one talked as we ate in silence. I could hear chatter further down the table and felt envious of them. I was not certain if this was common or if it was because I was sitting here. I felt Gideon's foot brush against mine. I looked up from my food and found him giving me an encouraging smile as he brushed it again. I meekly smiled back.

The King never once even paid us any attention. He ate his food without a word, not even looking up from his plate. I wondered if he had even noticed my attendance or when his son had introduced me to his wife.

I was already preparing for the moment we were dismissed. I would be doing everything in my willpower to reframe myself from jumping out of this chair and running away from here. I would need to navigate so as not to be ensnared by any of the other guests, questioning why I was receiving special treatment. I knew I had not posed an issue prior, and now I sat here, becoming every single person's biggest threat.

I felt the weight of the room, barely acknowledging the taste of the food I ate. Gideon continued to rub his foot up and down my calf. I stiffened, realizing there were tables behind me; those vipers had a clear shot of potentially seeing what he was doing if my dress fabric was moving underneath the table. I sat up straighter and tucked my legs underneath my chair, hoping to escape his foot reach. He gave me a raised eyebrow, and I turned my head slightly, flicking a gaze to the guests behind me, hoping he understood my meaning. He furrowed his brows, and I watched as realization spread a crossed his face. I noticed Regalius looking back and forth between us with a questioning look. Queen Opal was scrutinizing every little detailed reaction between us. Finch was the only one not paying attention as he continued to dig into his food.

When the last bite had been consumed, we were finally dismissed. King Lucien rose from his seat, announcing the end of the meal. The three princes that had brought me here, stood up, and I followed suit. Thankfully, they continued to escort me as we left the banquet hall. I was spared by anyone needling me with questions, but I knew I could not escape it. I had been hopeful they would take me back to the private library, but I was met with disappointment.

"I know I promised I would take you back, but I cannot tonight," Regalius informed me. "I will come collect you from your rooms tomorrow." Disappointment must have shown on my face as he added. "I did not mean to break my promise tonight; I just have some urgent princely duties."

"I understand," I replied dully. With no words being exchanged at the meal, I was confused on what I had missed for something to have come up. I looked at the two prince brothers to see if they were still up for hanging out.

"Unfortunately, this is a matter that we need to attend with Regalius; we are sorry, Serenity," Gideon replied, turning me down as well. I was going to need to bolt my door this evening to prevent Lydia from crashing through it.

"When did this matter come up?" I inquired cocking my head to the side to look at the princes as they were ready to leave me at the end of my corridor. There had been no talk at the evening meal, and I had been with the princes for hours now.

"It is a matter I forgot about earlier," Regalius stated with ease.

"I see." My shoulders fell slightly. "Okay, well, have fun then." I barely waved them away as I turned and hurried to my room. I was not quick enough to get inside as I heard Lydia's voice coming from behind me. Her hand smacked against my door frame before I even opened it fully.

"You have a lot of explaining to do, Serenity," she warned.

"I do not have to answer to you, Lydia," I replied coolly. Who was she to bark orders at me. She rolled her eyes at me.

"You are right, you don't. But I am your friend, and you have been gone all day, and then you waltz into the evening meal with not one or two but three princes, and one of them just happens to be Prince Regalius Baylor. Cough up the information about what is going on," Lydia demanded angrily.

"What I do with my time is none of your concern, and if you wanted people to take you seriously as a lady, you would say 'do not'. People of higher birth do not say don't. It becomes quite noticeable when you talk," I snipped. Her hand came off my doorframe, and she placed it on her chest shocked by my statement.

"I am insulted!" she screeched. I rolled my eyes.

"I am too, now, if you do not mind. I am going to retire for the evening. Good night, Lydia." I opened and shut the door in her face, locking it in place. I could hear her raging on the other side, and I was grateful her room was two down from mine. I had a sneaking suspicion if we were next-door neighbors, she would purposely be banging on the walls to get my attention.

Chapter Seventeen

I AWOKE TO SOMEONE KNOCKING ON MY DOOR. WHO would be bothering me this early in the morning? If it was Lydia, I would make her regret coming to wake me up. Getting out of bed, I wrapped myself in the silken olive robe and exited my bedroom to the entertaining room. I unlocked and opened the door to the corridor, but it was Gideon who greeted me by pushing past me. I glanced out to the empty hallway before immediately shut the door and locked it behind him.

"What are you doing here?" I whispered a bit crossed. I'd been expecting him to show up last night, like he had all the previous nights. When he never showed, I tossed and turned in bed annoyed and continuously thought I heard a knock on my door at all hours of the night.

"I miss you, and when I didn't see you after dinner... I could not sleep and decided to come now," he answered matter-of-factly.

"Gideon, it is early. Someone could have seen you." I continued to whisper for some unknown reason. Usually, he would already be gone by this time in the morning. I tried to argue with him, but he was already stripping out of his clothes and heading to my bed. I glanced at the lock, double-checking it. When I followed him into my bedroom, he was already pulling his boots off.

"Gideon," I quietly said while he unbuttoned his pants. "Gideon, I want to go back to bed, I am tired." I tried to keep the whine from my voice. I could feel the headache forming from exhaustion, which doubled with how reckless this all was, it was a bit much for me.

"Then let us cuddle." He flopped back on the bed, turning his body so his legs were no longer hanging over the edge. His arms stretched wide open, expecting me to curl up in them.

"Gideon, someone could catch us if they see you leaving my room," I warned.

"Does it really matter when you are already my fiancé?" He lazily smiled with not a single care in the world.

"I see your reasoning, but that is not to be announced for another two months. Until then, we are supposed to be acting like two participating individuals in The Courting Seasons. That means I cannot have you sneaking in and out of my rooms at all hours of the day, Gideon." I gave him a pointed look, trying to emphasize my point.

"I know, Serenity, but I miss you is all. Come here." The tips of his fingers wiggled, motioning for me to crawl into his arms.

"Gideon, no. You need to leave now." I tried to not give in to his charm. I did not have time for this, I wanted to go back to sleep without worrying.

"Fine," Gideon sighed, getting back up to retrieve his clothing. "You are no fun."

"Yes, well, unlike you, who is a royal, I have to deal with all the vipers and their jealousy issues if you are caught leaving my room. It is not safe out there being a female." I wrapped my arms around my waist, hugging myself as I slightly rocked back and forth, watching him.

"Yeah, I understand. I am sorry for being selfish there, Serenity. I was not thinking," Gideon replied not looking at me. He stood up, completely naked. "Can I at least have a hug?"

"Yeah, I supposed." I opened my arms up, and he embraced me with a squeeze. I could not even react as he hauled us onto the bed. I withheld the squeal I wanted to let escape my lips.

"Gideon!" I hissed. He nuzzled my neck.

"It is a lot more difficult to be a royal here than it is back home," he whispered in my ear, sighing.

"I prefer the quiet side of life to all this hustle and bustle," I whispered back. He kissed me softly. I gave into his wiles. Curling into his arms, I breathed in his scent as I let the sleep take over.

The second time I woke up, I found myself alone. Gideon must have snuck out at some point without disturbing me. I could only hope no one had seen him and that he did not choose to make a habit of coming in the mornings. I lay there breathing in the lingering familiar scent of Gideon.

Regalius had said he would come to collect me and take me back to the private library. I was adamant about staying put, not wanting to miss him by chance. Forcing myself out of bed, I pulled open the wardrobe and grabbed a simple almond-white dress. I suppose the color would fit the theme of strawberries if one counts the yellow-white seeds in them.

I took my seat at the writing desk and grabbed parchment paper. I wrote as much as I could remember from yesterday's scrolls. I filled dozens of sheets as I made notes on my speculations about various theories and questions that I still had. I only hoped that some of the questions could be answered either by the historical texts in this private library or by visiting another.

I tapped the ink quill feather on my lips. If someone had told me on my birthday this year that not only, would I be milestones ahead on my research due to having access to two monarchy libraries but also mingling with princes, I would probably have laughed outright on the spot. Sometimes, I still anticipated waking up, to find this would've been a fevered dream. I'd be thrown back into the monotony of rereading the same book multiple times, trying to find a new detail. Only when a new historical book arrived would I feel any form of excitement as I devoured it, knowing it wouldn't be my first read-through of it.

Now, it was the opposite. I did not have the luxury to reread, I got one shot and then moved on to the next to save on time. Time. It was limited these days. After I left this place, I wondered if I would have the opportunity to come back and reread some of the books to verify my work? It would help tremendously. This library added a whole new section to my research.

A light tap came at my door. I hurried towards it and, throwing open the door, I was greeted by Regalius. I had assumed he would have sent a servant to fetch me. It was quite a shock to see him on the other side.

"Serenity, that is probably the quickest I have ever had someone open a door for me," he chuckled.

"Well, I, um. . ." I stumbled over my words, not knowing exactly how to respond as I was a smidge out of breath.

"I know, come on." He turned and did not wait for me to follow him. I hesitated for only a moment, and then I was chasing after him. I stayed walking behind him to show respect in case we passed by anyone. He halted, causing me to stop abruptly. He looked back at me over his shoulder, took a couple steps backward, and looped his arm with mine.

"Walk with me, not behind me. You are not inferior to me, Serenity," Regalius commented.

"Your Highness, you are a Prince, and I am a Lady is that not the very definition of inferior?" I countered.

"It is, but stop. I thought we were past all that. I told you to call me Regalius, just do not call me Reggie. I hate that wretched nickname," he warned with a shudder.

"Why do you not like Reggie?" Curiosity stirred within me. I did not have a nickname I despised, so I wondered why he did.

"Reggie does not sound serious. It sounds like someone who goofs off all day and is not meant to be given respect. It is fine and dandy for others to sport but not for the Crown Prince Heir," Regalius responded indignantly.

"I have never met a Reggie, so I really have no comment on the matter," I replied thoughtfully.

"What about you? Do people call you Serry? What about Sara? Or is there some other spin-off of a nickname for Serenity?" Regalius teased.

"Actually, my sister, Quiet, sometimes calls me Nitty. Sometimes, it does not matter who is call me it, I do not even realize I am responding to it, even when it is not her." I laughed. I never anticipated telling him that and was surprised when it came out.

"Nitty, huh?" He prodded.

"Yeah, when she was younger, she could not say my full name, and it only came out as Nitty. Surprisingly, my youngest sister Pulchra never picked up on it."

"Do you have any other siblings?"

"Two older brothers, Ace and Loyal. And then my older sister, Amity, is the head of the manor since our mother passed."

"I am sorry for your loss," he murmured.

"Thank you. She passed a few years ago."

"I am an only child, and I have always wanted a sibling. I am a little jealous, what is it like?" I could hear the longing in his voice.

"Well, my two older brothers let me trail after them all the time. We joked in the family that our adventures were what gave our father silver hair to match the rest of us." I laughed at the memory. "I was five when Quiet was born, and we are pretty close. Then fifteen years later, Pulchra, the baby of the family, was born."

"What about your older sister?" He prompted, and I pursed my lips.

"Amity and I had never been close. For a bit, I blamed the seven-year age difference, but it never made sense considering I got along with Ace, who is only two years younger than her."

"That is unfortunate. Did your parents not want any more kids after Pulchra?" Regalius asked, causing me to pause. When I didn't reply right away, he searched, trying to figure out what was wrong. "Was it something I said?"

"My mother died giving birth to Pulchra." I bluntly stated. We continued walking at a slower pace.

"I am sorry to hear that Serenity, I did not mean to . . . Do you blame your sister?"

"At first, I did, but not anymore." I smiled to myself. I missed my little sisters. I had never been away from any of my siblings, and my younger sisters had never known a life without me. I was curious how the two were getting along by themselves.

"I am sorry to have taken you away from them," Regalius murmured as if he could read my mind.

"You did not take me away from them. This whole trip began with me visiting Theorines's castle as a guest for their library," I tried to reassure him. I was not certain why though?

"I am sure you would rather be home with them than here," he nosed again.

"While I do miss them terribly, I currently have a historical section calling my name. I may never have another opportunity to have my hands on some of these books and scrolls." My walking pace picking up as I became excited.

"You know, if you ever wanted to return, I would have you as an honored guest." His words caught me off guard. My head whipped to look up at him, causing me to stumble. He managed to catch me as I crashed into him. I murmured my apologies as he helped me stand upright.

"Pretty certain after that, you may regret that offer," I teased, feeling slightly embarrassed and flustered.

"I knew you would fall for me sooner or later," he flirted.

I rolled my eyes. "Far from it, but you can keep dreaming." I flirted back as we made it to the double doors to the private library. The conversation between us flowed that I had not even paid attention to our surroundings as we walked together. I felt we had blinked and were already at our destination.

When Regalius opened the door, I had expected to see Gideon and Finch already there. Instead, we were greeted with an empty room. I turned, giving Regalius a questioning look.

"It will be the two of us. I hope that is alright?" He inquired.

I nodded. It caught me off guard slightly, but it was his home after all. Maybe the brothers were occupied elsewhere? Either way, I was not going to reject this opportunity.

A few hours later, I was curled up on one of the couches reading about a famine the lands endured two centuries back. It was quite intriguing learning how they had adapted with the little food they had left and the creative uses they stumbled upon. I must have been a little loud in my musings because Regalius shifted on his couch.

"You read history as someone reading an epic fantasy novel," he commented. I found him watching me, and I ducked my head. How long had he been focused on me, instead, of reading his book?

"Not all authors are dry and dusty. Some have a way of weaving words together," I defended. "Besides, what are you reading?" I tried to lean forward to see the cover, but his knee blocked my view. The way we sat on these couches was completely immodest, but having fallen into an ease of comfort had relaxed our etiquette. As long as no one of special interest walked in, they wouldn't find me half sprawled and slouching on the couch. With my shoes kicked off, feet curled under the pillow, and my dress hiked up over my right leg to regulate temperature. Meanwhile, Regalius had also forgone his shoes and was completely lying down on the couch with his knee propped up, his head resting on the throw pillows.

"An epic fantasy," he replied matter-of-factly and very proud of the statement.

"Ah." I nodded. It didn't phase me what he was reading. I found comfort in sharing the space with him as we both read in silence. He was not as nosey as the royals of Theorines who constantly pestered me about what I was reading and why I was copying down specific pieces of text. Regalius was kind and had snuck in paper and ink for me to write my notes. Believing I wouldn't be able to copy notes here, the self-inking quill from Finch remained in my room. Regalius let me go about my business, providing me with any materials I required.

"Does it bother you to spend this much time in here with me?" I inquired, the realization of how much of his day I was monopolizing.

"Not really." He shrugged, not taking his focus from the book.

"Why is that?" I pushed. Surely, he had better things to be doing than being crammed up in this room babysitting me.

"You do not demand much of me, and aside from my parents, no one else can come to this library." He flipped a page.

I hummed, not knowing how to add to the conversation. Only the servant, Muriel, came in here to deliver food or additional supplies. There had never even been the sound of footsteps walking past the private library. The nagging fear that The King or Queen would walk through that door remained constant in my mind, but with Regalius here, I knew he would handle it. While it intrigued me to know how the situation would play out, I personally did not want to witness it firsthand.

Lydia's knock came on my door, and I had been prepared for it. Bracing myself, I opened it to find the brightest yellow dress I had laid eyes upon. The fabric almost glowed, and yellow ostrich feathers were fanned out behind her head. Giant citrines were sewn into the fabric that surrounded the big hoop bottom. I blinked a few times, trying to save my eyesight.

She looked down at my steel-blue dress, the hoop skirt not billowing as big as hers as the tulle layered to create a shifty effect. The top was a simple strapless that corseted in the back. I had picked out a sapphire drop pendant with matching earrings and a sapphire bracelet.

"Your dress looks *nice*," Lydia commented.

"Thank you, yours is... something else," I surmised.

"I know!" She gushed, brightening up to talk about it. "I absolutely love the feather aspect."

I made a sound of understanding as we walked to the ball.

When we entered the ballroom, I led us immediately to one of the tables along the wall with a perfect view of the dance floor. I figured it wouldn't be long until Lydia had swindled someone into a dance, and I could stand there enjoying my wine while watching everyone.

She incessantly chatted about something that I wasn't paying attention to while grabbing my first glass of wine. Taking a sip, I savored the taste of strawberry that burst across my tongue.

It took only a matter of minutes, and I watched Lydia being twirled a crossed the dance floor from her first dance partner. I had to give the girl credit; she was bold. She had minimal fear of asking any passing male if they would care to be her dance partner, and before they could give her an answer, she was dragging them to the floor. I finished my first glass and grabbed a second one, I would need to find out who created this wine. It was divine.

Lydia came hurrying back after her first dance, flushed and beaming in excitement. I passed her a glass that she happily took and drank from greedily. I didn't bother to correct her on etiquetteness; she would be gone before I could finish the lesson.

"*Ohh,* this is so fun!" She exclaimed, discarding the empty glass. She barely turned to survey for her next dance partner when I watched in horror as she lost her balance and came crashing into me. Her hand grasped the top of my dress, and I heard the fabric ripping as I went down with her.

Her yellow dress swallowed me, and I gripped at the fabric covering my front, feeling it loose and a coolness caressing my skin. Lydia groaned beside me as she pulled away from me, standing back up. With one arm clasped tightly across my chest, I shakily got to my feet. I forced myself to look down and was met with horror. My dress was ripped from the top down to around my hip.

"Oh no! Serenity! I didn't mean to!" Gasped Lydia. I tried to wave her away, noticing the amount of attention we were drawing to ourselves. I tried to calculate how quickly I could get to the exit and how many people would witness the state I was in. Tears brimmed my eyes, but I dared not shed a tear until I was in a secluded room.

"Serenity, I—" Lydia began but was cut off.

"—You have done enough, come on, Serenity," Finch growled while draping his smokey lavender jacket over my shoulders, attempting to conceal the damage. I didn't know where he came from, but he was now leading us through a different side door that was not the entrance. I gripped the front of his jacket tightly to cover myself. Guests moved out of our way, and I refused to meet any of their eyes. I kept focus on breathing and not letting the tears that threatened to fall, escape.

The doors closed, and the ballroom became muffled noise. Finch continued leading until he was shoving us into an empty room and placing me on a couch. He knelt before me, his fingers gently caressing my cheek. I met his eyes through blurry tears and pulled his jacket tighter around me as I looked away from him, closing my eyes. The first tear rolled down my right cheek. He pulled me into his arms, rocking me as I cried while he held me.

When my sobs subsided, I pulled away from him, swatting at the stray tears on my cheeks. He looked at me grimly and I clenched my jaw.

"Are you okay?" He asked quietly.

"Yeah." I dug my palm into my eye. "I will be fine; I need to get back to my rooms."

"She should not get away with that," Finch growled.

"Lydia had not meant to do it," I defended. I knew it had been an accident; she lost her balance, and there was no reason to punish her for it.

"She—" Finch began, but I cut him off.

"—Lydia is many things, but I can promise you. She did not mean that."

He looked in disbelief, the silence stretching between us, and eventually, he nodded, accepting my answer. Getting up, he escorted me back to my rooms. At my door, I thanked him for rescuing and comforting me. He shrugged it off and departed without another word. I slipped into my rooms, not wanting anyone else to see me in this state. I still wore his jacket and would need to somehow have it returned to him.

An hour had passed, and I had slipped out of the destroyed dress. I was now in the olive-green nightgown, sipping a glass of the strawberry wine. I had flagged down a passing servant in the hallway, requesting a bottle be brought to my room. A knock came to my door; I wondered if it was the same servant returning for something else.

Crossing the room, I answered the door to find Lydia on the other side with a covered platter. She was in her own pink nightgown; long gone was the flashy dresses.

"I wanted to apologize for earlier. I feel bad." She held up the covered platter as a peace offering.

I sighed, letting her in. "There is nothing to forgive. I know it was an accident," I replied as we sat in the oversized chairs. I procured an additional glass and poured her some wine.

"I would never do something like that to intentionally ruin you," she continued.

"Lydia," I stated firmly, and she quieted. "I said there was nothing to forgive. Let it lie. What is under the platter?" I nodded at the still-covered food.

Her eyes widened, and then she jumped into action, undercovering a variety of pastries and sweets. We nestled in the chairs while sipping our wine and eating the pastries. Lydia filled me in on how the rest of the ball had gone. Most of what she said was laced with how handsome Prince Regalius Baylor was. I nodded while reframing from rolling my eyes at her obsessive crush on the prince. She was certain he would ask her to dance at the next ball or so. I responded with the correct words. Meanwhile, my mind wandered to Finch.

Who knew what state I would have been in if we hadn't been friends prior? It made me wonder how many future situations he would need to save his soon-to-be sister-in-law from. I doubted he would be informing Gideon of the event, but then again, probably, the gossipmongers would get to Gideon first. I would deal with it if he brought it up. A shiver coursed through me; I still did not like how he had cornered me at the last dance. My track record of dances was not going well, and it made me look less forward to the rest of the season's participation.

Chapter Eighteen

A FEW DAYS LATER, REGALIUS CAME TO COLLECT ME BUT didn't follow me into the room. I looked at him surprised.

"Can I trust you?" Regalius asked me.

"Uhhh?" I was uncertain as to where he was going with this.

"With the books, Serenity," he supplied, his voice warming.

"Yeah, why?" I gave him a questioning look.

"Because I plan to leave you here by yourself to read, I snuck in paper, an ink quill, and a jar. Just please be careful," he emphasized.

"But you said." My eyes widened in shock.

"I know what I said, but I would like to have the first signed copy of your historical book when it is published." He smiled at me, and I warmed.

"Thank you, thank you!" I threw my arms around Regalius, hugging him tightly. I felt him awkwardly pat my back.

"You are welcome, Serenity." He chuckled. I removed my arms, instantly realizing my actions. My hands covered my mouth from embarrassment.

"I am so sorry! I did not mean to hug you. That is not like me."

"You are fine. I can understand why you are overcome with emotions."

"I am not overcome." I tried to defend myself.

"I just handed you a secluded private library and smuggled in writing materials for you." He gave me a point-in-case smug look.

"Okay, maybe I am a little overcome," I dipped my head in a shy smile.

"Well, now I know how to make you happy." Regalius led us into the private library. I instantly grabbed my next scroll to read. "Now, if anyone comes in here and raises questions, tell them I gave you permission. If they do not believe you, tell them to come find me. If they still fuss, just state if they harm you, they will be dealing with the consequences from me."

My hand stilled on the scroll as I looked up at him. "Should I be worried?"

"You are in the private library of the largest monarchy, unguarded, unsupervised, and with contraband. You tell me." He raised an eyebrow.

"Dually noted," I replied crisply. Regalius promised he would return for me in a few hours. He made sure to give me instructions on how to get to the bathroom as well.

I made it through all the unread scrolls and began copying the ones I'd read the previous time. A soft knock came to the door, followed by someone opening it. I glanced up to see the maid, Muriel, coming in carrying a tray. She had long black hair in two braids down her front. Her glasses covered her warm brown eyes. It was evident she was very insecure about herself with how she moved and glanced about the room.

"Oh, um, hello," I greeted cautiously. I slid the ink jar further away from the scrolls and tried to conceal it being in here. Muriel carried the tray toward me; she did not say a word as she set it down on the table next to me, and with a curtsy, turned to leave. "Wait!" I called, halting her.

She turned around to face me. Her face in complete alarm. "Is something wrong, Your Highness?"

"Oh, I am not a Princess, just a lady," I corrected her hastily, and then nodded to the tray. "What is this?"

"The Prince sent orders to bring you food in here," she answered, adjusting her glasses.

"Oh, well, that was nice of him." I smiled. I hadn't expected him to inform anyone else of my whereabouts in here. I assumed when I became hungry, I would need to seek out my own source of nourishment.

"Is there anything else you need of me, Mi'Lady?"

"No, no, that is all. Thank you, Muriel."

"You are welcome, Mi'Lady," she answered, bowing her head and folded one hand on top of another.

I dismissed Muriel and looked at the tray with food; how thoughtful of Regalius to ensure I ate.

"Serenity. . . Serenity." Distantly, I heard a voice calling my name as I was being nudged.

"Go away, Quiet." I swatted in the general direction I believed my sister was, keeping my eyes closed, hoping to fall back asleep.

"Serenity." Another nudge, a bit harder than the previous ones.

"Mmh, be like your name, *Quiet*," I mumbled, still swatting at empty air, becoming more irritated.

"Serenity." Another nudge.

I bolted up from my sleeping position. "Quiet, please! I am trying to slee—" The word became stuck in my mouth as I came face to face with Regalius. "You. . . are. . . not my sister."

"No, I am definitely not." He wore an amused expression while lightly chuckling. I looked around at my surroundings. I was still in the private library but I had moved to the couch to read and must have fallen asleep. I gasped, instantly searching for the book I had been reading. Had I damaged it?

"If you are looking for this." He waved the book in front of my face. "It was not damaged. You were gripping it tightly to your chest."

"Glad, it is okay." I swung my legs over the side of the couch to sit up properly. I glanced down at my wrinkled dress and attempted to smooth the creases away. I could only imagine what my hair and face looked like. "What time is it?"

"Nearly midnight," he answered casually and a bit amused.

I shot up to my feet, panic lacing through me. "Midnight?!" I need to get to my room. My whole day would be off tomorrow. That was fine at home, but here, I was never certain when something would be required until the last minute. If I was caught galivanting in the corridor with Regalius, what would the whispers say? How would I even explain this to Gideon? I twisted my lips from the thought, rationalizing to myself that we had been sent here to find potential love in another. My eyes roved over the prince before me, although I hadn't been looking for love in him.

"It is fine, Serenity. I will escort you back. You are fine," Regalius soothed, placing the book on the desk with all my notes. He surveyed the stacks of papers, letting out a low whistle.

"Are you certain? What if someone sees?" I rushed out.

"Are you worried about being seen with me in the middle of the night?" He continued to rifle through the sheets, lingering on a few before moving on.

"Yes." I did not even think about my answer.

"Well, that would be a first." He looked at me speculatively. "Come on." He held out his arm, and reluctantly, I looped mine within his.

"Why did it take you so long to collect me?" I looked at him cocking an eyebrow. Nearly midnight, and to my knowledge, there had not been any mandatory events to attend. Did he perhaps forget about me?

"I was wrapped up in prior engagements." He cleared his throat, leading us out of the private library.

"Prior engagements until midnight?" I noticed his disheveled hair and misbuttoned clothing. His face was flushed as well.

"Yes, prior engagements." He tried to maintain a regal appearance, but his cheeks reddened deeper, the dimple nowhere in sight.

"Do these prior engagements involve another person?" I inquired. I had tried to keep the humor from my voice, but I could not contain my knowing smile.

"Possibly." His eyes flicked to me and then quickly away, his pace picking up as we turned the corner.

"And the fact your buttons are mismatched?" I nodded to his chest. I found a great deal of entertainment in causing him this discomfort of being found out.

Regalius, instantly looked down at the front of his shirt and unlooped our arms to fix the mess. His face and neck becoming completely flushed as he worked quickly on the buttons.

"Pretty sure walking with you alone in an empty corridor as you unbutton to show off your bare chest will not give the wrong idea," I commented nonchalantly. I glanced down at my wrinkled dress, knowing it, too, would give the wrong idea. "Not to mention the state my attire is in."

A warm, rich laugh filled the empty corridor. "Afraid the whispers will link you to me?" He teased, attempting to retain his composure.

"Absolutely," I replied once again without thought. I realized I did not mind offending him in the slightest, which I found odd. When I was in Theorines, I made certain never to displease the royals, but with Regalius it came all too naturally to take him down a peg at each step. Which I didn't understand why when he had been nothing but kind to me. He didn't swagger around the cocky arrogance as some of the royals did in attendance.

"Which eligible person here are you so worried about hearing the rumors?" He tilted his head. We were no longer walking as we stood there while he continued to fix his buttons.

"None," I defended while glancing around the empty hallway for prying ears.

"If that were true, you would not be as on edge." He glanced up from his buttons to emphasize his point, before resuming to his task.

"Someone is really sure of themselves."

"Sweetheart, when you are me, people throw themselves at you." He rolled his eyes and shook his head.

"I never have," I stated pointedly. I never had even a fleeting desire to as he said, throw myself at him. However, with the way he'd said it, I didn't fully believe he enjoyed everyone vying for his attention.

"No, you have not. You are the exception in my life, although you did fall for me that one time." He chuckled to himself.

"That was literal, not figuratively, Reggie." I dropped the nickname, hoping to distract him enough to change the conversation.

"Hey! I said no to Reggie." He made a move to grab me, and I moved out of his reach, giggling.

"Then do not patronize me by calling me *Sweetheart*," I countered.

"I was not patronizing."

"Sweetheart, when you are me, people throw themselves at you" I air quoted as I mocked him, laughing from the expression he wore.

"Well, they do," he grumbled in a pouty voice.

"Must be difficult to be Prince heir to the highest-ranked monarchy," I commented in a babytalk voice, still giggling from his pouting.

"I never know who my true friends are." The loneliness crept into his voice, catching me off guard. "And who are in my life to use me." His sad eyes caught mine, and I sobered up. I had not expected him to be this honestly vulnerable. I placed my hand on his arm gently.

"Regalius, you can consider me a friend."

"What about the library?"

"You do not need to gain my friendship with private libraries."

"No?"

"No, if Gideon and Finch trust you as a friend, then so do I." He looped his arm with mine again as he continued to escort me to my rooms.

"I have been wondering, what is your relationship with those two?" I could hear the curiosity in his voice.

"What do you mean?" I prevented myself from yielding any facial expression or body movement to make him question my reaction to his question.

"Is one of them your love?" He pushed.

"That is quite blunt." My voice raised slightly, and I cursed myself.

"Well?" He raised an eyebrow.

"It is not as simple as that."

"How complex can it be," he continued pushing, wanting an answer from me.

"I cannot tell you." I thought to my future in-laws and how they wanted their son and me to keep things a secret. I couldn't betray them like this, they had come off as decent people and the last thing I needed was to anger not just my future in-laws but also the royals of a kingdom I would be residing the rest of my days in.

"Why not? Did the Theorines Princes swear you to secrecy" The slight teasing of his voice was underlaid with seriousness. I didn't know why but I felt if I told him the truth, he would attempt to rescue me from the situation. Which was a silly notion in it of itself considering what could he actually do to save me? He would have to marry me and since he had never attempted to court me, I highly doubted he wanted to shackle himself to me. I shivered, thinking of how his mother would react to her son marrying a lady, instead of a princess.

"Not them."

"Then who?"

"I have said too much already," I replied hastily.

"Fine, I will let it go, but we are to your room." He nodded as we stood in front of my door.

"Thank you for escorting me here."

"You are welcome." He bowed and left me to retire for what was left of the night.

However, sleep did not find me. Instead, I tossed and turned, rehashing my conversation with him and what he was currently speculating. I did not believe Regalius would cause me many problems, but I was uncertain if Gideon would be okay with his friend knowing. We had never talked about what would happen if someone did come to find out while we were here. I could only hope he would not be mad.

Chapter Nineteen

Lydia despite claiming to be quite crossed with me did not act it. She begged and tried to course me into telling her where I had been the last few days, but I refused to give in. If Lydia knew, she would cling to the fact I had been spending personal time with more than one prince. Especially a very peculiar prince that she had her sights set on. Lydia would twist it in her mind that I was holding out on her, which was by far from the case.

We were sitting together in an empty room that she had dragged me into. I supposed she thought if she could get me alone and away from everyone, I would begin to talk. Instead, I had diverted the conversation by asking what she had been up to the last few days. Flirting with men, of course, and hanging out with all the ladies. I knew what it really meant, but I did not lead on.

The door creaked open, and Finch's head popped in, and then he called over his shoulder, "Found her!" I was not certain how I would explain that one to Lydia as she looked at me for answers. The door swung wide open as Finch, Gideon, and Regalius strolled in and shut the door behind them. Lydia immediately jumped to her feet to curtsy, muttering Your Highnesses. I forgot my manners and remained seated; it was not until Lydia's confused side eye that I realized my mistake in comfortability with these three.

"You may take your seat, Lydia," Gideon said, releasing my friend from her curtsy.

"We have been looking for you," Finch jumped in, ignoring Lydia as he looked at me.

"I *heard*. What do you *want*?" I asked, trying to keep my tone light with a sprinkling of warning in it.

"Is that any way to speak to three princes, Lady Serenity Novena?" Regalius chided. I rolled my eyes. Lydia jumped in before I could respond.

"Apologies, Lady Serenity Novena is not perverse in speaking with princes. Please forgive her." *Oh, the little suck-up.* I looked at her unamused as I caught all three princes trying to hide their smiles. We all knew she was attempting to portray me in a bad light.

"Oh, we are *quite familiar* with Serenity," Finch responded with a smucker. I shot him a look. *What was he doing?* "So familiar that we had asked her to be informal with us."

"Finch," I warned. Where was he going with this? I wanted to stay under anyone's notice and here he was serving me up on a silver platter to Lydia. She'd nagged me non-stop about how well I knew the three of them, especially Regalius. I let out a breath of frustration. Finch was supposed to be the one who caused me the least amount of trouble out of the three, but yet here he was creating the most chaos.

"See, she is just so used to calling us by our first names that she forgets to add the title." Finch gave me a cocky grin. Lydia pursed her lips as she looked between me and the three Princes.

"Serenity, why have you not told me of your familiarity?" She asked in a sickenly, sweet voice. The undertones of accusation lay heavy.

"That would be our parent's fault, Finch and mine," Gideon interrupted to answer her question and saving me. "Regalius is on his own for this one." Gideon looked over at Regalius to fend for himself. I could've imagined it, but I swore there was a bit of tension between the two.

"Titles are stuffy," Regalius responded, not letting on more than that. He shrugged almost as if testing how Gideon would react to his minimal answer.

"Why would your parents be at fault?" Lydia pushed, clinging to Gideon's words. It was a first that she had not completely become hung up on Regalius's words. Most likely due to the fact that The Theorines's Royal gossip was far juicier than The T'Lovoness heirs' response.

"Because I lived with Gideon and Finch for a bit," I jumped in, needing to control how I wanted this conversation to play out. "And if it got out, I could become ostracized. You know how vicious they can be." I tried to play on the sympathy card. I needed to get Lydia off this topic and onto another. I needed for her to believe. She stared at me for a moment, mulling it over.

"I guess that makes sense," she finally replied, "but I thought we were friends. Why did you never think to tell me?" Her lip protruded outwards a bit as she glanced between me and the brothers.

"Would you go against the King of Theorines's orders?" I raised an eyebrow at her. I realized at some point I had gone from thinking of her as a merchant's daughter to my friend. I hadn't even bristled when she said the term to me.

"I guess not." Her lips quirked to the side, and then she looked at the princes. "Can I call you by your first names without the titles?" She wasn't shy in asking. The three looked at each other, silently communicating their thoughts. Regalius and Gideon shrugged, while Finch shook his head against it.

"Sure, I do not see an issue with it," Regalius stated before continuing, "but only if it is in private. Like Serenity said, if others heard, it could become *vicious*, and I will not protect you in the event of a slipup." He gave her a pointed look. He would the one throwing her to the wolves without remorse if she made one little mistake.

"I understand. . . Reggie." She smiled sweetly. Regalius gave her a very tight smile. Lydia hadn't the faintest idea how that nickname caused her the opposite effect of what she was going for.

"What did you want that you were seeking me out?" I repeated, looking at the three princes. Gideon was the one who decided to speak first.

"We were bored and wanted to see what you were up to."

"Why?" I asked, a bit annoyed. While I didn't mind their company, it was a recipe for disaster with Lydia in attendance. They could have easily requested my presence and taken me somewhere else, or better yet, left me alone.

"Serenity," Lydia jumped in, "don't be mean, let us entertain them." Despite her smile, her eyes were a cross of begging, and *if you say no I will make you regret it.*

"Do not be mean," I corrected. I was not certain why she had gotten under my skin like she just had, but if Lydia wanted to try to make a fool of me more than once in front of my friends, then I had no issue correcting her poor speech. Her eyes widened as she blinked rapidly. I stared at her, raising my eyebrow slightly. I did not even hide my eye roll as I looked at the three males. "Why?"

Regalius and Finch wore amused expressions while Gideon scratched the back of his head and gave his nervous chuckle. Gideon, of course, was the one to respond.

"Because we can be ourselves with you and do not half to hold up appearances like we do when we are out among the mob." He shifted.

"Fine, fine, just do not be distracting," I consented. Finch whooped as the three came to sit amongst the surrounding chairs. Lydia gave them all excited smiles; out of my peripheral vision, I caught her flicking her attention to me.

"Let us get to know each other better!" Lydia clapped her hands together. The small action slightly reminding me of Queen Izralda and how she would clap excitedly at everything. The difference was that The Queen was genuine in her bubbly nature, while Lydia was looking for something to gain from the experience.

"What an excellent idea, you go first, Lyla," Regalius said, causing everyone to pause in the room from his intended mistake. Apparently being called 'Reggie' had not been forgiven.

"Lydia," she corrected, her smile stretching wider. She shifted slightly, trying to restrain herself from chastising a royal. If it had been anyone else, Lydia would have easily corrected them in the vilest way possible. Lydia loved nothing more than causing another to feel shame and embarrassment.

"What?" He asked, feigning ignorance. It appeared, Regalius must have had practice dealing with people who annoyed him. Most likely, only his parents he wouldn't be able to get away with this kind of behavior, but then again with a mother like his, who knew?

"My name is Lydia, Reggie," she answered, batting her lashes a few times. While she smiled, it could not cover up her apparent annoyance.

"Ah, Lydia. . . right. Anyway," Regalius dismissed, as if it were no consequence to him. "You go first in telling us about yourself." He did not apologize, a royal should never admit error to the lesser common folks. This was a colder side of Regalius that I hadn't witnessed prior and it was both scary and intriguing to me.

"Well, it is not fun to just tell about oneself. Let us play a game!" Lydia clapped her hands together again. Once again reminding me of The Theorines's Queen and wondered if her sons thought the same thing.

"What is the game?" Gideon asked, leaning in with his elbows on his knees.

"Here is how we play," Lydia began, "I tell two truths and a lie. If you guess my lie, you can dare me to do anything you like. If you do not guess my lie, then I can dare you to do anything I like." She giggled. We looked at each other and silently agreed to go along with it.

"Alright, tell us your two truths and a lie," Regalius encouraged.

Lydia looked up at the ceiling as she thought about it. When she finally had it figured out, she let out a little breath of air and began. "I am an only child." she ticked off a finger. "My Mother died." She ticked off a second finger. "My brother tried to sell me into slavery." She ticked off her last finger. We all sat there blinking at her while she sat looked at us innocently.

"Brother tried to sell you into slavery," Finch stated as he leaned back in his seat with a knowing look.

"Are you sure?" She asked wide-eyed. I couldn't tell if he had guessed correctly or not. Two of those scenarios had appeared normal that I would never have thought of a brother selling her off into slavery. I had been going between being an only child by her need for attention or her mother dying due to my similar situation. Lydia had never mentioned a brother to me prior, and for as much as she chattered, it would have come up eventually by now.

"Yes. Tell me I am wrong. I dare you," he challenged. She sat there, and we all glanced between her and Finch, awaiting who would be daring who. She finally broke with a sigh.

"You are correct; what would you dare for me to do," she replied helplessly.

Finch remained leaning back as he thought about it. "I dare you to walk around the room pretending to be a duck and quacking until I say to stop." We all broke out laughing at the notion, except for Lydia. "Well, go on." He urged.

We watched as Lydia slowly got up from her seat and began to flap her arms at her side while making quacking noises and walking around the room. It was quite an absurd sight to see.

"How long are you going to make her quack for?" Regalius asked, mirroring my exact thoughts.

"Until I feel like it," Finch responded coolly and under his breath I heard him say, "she deserves to be punished a bit." I blinked at him to make certain I heard that right and he gave me a wink. It barely took a minute for Gideon to speak up.

"You probably can make her stop quacking." Gideon nervously chuckled.

"No, she could learn to be a bit more *humble*," Finch stated coldly. I had never seen this side of Finch before. Did Lydia get under his skin that much? I did not think he was biased against the classes like Queen Opal, but maybe I was mistaken? Lydia continued to quack around the room, looking at us with a red face for the next minute.

"That is enough, Lydia; you may stop," Finch ordered. Lydia was mid-flap of her arms when Finch released her. She slowly lowered her arms to begin smoothing out her dress as she walked stiffly back to us.

"Was it necessary to make her do it for that long?" Gideon asked his brother.

"Yes, she needed to be taught a lesson," Finch stared Lydia down as he said it.

"What lesson?" Gideon's voice was beginning to rise.

"That she may be here at The Courting Seasons, but she needs to learn her place. If she wants to be a nuisance, then I simply dared her to act like a nuisance." All the friendliness was gone from Finch's face. This wasn't the same prince requesting for me to look at the stars with him, I didn't recognize him.

"That is bullshit! Mother raised you better!" Gideon shouted. Lydia was still standing and fidgeting in place. She was fighting tears, and I really did not blame her. I hadn't expected the innocent dare to turn into something this cruel.

"No." Finch turned his head to look at Gideon. "Mother raised you to be better. She raised me to see through the bullshit to protect you and your bleeding heart."

"What is that supposed to mean?" Gideon demanded. I glanced over to Regalius, trying to gauge his reaction. I had never witnessed the brother's fight and this wasn't the appropriate time for it. Regalius, unfortunately, was not revealing any hints of his thoughts on the matter.

"We were raised together, but we never had lessons together. There was a reason for it." Finch stated in his cold voice, his gaze flicked to mine before flicking it back to Gideon. "Just know, brother, if you do not watch it, you will hurt the one thing that you believe matters to you before it has even begun to truly matter."

"What are you talking about?" Gideon bolted to his feet to stand over his younger brother. The two were glaring at each other.

"If you do not know exactly what I am talking about, you are a bigger idiot of an heir than I thought you were. That thing-" Finch gestured to Lydia, who was still standing awkwardly "—is what I am talking about." Harsh, not even I thought Lydia should be called a 'thing'.

Lydia squeaked from the insult, bringing our full attention to her. Her hands were knuckle white by her face as she held back tears. I was not certain what I could say to console her right at this very moment. I went to reach my arm out as she turned and ran from the room. Gideon, who was already on his feet from looming over Finch, chased after her as he yelled over his shoulder, "Look what you did!" The door slamming shut behind them.

"At least he had the decency to remember to close the door," Finch commented.

"What was that really about Finch?" I asked. Regalius had yet to say a word, his attention still on the door, deep in thought. Finch turned his cold expression to me, and I watched as it turned from a stranger back to the Finch I knew.

"Gideon will fall for any sob story given to him. The moment she started with her two truths and a lie, and all three of them could have been weaved as depressing, I knew his heart would break for her. That thing is a manipulative little bitch. She leeched onto you to raise her social status here; she will play the pity card to have any of us feel a remorse of sympathy for her and to keep her around. I choose to weed people like that out." Finch uncrossed his leg to get up from the couch. "Now, if you will excuse me, I need to go save that bleeding heart from a viper, as you like to call them." He didn't wait for our response as he dismissed himself and left Regalius and me in the room alone.

I looked at Regalius to find him already watching me, both of us trying to understand what had just happened. I knew Lydia was desperate to climb the social ladder, and I knew I was one of the few who allowed her to hang around me, even despite her gaudy dresses.

"Well, that was entertaining, to say the least," Regalius commented, leaning back in his chair.

"The very least," I agreed.

"I was getting the distinct feeling there was more to it than Finch was leading us on to believe." Regalius mused, waiting to hear my answer.

"I was too, but not certain of what," I commented dryly. The way Finch's gaze flicked to mine made me question if it had something to do with my secret engagement to Gideon. But Gideon had fought to steal my unknown engagement from Finch to himself. Why would he ruin something he fought for? Was Finch claiming he cared for me more than his elder brother's feelings? I hindered no romantic feelings for any of them. The physical intimacy I shared with Gideon was more out of distraction and future obligation. Eventually, I would like for more than feelings of friendship to blossom between Gideon and me, but for now, I was content with where we were.

"I am sure in a matter of time, we will find out," Regalius surmised.

"With how vague Finch was, I am not as certain. . . Is it common for royals to raise their children differently?" I asked. Finch stating their mother raised them differently had my mind working. There was nothing about it in the historical texts I had read, but maybe it was a common private thing to not discuss or be important to document? Then again, Gideon and Finch's mother had not been born into royalty; rather she had married into it. I questioned why she would have chosen to raise her two sons completely differently. Gideon being raised as heir to the throne made sense, but it felt as if Finch had been raised to be like a sellsword and protector to his older brother.

"I am an only child and do not have much experience in the

matter. However, it is not uncommon for children born from royals to have vastly different upbringings than their siblings. . . Is it not the same for children from Lady's?" He questioned me back.

I tucked away the new information while I mulled over his question. "Honestly, I could not tell you, my siblings and I did not experience a normal upbringing compared to other children with Lord's or Lady's for parents," I replied slowly thinking it through.

"What do you mean? How was yours different?" He leaned forward to brace his elbows on his knees, giving me his full attention. Something about the gesture and his interest both unnerved and exhilarated me. Rarely did I find the need to talk to myself, but Regalius was constantly curious about my life.

"My mother preferred having us grow up and be a part of the neighboring villages. We spent every holiday participating in their festivities, and she would send us out to help them with physical labor as well." I paused to let it sink in a moment. "To my knowledge majority of Lady's and Lord's are not as active in their villages and definitely do not send their offspring out to help the people collect eggs or harvest crops."

"You were sent out to do farm labor?" Regalius asked incredulous. His eyebrows raised, and he leaned in even further.

"Yes, as were all my siblings except Pulchra since she is only five currently." I supposed a prince had never been sent to do chores. He probably had been gifted a golden spoon since childhood always having a flock of nursemaids to tend and care for him. I shouldn't be so contrite in my way of thinking, most of the neighboring Lady's children in Grewt'en had grown up the same way. If anything, my family had been the anomaly in the Queendom.

"Was it regularly?" He asked.

"Usually, if someone took ill or became injured, Mother would send us to step in and help."

"Did you stay at their homes as well?"

"Yes, it would be quite tiring to travel back and forth to the neighboring villages if we were not close by. . . Let alone, as Mother would put it, *'Did not teach us to appreciate everything that everyone does in our community'*".

"Your mother sounds like a very honorable lady," Regalius commented. I could not contain my laughter. He gave me a perplexed look. "Was it something I said?"

"Yes and no. My father's name is Lord Honorable Lambert. I am sure you can see why I laughed." I wiped away the tears from the corners of my eyes, still chuckling over the matter, even if we had been discussing my mother. Regalius joined in my laughter.

"She married a man that fits her then."

"Tis, she did. May I ask you something?" I decided to push since we were on the topics of names.

"Of course, Serenity Dear, what is it?"

"Why did your mother name you Regalius? She is not from Grewt'en; it strikes me odd."

"She always had a fascination with Grewt'en's beliefs on names being a powerful influence on a child's character growing up. My mother wanted me to be regal and felt it would fit me when I became a king. Being regal is stuffy." He appeared unphased by being asked the question. Most likely, he or his parents had been asked the reasoning of his name many of times. It had not been the first I heard of someone adopting The Grewt'en ways when it came to names. However, it was a first when it came to a royal not from my home.

"Being serene is boring." I laughed. Nothing about me was serene and living up to that expectation was quite dull.

"If you could choose a different name, what would it be?" Conversation with Regalius flowed seamlessly. His apparent interest was genuine, and he never attempted to move the topics along to fit his agenda. Very minimally did he take the time to boast about himself. For an heir, even with his charismatic nature, he never came off as conceited.

I pondered his question for a moment and came up blank. "Never really considered it. Usually, the only time I wish for something different is when I do not want to be nice."

"And what would those names be?" He pushed, a twinkle of delight entering his eye.

"Pricella. So I could be prissy, or Sassy so I could be fun or maybe even—"

"I think you are fun with the name Serenity." Regalius cut me off.

"I know that, but there are people who expect me to be serene at all times based on my name." My voice was beginning to rise.

"Did I strike a nerve?" He asked calmly.

"Apparently." I laughed to mask my embarrassment. I had not anticipated that to bubble out of me.

"Just so you are aware, you never have to act serene around me because of your name. Just be yourself like you always have been," he said. He did not wait for me to reply as he rose and left me to my own thoughts in the room.

I flopped back in my chair to ponder everything that had happen within the time the princes had arrived. This day could have gone completely differently if I had never left my room. Now my betrothed was off comforting Lydia, Finch had shown another side to himself, and ironically enough, Regalius had been the only normal person out of the entire encounter.

Chapter Twenty

I WITHHELD MY SIGH AS I RAPPED MY KNUCKLES ON
Lydia's door. The least I supposed I could do as her only friend here
was check on her after the way Finch had treated her. I was sure
Gideon had become her knight in shining armor by comforting her. I
rolled my eyes, chuckling to myself at what she would be dramatically
telling the story for anyone to hear. I questioned if she would portray
Finch in a bad light or omit him from the story completely.

Lydia did not answer the door, and I knocked again. I suppose
she may not have returned to her rooms yet. Who knows where Lydia
could have run off to when she had left us. Perhaps she was already
galivanting around to tell every one of her brave hero.

I turned away and paused, glancing down at her door handle. I
quickly looked up and down the hallway and, after finding it empty,
lightly rested my fingertips on the gold knob to turn it. The door was
unlocked as it opened. I peeked inside, and glancing back down the
hallway to ensure it was indeed still empty, took a step in.

Her room was set up similarly to mine. However, the color
scheme was completely different. Her walls were painted a metallic
gold, and emerald-green curtains adorned the big windows. I noted

how she had hardwood flooring scattered with area rugs. Her furniture was simple in a light sky blue. It made me curious if every room had a different aesthetic to it.

I tilted my head to the side when a sound came from her bedroom. I wanted to call out her name but thought better of it because I should not be in here. I took a step toward the noise and then heard it again. Tilting my head to the other side, I tried to decipher what I was hearing. I took one more step, and then I recognized the sound. The bed was creaking and those were moans. I took half a step back, but then my stomach dropped. Gideon had gone to comfort her; could he be in there with her? We had never agreed to be exclusive. He was free to do as he pleased.

My curiosity was getting the better of me and I took a tentative step forward. I crossed the entertaining room and stood outside of Lydia's bedroom. The door was ajar, and I took a deep breath in as I braced myself for who I would see with her. Relief flooded me when I caught sight of the male's blonde hair. It was not Gideon. I backed away, not wanting to be caught. When I was out of sight of her bedroom door, I turned to make my hasty escape. I knocked into an end table, clapping a hand over my mouth to prevent myself from making more noise. I hurried to the door leading to the hallway when the male asked, "What was that?"

I, as quietly as possible, escaped Lydia's rooms. The hallway was still empty as I hurried to my room two down from Lydia's. I yanked the door open and closed it, breathing heavily as I leaned against the wood. *What had I been thinking?*

No, I knew what I had been thinking. My good intentions turned into thinking the worst of a situation. I should never have considered entering Lydia's bedroom. The only reason the thought had crossed my mind was because I still had an inkling that she had been the one jiggling my door handle a while back. That, however, did not make it right for me to do the same. My heart continued to race as my breathing slowed.

Lydia must not have been too upset with how Finch had treated her if she had a male in her room. I had not even been aware she had an interest in anyone here who was not Regalius. I realized I would need to keep quiet about this, least I give myself away.

I looked up at the ceiling. As much as I would have preferred to do more research, there was a mandatory ball tonight that required my attendance. Pushing off the door, I headed toward my armoire to pick out a dress.

Tonight, walking into the ballroom alone, I chose to wear a red satin dress with a slit in the right leg. A hoop skirt was not required for this one, and I was able to move with ease without stressing that I would knock into something. I chose to be more elaborate in my accessories than I had the previous ball, shaking my head to dismiss the memory of how that one ended. On my right thigh was a gold circlet with a simple chain hung from it. The chain ended with a diamond cut ruby that swayed with each step when I walked. I had an elaborate ruby scalloped necklace surrounded by clusters of diamonds and the matching earrings. I painted my lips to match the dress while wearing my hair down.

I kept my head held high as I entered the ball, this time not lingering at the entrance as I crossed the distance when I spotted Ivy and her sisters. Greta was the first to notice me and gasped as her eyes looked me over and how tight the dress hugged my figure. I gave her a pursed lip smile.

Greta's granny-smith apple green dress had a sweetheart neckline. It layered with a very intricate black lace overtopped. She wore her hair half up with the curl spirals fanning down her back. Single pearl droplet earrings hung from her lobes, and a matching pearl necklace that nestled an emerald above her cleavage adorned her chest.

Ivy turned to see what Greta was looking at, and her face blanched. "Serenity," she gasped while wearing a dusty rose dress filled with small pearls that were sewn in a crisscross pattern along the bottom half. Similar tiny pearls were lined across the top of the strapless gown. Her hair was styled in a high bun, except for two very thick hair coils that swayed each time she moved her head. Simple silver hoop earrings adorned her ears, and a darker pink velvet choker was tied around her neck.

"Ivy." I dipped my head and repeated the process with the other two sisters.

"That dress," Ivy began, trailing off.

"Ah yes, my designer decided to add a few showstoppers into my wardrobe." I smiled sweetly. I had not yet spotted Lydia, but I was sure she would find me quicker than I found her.

"You never did mention who your designer was," Greta stated, her eyes making multiple passes over my dress.

"Then it would not be a secret." I brought my index finger to my mouth, giving her a small smile and winked.

"I think you look beautiful," Mimzy complimented. She wore a dress similar to Greta's but instead of green it was a deep blue that the black lace barely was noticeable. Her curly locks were left down, and she hadn't adorned herself with any jewels.

"Thank you, Mimzy. I like your dress." I smiled, and her face brightened.

"Thank you! It was one of Greta's from last year." She beamed, and I did not miss the way Greta cringed at the knowledge of a second-hand dress being recycled for her younger sister.

"It suits you," was my reply to the youngest sister. Reaching through the sisters, I grabbed myself a glass of wine, not minding the slightest irritation I caused Ivy. I turned to look out upon the dance floor while sipping the sweet wine. Regalius was dancing with a princess while Gideon and Finch stood talking in a group of males. Slowly, I picked out other recognizable faces in the crowd.

King Lucien appeared to enjoy watching the dance while Queen Opal surveyed the members wearing her permanent pursed lips. Servants standing beside her fan The Queen with the pink and green dyed ostrich feathers. Tonight's dress was not as overly extravagant, but it made a statement. A deep blush wine pink color with layers of tulle deepening the color. There were white silk swags that bunched into the resemblance of a rose. The dress overall was quite beautiful; it was a shame someone with such a sour disposition wore it.

"Think someone will ask you to dance tonight?" Ivy sidled up next to me. She made a noise as she sucked on her teeth.

"If I thought that, then why would I stand along the wall in the shadows," I commented dryly, and she hissed.

"What are you trying to say?" She challenged.

I didn't look at her, still watching the guests dance on the floor before us where I knew she and Greta longed to be. "If I had wanted to have someone ask me to dance, I would be occupying one of the empty tables near the male circles. I would flirt using my eyes at the males of my choosing until one felt bold enough to ask me. I would not be standing the furthest out of reach, hidden in the shadows in a cluster." Finishing, I took a sip of my wine.

"Alright, show me. Prove it." She spat. From my peripheral vision, she was glaring at me.

"Who do you have your eyes on?" I asked instead.

"Why? Are you going to take him?" She accused, and slowly, I shifted my focus to her.

"No, I have no desire to *take* your crush. I am merely asking to know where to move to."

She held my stare, her eyes searching mine, trying to detect the lie that was not that. Her sisters remained silent, watching us.

"Fine," she huffed. "I am interested in Lord Bryon; he is over there. The tall blond hair." I followed to where she indicated, spotting the Lord in question. Setting my empty wine glass down, I grabbed a full one.

"Alright, Ladies, time to relocate, let us go." The trio scrambled to keep up behind me. I situated us at an empty table where Lord Bryon would have a perfect view of us. I stood with my back to him, not wanting the attention drawn to me, and informed Ivy to stand in perfect view of him. I told her to make eye contact with him and immediately look away and then look at him again, feigning a shy smile. In the meantime, we talked idly, and I encouraged them to laugh and giggle at something funny.

It took only two dances until Lord Byron asked Ivy to dance. She gave me a startled expression as he led her to the dance floor.

"How did you know?" Greta asked incredulously.

"With all these mandatory social events occurring, I started observing people. It was a pattern I witnessed occur over and over again." I shrugged.

Lydia had not made an appearance, and I wondered what happened to her. It was not like her to miss a ball, even despite her earlier disaster. Although, stumbling upon her and another male proved she had to be doing okay. I didn't know why I cared about her attendance either. Dismissing myself from Lady Malevolent's daughters, I decided I was ready to return to my rooms. I had a minimal desire to dance with anyone, and something about watching Regalius dance with another bothered me.

Chapter Twenty-One

"Serenity, you have a letter from your family," Muriel said as she breezed through the room, holding the tray with a single letter. Somehow, through my countless hours spent in the personal royal library, had caused Muriel and I becoming close. Regalius had permitted the maid to be my personal handmaid if I required help. This must have also translated to her delivering my letters on top of my meals. Slowly, she moved her items into the unoccupied maid's room in my living space. I didn't mind her company; most times, I rarely vacated the space, and when I was here, she was not.

"You know you could just hand carry it to me?" I stated.

"My job entails a tray, then a tray it will be," she replied. Murial's comfort also became apparent as her shy nature became overshadowed by her saucy personality.

I took the letter off the tray, shaking my head at her. I flipped the envelope over and could see the handwriting was Amity's. Breaking the seal, I withdrew the four pieces of parchment. The first one was from Pulchra:

Serenity,

I miss you and hope you are dancing with all the princes and kings. Maybe some other princesses too? Quiet says you will not be coming back unless it is to visit us, but we can come to visit you. I want to visit you every day.

Love,

Pulchra

I crushed the letter to my chest. Oh my sweet baby girl. I flopped back in the chair, looking at the ceiling. I only hoped Quiet would raise Pulchra right, not that she had agreed to that, but neither did I at fifteen.

The next letter was from Father:

Dearest Daughter Serenity,

I hope you are enjoying your time in T'Lovoness at the Courting Seasons. Your Mother always enjoyed hearing about them when Queen Opal first began them. If she were still alive today, she would most likely be writing to you every day, begging for details. She would not want you to leave out one little thing that happens.

I, however, hope you send all those details to your sisters. I am certain they will be delighted to read everything that is happening. Although I am certain if you write to them about the library and all the time you spend in it, I am quite certain they will be disappointed. I will send every single one of their letters of disgruntlement if that is all you write about.

We did not discuss this before you departed, but it has been decided once The Courting Season has come to an end, you will travel back to Theorines to live. I have already begun the process of sending your items over. Quiet has been the one packing everything. If there are any issues, you will need to take it up with her.

Sending all my love,
Lord Honorable Lambert

I was fearful of how my items would be packed by Quiet's hand. I already knew my books would not be placed as lovingly into the chests as I would have liked. I would need to cross that river when I got to it within the month. The courting season was already coming to a close, and I was still not done with either library. At least I could beg Gideon to come back here to continue my research.

The next letter was scrawled in Amity's fine penmanship.

Serenity,

There have been minimal letters from you sent home. Hope all is well with you and the heir of Theorines. Please send Prince Gideon Orion my regards. I hope to not hear of a different future brother-in-law than the one that was agreed upon. You best behave yourself and not always be colluding in the library. There is more to life than books. Do not disgrace this family. There are still other children at Wyndmeer Manor in search of a spouse.

Sending love,
Lady Amity Lovanna

I snorted at my older sister's letter and folded it up. I braced myself for the last letter. Quiet had written quite a bit.

Nitty,

You will never believe it, but Amity says I too can attend The Courting Seasons in three years! I am ecstatic! You must tell me everything there is to know to help me have a hand up above the competition. With being a future Queen's sister, I am certain that will help me immensely in finding a match.

Do you sit around and have tea parties all day and then go directly into balls with dancing. Silly me, I know you probably are too busy with your nose in a book to even notice what is happening around you. Please tell me Prince Gideon Orion has taken you out on a few dances or midnight strolls in the garden. I am just swooning over the idea! Father says we can visit shortly after you are settled in at Theorines. I want to see ALL of the dresses King Ashborn had ordered made for you! I may just have to permanently borrow one or two.

What is Prince Finch Azrael like? I was thinking maybe two sisters could marry two Prince brothers? We could continue to live together; would that not be magnificent?

I shook my head, laughing at Quiet's enthusiasm. I had to remind myself she was only fifteen and completely boy-crazy. She probably was already beginning to fill Pulchra's head with silly Princess nonsense. I could already think of five dresses Quiet would love that I would most likely never wear again that she could permanently borrow. Flipping to the next page, I continued to read.

Now, onto the bad news. I am not sure how to write this delicate matter that will not end in tears . . . I was able to find out your stable hand's new place of employment after Amity let him go. Unfortunately, there had been a freak horse accident with a new skittish wild stallion. Theo took a blow to the head and has passed on. I am so sorry, Nitty.

I reread those sentences over again. No, no, no, no. This could not be. I reread the previous paragraph and then read again, but did not read any of her following paragraphs. I dropped the letter on my desk, staring ahead at the wall. There had always been a small part of me that felt bad for the way things had ended between Theo and me, but that had been out of my control. I had barely been gone for five months. The guilt choked me on when was the last time I had thought about Theo.

I sat there staring at the wall, lost in my mind. I was uncertain how much time had passed by as all the feeling I had left within me disappeared. When the walls felt like they were closing in on me in this room, I stood up abruptly, letting the chair fall backwards to the ground. I did not even bother to glance back at it as I raced toward the door leading to the hallway. I needed to be out of this room immediately. I realized my mistake of people seeing me as I ran for a secluded area. I could not handle the thought of returning to my rooms where those letters lay.

My eyes burned as I hurried down the corridor. People I passed were giving me wary sideways glances. I did not care about the appearance of my current state. I needed fresh air. My eyes found the room I had occupied with Lydia when Finch had made her pretend to be a duck. I grabbed the handle and wrenched the door open, relieved at finding it empty.

Slamming the door shut behind me, I ran to the couch, as tears rolled down my cheeks. Grabbing a throw pillow, I clutched it to my chest, bawling into the soft fabric. The heartbreak grew within me.

"Serenity Dear, why is someone like yourself crying?" Regalius's voice interrupted my spiraling thoughts. Why, of all people, did he have to be the one to find me. I knew I should have stayed in my room, but I felt suffocated in there.

"How did you know I was in here?" My voice was shrill, and I hugged the pillow tighter tucking my head into it. My body was shaking as I fought for composure against the tears instead of answering his question.

"I saw you run in here. I figured I would give you a few moments before I came to comfort you." I heard his footsteps approaching. I did not want him sitting with me. I just wanted him gone. Let me wallow in my own misery alone. I felt him sit down on the loveseat next to me, and I tried to scoot away from him. I kept a giggle to myself from the situation of being on a loveseat with him when I felt no romantic feelings for him.

I tried to scoot further away, but there was not much space, and I opted to lean as far away from him as possible. I felt his arm rest on the back of the chair, trying to encourage me to use him for comfort. I resisted.

"Come on, Serenity Dear, I will make you feel better," he promised.

"I am quite fine managing on my own." I sobbed.

His arm came down behind me as his hand wrapped around my right shoulder, pulling me into him. "oof!"

"What set you to crying? You are a lady of iron steel."

"It is none of your concern." The letter flashed in my mind. *Unfortunately, there had been a freak horse accident with a new skittish wild stallion. Theo took a blow to the head and has passed on.* Pain coursed through me fresh again. My throat burned as fresh tears pricked my eyes. I tried to keep them from falling with the rest, my teeth clenched as tightly together as possible, hurting my jaw to keep these tears from falling. I did not want Regalius to see me like this.

"That bad, huh?" His voice became soft as he gave me a slight squeeze into him. Maybe it was the warmth of his body, maybe the smell of smokey cedar and fresh linens, or just the comfort of another person, but the flood gates broken open once again. I clung to him, sobbing as the heartbreak racked through my body. He wrapped me in both his arms, pulling me tighter to him with a slight rocking motion back and forth.

When the sobs subsided, and the tears slowed, I took deep, steadying breaths, my lungs burning. Breathing in Regalius as I calmed my nerves to gather my wits about me. I took one last calming breath of Regalius's scent before I pulled away from him. His arms released me from their embrace, and I was not certain how to proceed from here.

"Thank you, Regalius, for comforting me." The least I could do is have manners. I was not a heathen. I had been raised properly.

"You are welcome. May I ask what caused the tears?" He pushed. The concern and worry I found in his eyes touched me. Something stirred within me that I felt compelled to trust Regalius.

"I received a letter from home," I started, "and it had some heart . . . distrauting news." I felt new tears threatening when I was about to say the word heartbreaking.

"Is everything okay? Did something happen with your family?" The concern in his voice was endearing. I gave him a pathetic excuse of a small smile.

"They are all fine. Marvelous, actually, as Father put it. My sister, however, is the one who gave me the bad news about. . ." I had to mentally steel myself to say the words out loud. "I guess I should tell you, before I had been sent here, before even my trip to Theorines, there was a boy back home that I loved." I felt Regalius stiffen at my confession.

"You love another?" He asked, treading lightly.

"I do, I mean, I did. . . Well, I guess I still do, but it does not matter anymore." Regalius tucked a strand of hair behind my ear while he listened. "I have been trying to let my heart mend these past few months."

"Why does it not matter anymore?" He pressed.

"Because . . . Because." The tears warmed my eyes. ". . . my older sister found out and fired him from the manor, and then he went to a new place to work and was killed in a freak accident. If we had been more careful, he would still be alive!" I sobbed. Regalius bundled me back up into his arms tightly. Consoling me through the sobs racking my body.

I blamed myself for Theo's death. If we had never been caught, he would still be alive today, and I would only live with the guilt of being placed in an arranged marriage. I was grateful that I would not be going home before permanently living at Theorines. Otherwise, I would have to endure every memory I shared with Theo.

"Do you think you could love another?" Regalius's voice broke my downward spiral of thoughts. I pulled back from him, wiping away my tears as I studied him.

"My heart was just shattered; do you not believe that is a bit insulting to ask, given my current state?" I snapped defensively. I felt the fire crackle within me, readying to pick a fight with him. A heart that shattered two months ago when my arranged marriage had pieces be ripped apart again.

"I am not asking about present times. I am asking about the future," he replied, unphased by my lashing out. I did not believe I could think of something like that so soon with raw pain.

"I do not know; my heart cannot handle the thought of letting another in."

"The season is almost over; do you want to return home?" It felt like Regalius was purposely pouring salt into my wounds.

"Not particularly, no, but I will not be returning home. I will be sent back to live at Theorines." I snapped, the words leaving my mouth before I could consider what I was telling him.

"Why would you be going back to Theorines?" He cocked his head to look at me. I clapped a hand over my mouth as I lunged away from him wide-eyed at what I had admitted out loud. "Serenity, why would you be going back to Theorines? Answer me." He gave me a leveled gaze.

"Because if neither Gideon, Finch, or I find someone during the courting season, Their Father and my sister have an agreement to arrange my hand in marriage to Gideon first, and I have deduced probably Finch second if Gideon would find someone."

"I knew something was up with you and the Theorines boys. I just did not know what it was. Is that what you want?" Regalius pushed.

"Gideon is nice and would be a good husband, but . . ." I trailed off, looking at the far wall.

"But?"

"I never knew my older sister was arranging a marriage for me. Initially it was with Finch, but then Gideon argued to be changed to him, and then somehow it turned into we should all get a shot of finding love at The Courting Seasons. Instead of looking for love, I took the opportunity to read through your historical section because

I never saw the value in seeking out love when I was still nursing a broken heart."

"Do you love Gideon?" I took my eyes off the wall and looked at Regalius; the concern he held for me was causing my heart to feel additional cracks within it.

"Not in that sense. He is a good guy, but I love him as a friend and nothing more." It was the first time I had admitted the truth out loud. The same could be said about my feelings with Finch, there was nothing more than the love of friendship for both brothers. Truly, I didn't believe there was room in my heart to give past Theo and now my heart would be buried with him. The warmth of fresh tears stung my eyes.

"Do you want to live in Theorines?" Regalius pushed; his needling questioning was unlike him. What was he getting at? He pulled me slightly back into his arms, comforting me as the tears brimmed my eyes.

"I really do not think I have much of a choice. The letters I received today indicate my items are being packed up and sent there as we speak." Everyone had a hand in controlling my future but myself. I would be shipped off to Theorines to live out my days as their future queen and then eventually as their ruler. The entire while as, I secretly grieved over my first love.

"Do you wish you had a free choice in the matter?" Regalius's questions were quite random and border lining what-if scenarios. Even as a prince, there was nothing he could do to help in this situation. He had his own troubles to worry about instead of meddling with mine.

"Yes, but would not anyone in my situation?"

"I suppose not. I could give you an option to not return to either place." He let his words fall between us. Everything about his manor remained serious that he was not joking about what he would be offering.

"What do you mean?" A small bubble of hope began rising within me.

"You could stay here instead." He offered. His closeness was startling apparent, from his body heat, but he didn't appear to mind.

"But how?" Confusion began lacing with the bubble of hope.

"Marry me, instead."

I blinked as a roar of whiteness filled my ears. The bubble popped. I did not just hear him correctly. "Regalius," I began, only to be cut off by him.

"Hear me out, Serenity. I am giving you the one chance in life to make a decision for yourself, and for your future. You can say 'no'. I am giving you that option to decide your fate." Did he not realize he would be giving up his future for me? The only time we had spent together was reading books or when he was saving me. Even during those times, there was no romance to be found. Did he not want to find the love of his life? There was nothing special about me for him to give up his freedom for.

I studied him, not detecting anywhere that he was joking. His offer appeared genuine. Weighing all my options until I finally sighed, conceding to hearing his offer. I nodded, indicating for him to continue.

"You do not want to go home and you have no feelings for Gideon. Why would you shackle yourself like that?" His questions didn't come off as accusatory, but I felt the need to defend myself anyway.

"Because I felt I had no other option, and while I do not hinder any feelings for Gideon, you out to know with that marriage proposal that I have been sleeping with him." I figured, if he wanted to retract his marriage proposal, that fact may give him the out. I didn't think I would be confessing my nightly rendezvous with another, but if he was going to be asking me appalling questions, then I might as well make him reconsider a few things.

"You have?" Regalius asked, shocked.

"Oh, come on, I have found you are up late and all rumpled. Do not tell me you love any of the people you are sleeping with." I pointed the finger back at him.

"Alright, so why are you sleeping with Gideon?"

"Because pretty much we knew we were getting engaged, and sometimes you just need the distraction from life," I defended.

"I concede, now as I was saying, you have no choice but to return to Theorines and visiting home will be painful for you. I need to find a future Queen. Despite all my endeavors, you have never been interested in my crown or wealth. Meanwhile, everyone else here is vying for my hand in marriage." He hadn't even paused in his thoughts about my confession. Apparently, a virgin bride was not the top priority for the T'Lovoness heir.

"Way to rub it in," I interrupted. He held up his hand to silence me.

"Serenity, I know they want my crown, not me. My birthright could be anyone. They would not care so long as they are married to this crown and what the future would hold for them." He inhaled a deep breath before letting out a sigh. It was evident, that this bothered him, and began to wonder how many used him for his position and did not get to know the real him. They saw the crown, his heritage, and their future by marrying him.

"Go on," I encouraged. He looked up at me.

"I am proposing you marry me out of friendship. I know you to be genuine and true. I will not push, force, or expect anything of you as my wife, just your happiness." He studied me, awaiting my response. I knew I would be jumping from one secret engagement to another, from one prince to another. Gideon would be a great husband, but I did not have a choice in that marriage. I could have free choice with Regalius's offer.

"What about children? T'Lovoness demands heirs," I countered.

"When you are ready, we will. I cannot promise not to lay with you. That is one of my duties as the future King to produce heirs." He did not appear ruffled by the notion. I gulped. He was offering me a bright future on a golden platter encrusted with jewels.

"You do not expect me to fall in love with you?" I questioned. I saw a momentary loneliness flash in his eyes before he blinked it away.

"I cannot force your heart, Serenity Dear. All I ask is for your friendship to rule together and to fulfill your intended duties as my Queen."

I searched his eyes, confirming he spoke the truth, making certain it was all not a trick. Taking a deep breath, I made my decision.

"Yes, Regalius, I will marry you."

PART 2

Chapter Twenty-Two

26 YEARS LATER

I BARELY NOTICED THE SUMMER BREEZE THAT CARESSED my skin, which blew through the opened ballroom windows, or the cats vying for my attention. They twined in between my legs beneath my dress, unaccustomed to me ignoring them. I stood in the middle of the wooden dance floor, freshly shined to a brilliance that I could see my reflection when I glanced down at it. It reflected the ceiling mural off it. Despite the bustle of the castle in preparation, I was the only one surveying last-minute details in here. The silence was almost a welcome compared to the hustle and bustle I had endured the last few months.

"Everything needs to be perfect," I whispered to the empty room. I could not allow a single mistake to occur, or it would be chastised for years to come. It had been a daring move to pause T'Lovoness's Courting Seasons until my eldest son and heir, Prince Rafael Baylor, turned twenty-five. After all, the founder and my late mother-in-law of the courting seasons started it right here in this very castle; it had been her pride and joy. While the event and its planning had never been my thing, it was Regalius who wanted to pause everything until our son was twenty-five. Involuntarily, I shivered from some of the

234

horrors my husband had revealed to me while he grew up. Far too many guests had tried to seduce and ensnare him when he wasn't of age to participate yet. Regalius would beg his mother to allow him to live temporary in a different home during the three months the season ran its course, but the late queen always denied him. Regalius wanted our children to grow up away from it all. He didn't want our sons to grow up feeling unwelcomed in their home while simultaneously being accosted by guests.

I never refuted Regalius's desire to pause the courting season or to shorten it when we resumed hosting it. I had been relieved at not having to host the event on my own. The mere thought of learning to be a ruler while simultaneously holding such an extravagant and tedious event overwhelmed me. Queen Opal refused to divulge details on how to plan and host her courting seasons. The only thing I was allowed to do was sit by her side while she hosted. Shortly after Queen Opal passed, King Lucien chose to pass the crown to his only son and then followed his wife into the afterlife.

It caused quite the scandalous outrage when Regalius and I announced we would be putting the event on hold for twenty years. At the time, I had rolled my eyes at how many parents were being melodramatic from the thought of having to figure out ways to match their children with a spouse. The Courting Seasons had made its attendees lazy and complacent. Many had become bitter at first, an entire generation being denied participation in the infamous T'Lovoness's Courting Seasons, a most highly anticipated yearly event. Reluctantly, they turned their focus to Kingdom Hayverton and Queendom Grewt'en for their courting seasons. While they weren't as large or extravagant, they appeared to satisfy the disgruntlement. From my conversations with Queen Fairness of Grewt'en, they had not been prepared for the abundance of guests that arrived when we didn't host one. Now her letters were filled with of curiosity about whether their attendance will decrease with us resuming again.

Silver hair caught my attention, and I found my eldest son

approaching me, his footfalls silent against the marble flooring. Rafael's blue eyes pierced through me as he tilted his head to the side, attempting to figure out what bothered me. There was no denying he was my son, with the matching cheekbones and nose. Instead of formal attire, he wore a loose white button-up with the top few buttons undone to expose his chest and black slacks with a few wrinkles.

"Mother, you have that indent in the middle of your forehead when you are worrying yourself senseless," humor laced Rafael's voice.

I shook my head, relaxing my face while silently telling him to not worry about me.

He turned his focus to the ballroom. Every flower spray and bouquet decoration had been strategically placed. I had chosen white and gold with a pop of color in the range of pink shades. New banners hung with our Kingdom's colors and history weaved within. Like the flooring, the gold had been polished until it glowed its reflections back. I wouldn't admit we had allowed things to become neglected, but I never understood the importance of working our servants into the ground with cleanliness through the years. The castle was far too vast for that amount of work. Ghosts of memories flitted to the forefront of my mind, reminding me of my first time here. Aside from the decorations and minimal renovations, the ballroom has remained unchanged all these decades.

"This ballroom is unlike you," Rafael stated in a mixture of unimpressed and awe. To anyone else he would have appeared bored and almost insulting in nature, but I knew after all these years he was merely putting on a façade. Somewhere along the lines, his expressionate and happy nature shifted to reserve with a neutral expression.

"I know, but it needs to be perfect," I sighed. The nagging awareness that for the next few weeks, I would need to be present in entertaining and unable to write.

"It does not even look like our home." His gravelly voice

commented. He could wear the most unamused expression, but the light in his eyes always gave him away. How much of a stranger did he feel in this room, and would he begin to resent the upcoming weeks. Guests would be pouring in any day and then his casual dressing ways would be put aside as they chased after him.

"No, it does not." I surmised. "This will be our life every summer after. After all, we had not paused this event for the return to be mediocre." I had been meticulously planning for the last five years, my time spent pouring over researching every single one of my late mother-in-law's documented events. It came to no one's surprise that Queen Opal had kept a personal collection of every book written about her courting seasons. What I found astonishing is she even collected the books that spoke ill of the event.

It was on one rainy day a few years back that I discovered Queen Opal's personal notes on planning each year's theme and events. I used this hidden book as my baseline for planning out each day's itinerary, tediously following her formula. Unlike her, I would have the itinerary delivered to each guest. I never shared my mother-in-law's delight in watching guests scramble to prepare for unannounced mandatory events.

"Why though?" He tilted his head to the other side. "Mother, you are a queen who hides herself away behind books. Not someone who puts on airs for others." He smirked at me.

I tried waving him off to which he ignored, and I rolled my eyes. My son was not wrong, but for this occasion, I had to become someone I was not. Both of my children had grown up within these palace walls, sheltered and protected; even on our trips to visit the royals at Queendom Grewt'en. While courting seasons still continued onwards in Kingdom Hayverton and Queendom Grewt'en, Rafael and Killien had never experienced it. They had not the faintest idea what was riding on this courting season.

Rafael knew his responsibilities; we had been preparing him to ascend the throne and claim his future title of King of Kingdom T'Lovoness. He, however, still had a great deal to learn when it came to keeping a monarchy in prosperity. Minimal doubt clouded my mind on the kind of ruler Rafael would be. He would excel at it like he did with everything else, even with his reserved mannerisms. Only a small part of me worried how the people would react to his lack of showing empathy, but Regalius would remind me of the benefits of it when it came to business dealings.

"Rafael, there are times when we need to do things that are expected of us," I began.

He responded with a droll look. While he may be twenty-five, there were still days he reminded me of a stubborn, sulking teenager.

"One of those things is to present to the other royals and all of our guests an image that aligns with being the –"

"—wealthiest and largest monarchy in the lands. *I know, Mother*," Rafael cut me off and crossed his arms. He had heard the speech numerous times in the last few years; between my planning of this event and his lessons, he had become quite familiar with the words that we drilled into his head.

"Then, if you know, why must you act this impudent?" I countered. Guests would begin arriving any day now. Glancing down at my dress, I found not a single wrinkle in sight, but I still smoothed the fabric out to chase away the invisible wrinkles. I had forgotten about the cats that had stopped brushing against my calves. They either were sleeping at my feet or had left the protection of my dress.

Searching around the ballroom, I realized there was not a mirror in sight to check my appearance. How utterly ridiculous, considering this was a room where multiple guests would be vying to look their best. Removing my hands from the fabric, I began patting my face and head, trying to feel for anything out of place. I didn't need to be caught unaware by guests and their first impression was me looking a mess.

My son's warm hand caught mine, worry reflecting in his eyes. "Mother, you have that indent forming again in between your brows. You look beautiful. I know my role to be the perfect prodigal heir."

"And?" I pushed, withdrawing my hand from his.

"And to find myself a wife that is not an heir herself."

"Excellent. Without further ado, I will do what I do best. Hole myself up in my library. In three nights, we will welcome all our guests in this room. In the meantime, your father and I expect you and Killien to be scarce around our guests until then." I gave him a pointed look. He nodded, and that was the end of our conversation.

Chapter Twenty-Three

THREE NIGHTS LATER, I STOOD IN THE FULL BALLROOM TO greet our guests. The once-empty room had become a sight to behold with all the bodies that filled it. The nagging fear of no one attending had disappeared, but it was replaced by the worry of everything that could possibly go wrong. We needed this event to spark stories that withstood the test of time in history. Not only had minimal expense been spared on our side, but judging by the extravagant outfits worn by the guests it had not been spared either. If it were not for the crowns and tiaras adorning the prince and princess's heads, I would not be able to depict them from the crowd of guests. I had momentarily considered opening the guest list up even further to be like the original Courting Games that allowed for all to attend. However, we did not have the capacity to hold everyone.

In my research, I was able to piece together information about the Courting Games. It astounded me that my late mother-in-law could even stomach reading about them. Let alone be inspired enough to create The Courting Seasons. The Courting Games had been barbaric. Participates battled for their spouse in an enclosed area. Everyone was dumped in with no rules, allowing death even upon royals. Back when, there were twenty-six monarchies instead of the six we have in the present day. From the little I could gleam, the enclosure was vast, with wooded trees and brush to hide within. However, the location has long since been lost to history. A few of the scrolls indicated it may be closer to where our neighbor, Kingdom Theorines, resided. I was basing this off the landscape and a few of the past fallen monarchies that had been loosely mentioned.

"Serenity-Dear, is something weighing on your mind?" Regalius broke my thoughts as he took his place by my side. Rafael entered the ballroom from the other side, and the sound of whispering and giggles filled the room. He glanced out to the crowd, taking notice, and gave them a flirtatious, confident smile. A few girls squealed in delight as I heard the snap of multiple fans opening to cool themselves while flirting with their eyes behind the fan. I had not prepared myself for the reaction of guests to the heir.

"Everything is fine, Regalius. I was simply thinking back to the history of the courting games," I replied while analyzing every little detail around the room, ensuring I did not need to send a servant on a last-second errand. I sighed to myself; Killien was nowhere in sight. We both knew he would struggle through this. If he could find a wife this year, he wouldn't ever have to attend any more of these events, but with how reclusive he was in nature, even that was a high demand.

"Interesting thing to be thinking about before we greet our guests." He chuckled as I amused him. He had over a quarter of a century of time to become accustomed to my constant obscure thoughts that mingled history with the present.

Our loyal servant, Maxwell, crossed the ballroom towards us. He was ten years younger, unmarried and unattached. His coppery locks had started becoming streaked with silver strands that matched my own a few years ago. His deep green eyes never missed a single detail in our daily lives as they currently scanned each guest he passed. Despite not being required of him, he trained regularly amongst the castle guards, claiming it to be for additional protection if something would occur to us. He took his job more seriously than we had ever expected, and based on his physical training, many guests turned their heads to stare at his sculpted biceps on display.

Regalius had hand-picked Maxwell to personally serve us when we wedded, and he has remained loyal ever since. I had attempted to play matchmaker a few times, but it never worked out. He was far too married to his job in more ways than one. A small part of me hoped that, with the additional guests and their servants in attendance here, he would find someone to have fun with. We only wished for the man who has served alongside us for almost thirty years to find love.

With Maxwell halfway to us, Rafael took his place next to me. We planned to stand the entire evening to greet our guests; I didn't want to appear lazy or sloth-like by sitting. Without a whisp of appearance from our youngest, there would be no point in delaying the introductions. Killien would stay hidden away. Eventually he would need to show his face. While the castle may be vast, it was now overfilled with guests. Even the servant's secret passageways wouldn't be able to hide him away.

"Your Highnesses." Maxwell dipped in a low bow to show his respect, the act catching me off guard momentarily. We had instructed all the servants to be on their best behavior and to act in what was expected of them as members of the royal staff. Normally, our servants were informal, even Maxwell, with how seriously he took his position. I preferred the informalness, which probably had more to do with my heritage than anything else. For the next few weeks, I would grin and bear every bow, curtsy, and polite respons until things could return back to semi-normal.

"Rise, Maxwell," Regalius replied casually, not breaking character.

"Shall I instruct everyone that you will begin the procession of receiving guests?" Maxwell asked. Unlike Queen Opal, I chose not to receive introductions based on societal status. It was a bold move, but the entire premise of The Courting Seasons was to have an equal chance of finding love, despite titles.

Regalius and I glanced at each other and nodded. We were ready.

"Let the fun begin," Regalius replied joyously. Which surprised me, considering his past experiences of the event, that he would be this excited. I chalked it up to his charismatic skills, something I did not possess. The King of T'Lovoness could befriend a rattlesnake within seconds. I, on the other hand, would be bit before I even noticed the snake in my path.

A couple of hours later and a blur of introductions that I had all but forgotten the names to the face stood a princess before us. I didn't need Maxwell's announcement to know Gideon's daughter stood before me. She had her father's long black hair and violet eyes; the only hints of her mother were in the girl's face shape, and that was where the similarities ended.

Princess Persamina Rowena of Theorines did not possess her mother's haughtier-than-though attitude; instead, she looked completely petrified to be here. While the other girls giggled and flushed to be introduced to Rafael, her red cheeks were from complete embarrassment and shyness. It shouldn't be any surprise, considering Lydia had kept her daughter locked away all these years. The reasoning remained unclear to us as to why the Theorines's royals would do such a thing to their own child. Princess Persamina Rowena was pretty in her own way, but it was evident she felt out of sorts amongst the rest of us royals. I surmised being in a room with this many people would be quite overwhelming for her. Her parents never prepared their daughter for what they were sending her off to by participating in the largest event of the year.

Rafael immediately caught on to the poor princess's anxiety and chose to toy with her. She had been the only princess in his life that he hadn't met prior to tonight, and he chose this opportunity to test her. My gaze roamed over the room where many guests were chattering amongst themselves as they caught up with the latest happenings in their lives. The Theorines's heir was an outsider to these people, and I wondered would she survive her time here?

As the princess held her extended long curtsy, she didn't react like any other in her same position. Instead of seething with rage, she appeared to be on the verge of tears. While her posture was impeccable, it wouldn't save her from the vicious vipers about. I searched the ballroom until I found the two individuals I had been seeking for.

The Ice Princess, Iryse Skyvian of Kingdom Hayverton, caught my attention, and when her eyes met mine, I gave a slight nod, indicating I wished to speak to her again. She nodded and turned her head to whisper to her twin, Princess Tearani Ryver. The Hayverton twins had been introduced to us earlier in the evening, but we were already well acquainted with them prior to tonight. Their kingdom neighbored ours to the north, and with us being their closest neighbors, their king and queen liked to have regular visits.

Despite them being twins, there were no similarities between the sisters. While Iryse received her title of Ice Princess due to her snow-white hair, cerulean-blue ice eyes, and pale skin, it was her sister Tearani whose personality should have received the title. Tearani's golden sun-kissed skin and dark violet eyes with black hair radiated warmth, but her monotone voice and lack of expression were void of it. She now stared at me with those violet eyes that were almost black as her younger sister parted through the crowd to me. I nodded my head in acknowledgement. She blinked unphased and nodded her head slowly back before turning her attention to people watch. While another Queen may have been offended by being dismissed by a princess, I found it humorous and very much like Tearani.

Bringing my attention back to The Theorines Princess made me grateful for how easy my courting season had been. If Queen Opal were still alive, all the royals would have been doted on by her, but their wings would've been clipped. She never allowed the royals in attendance to have any freedom while here. Simultaneously, I witnessed first-hand how cruel the guests could be to one another, sometimes even to me. Some of the bolder females would go to the extreme of attempting to weasel their way into my marriage bed with Regalius.

In our early years of marriage, when it was an open relationship, it was not uncommon for me to accidentally walk in on Regalius in bed with a courting season guest. Some of the girls would look affright while others smiled like they were stealing him away from me. The scared guests, I would give respect and leave, but for the hoity-toity ones, I would walk in and act like they were not the first, nor were they special. None of them realized at the time that Regalius and I had chosen to marry each other out of convenience and friendship. As long as we produce an heir to the throne, why should we be miserable together? However, that thought faded away rather quickly, considering I had become pregnant with Rafael within a few months of our wedding.

Looking at my husband, a swell of love surged through me. Slowly, our feelings grew from friendship to love. Somewhere along the lines, our relationship changed from open to only the two of us, or at least I assumed so. It had been about two decades, shortly after Killien had been born that I accidently stumbled upon him with someone else. Regalius feeling me stare at him, turned his focus on me. He smiled, causing the crinkles to form around his eyes. I smiled, forgetting we were not the only two in the room.

Our attention shifted when Rafael finally released Princess Persamina Rowena from her curtsy. She rose shakily, her face redder than before, with fresh tears stinging her eyes. Quickly, she glanced between Regalius and me, giving another curtsy while addressing us. I nodded in a dismissal response, and she attempted to escape but was only able to take a couple of steps when Rafael spoke out of turn.

"You are most welcome, Princess Persamina Rowena."

A multitude of emotions flashed across her face. She stood there frozen like a petrified rabbit, uncertain if she should stay or go. My eldest waved his hand lazily with a smile of ease that she was released from the conversation. She gulped and then disappeared into the crowd, only to pop up again as she headed to the wine table. She would need more than a drink to survive here.

"Rafael, please be nice to her," Regalius murmured. Our son gave his father a questioning look, surprised to be chastised. "Her father was one of my best friends growing up. We cannot help her upbringing, but it is evident she will be completely lost here amongst society. Do not make her time here even more difficult."

Rafael simply shrugged as he turned his attention back to the next lady being introduced to him by Maxwell. I turned to murmur to Regalius. "That was quite kind of you. Think he will listen?"

"He ought to if he knows what is best for him," my husband grumbled. His displeasement of Rafael's actions was evident, and it would be best if our eldest had made himself scarce after the greetings. Before I could think more about what was to come, the ice-princess bubbly voice broke through my thoughts.

"You wanted to see me, Queen Serenity?" Princess Iryse Skyvian asked warmly. Her friendly and bubbliness outshined everyone I knew, including my sister Pulchra and Queen Fairness of Queendom Grewt'en. Her beauty went further than her lovely appearance and I had yet to ever witness her show unkindness to anyone.

"May I request a favor from you?" I asked.

"Depends on the favor," she countered with ease. *Smart girl.*

"You know the princess from Kingdom Theorines?"

"The Tower Princess?" She tilted her head to the side, her eyes quickly scanning the room trying to find who we were talking about.

"Yes, Princess Persamina Rowena." I confirmed while correcting her from the nickname already floating about. The princess in question had reached the wine table, and a shadowy figure stopped at the table at the same time. Killien, dressed in all black, had finally made an appearance. Interestingly enough, he chose to show when he had a chance to encounter another royal similar to his own personality. My mind already calculating the possibilities.

"Would you perhaps befriend her?" I nodded my head in the direction as we watched Killien's hand entrap the scared princess's hand on the wine glass. She looked up at him, petrified as he glared down at her, uncertain what to make of the situation. Killien had kept himself holed up away from everyone for far too long. His shy, reserved nature had never been prepared for an event like this.

Princess Iryse gasped next to me, the scene holding both of our interests. I kept my face neutral, lest anyone else catch on to what we were watching.

"Oh, this is going to be fun!" She squealed with delight. I didn't take my attention away from the two who stood there staring at one another. My son looked like a wolf ready to terrorize the poor, scared rabbit who remained frozen in her spot. If it had been any other female, they would've already yanked their hand from his grasp. I had been asked many times over the years if I regretted naming my youngest Killien. The only thing I ever regretted was the stigmatism that came with his name due to my heritage. Many still believed I had named him Killien to protect his older brother against threats. I rolled my eyes at the notion every time. My youngest was far too soft and fragile for that kind of behavior.

"Have fun befriending," I commented. Without another word, The Ice Princess happily skipped across the room in an undignified fashion. The guests, unfamiliar with her ways, eyed her tiara suspiciously while they moved out of her way. I withheld my amusement, focusing back on Killien as he yanked his hand away from Princess Persamina Rowena. Reacting like she had burned him. He quickly grabbed another glass and stalked off, leaving the scared princess confused. She didn't have time to ponder the occurrence when Iryse began chatting with her.

Feeling someone staring at me intently, I looked to where the remaining twin stood. We locked eyes. Tearani Ryver blinked and slowly turned her head to watch her sister socialize with The Theorines's Princess. Most likely the frigid princess was trying to calculate what I was up to. Where she lacked warmth, she made up for with her protective nature of her younger twin. I had only caught on one rare occasion, Tearani smiling, and even that had been unbeknownst to her that I had witnessed her mask break.

I couldn't give my former lover's daughter many things, but if guiding the twins to be her friend could possibly detour away some of the vipers, then it would have to be gift enough. Between Tearani Ryver's formidable presence and Iryse Skyvian's bubbliness, the daughters of the second-largest Kingdom would be enough to protect the scared princess. She had been isolated enough, so why not experience life with some friends by her side.

Chapter Twenty-Four

"Tonight reminded me of what I do not miss," Regalius commented while undoing the top button on his shirt. We were back in our bedroom chambers, both completely exhausted after hours of introductions. I rolled my neck, attempting to ease some of the tension that had formed between my shoulders. I recalled the last time I felt this much tension was twenty years ago when Queen Opal still reigned. Despite Regalius's attempt to protect me from his mother, I still walked on glass shards when in her presence.

I laughed, removing an earring. "I am just grateful I removed the themes." Queen Opal had delighted in watching her guests scramble last minute to fit her mystery theme. No longer would T'Lovoness host a random berry courting season. I met his eyes in the vanity and raised an eyebrow. "Think anyone will attempt to climb into our bed this year?" I removed the other earring, earning me a laugh. At this point, we were old enough to be the majority of the attending guests parents' age. However, it never stopped the delusional, determined ones.

"If they are ever *so* bold, I will be certain to send them *your way*," he teased, and I scrunched up my nose at him. He probably was thinking back to the beginning of our marriage.

"I prefer that you did not."

Regalius crossed the room, and bending down, wrapped his arms around my waist, pulling me close to him. We stared at each other in the mirror. While we were the same, the image reflected back to us was of a couple that had aged. No longer were we the young newlyweds. Instead, we were now preparing to step down and give the throne to our son.

"A lot has changed since we were first wedded. We both agreed back then we could have our own separate lives and lovers as long as no bastard children came into play. We both upheld our agreement, and now I do not want anyone else but you." He nuzzled my neck.

"It sure took us a bit to fall in love with each other," I commented.

"I think it was accelerated with you already being pregnant with Rafael from that one night."

"Do not remind me." I tried to remove myself from his arms, but he just held me closer to him. My memory dipped back to that evening almost twenty-six years ago.

I knocked three hard raps on his door. The sound deafening as it echoed off the walls of the silent hallway. It was the dead of night. Everyone was in bed sleeping, most likely including the occupant of whose door I stood before. Inhaling deeply, I steeled myself for rejection as I released the slow and steadying breath. I was being ridiculous, but I wouldn't know his answer if I never asked.

In the quietness the sound of footsteps approaching on the other side of the door could be heard. I prepared myself for the servant that would open the door to greet me, I believed his name was Maxwell, but my nerves had me questioning everything. The entire trip here, I had been reciting in my mind what I would tell the servant. A simple sentence, really. I need to speak to The Prince. Seven words that I had been playing on a loop with every step. They were seven simple words, but yet my stomach was in knots. I forced my hands to stay bunched at my sides lest I fiddle with anything to give away my nervousness.

I planned to lay myself out to The Prince; my nerves frayed if he would accept or reject my request. I was prepared for everything I planned to say, what I had not prepared for was Regalius, who was the one opening the door. He stood in a robe with his bare muscular chest on display. Our surprises mirrored one another.

"Serenity Dear?" He asked, confused, his brow furrowing.

"I-I was not expecting you to answer the door," I sputtered. My mind backpedaled on how to proceed and jump forward to my proposal. How was I going to drop my request smoothly?

"I dismiss my servants in the evening. I like my privacy," he answered, crossing his arms over his chest. His eyes roved over me, trying to assess why I was standing at his door.

"Oh, that makes sense. . . May-may I come in?" I glanced past him to his chambers lit with candlelight, not seeing anyone else, before looking back at him for confirmation. He nodded, standing to the side and allowing me to pass through. The door clicked shut softly behind me. All the courage I had been mustering vanished, and I kept my back to him. I tried to gather an ounce of strength as I focused on the details of his room.

The expanse area was decorated with dark wood furniture draped in T'Lovoness's blood-red colors and gold threading. Very minimal of the T'Lovoness's blue could be found in the room, which I found odd; even the carpet was blood red. Despite the large space, it was cozy and held an air of power about it. I believed if I stumbled upon his room without him in it, I would still know it was his.

"What brings you to my rooms, Serenity-Dear?" He asked. The sound of his weight leaning against the door filled the silence. I had played out every scenario possible of me coming her, except for him opening the door. I could only hope, the words that came out of my mouth sounded like the ones I had practice. Keeping my back to him, I took another deep breath.

"Is your offer still on the table?" My voice didn't shake, but I hid

my balled fists within the folds of my dress. I steeled myself for his rejection while a tiny voice whispered with hope that he would accept. His weight shifted against the door, and I forced myself to take another even breath.

"And which offer would that be?" Amusement crept into his voice.

"The one where you promised to help me forget him." I clenched my teeth. I felt my cheeks heating from the admission. He had told me after we announced our engagement to his parents that he would never push me for sex, but if I came to him willingly, he would help ease my heartbreak. I had thought I made peace with not having a future with Theo. However, upon receiving that letter from Quiet, my heart shattered. I supposed I had prepared myself to end up with someone else, but I hadn't protected my heart for Theo's death. Although I didn't think anything would lessen my grief.

My resolve finally broke as I stood there in his bedroom. The Courting Season had ended but a day ago, and now our wedding was looming near. I questioned if I had made the right choice in agreeing to marry Regalius out of friendship and convenience; maybe I was being rash. Until now, the thought of backing out hadn't crossed my mind. No, I was here because he offered, and I wanted to start a future together on a positive note. After all, heirs would be required of us, so eventually, we would need to get this over with. I was making it out to be a chore and realized I was overthinking this.

Regalius pushed his weight off the doorframe, the sound of his footfalls muffled slightly from the red carpet. My heart picked up, dreading his rejection, but instead, his arms wrapped around me, pulling me close to him. The heat of his bare chest pressed against my exposed back sent a zing coursing through me. His head came down and softly kissed me in the crook of my neck and shoulder, sending another zing crackling through me. Every hair on my body rose from the sensation, and he yanked my hips firmly against his. Giving my neck a peck, he then trailed his tongue up to my right ear, where he nipped my earlobe. I shivered from the feeling.

His hands skimmed my body until he held both of my breasts.

Giving a slight, firm squeeze, his thumbs massaged circles on my nipples through the fabric. A small moan left my lips, my head falling back to rest on his shoulder. I turned my face away to give him better access while he kissed and nipped along my jawline. His hands abandoned my breasts to skim to the back of my dress.

He didn't stop his nips while blindly undoing my corset. The fabric becoming looser with every few inches undone, allowing my breathing to come easier. Without warning, he pulled away from me, and I stumbled, trying to catch myself. He caught me, and our eyes locked, causing my heart to beat faster. Slowly, he righted me and, without a word, lifted the dress over my head. He tossed it on the back of a nearby chair and didn't waste any time by removing my slip dress as well. I stood before him in only my panties. The mirror across from us reflected the raw desire emanating from Regalius's gaze locked on mine.

He wrapped his left arm around me, possessively cupping my right breast while his other hand's fingers moved down my hip to my pantie line. He didn't hesitate as he pushed his hand into my panties, delving his fingers through my curls to find my clit.

His eyes remained locked on mine as he watched me while he rubbed his fingers back and forth, sending pleasure through me. I pushed up against him, wanting more, and a dark smile graced his lips. His fingers slid past my clit and to my entrance, where he played with me. Another moan left me as he continued to taunt me.

"Place your foot on the ottoman," he murmured in my ear. I quickly obeyed, my weight shifting between my left foot and pressing against his body. The angle gave us both a better view of what he was doing. Watching him tease me neared me to the breaking point of begging, and I nearly cried out when he pushed two fingers in.

My hooded eyes met his molten ones in the mirror as he withdrew and pushed his fingers back into me. My breathing came out in quick pants as he picked up speed. The hilt of his hand grinding against my clit, sending sparks of pleasure. I moaned again, closing my eyes as I leaned all my weight against him.

"Bedroom now," he growled, removing his fingers from me; he guided me to turn around to face him. I felt the warmth of his breath from how close our faces were, my nipples barely grazing his chest. With his hands firmly holding me, he led me step by step to the entrance of his bedroom door. Candlelight flickered on the walls in the room, but I paid no attention to anything else in the room; my focus stayed solely on him.

"Get on the bed," he ordered. I obeyed without complaint, climbing onto the massive, soft bed. I laid on my back and watched him drink me in.

"Spread your legs wide and bend your knees up, feet firmly on the bed." I followed his instructions, feeling beyond exposed. "Play with your nipples. Pinch them."

Pinkness graced my skin as I obeyed. I had never touched myself this way before, and I pinched them slightly, testing how it felt. His gaze did not miss a single thing I did.

"You. Are. So. Beautiful." He crawled onto the bed, placing his head between my knees. While I lay completely naked, he still wore the robe, keeping the rest of his body a mystery to me. My heart was racing, uncertain what he would do next.

Regalius lowered his head; he wouldn't dare... would he? He pressed a kiss against my clit, sending another zing racing through my body. I arched into him as he sucked my clit into his mouth. His teeth grazing slightly with a nip and I shattered apart unexpectantly. I had never cum this quickly before, the pleasure coursing through me. He didn't let up as he continued to suck, causing wave after wave of pleasure to run through me. I moaned loudly, conflicted about whether I wanted to grind my body against his mouth or pull away. I begged him to stop when I felt the pleasure beginning to build again, becoming too much. He didn't listen to my wishes, ignoring me as he sucked hard, his teeth continuing to graze ever so slightly. The bud becoming more sensitive to each graze had me hissing with another bucking arch in a futile attempt to escape. Tears formed in my eyes, but he wouldn't release me.

"Regalius! Please stop! It is too much!" I released my nipples, unaware of how tightly I had been pinching them. My hands, instead, dug into the sheets, clutching them tightly.

He chuckled darkly against my clit, sending more vibrations of pleasure. My thighs clenched his head tightly enough that I thought I might break it. Tears continued to stream down my face when he finally released his mouth from my clit. I was left a shaking mess. His tongue flicked across my clit, jolting my body upright from the pleasure. He repeated the action three more times, and I sobbed his name.

Regalius shifted his weight, pulling himself up and braced both his hands on either side of me. Lowering himself, he kissed me. I tasted myself through panted breaths. I let go of the sheets and wrapped my arms around his neck to bring him closer to me. I needed more of him. I wanted him to erase every memory from me. I wanted to forget about the boy who broke my heart with his death, and only remember the man I would spend the rest of my life with.

The head of his cock pushed at my entrance, and I shifted myself to help him. I felt the stretch from his thickness, not accustomed to his girth. He paused, breaking the kiss to watch me in the candlelight, allowing me to relax when he sensed me tensing, bracing from his size. He pulled out slightly, giving me momentarily pause before thrusting all the way in. I yipped from the unexpectedness. He settled there, my sensitivity feeling every little bit of him.

He created a rhythm, thrusting in and out slowly. Watching me as I moaned from the ripples of pleasure he brought. His left hand trailed down to my thigh, gripping it; he hiked it up to give himself better access. I moaned from the extra depth the angle gave him.

Lowering his lips back to mine, he kissed me, picking up pace. His pelvis grinding against my clit, bringing upon more waves of pleasure. His movements became rougher, and he moaned into my mouth. He pounded into me three more times before collapsing onto me, breaking the kiss. He nuzzled my neck. We both were panting heavily. Our sweaty bodies were breathing in rhythm together, and I was coming back down from my out-of-body experience.

"Regalius," I breathed his name.

"I know," he stated. He shifted slightly to roll off my body, curling up beside me, and nestled me into him. I let go of a sigh. I was not ready for sleep; and I wouldn't mind taking a bath before bed. But right now, in this moment, I was content. Regalius shifted, pulling me even tighter to him as he kissed my neck, nuzzling me. My heart warmed at the tenderness. This was everything I had been searching for and everything I had been wanting. I just had not known it until this moment. If it was like this for the rest of our lives, I would be forever grateful for this man.

"I never did inquire how many lovers you have taken over the years," Regalius stated, breaking my thoughts from the memory of our first time together. He still had me wrapped in his arms as we rocked back and forth.

"Is that something of importance right now?" I cocked an eyebrow at him. Where was all this coming from? He never cared before we were married, never cared as our sons were growing up. Why did he care now?

"I suppose it is not important, but I am curious, considering how secretive you have been all these years. I never once stumbled upon you with anyone else."

"There was never a doubt in my mind who sired our sons if that gives you a peace of mind," I commented. He double-blinked, letting my reply sink in. The rocking slowed until it came to a halt altogether.

"Are you telling me you have never taken anyone else to bed since our engagement?" We both knew he could not say the same thing.

"Aside from the few dalliances I had with my former betrothed before our engagement, there has been no one else. I was far too busy researching to notice or give anyone else the time of day." His arms squeezed me tightly to him.

"Oh, Serenity-Dear, I am sorry if I caused you misery with—"

"—Do not be. We had an agreement. The only *misery* you caused was me accidentally stumbling upon you and your lovers at various times. That was quite awkward." Too many memories I had attempted to forget fluttered to the forefront of my mind. All the positions, places, and females that I had found Regalius in.

"If you wanted to sample any of the princes or lordlings this season, I would understand, given my past." His voice was apologetic.

"Are you implying for me to go out there and have a tumble in the sheets with someone the age as our sons?" I gave him an amused smile.

"Might teach you a few new tricks in the bed," he joked, causing me to laugh.

"Are you saying my charms are becoming old and dusty?"

"Like the books you love to read."

We broke out with laughter, and I leaned back into him, the love I had for him coursing through me.

"I probably will not find anyone, but I will keep the idea in the back of my mind."

"How about, for the time being, I just focus your attention back to me." He kissed my neck, indicating what he wanted to come next.

Chapter Twenty-Five

The following evening, my family relaxed in a private parlor with the three royal children of Queendom Grewt'en. It had only been day one of the official events, and as I gazed around the room, it appeared we were all exhausted. I had specifically chosen this room for its calming aesthetic; the walls had been painted in sage green, with the furniture ranging from navy to sky blue. Even the carpet was a deep green, adding to the comfort that cold floors could not provide. As an interior room in the castle, there were no windows. Instead, they were replaced with calming landscape paintings that hung throughout the room.

"You have outdone yourself, Serenity," commented Queendom Grewt'en's heir, Princess Regina Isadora. Titles had long since been discarded between the members in this room.

"Thank you. Your mother has the letters to prove how much I relied on her advice for things." I laughed, and took a sip of my chamomile tea, enjoying the warmth the mug provided. It may be summer, but the coziness was needed as I curled my feet up underneath me in the oversized chair. Nothing about my posture was queen-like, but here, I needn't worry. Upon meeting her mother,

Queen Fairness, we had become quite close friends. As the years passed, our families often visited one another, and her children had become Regalius and my adopted nieces and nephews.

Regina sat across from me, sharing one of the deep plush loveseats with Rafael. Her long red hair fell in loose waves after a day of being styled back in braids. She had swapped the elaborate long dress from earlier that shifted colors from a pastel mint green to a bold grass green in the lighting to the short silk lavender dress that revealed her long legs. The top portion only held up by two thin straps, revealing an ample amount of cleavage. She brushed her calf up against Rafael's innocently. It had been no secret the longstanding crush she had on him. Unfortunately, for Regina, it would be an unfulfilled love as they were both heirs to their own monarchies.

This was probably the only place The Grewt'en heir was able to relax and be herself. As a child, she had been bossy and took on the responsibilities of being a parent and adult to her younger siblings. Slowly, through the years, I observed that bossy confidence shift to doubt in her teenage years. Now, at twenty-three and nearing the time for her to take over the throne, her anxiousness had already begun to reveal itself today as she lashed out at other guests. Her main target was the Theorines's princess, which I suspected was due to the additional attention Rafael had given her last night.

"Fairness had me often reviewing your letters and questioning how I would respond," Regina replied with a proud smile that was twinged with a bit of cockiness.

"Pretty soon, it will be you planning Grewt'en's yearly season," her brother, Montgomery, teased. He delighted in keeping her ego in check. Regina's smile faltered at the realization, her eyes widening slightly as she leaned into Rafael for comfort. My eldest draped his arm over her shoulders and gave Regina a slight squeeze. While she had romantic feelings for him, I had never witnessed a sign of those feelings being requited. If anything, he kept her at a distance in the friend zone.

The second eldest Grewt'en royal, Prince Montgomery Victory, lounged with his leg crossed over the armchair positioned between Regina and Killien. His black hair layered in a stylish well put together way, unlike my youngest son's black hair that shagged downward. The two males sitting beside one another at a distance could pass more as brothers than Killien and Rafael could. Killien, being two years older, had behaved as an older brother to Montgomery in their younger years. Somewhere along the lines, it shifted when Montgomery's suave nature appeared, and Killien became reclusive. The former years must have stuck with Montgomery as he always chose to be near Killien.

Montgomery sipped his whiskey with a devilish smile, his flirtatious silver eyes peering at me over the rim. From the letters his mother had written and my own observations, my nephew already had a list of lovers who could fill this room alone. His charismatic nature, radiating off him, was a magnet for anyone interested in a tussle in the sheets. The prince had gone from a suave boy to the twenty-one-year-old who held the swagger of a king. I fully believed he had skipped the awkward teenage years. Despite all that, he still showed kindness to Killien, who sat next to him with a scowl. No one had forced Killien to attend, but his behavior cried otherwise.

The last Grewt'en royal in attendance, Prince Percival Chivalry, sat between Rafael and Regalius in a chair with perfect posture. The nineteen-year-old, blue-eyed, blond-haired prince was deep in conversation with my husband about monarchy politics. The third eldest Grewt'en royal would have made a wonderful ruler with his attention to detail and knowledge. Unfortunately, the hand he had been dealt would never allow for it. While his personality came off to the majority as indifferent, it was because he found the conversation lacking and the individual simple-minded. Percival was rather bright for his age, and instead of partaking in typical teenage mischievousness, he strived for a battle of the wits. If Regina was smart, she would keep him on her royal council to help her reign.

Percival differed from me in the sense of being a book dragon, but he thirsted for knowledge. Quite often he would arrive to our home unannounced to simply visit my library. He knew I had new books continuously arriving to add to my ever-growing collection. I had gotten into the habit of setting the new books aside until he had a chance to peruse them before the books found their permanent home on my shelves. Often late into the evenings, I would find myself in a lively discussion with Percival about various historical topics. He regularly helped me with my research and while he didn't know it yet, I would be crediting him when my book was finished.

"I am certain Regina will do just fine," I replied, giving the Grewt'en heir an encouraging smile. She smiled meekly back at me. "Besides Grewt'en's season is already established, all she will need to do is take over with some minimal guidance from Fairness."

"I suppose." Montgomery leaned back and took another sip of his whisky.

"Why do you even care?" Rafael asked, the bite of suspicion lingering as he pulled Regina closer to him. "You are going to seduce everything that you can crawl into bed with."

Montgomery let out a bark of laughter, not even slightly offended by Rafael's words. Killien's scowl deepened as he leaned slightly away from Montgomery and the noise he produced. Even Regalius and Percival paused in their lively discussion to take in the scene. Percival rolled his eyes and brought Regalius's attention back to the conversation at hand. Regina curled her lip as she nestled deeper into Rafael for comfort. I found the entire situation comical, reminding me of my years living at home in Wyndmeer manor.

"Come on, Killien." Montgomery leaned over his chair to Killien's space and wrapped his arm over my youngest son's shoulder, yanking the scowling prince to him. "Let us both go seduce anything that will allow us to crawl into their beds." Montgomery continued to laugh in delight. Killien attempted to untangle himself, but Montgomery wouldn't release his hold. Killien looked him up and down as if he had never seen the prince a day before in his life.

I tried to smother the laugh, attempting to escape by covering a hand over my mouth. I was not unaware that the once children were now all consenting adults in this room. Nor would I be naïve enough to not know the happenings that occurred during the courting seasons, even with my children. I highly doubted Montgomery would be able to convince Killien to be a wingman. My eyes connected with my eldest, and he gave me a slight glare with a scowl that matched Killien's. There had never been signs of Rafael flirting with anyone. He had either been secretive or never engaged with anyone. Something that would need to change for his future and the future of this Kingdom. I had a minimal desire to arrange a marriage for my eldest, let alone it be a mockery that T'Lovoness's courting seasons proved fruitless for the heir.

"Mum," Killien called out to me hours later. Everyone was departing from the parlor to retire for the evening, and I paused. I didn't miss the way Regina rolled her eyes at my youngest. Somewhere along the lines, she had lost her friendliness to him. Long gone were the days she was making him join in on tea parties as she now treated him like a pariah. Regalius raised an eyebrow, and I shooed him away to indicate that I would handle it and talk to him later. When it was only Killien, and I left in the room, he waited until the door was clicked shut to begin speaking.

"Mum, I need to talk to you," his voice twinged with nervousness. He feet shuffled, and he looked to the ground, unable to make eye contact. At one point, my sole mission was to break him of the habit. While it was not as bad as it used to be, the nervous tick still persisted. I would chase him around the castle, attempting to help him conceal his agitation. When he started avoiding me a few years back, I gave up.

"What is it, Killien?" I laced my voice with tender, concern so he wouldn't feel like I was attacking him. With my youngest, the range of what he would want to talk about could be from anything to everything. The nervous tick would be present even if he asked for a special dessert recipe for the castle staff to make or to go riding horses. The evening conversation had been relaxing after the initial teasing; the discussion of memories and what was in store for this season was the main center of focus. I ran through every detail of tonight to see if anything from it would cause Killien the need to talk.

"Can I go live in the summer home until this courting season business is over with?" He continued shuffling, still not meeting my eye. His shaggy black hair partially covered his face, and what most would deem as a scowl was him trying to mask his shyness.

"May I ask why?" Concern washing over me. Prior to the season beginning, I made sure to have many discussions with Killien on what to expect and how he was expected to act.

"I hear people whispering that they believe I will kill someone. Why did you name me Killien?" He finally looked up at me, his eyes rimmed red, filled with sadness. My heart completely breaking for my son, and I crossed the distance to wrap my arms around him, pulling him into a tight embrace. I could prepare him for everything, but not for how guests would treat him, especially not at this velocity.

"Ignore them sweetie. We named you Killien because your father and I liked the name. We also knew your older brother would need someone strong by his side."

"But you were from Grewt'en, where names hold power," he tried to argue, the strain entering his voice. He attempted to pull away from me, but I did not allow him to get far.

"I am, and that is the belief of the people from Grewt'en. However, do you think I am serene like my name indicates I should be?" I pulled back for him to see my face, and I raised an eyebrow.

"I think you try to be serene but fail," he stated matter-of-factly, not even trying to soften the blow.

"Oof, thanks." I laughed from the jab, and a timid smile graced his lips.

"Sorry, Mum." He tried to shuffle his feet while still in my arms.

"Do not be sorry. I am giving you an example of what my name means and what I am not. When I was younger, I wished my parents had named me Malicious, Prissella, or Solitude just so I could be left alone to read and research."

"Malicious and Prissella does not fit you mum; Solitude would be a better fit." Killien pulled out of my arms, and I let him as he absently stared at the paintings on the wall. His focus mainly on the large landscape with a grassy knoll with a cottage on top, wind blowing through the grass blades on a clear summer day.

"How about you talk to the princess from Theorines. She appears to be nice," I encouraged. I watched her at tea this morning; due to her unfortunate fate, she had ended up at a table with Regina and the Shediwark princess. I never understood Regina's decision to hang around Princess Olivia Jade, but the Shediwark girl trailed behind my niece. I had found myself thinking Princess Olivia Jade to be quite rude and daft, but I kept my opinions to myself. For Princess Persamina Rowena to be stuck at a table with those two, her timid and shyness became apparent as her shoulders curled in on herself. The excited nervousness she had entered the room with was replaced with complete fear as she attempted to shrink herself to be forgotten. From Montgomery's comments earlier, I believed the Theorines's princess would be an excellent person for Killien to gain some confidence from.

"I think she is scared of me too." His shoulders slumped.

"Oh? Why do you say that?"

"I trapped her hand in a wine goblet last night, and I forgot to let go. She looked like she was ready to cry and run away." He paused and then continued. "Then today, she collided into me crying. I think she felt obligated to tell me to call her Mina." He scratched the back of his head.

"Why is that?" I pressed, needing to know more.

"I told her to call me Knox, and she immediately said to call her Mina, I had been gripping her arm on accident, and she still looked scared." I tucked away the knowledge of her preferring to be called Mina.

"If I had to wager, I bet she is quite frightened to be here. After all, she had been locked up her entire life. Probably being surrounded by everyone and all these interactions is overwhelming. She probably could use a friendly face around here." I encouraged. Mina had not attended any of the other events on the itinerary today, and I wondered if she would be attending any tomorrow or in the near future.

"I doubt she would want my company," he replied, disheartened.

"How about this," I began, taking a deep breath knowing what I would be offering. "Try being friends with her, and if it does not work out, you can go live in our summer home until the end of the season." I dangled the offer in front of him, but my sneaking suspicion was that once Killien befriended Mina, he wouldn't want to leave as readily.

"You promise?" Hope filled his voice as he looked at me, trying to detect the lie.

"I promise, but you need to try Killien." I leveled my gaze at him. "And please remember she has been locked away from everyone her entire life. She most likely will be a bit skittish and shy. It's entirely possible she may not respond normally to things." I needed to emphasize these points. Killien had difficulties navigating normal situations, and I was forcing him to potentially respond on the quick to the Theorines's Princess. If this had been Rafael, I wouldn't have worried as much. No, my eldest, I would be admonishing for toying with the poor girl.

"Yes, Mum," he replied with hope, but I didn't miss the small bit of protectiveness that had entered his voice. Determination spread across his face, and my heart swelled. I wish I could say that I didn't know either of my sons this well, but Killien had always been far too softhearted and overly protective of anyone or anything that was treated as an outcast. It had not gone unnoticed how servants and guests would give him a wide berth while growing up. Maybe I was playing a little matchmaker in hopes that the Theorines's heir would be the girl for him.

Chapter Twenty-Six

Four days later, I cursed myself. Why did I make any of these events mandatory for me to attend. Would anyone truly notice if I didn't make an appearance? I had left the wretched needle-work hour and was now occupying the exterior room dedicated to Kingdom Hayverton. In T'Lovoness castle, each monarchy had a room that honored them with their respective colors. A previous royal had designed it this way to make guests feel welcomed among their home colors.

Kingdom Hayverton's colors filled the room with gray granite flooring that rose up to slate light blue walls. Navy rugs were found under all the furniture, which ranged in a mix of the three colors. Sunlight shined through the stained glass window that depicted a rendition of Hayverton's castle.

I had free time between now and the evening meal and took the opportunity to invite the Hayverton twins to meet with me here. A soft knock sounded on the door, but they didn't wait for an invitation as Tearani glided in with a gray wrapped gift in her hand. Iryse breezed in behind, closing the door after her.

Tearani's face gave nothing away as her dark violet eyes bore into me. She didn't even glance around the room. She wore a two-piece burnt-orange dress that complimented her sun-kissed skin. While the bottom portion of the dress was long with silk and tulle, there was a slit on both legs that were exposed with each of her steps. A golden circlet wrapped around her upper right thigh. With her naval exposed, it showed a blood ruby piercing. The top portion of her silk dress dipped down in a sweetheart neckline and sleeves that lazily fell off her shoulders. Aside from the naval ring, the only other jewelry in sight were the tear-drop blood rubies adorning her ears. Her brown-black hair was straight, with an elaborate tiara upon her head, encrusted with blue-stones. She took her seat across from me.

Iryse walked as if she was made of the breeze herself, the way she flowed with each step. Her silver-white dress merely amplified her nickname of Ice Princess with the slate light blue thread weaving scalloped designs through it. The bottom of the dress's front stopped at her knees and became longer until it trailed the floor behind her. It cinched her waist in while being strapless. Unlike her sister, she had bracelets on both wrists, a large aquamarine pendant around her neck, and matching earrings. Her hair was loosely styled up with soft white waves flowing down her back, and one coil hung over her left shoulder. She sat next to Tearani and automatically picked up a mixed berry pastry, taking a bite without invitation.

"Thank you both for agreeing to come," I began.

"It is our pleasure," Tearani responded in her monotone voice. She held up the present that I suspected was a book based on its size. "This is for your collection." She leaned forward to place the book on the coffee table between us.

"Thank you, I will open it later." I left the book where she rested it; I could've opened it now, but I had more pressing matters to discuss. "Is the season treating you well?"

"I am having a blast," squealed Iryse, not bothering to conceal her excitement.

"That is excellent to hear. Is anyone capturing your interest?" I leaned in slightly, unable to contain my smile.

"It's still too early to tell." She gave me a secretive smile. I shifted my focus to the other twin.

"And how about you, Princess Tearani Ryver?"

"The season thus far has been quite comfortable. What is it you wish to discuss, Queen Serenity?" She blinked. Direct and right to the point.

"I was curious how Princess Persamina Rowena is adjusting after requesting your assistance?" If the eldest Hayverton twin did not want to mince time, then I wouldn't either. I had one encounter with Mina in the rose garden, where she was alone petting my beloved castle cats. The conversation had been brief but pleasant.

"I haven't really seen her." Iryse squirmed in her chair.

"The Theorines's princess barely attends events," Tearani added, swooping in to save Iryse's guilt.

"That is something, I had noticed as well." I tapped my finger to my lips. "She had attended the ball the other night where she danced with both of my sons." I dropped the nugget on the table, waiting to see how they would react.

"We were not in attendance." Tearani held my stare, challenging me to dispute her statement. I couldn't and we both knew it.

"Well, let us hope in future events, it will all work out." I leaned back and clasped my hands together to rest on my belly. I refused the urge to twist or bite my bottom lip from frustration. We were nearing the end of the first week of the season, and I worried that I would be shipping Killien off to the summer home soon. "Is there anything else of note, I should be concerned about?"

Tearani rattled off various pairings she had observed over the last few days with Iryse chirping her opinions on the couplings. Neither twin revealing who they were interested in. I'm not certain when it occurred, but somewhere along the years, it had become common for me to swap information with the twins. I didn't believe Tearani trusted me much, but she kept her suspicions to herself. Iryse, on the other hand, delighted in sharing and receiving any juicy gossip. It was the main reason I had chosen these two to get close to Mina, even if they were currently failing the matter. Between Iryse's friendly disposition and Tearani never missing anything, it was the perfect match.

When the twins had left, I barely waited for the door to click shut as I dove for the gift that had been taunting me the entire time. I ripped the blue paper off it and held the freshly bound book, the title depicting it was of Hayverton's history. I opened to the front page, and in perfect, neat penmanship, Tearani had written:

Queen Serenity,
I had one of our personal collections of royal historian books copied and bound for you. You are now in possession of the second book to ever exist of these subjects. Please do with that as you will.
-T

Eagerly, I flipped to the next page but closed the book quickly. No, I needed to head to my personal library otherwise I would be in this room all evening with any guest able to stumble upon me. I did not wish to be disturbed with this forbidden information. Maybe it wasn't to that extreme, but if there was only one other book that contained this information, it must be important. Only a small nagging in the back of my mind questioned why Tearani would offer me a book like this, but I suppose the answers would be revealed soon enough. If not, maybe it would clear up some confusion I had on certain events that had never been properly recorded in Hayverton.

I left the room dedicated to Kingdom Hayverton and started my travels to my destination. I debated slipping into one of our private rooms that would lead me to a servant's passageway to stay out of sight when movement caught the corner of my eye. Montgomery had a lordling son pressed up against a pillar, kissing the male deeply. Neither of them paying me much mind as I passed by, not wanting to interrupt. They would find a room without me needing to state the obvious. It had not been the first coupling I had encountered in my travels around the castle and it certainly wouldn't be the last. The loud moan that escaped from the couple had me glancing back before I could help myself. Montgomery was watching me and smirked against the lordling's lips when our eyes met. I let him see my eye-roll and walk away to the sound of his muffled laugh. It was a good thing he was not my son and heir; he would be giving me a run for all I was worth. My already silver hair would be completely white from the amount of stress he'd give me if he was mine. Even as an adopted nephew, he stressed me out. He would walk out of this courting season, breaking more hearts than I cared to know about and hopefully with no pregnancies.

The rest of my travels were less eventful. My personal library smelled of vanilla from the pages of my books, enveloping me in the welcoming scent. I inhaled a sigh of relief, collapsing into my lounge chair and opened the book to reveal the secrets this book held.

My reading was short-lived. On page two, Rafael came barging in with Regalius following. Both of them were furious. I exhaled, annoyed at what these two were arguing about now. One of the few times I ever witnessed Rafael become ruffled was when at odds with his father. I closed the book, sitting up to hear what they would begin to shout at me in their disagreement.

"You will never believe who I caught our son coupling with!" Regalius's rage seethed through him. Rarely did he allow his temper to simmer through, but when it came to our oldest child, there was a special reserve for it. I believed it primarily was because he had various expectations for his successor, some of which I thought were a little difficult to attain. I would try to reason with Regalius on the matter, but once Rafael was crowned, there would be nothing we could do.

I did not have an opportunity to answer when Rafael interceded.

"It was not what it looked like! You walked in at the wrong time!" Rafael shouted.

The two were yelling at each other simultaneously, and I couldn't translate what either was saying. I had to shout to silence them, while giving both a firm glare.

"Regalius, what did you find?" I directed my attention to my husband first.

"Rafael and Regina were about to have a tumble in the sheets," he spat.

I inhaled sharply. I held up my hand to silence Rafael from what he was about to argue, trying to collect myself. "Calmly, Rafael, tell me what your father had mistaken?" I pinpointed my eldest with a stare, trying to detect any possible lie he would give.

Rafael glared at his father as he replied, "Regina and I were in a tickle fight, and Father walked in on us."

"Tell the whole story, boy!" Bellowed Regalius.

"Regalius!" I scolded.

"Rafael only had his pants on while being on top of the Grewt'en heir, and her short dress was up to her hips. I could see her damn undergarments, Serenity."

"Why were you in my room to begin with?!" accused Rafael.

"I can come and go wherever I please," Regalius answered, throwing his weight around.

I massaged my temples at this mess. I had been dead wrong in my thoughts of Regina's crush being only one-sided. "Regalius, I need you to be quiet. Rafael, I cannot stress this enough. You *cannot—*"

"—produce an heir with Regina," Rafael cut me off. "Well aware, Mother, and that was not what was happening."

"Regardless of what was happening, you know what is expected of you." I continued to massage my temples roughly, closing my eyes. I considered adding that I was not ready to be a grandma to a bastard child that would be in a custody battle between two monarchies because two heirs decided to have some fun.

"I did nothing wrong, *Mother.*" Rafael turned on his heel and stormed out, slamming the door behind him. Regalius glared at the door, and it was apparent he was debating on chasing after him to give our son a lashing for slamming the door. After a few seconds passed, the anger released from my husband as he plopped, defeated, on the lounge next to me.

"Serenity-Dear, what are we going to do about him?" He asked, exasperated, glaring at my books as if they would give him the answers he sought.

"As long as a child does not come from it, it will be fine. Are you certain of what you saw?" I questioned, I believed him, but in a calmer manner I wanted him to recount the events.

He went into detail about how he noticed the two had been quite cozier prior and that Rafael was leading Regina to his rooms. He waited a bit to follow suit, and that was when he found them in the obvious position. He heard no giggling prior, and while all hands were accounted for in appropriate positions, he didn't for one bit believe that a couple of horny twenty-year-olds were in a tickling fight.

"We cannot keep eyes on them at all times," I said quietly. "This is the courting seasons. Those two cannot end up together, but we cannot micromanage the courtings."

Regalius attempted to argue against me, but I shushed him.

"This whole event was created to find love without intervention. Those two, because of their birthrights, cannot be together. We can only hope that if they are reckless, a child does not come from it." I thought back to the rules of a Queendom. If they would have a girl, it would become the heir of Queendom Grewt'en, but on the flip side, if it was a boy and Rafael claimed it, he could name the child his heir. In Grewt'en, it would be no issue being fatherless as many of the children of the Queen rulers rarely shared the same father. However, having an illegitimate heir in T'Lovoness would complicate matters. I shook my head. These were all what-if scenarios I was worrying about.

Chapter Twenty-Seven

A few days later, when everything cooled down, I invited Regina out on a horse ride in the beautiful summer weather. We saddled up directly after breakfast, skipping tea time on the daily itinerary. There were more than a few reasons I had decided to single Regina out on this ride. Her put-together behavior had started cracking as I witnessed her continuously lashing out at all the guests and being overwhelmed. As a future Queen, she needed to learn how to handle her emotions in the future, but for now, as a queen in training, I could steal her away. I worried that if Regina continuously reacted irrationally that, she'd create irreparable damage to her reputation.

Queen Fairness was not ready to relinquish the crown, giving my niece some time to grow and mature. She would always be the little girl I watched chase after butterflies in the wild fields, but now I had to change my mindset. Fairness had sent a letter requesting for me to guide Regina while being here. After recent events, I felt I was being given a larger chore than I had bargained for. Aside from Regina's cattiness coming through, what I deduced down to was anxiety and hoped it wasn't her true personality when she didn't think I was watching. There was also the conversation I needed to have with her regarding what Regalius had stumbled upon the other day.

"Do you plan to visit us after this season is done?" Regina's hopeful voice broke the strained silence between us. She sat with perfect posture, and if it weren't for her white knuckles on the reins, I would've believed nothing was a matter with her.

"It is a high possibility. I miss your mother and the warm, dry climate," I replied. While my manor was further away from where Grewt'en's castle was nestled, it still held the same dry climate. T'Lovoness's heat held humidity in it, which took me by surprise, and I had to become accustomed to the change in weather.

A breeze blew through Regina's beautiful, loose red locks, little braids mingled within that attempted to keep the crown of hair in place. Glimpses of light splashed across her body as the leaves shifted, allowing sunlight to pour through. The heat of summer was upon us, and we were both grateful to be hidden beneath the shade of trees that covered the walking trail.

"Fairness misses you as well," Regina replied. "She was quite poutful that she could not come to visit."

"She should not be traveling in her state." I laughed, worried about my friend. She was pregnant with her sixth child, due any day now. Fairness was filled with life and laughter, unlike her eldest, serious child. When The Grewt'en Queen entered the room, it lit up. It was difficult to not fall in love with her. Regina, on the other hand, had a chip forming on her shoulder, something that had never been there prior. With each passing year, I had a feeling it was because my niece felt the pressure of her future racing towards her. She was an observant girl and most likely noticed how others fawned over her mother. Meanwhile, the Grewt'en Heir struggled with her sharp tongue. Somewhere in Fairness's mind believed I could be the one to help soften Regina, I inhaled. *I had my work cut out for me.*

"That is what I told her, but you know how she is." Regina

shrugged in indifference to her mother's actions. It was quite surprising that Fairness hadn't made the trip regardless of her state. Her whimsical way of living, covered up how stubborn The Grewt'en Queen could genuinely be. When she was determined, nothing could stop her.

"I do." I laughed, but Regina remained silent. "Is something the matter, Regina?"

Her lips pursed while glaring down at her horse's neck. I chose to remain silent, letting her battle the war in her mind. The quietness stretched between us. The only sound filling the empty void was the sound of horse hooves against the soft, packed dirt. Leaves rustled in the trees around us from the welcomed summer wind, and a few birds sang their songs, flitting from one branch to another. In years past, Fairness confided that Regina looked up to me for wisdom and guidance, something that, she as a mother, was unable to give her. Regina fought between attempting to mimic her mother's free-spirit personality and being somber and serious.

"Do you believe that I will make a great queen?" Regina's quiet voice lacked the confidence she normally swaggered around with. She reminded me of her teenage years when the bossiness faded into questioning her every decision.

"Is there a doubt in your mind?" I countered. Regina tilted her head to the side, mulling over my question, not taking her glaring focus from the horse's neck. I hardly believed any great ruler ever actually thought of themselves as great. If one went into ruling with that pompous of a disposition, it could only end in disaster from narrow-sightedness. The simple fact she fretted, despite the mask she wore daily to hide it, gave some indication on how serious she was about what her future meant.

"Fairness is . . ." She sighed. "You know how my mother is. I do not believe the people will love me as much as they cherish her." Her shoulders curled forward, trying to withdraw within herself.

"The people did not like your mother when she began her reign,"

I commented lightly. Regina perked up, looking at me, completely surprised. I continued, "When I met your mother, she had been battling a power struggle of transitioning from princess to queen. Your grandmother was a solemn, cold, and bitter woman."

Regina gasped at my blunt description of Queen Spite. I ignored it.

"The people were not familiar with your mother's colorful personality." I smiled, reminiscing on the first time I had met Fairness. She had worn hot pink and sky-blue silks. While other royals remained distant friendly upon meeting the new wife of the future king of T'Lovoness, Fairness had come running to embrace me in a welcoming hug. It only took a few interactions to realize she did not take many things seriously and lived in the moment she occupied.

"I had never met my grandmother; there is not much said about her," Regina replied slowly.

"Be grateful. I fear how you would have turned out if she got her claws into you." I shuddered. Due to the unsurprising friendship of Queen Opal and Queen Spite, I saw the latter queen often. Thankfully, if The Grewt'en Queen was around, then so was her daughter. They did not like the males meddling in their affairs and would entrap Fairness and me in their conversations. The entire time looking down their nose at anyone below princess rank. More often than I could count, I was included in their snide remarks. The first chance Fairness and I could escape The Queens, we did. The world was a better place without either of them in it.

"Why?"

"Because she was a cruel, cold woman. She always tried to dim your mother's light." Defensiveness entered my voice for my dear friend. The former Grewt'en Queen had lived up to her name of being spiteful when it came to her daughters. I was astounded when Fairness had indulged me on who the fathers were for her and her sister's. Along with the whispers she heard on how they had been conceived. Even in the bedroom, Queen Spiteful was bitter and conniving.

"That sounds impossible," Regina countered.

"Fairness is far bubblier with your grandmother gone."

My niece chose that moment to remain quiet again. Her thoughts most likely settled back to the original question she had asked.

"Regina, you have turned into a beautiful, strong young princess. I have no doubt you will be an amazing queen. However," I paused, taking in a breath to steady myself on what I planned to say next. "You need to lose the chip on your shoulder. Soften a bit. You are becoming a bit shrew in your ways."

My niece startled, her eyes widening from the audacity that I would be bold enough to say those words to her. As a lady, it would be frowned upon to be insulative, regardless of the manner of truth. As a royal, it could be the thin balance of peace and war. Far too many royals had lived, never hearing the harsh truth about themselves, and it showed. They always danced pleasantries about each other, regardless of how insufferable their company was. However, a lower-ranked person was too fearful if they would speak their thoughts out loud about the royals. Thus creating a vicious cycle of royals being pompous creatures with minimal self-awareness.

"I do *not* believe you should be speaking—" Regina started in a snippy tone, but I cut her off.

"*Regina Isadora*," I scolded. "That there is the shrewdness I am referring to. Do not think you can prance around *my* castle acting like you own it. Start showing a bit more kindness to those around you. One day, they could be your alliance." I pinpointed her with a leveled gaze, thinking of her treatment to the Theorines's heir. "One day, that alliance could mean the difference between your Queendom thriving or barely surviving." Queendom Grewt'en sat nestled in the bottom of our continent. Only three major travel routes ran to the Queendom, one from T'Lovoness, but the other two passed through Theorines.

While the latter remained a peaceful monarchy, albeit falling into ruin from the way their Queen spent money. Everything could change with the right nurturing hand of a new ruler. What had once been a beautiful castle full of life now was dreary. All the gardens had shriveled up, the trees long since dead; there were no gardeners present to remove what remained. It had given the castle an eerie, haunting presence.

If Regina didn't watch herself, eventually the next ruler on that throne may not take kindly to her. Theorines had switched between being a Kingdom and Queendom through the years. I assumed Lydia had sent their daughter here to find someone to rule by the princess's side when she took the throne. After all, the last time Theorines had been a queendom was when Gideon's grandmother ruled it. If Regina continued to bully the Theorines's heir, what would stop Princess Persamina from closing up trade routes from one queendom to another. From the way Regina acted, I didn't believe she would be all too thrilled to no longer be the only queendom when King Gideon announced his daughter as the next ruler. I'm a little surprised he hadn't already made the announcement; it would grant her more potential for interested suitors to rule alongside a queen.

Regina gritted her teeth, her lips twisting as she grounded her jaw back and forth.

"Keep that up, and you will give your hand away every time to the enemy when you are upset about something." I chirped back to her.

Her eyes narrowed on me, but I merely raised an eyebrow, waiting for her to backdown. A few beats passed by until she finally huffed and glanced away.

"Your mother asked me to help guide you while you were here, so tell me about Devereux." I smiled sweetly, giving Regina a knowing look as her head whipped back to me, her eyes wide with surprise.

"How did you know that?" She gasped.

When my presence was required to sit and behave like a queen, it became rather dull after a few minutes. The idle chatter of anyone who sat with me was always catered to what would please me the most; females vying to be my future daughter-in-law. It wasn't difficult to place a warm smile or head nod at the right time in conversation while I surveyed the other guests. It had taken only four days into the start of The Courting Season for me to figure out who her main lover was. There were a few others entangled in the mix, but Devereux had been her main favored partner.

"I have known you your whole life, my niece." I watched as the smile graced her lips. "I know when someone has captured your interest. Now queen to princess, how is he in bed?" I smiled. "Unless you want to talk about Regalius finding you in Rafael's bed the other day."

Regina's smile faltered, and she shook her head quickly. "That was not as it appeared, I promise," she rushed out. I smiled kindly, pretending to give her the benefit of the doubt. She chose my smile as acceptance of her response and quickly began to gush about Devereux's attentiveness. While I was not one for idle gossip, Regina had come to me for numerous personal things in the past, and I wanted to extend this olive branch to her again. Despite the possibility of what she and Rafael could be doing in secret.

Regina mentioned a few other names she had been sampling, along with ones she intended to try out. She worried whether Devereux would be willing to follow her back to Grewt'en or if she would even want to add him to a more permanent list of lovers. It hadn't surprised me when Regina stated that she had no intentions of ever marrying. She wished to be like her mother and other past queens in that regard. However, when she made the statement, she was nervous. Worrying that I would judge her for it, a silly notion considering I came from Grewt'en. When she found no judgment and only encouragement, she continued onward.

The gossip of Devereux and the others faded in the conversation, changing over to her annoyance with her brothers. We rounded the bend, leading us back to the castle. Regina had become a completely different person during our ride, I made note that I would need to invite her on more outings. All of my niece's burdens and anxieties melted away from the little escape of prying eyes. As I had assumed, her nerves had become spent being surrounded by this many people with no escape. She had been trying to keep up appearances, but it resulted in her becoming snippy and difficult to be around. Once a week at a minimum, I would take her out riding; when that wore its welcome, I would change my tactics as need be to keep my niece from spiraling.

Chapter Twenty-Eight

According to the itinerary, I had scheduled morning tea at this time. However, similar to when I had attended my season twenty-six years ago, I chose to skip it. I had minimal desire to participate more than needed to be of me. In my absence, the guests were more likely to be relaxed and enjoy their time here. No one enjoyed the host queen watching their every move.

Instead, I hid in my personal library rereading the Hayverton history book while taking notes along the way. Unlike the sounds of clinking porcelain cups on their saucers and the incessant gossiping chatter, the only sound to be heard in this room was from my self-inking quill.

Truly, I loathed the itinerary. Instead of curating my own, I had been lazy by using one of my late mother-in-law's years past itinerary. I sighed; I should have rethought that as I now remained hidden away from everyone. I had minimal desire to participate in this courting season any more than I had in all the ones Queen Opal had forced me to co-host with her. Even during those years, I would attempt to hide and avoid as many of the events as possible. Dealing with her disdain for me was easier than sitting there and exchanging pleasantries for hours on end with the snippy, spoiled royal brats. Especially when one of those royal brats had their eye on Regalius or if I had already found them in his bed. Queen Opal was completely oblivious to it all.

"Mother." Rafael's soft but firm voice came from behind. He always had this insane in-apt ability to stand behind me unnoticed. In his youth, he gave me a fright every time, but now ,even with the slight startle, I didn't glance up from my writing.

"What is it, Rafael?"

"Killien appears to be interested in a girl," he stated calmly, but I could hear a twinge of questioning in his voice. I chose not to react, curious as to why Rafael felt the need to inform me of this. The two brothers had been quite close at one time, but as they became older, a wedge grew between them. It started around the time Rafael began taking his role as the heir seriously. Meanwhile, his younger brother had become reserved, donning black attire and barely participating in family gatherings. Initially, I had written it off as a moody teenager, giving him his space, but maybe I had been a little too absent.

"And who would that be?" I kept my voice neutral, my attention not wavering from the parchment as the words continued to flow from the wet ink. Even all these years later, my name could still be read between the swirls of the self-inking quill. I knew who my eldest son was going to name. After all, I observed the ball from a distance last night. Only later on, I heard the snippet gossip about the conversation that had occurred between all parties involved.

"Appears to be *The Tower Princess*," he answered. His attempt at hiding his intrigue, failed.

"She has a name and a genuine title, and we both know that you know it by now," I countered; abandoning my task at hand, I turned to face him. Arching a brow, I dared my eldest son to argue against my statement. Rafael already had a piling list of ways he was well acquainted with Princess Persamina Rowena, from the first night he made her hold that ridiculous long curtsy to the way I often caught him watching her. Whenever any male gave her attention, he would glower, which caused him to cut in and steal a dance from her at the first ball. I had been so focused on how he paid attention to Mina that I had missed what was going on between him and Regina. According to my source, when Rafael found out Mina and Knox shared a kiss his jealousy had become apparent for all to see. Instead of handling his emotions, he had strolled off with Regina, and a small part of me fretted about what they did together.

Instead of replying, he merely blinked. To anyone else, he would have come off as bored and irritated. It was the mask he had begun practicing as a teenager, not wanting others to know his thoughts, intentions, or feelings on a topic. If I had not been observing previous interactions, I wouldn't have any idea why he was bringing this up.

"Do not think I did not witness you steal her from your brother's dance or the time you followed her into the rose maze after Regina had cornered her."

Rafael tried to interrupt me, but I didn't allow for it as I continued onwards.

"Every time Killien begins gaining a little bit of confidence, you choose to swoop in and take away Princess Persamina Rowena's attention from him." I didn't add that it made me scared every time Killien would be chipping in on our agreement. He was making an earnest attempt to befriend Mina, but if Rafael kept ruining it, I would have one less son living in this castle for a while.

"I was merely intrigued about the girl who captured his interest, is all. Can I not be protective of my younger brother?" He gave me a persuasive smile that didn't quite meet his mischievous eyes.

"I would believe you if I did not see the way you looked at her as well." I let the fact drop between us, waiting to see how he would meet the challenge. There had never been a doubt in my mind about who my eldest child took after. I may have been naïve in my youth, but that girl had disappeared. As queen, I needed to stay multiple steps ahead of everyone around me, and with Regalius by my side, we were a formidable pair.

"I have not the faintest idea as to what you are referring to, Mother." Despite attempting to appear innocent and bored, the corner of his lip tilted upwards. We stared at each other, waiting for the other to break. I conceded with a sigh.

"Always so formal, I miss the days when you used to call me mommy." I leaned back in my chair. The buzzing tension I had paid no mind to broke in the room.

"I am heir to the throne," he answered as if that was all the explanation he needed for his behavior.

"You need to not be this stuffy. Your Father and I are not." We had never been certain where his need to put on an act came from, if it had been for our approval, or if there were another reason. Now, there were only glimpses of the kind, sweet boy who showed all his emotions as a child. It was in the way he smiled to himself while watching the same princess he claimed not to know. I never had wanted to meddle in my children's love affairs, but another would need to capture his attention to re-direct his focus away from The Theorines's Princess. She was not to be his queen.

"Regina mentioned you called her shrew." He accused; the way he changed topics did not go unnoticed.

"Do you plan to be her knight in shining armor?" I mused. "Regina does not need you to protect her, and yes, I did call her shrew. You know how she becomes when overwhelmed. She is also not the friendliest to Princess Persamina Rowena, as you already know from the rose garden ordeal." I decided to casually plant that seed further into my eldest's mind. Rafael stiffened, temporarily losing his composure. "Furthermore, it was said after you found out Killien had kissed Princess Persamina Rowena that you and Regina had wandered off together. Shall we discuss more into that?"

Checkmate. While I didn't want to meddle in my children's lives, I did need to start moving other pieces into place where I needed them to be. I could never nurture the Theorines's princess; she was far too skittish and wouldn't be able to handle the ostracization. However, the twins had been the perfect start to growing her confidence. Topple that with the male attention she had been receiving from Killien and my nephew Montgomery, it continued to grow. I had never planned for Rafael to enter the mix, but I was adjusting to it as need be.

"Is there anything else you needed?" I asked when he remained silent. Instead of choosing to think of a reply, he stood there staring me down.

"No, that is all," he replied in annoyance while turning on his heel to leave.

"Rafael," I called, halting him as he turned back to face me, waiting to hear my next words. "Be careful about who you dally with . . . I am not ready to be a grandma." His face scrunched up at my implications. Both of us thinking of the last conversation that had occurred in here. "And just remember, no courtship with other heirs."

He left, not saying a word. I shook my head, looking up at the ceiling, wishing it would give me answers. Instead, one of the castle cats, who often accompanied me around the castle, let out a trill. I glanced down to find two of them curled up together sleeping on the chair next to me. I was envious of Pumpking and Sugarplum. Their carefree lifestyle in the castle was one of luxury and ease. They did not have to worry about their children's broken hearts or the futures I had to maneuver. The only heartbreak the cats had given me was when Sugarplum's father, Mistletoe had passed away a few years ago. He had been my first pet and gift from Regalius shortly after being married. He had been my heart-cat and while others have never been able to replace the residence he had taken within me, his offspring helped fill some of the void.

Chapter Twenty-Nine

A LETTER ARRIVED, AND BY THE PENMANSHIP, I KNEW IT was from Lydia. Bracing myself, I opened the envelope. A mixture of dread and curiosity swirled through me of the contents. We had barely exchanged letters in all these years, but I supposed with her daughter here, she would choose to make an exception.

To my dearest and closest friends,

We are currently arriving to stay in your Kingdom during our daughter's courting season. It will be nice to catch up after all these years that have passed by us. We should not have allowed the time to get away from us like this. We look forward to dining together tonight.
Sincerely,
King Gideon and Queen Lydia of Theorines

I looked up to meet Regalius's eyes, gulping.

"Gideon and Lydia are arriving right now in the castle," I informed him. His eyes accessed me, taking in the information. It was not uncommon for other royals to visit one another while their children participated in the courting season. However, generally, a request to stay occurred first, instead of self-inviting themselves unexpectently like Lydia was doing now. They would be the first parents to stay while the event was in full swing.

"Well, things are going to become a bit more exciting . . . Is it too late to hide the valuables?" He joked.

"Regalius." I laughed and then turned to Maxwell. "Anything that is not nailed down and valuable have a servant standing near it. I do not trust Lydia and her sticky fingers." Maxwell nodded quickly and hurried out of the room. I leaned back in my chair. "This is going to be exhausting."

Regalius crossed the room and kneeled down in front of me, taking both of my hands into his.

"It will be alright; we have the higher ground here. They are in our home," he comforted. We had only seen Gideon and Lydia a few times since the day they had left from our courting season. After they announced their engagement, it had come down to occasionally exchanging letters. Each time we had been in the same room with Gideon, it took me back to when he cornered me two days after Regalius and I had announced our engagement.

I read the borrowed book in the quiet, private library. My nerves still made me fearful of everything that would be changing. The other small part of me worried it would all be taken away and I would lose access to all the wealth of history at my fingertips. My mind darted back to the thought of becoming a future queen. I had agreed to marry Regalius, but I didn't believe I was fully prepared for the expectations of my future.

I didn't love Regalius. I barely knew him. He was a kind prince that had never attempted to win me over. Maybe I had been rash with my decision to accept his proposal, riding on the emotions of Theo's death. Every night I tenderly touched the dried flower he had gifted me months ago. The heartbreak still stinging in my chest.

I reasoned with myself that my options were slim pickings at this point. I had spent the entire season not bothering on getting to know anyone, instead spending my time reading. I reflected over the last few weeks; I had merely accepted my fate of being in a secret arranged marriage to Gideon. I hadn't fought against it; I also hadn't given up hope to be with Theo either. I told myself I had, but receiving that letter from Quiet was all it took to shatter my delusional hopes. Finding out that I initially had been intended for Finch but feeling the betrayal at Gideon's hidden secret unnerved me. I suppose when Regalius offered his hand with minimal strings attached, I had accepted it way too graciously. But what's done is done. Our engagement was announced to the public two days ago. I shook my head at the mess I had placed myself in. Secretly engaged to someone I had called a friend while still loving a stable boy, only to end up engaged to someone who didn't desire me. No, it was better than the alternative of marrying someone who had lied to me, I tried to convince myself.

The door to the private library clicked open, and I assumed it was Regalius. I lounged in the settee, my back facing the door while I leisurely read. It was one of the few moments I gave my mind a break. I picked a steamy romance novel that caused me to blush more times than naught.

"Give me a moment; I need to finish this passage," I called absentmindedly over my shoulder. The footsteps approached closer through the lush, thick carpet on the floor. He stopped behind me, waiting patiently. At least I wouldn't need to answer to someone who demanded my attention at their convenience. Regalius respected me and my time, which I appreciated. I flipped the page and read the last paragraph of the chapter before closing the book. I turned and startled when it wasn't Regalius. Instead, Gideon stood there with red-rimmed eyes and a sneer on his face.

"Gideon?" My eyes went wide as fear crept through my body, knots forming in my stomach. I sat upright from my lounging position, debating whether to stand or stay seated.

"I thought you wanted to be with me?" He accused, his body slightly vibrating with anger.

"Gideon, it is not like that," I tried to defend, my heart hammering. When I had agreed to marry Regalius, there had never been a moment for me to talk to Gideon about the new arrangement. He had found out like everyone else when it was announced at the ballroom in front of the other guests. It was never my intention to hurt him, even if he had hurt me, too. All I had ever wanted was to live a simple life, but thanks to my scheming older sister, my life had become far more complicated than I had ever wished.

"No? Then what is it like, Serenity? One minute, you are my fiancé, and the next thing I know, you are announcing to everyone at the ball that you are marrying my best friend." He shot back. I should have listened to the nagging voice in the back of my mind to urge Regalius to hold off our announcement until we talked to Gideon. Instead, I sat here trapped by my former fiancé.

"Gideon, you are upset. Can we not talk this out like civilized adults?" I offered, trying to find a safe ground. He towered over me, and while I didn't believe he would ever physically harm me, it did not ease up the fear I felt.

"Serenity, I love you." He desperately confessed, trying to prove his feelings for me overrode everything else. His eyes pleaded for me to feel the same.

"You do not mean that," I breathed. My stomach dropped while my heart hammered in my ears. I needed to get out of here, my eyes darting to the door, but there would be no way I could get past Gideon.

"Yes, yes, I do. I have loved you for quite some time. I thought you felt the same." His desperation turned back into accusation. His pleading eyes changed to a burning glare. He was riding on too many emotions now, unable to pick which to present me with. No matter what he said or did, it wouldn't change my decision. I tried offering him a kind smile as I attempted to let him down softly.

"Gideon, you are a dear friend to me as is Regalius –"

"Oh, so you are just marrying him for his kingdom. Is mine not big enough for you?" He spat.

"That is not it either, Gideon." Tears pricked my eyes. My fear

mingled with frustration and feeling bad for hurting him like this. Logically, I tried to reason with myself that he had attempted to entrap me in a marriage to him, too. I may have confronted him about it, and he may have worked towards my forgiveness, but that betrayal still lingered in my mind. "I just, I—"

"Serenity, I am begging you, please choose me. Please," he pleaded, tears filled his eyes. The anger completely left his body, and I breathed a small sigh of relief as I felt the tears run down my cheeks.

"I am sorry, Gideon." My voice cracked. I was sorry; sorry for the prince who had become my friend in his home. Who had taken me on adventures and gotten us into mischief, for the one who, at one point, I had begun welcoming into my heart as I thought of our future together. Sorry for how things turned out, and maybe if he had been honest and not had a hand in taking away my choice, things could have been different. A wedge had formed between our friendship, causing a strain, and I was not innocent in the matter either.

"Serenity." Gideon took a step to me. I shook my head, but he pulled me up to him, wrapping his arms around my waist and pulling me close to him. We comforted each other through all the warring emotions, and I needed to pull away. Somehow, deep down, I felt I was losing my friendship with the prince who had charmed me. It was a selfish thought, considering I had broken his heart.

"Serenity, I will never stop loving you. You will forever be the love of my life." Gideon declared, kissing the top of my forehead. I had no words to speak, how could I even respond to that? He hugged me tightly, and then I felt the absence of his body heat as he turned, leaving me to wipe away the tears from my cheeks. I shook my head, inhaling while trying to gather my wits about me. I looked at the abandoned romance novel, no longer feeling in the mood to read about someone else falling in love. The desire to read history had left me as well. I plopped on the settee, lounging as I threw my head back, and covered my eyes with my arm. How did we all end up like this? I knew the answers, but it still made me wonder.

"Quite a touching scene you two had." Regalius's voice drifted *through the room, and I peeked beneath my arm to find him walking out of the secret servant passage. I sat up, my face flushing, but he appeared unruffled by the whole affair.*

"You heard everything?" I asked hesitantly.

"For the most part." He shrugged. "I never realized how deeply Gideon's feelings were for you."

"I had not been aware myself," I paused for a brief moment, gathering the courage to ask my next question. "Knowing that, do you regret asking me to marry you?" The two, after all, were best friends.

"Is there a reason I should?" He countered.

"You tell me." I searched his eyes, bracing for the rejection that may come. All it would take is for him to call off the engagement and then I would be marrying Gideon again. I held my breath, my fate resting in Regalius's hands.

"No, it's not a deal breaker. I was aware of your involvement with Gideon . . ." he trailed off, my hope soared for a fraction to now wait for what he would say next. ". . . I chose to ask you to marry me for your friendship. We agreed to have an open relationship; if you wanted to shag my best friend on the side, it would not faze me." He shrugged.

"Regalius, I could never –"

"—Serenity, as long as no bastards come from it, I do not care."

"What I was going to say is I could never give Gideon that kind of false hope, let alone I do not think he is the sharing type."

Regalius and I walked into the banquet hall, our arms interlinked. Similar to most nights, guests filled the long banquet tables. Tonight, on a rare occasion, the head of the table would be full. We had demanded the presence of both of our sons to attend with the understanding that Mina's parents would be present. Rafael had stiffened from the news, while Killien looked aghast. I was under the impression the latter had been told a few of the horrors Mina endured by her mother's hand by his reaction.

While my husband donned the traditional kingdom's colors with his navy pants and blood-red jacket that gold thread swirled with intricate designs upon his sleeves and waist, I did the opposite. I wore a long golden dress that shimmered in the light. A hoop had been placed beneath to give the dress a fuller appearance, with a sweetheart neckline showing off minimal cleavage. The other two T'Lovoness colors could be found on my right pointer finger in the large blood-ruby marquis cut stone, surrounded with blue sapphires. The matching necklace and earrings were my only other accessories, besides the golden crown that the same stones were encrusted in. My silver hair had piled, weaved, and braided upon my head, allowing only two long coils to drape over the front of my left shoulder.

When guests took notice of our entrance, they rose and bowed or curtsied. I paid them no attention, my focus solely on the two guests standing at the head of our table. Lydia's sense of distasteful fashion had not changed. Instead of wearing her Kingdom's colors, she had chosen a gaudy, bold magenta dress with exaggerated puffed shoulders. Sometimes, I convinced myself that I had imagined her disastrous style, but here she was, proving I had remembered correctly. Her soft fawn hair had been styled back with elaborate twists, inlaid with pearls, and nestled within the hair was a crown that almost rivaled in size to her husbands. She plastered a smile showing her brilliant white teeth when she took notice of us. In twenty years, time had not been kind to her from the amount of wrinkles. The powder she had set her face with did not help matters, amplifying each crease.

I gave her a lukewarm smile, feeling Regalius's grip slightly tightening on my arm in reassurance. I shifted my attention to my former fiancé. Unlike his wife, time had been kind to Gideon. Only a few strands of gray could be found in his long, loosely braided black hair. He was cleanly shaven with his chiseled, strong jaw. Theorines's King proudly wore his kingdom's colors with black pants, a deep emerald silk button-up shirt, and the entire assemble stitched together with golden thread and gold buttons. He gave me a warm smile that attempted to hide the pain that shined through his eyes. My smile shifted between tentative and welcoming. A burst of nervousness coursed through me of not knowing where Gideon and I stood after all this time.

We took our places. Regalius sitting at the head of the table with me in my rightful place on his right and directly across from me stood Gideon. When my husband gave the order, everyone took their seats. Rafael sat to my right, and he appeared distracted. It took me a moment to realize that Mina was the only one not in attendance.

"Friends, it has been far too long," Regalius broke the silence with a hearty, warm welcome.

Gideon raised his drink to my husband. "It has been far too long." Shifting his attention to me, he raised his glass slightly higher. "Regalius your wife has become lovelier since the last time we had been together."

A warmth crept up my neck, and I gave him a tentative smile. Regalius's hand squeezed my upper thigh beneath the table to give me reassurance. I wasn't certain what Gideon was playing at, but by Lydia's pursed lips and slightly narrowed eyes, she was not pleased.

"Your daughter has been a wonderful guest," I chose my words carefully, attempting to divert the conversation.

"Well, she is a Theorines royal after all," Lydia interjected before Gideon could accept the compliment. Lydia looked at Rafael as she said, "You know she has been raised to be the perfect wife to a king."

"Could that not be said to be true for most of the guests in attendance?" Rafael responded smoothly. If I had not been sitting next to him and felt how he shifted slightly at her statement, I wouldn't have had the faintest idea her words affected him. The way she had said it made me suspicious. Mina should be the Theorines's heir; why would Lydia be raising her to be a wife to a king when, for a queendom, it should be the opposite. Something was not adding up here. Theorines had no other heirs. With Finch still lost to the world, who would take over Theorines if Mina didn't? I met Gideon's stare, and he gave me a warm smile before turning his attention back to Regalius, who chose to engage him on a different topic.

"I suppose so." Lydia smiled sweetly and shifted her attention back to me. "Persamina is excellent at needlework, although I am sure you are already familiar with her work."

I was ready to respond when Mina came hurrying towards us. Her face blazed red, unable to hide her embarrassment from being late. The red crept over her shoulders and exposed chest. Her white dress was unlike any I had witnessed her wear while in attendance. This dress had Lydia written all over it, from the size of the hoop bottom that swayed with each step to the cherry blossom branches decorated with morganite stones for the flowers. Her dress had the potential to be stylish, but the designer had gone too far, causing a serene look to be chaotic and cluttered. I assumed Lydia had kept urging the dressmaker to keep adding branches and flowers on the dress, believing it would do the material justice. The princess's long black hair had been swept up in a chignon with various frontal pieces loosely curled and flowing down the front of her dress and past her knees.

"Ah, there she is, my darling daughter, Princess Persamina Rowena." Lydia smiled at her daughter and we all watched as she hurriedly curtsied and then took her seat. Her light diminished while sitting next to her mother. She stole quick glances around the table, trying to decipher where everyone was at in the conversation.

"Your mother was telling us how you were quite exceptional at needlework." I smiled. I didn't mean to put Mina in an awkward position, but it was the first thing that had come to mind. She had not attended a single needlework session while here and I had no idea of her skill level. I didn't blame her for skipping the different activities; some of them were more in place for societal expectation than actual enjoyment. Next year, there would be no needlework. I would rework that blasted itinerary until it reflected what I enjoyed. After all, Queen Opal's choice of activities had either been things she enjoyed, such as tea, or found delight in watching guests struggle in embarrassment on something they weren't skilled in, like needlework.

"Ah yes, I started at a very young age and picked up on it quite rather quickly." Her smile pleaded for me to not make her mother believe otherwise. I once again caught Gideon's attention on me. If he hadn't been sitting directly across from me, I probably wouldn't have noticed it as much. Lydia was too focused on her daughter than where her husband's focus was directed. Regalius squeezed my leg again. He must have sensed that I wanted to look at him to see what he was thinking on the matter.

"Honestly, back home, she almost always has a needle in her hand." Lydia laughed obnoxiously loud while placing a hand on her daughter's arm. Many heads turned their attention to our end of the table from the noise she produced. I bit my inner cheek while flexing my upper thigh muscles under Regalius's hand to communicate my annoyance. He gave me a heartfelt squeeze.

"That is quite interesting to hear." I forced a smile upon my lips while I ground my teeth. I wanted to silence her attention-seeking ways. I would have thought after a couple decades of being a ruler and having her every need met, she wouldn't be as attention starved. Apparently, though, coming to my home proved otherwise. How had the late King Lucien and Queen Izralda allowed it to get this far? I tilted my head. "Lydia, remember how we used to skip needlework during our courting season?"

"Oh, I do not recall that," she rushed out. She quickly grabbed her glass and took a quick sip her eyes looking everywhere but me. Mina perked up with curiosity, probably having never heard of her mother being anything but perfect.

"Oh, come now, Lydia, we both skipped needlework all the time." I wasn't sure why I felt the urge to keep pushing her on the topic, but something about Mina's reaction fueled it. Lydia's face became pinched, her eyes blazing as she attempted to mask it with a sweet smile. To an onlooker, we probably appeared as old friends catching up, but the war that crackled between us was blazing.

"I highly doubt that." Lydia waved her hand, attempting to dismiss my words.

I maintained my smile while giving her a knowing look. *Try to maneuver your way out of this one.* "We were both atrocious with a needle and thread. Alas, thankfully, it has not trickled down to your daughter for bad habits. She is a delight in needlework hour." I had no qualms about revealing a skill I was inadequate in. Especially not when Lydia's smile tightened, her eyes revealing pure murder in them. As long as I could continue to put Lydia in her place, maybe this meal wouldn't be as bad as I had initially dreaded. Once again, I felt Gideon's gaze on me, and I swallowed, feeling as if there were words left unspoken between us.

Entering our room after dinner, I had become thoroughly disgusted by the treatment Lydia dealt her daughter. I had believed sending the twins to help Mina navigate society would've been enough. I couldn't have been further from the truth. Lydia controlled every aspect of Mina's life including her food consumption.

"Did you see the way Lydia practically attempted to starve her daughter?" I threw my arms up in the air, unable to contain my thoughts on the matter. "Persamina stared at that cake near tears until I finally said something. It was a pitiful disgrace. How dare she not even allow that girl to eat cake, especially considering how much she had eaten during our season!" I paced the room while Regalius watched me helplessly. In the short time, I had come to find Gideon's daughter to be charming. Everything had been coming together, maybe not the tidiest, albeit, but enough that she could be my future daughter-in-law.

"I was worried about the child's upbringing prior, but now I am completely fearful of it," Regalius commented, sharing my worry. "We need to get her out of there."

We had no rights to another monarchy's child or to meddle, but yet we were. Everything had been falling into place these last few weeks, but it needed further encouragement. Something that would not occur with Lydia present, her claws dugged deep in her daughter's back as she controlled the girl like a marionette.

"You are aware that Lydia is aiming for her daughter to marry our Rafael, right?" It had never been a conversation I had brought up to Regalius. He chose to leave me to my own devices as I kept nudging Killien to the Theorines's heir and thwarting Rafael's advances. My hands had been full enough planning the event and here I was doing the exact opposite of my intentions. Meddling in my children's love lives, but for what we had been planning, it needed to be done.

"Oh, I am aware, but we cannot have that. We need Theorines to change back to being run as a queendom. That will not happen if she marries our eldest. He has a soft spot for her." Regalius was speaking out loud everything I was thinking. Lydia had driven their kingdom into a poverty wasteland, and it was beginning to affect the other monarchies via the travel trade routes. Few merchants wanted to travel from one end of the lands to the other, all needing to pass through Theorines. Lydia had continuously raised the tariff taxes to travel through their lands.

I pinched the bridge of my nose, squeezing my eyes shut as a million thoughts raced through my mind of what to do. Gideon had yet to name Persamina his heir, which was peculiar considering his brother had been absent for decades. Disappeared on the wind without a trace, the next to inherit the throne would be some relative of his who most likely wouldn't be fit to rule or save the monarchy.

"I have been trying to take care of Rafael to no avail. As for Killien, I cannot force them to fall in love." I hissed. As possibilities came and were dismissed from my mind of what to do. There was a lingering thought that stayed present no matter how many times I tried to ignore it.

"While you are taking care of things, you should also take care of Gideon's hard-on for you," Regalius commented casually.

The absurdity of his comment had me whirling around to face him. I couldn't have heard him correctly; it had been twenty-six years. Who would still have lingering feelings for that long? I couldn't even speak as I waited for him to elaborate, believing he had been mistaken.

"Did you not notice how he still gazes at you? Gideon never got over you." He leaned back in his chair, the familiar gleam entering his eyes. He was already scheming a plan, but I just didn't know if I would care for this one.

"I- I mean, yes, I noticed, but. . ." I was at a loss for words. How did one respond to something like the news being delivered by my spouse none-the-less. I chose my next words carefully. On normal circumstances, I knew where his mind was headed, but this time, I knew it wouldn't be something to take lightly. This was coupled with the fact that the person in question was the King of Theorines and my former fiancé. "So, what do you want me to do?"

"I think you ought to sleep with him," he stated matter-of factly.

A beat passed between us, my face bewildered by the suggestion. I chose to remain silent, allowing him to continue. My curiosity dampened down every argument that surfaced about what he was proposing.

"If he has not changed since we were kids, he is malleable enough that you could convince him to place his daughter on the throne as his heir. Somehow, he has allowed Lydia to rule their marriage and their kingdom, which has thrown it into near poverty." I never understood how King Ashborn and Queen Izralda had allowed it after they had stepped down. Often, I attributed Finch's disappearance to them withdrawing from the public eye and not caring what occurred to the lands they had ruled. They raised Finch to protect Gideon's bleeding heart as he had so eloquently put it that one time. With the younger prince gone, it probably had left Lydia completely unchecked by everyone.

"You want me to use sex to control him?" I asked to confirm what Regalius was asking. I had never weaponized sex. It wasn't something I could fathom doing. I took in my husband, the only man I had laid with all these years. We had become so intimately familiar with each other that the idea of laying with another made me nervous.

"Yes, I do." Regalius became serious as he leaned forward. "We need their daughter to rule their kingdom, and she needs to marry our son, Killien."

We both knew what he was silently proposing. History would be repeating itself, except this time, there may not be a silent offering for those involved to escape it. I believed Persamina to be sweet on Killien, but would that remain if our plans went into accordance and she was arranged for our youngest son?

"If Gideon is still in love with you," Regalius broke my thoughts. "Or, at minimum, still has lustful feelings for you, then we need you to speed up convincing him and not allow Lydia to sway him against it. This is to our benefit that he could not keep his eyes off you tonight. Let's not pass this up."

"And you are sure you are okay with this?" I asked cautiously. Our relationship had been without much hiccups, and I worried that something like this could change everything. The idea of going through with seducing Gideon did not bother me as much as if my marriage with Regalius changed in any form.

"Serenity-Dear, you have caught me in the act more times than I care to think about with another girl." He sighed, leaning back while he scratched his head. "I feel bad knowing you never slept with anyone else outside of our marriage. I put you through hell, probably witnessing that."

I crossed the room, touching his lips to silence him. "We had agreed on an open marriage as long as no bastard children came from it. It did not put me through hell. Was it awkward at times? Yes, but never hell. I knew what I was agreeing to. We have been married for a long time. I only worry it will put a strain on our relationship if I go through with this."

He kissed the tips of my fingers before removing them away, and I kneeled before him.

"I have no worries in that regard. If we want those trade routes to keep our kingdom the strongest, then we both know what you need to do," he murmured. Supplies and items from T'Cudter and Shediwark were becoming less prevalent and at a higher cost than normal. I knew we were feeling the pain, and most likely, Hayverton and potentially Grewt'en were as well. I knew things needed to change before a war broke out because of Theorines's tariff taxes, causing us all to suffer.

"What if it is a fluke and he does not still have feelings for me" I asked, doubt clouding my heart.

"Trust me, Serenity-Dear, he does."

Chapter Thirty

The following morning, after breakfast, I sent a calling card in Regalius's name to Gideon's rooms. It left me with little time to prepare, and I had not felt this nervous since before Rafael's birth. There were too many factors outside of my control. Lydia could show up with Gideon, or maybe Regalius misread Gideon's thoughts about me. After all, I had not left on good terms or made amends in the last twenty-six years with my former fiancé and lover. Last night, I had been so focused on Lydia's treatment of her daughter that I had forgotten to pay attention to Gideon. I only hoped that what Regalius claimed would prove to be true.

The door opened, causing a wave of butterflies to fill my belly. Gideon strode in, his footsteps faltering as surprise flashed across his face. Confusion followed as he looked about the room for where his friend could be hiding. The entire time his eyes kept flitting back to me and the new outfit I wore.

I had changed my clothes and hairstyle after breakfast. When we had all sat together for the morning meal, I'd worn a dress out of my normal style. It had been Regalius's idea to wear something a bit more youthful, which is how I ended up in a pink polka-dotted dress and my hair in two long braids. The suggestion felt silly, but something about that dress caused me a rush of girlish giggles. During the morning meal, I caught Gideon glancing at me more often than naught.

From breakfast, I didn't have much time but I quickly changed into a simple pullover dress. I wanted something that was easily removable and accentuated my figure. The golden fabric that caressed my skin dipped low in the front, revealing an ample amount of cleavage as it hugged my body. My hair now hung in loose waves, making me feel ethereal with the clash of gold silk and silver hair.

Gideon's eyes slowly trailed my body, lingering where my hardened nipples pressed against the fabric. This morning, he had ditched the simple long braid he'd worn yesterday. Instead, his hair was decorated in tiny, long braids that latticed worked together. It was elaborate in the scalloped design, which was woven amongst the loose strands. His attire was casual with the black slacks and emerald button-up shirt with the top few buttons undone to expose his chest. I suppose when he received the calling card, he anticipated drinking, smoking cigars and reminiscing.

"Serenity." He cleared his throat. "What do I owe the pleasure? I thought I was to be meeting with your *husband*?" Gideon's nervous chuckle followed; at least some things never changed.

I crossed the empty space between us, choosing to stomp down the sour feeling from him mentioning Regalius. A small flash of anger coursed through me. If Gideon hadn't allowed his wife to get out of control, I wouldn't need to be here doing this. This was absurd, but, if I wanted to control the trade routes, I would need his daughter married to my youngest. Putting Princess Persamina Rowena on the throne did not guarantee my plans would work, but it was better than the unknown alternative. If she married Killien, there was a more favorable chance of being better allies with Theorines.

"Close and lock the door," I murmured with a coy smile, looking up at him through my black, sooty lashes. I could feel the fabric of his shirt against mine when he inhaled sharply.

"Serenity?" Another nervous chuckle. His focus lingered on the perfect view he had of my cleavage. He took a step back, and my smile widened. Surely, as a king, he had the opportunity to be seduced before.

"Gideon," I breathed. "Close and lock the door." Until he fulfilled my request, I wouldn't say or do anything. The room I had chosen was away from the majority of the guest quarters, with little opportunity for anyone to stumble upon us. However, I wasn't going to take any chances.

He gave me a wary look, his hand fumbling behind him to follow my orders; never once taking his focus off me.

"I knew if I sent a letter in my name, you would have never come alone." I bit my bottom lip. "And I preferred it to be the two of us." I stepped forward, placing a hand on his chest. His breathing hitched from my touch.

"Why, Serenity?" His eyes searched mine, trying to determine if this were a trick or not. I could feel his heart racing beneath the palm of my hand, even as he kept glancing behind me, waiting for someone else to appear in the room.

"Do you still have feelings for me, Gideon?" My voice came out sultry with a slight poutful tone to it. I batted my lashes, never anticipating to cause him to react like he was still in his early twenties. I leaned in slightly, my breasts pressing into his chest.

"S-Serenity, where is this coming from?" He gulped as a multitude of emotions crossed his face before finally settling on a cautiously guarded one. The spark of hope flickered in his eyes.

This was my chance; I needed to play my cards right and word everything correctly for this to work. I twirled my finger around some loose hair strands that hadn't been styled. Dipping my head and tilting it to the side, I focused on playfully playing with his hair while biting my lip. "Well, I noticed the way you have been watching me and . . ." I paused, pretending to concentrate as I tilted my head to the other side. I leaned into him more, moving my hips sensually. I let the next words come out as a breathy whisper, "I could not help but to wonder . . ." I let the unsaid words float between us.

"Serenity, please do not jest if you do not mean it." His nervous chuckle mingled with the way his voice raised in pitch.

I guided his hand to cup the apex of my sex, with only the golden fabric being the only barrier. "Gideon," I purred. "When have you ever known me to jest over something like this?" I rose onto my tiptoes, leaning in until our lips were close enough that I could feel the warmth of his breath on my skin. His chest rose and fell quickly against mine as I pressed completely against him.

"What if, what if Regalius caught us?" He rushed out but didn't withdraw his hand. We both knew it was a flimsy question.

"I would not worry about that. Regalius is quite *busy* today, and he is not concerned about who warms my bed," I purred. It had not been an outright lie, and in this case, he expressed his approval and permission in the matter. Not that it appeared I needed his approval, considering his past reputation.

"Are you certain?" Gideon's voice turned husky. His fingers pulled at the fabric as he attempted to touch me further through it.

I leaned into him, our lips almost touching, and whispered, "Kiss me, Gideon."

His resolve broke as his lips crashed down on mine, kissing me hungrily. My heart thundered while his strong fingers rubbed against me. The friction of the fabric adding to the sensation. I let go of his hand and looped my arms around his neck. I needed to convince him as I moaned into his mouth.

His other hand snaked into my hair, tangling it between his fingers. Kissing him was different than Regalius, and I felt clumsy at first trying to figure out our rhythm. He abandoned rubbing me as he started yanking the golden dress upwards to grant himself better access to me.

Breaking the kiss, I huskily murmured, "Let us move this to the bedroom." Removing my arms from his neck, I stepped back and grabbed his hand. The fabric of my dress fell back to the ground while I led him. We barely crossed the threshold when he removed his hand from mine to begin undoing the buttons on his jacket and shirt, discarding both as he kicked off his shoes. Gideon's pants followed to the pile of clothes. He stood naked and hard before me.

I inhaled. Time had favored him well as he was still lean with muscles.

"Serenity?" He prompted. I flushed, taking a step back.

"Sorry, I am just a bit self-conscious." I wrapped my arms around my waist, hugging myself as I rocked. "I have had two kids since the last time we had been together. What if you do not still find my body attractive?" I wish I could say I was playing coy, but I realized it was the raw, honest truth.

Gideon stepped closer to caress my cheek, drawing my attention back to him. "Serenity, you have nothing to be self-conscious about, trust me." I barely nodded, and he trailed his other hand down my body to my hip. His fingers bunched up the fabric, pulling it up higher once again. His hand left my cheek to assist the other. When my dress was removed, he discarded it to the growing pile of clothes. The heat of his body radiated on my naked flesh, and I could feel the tip of his hard cock pressed against my abdomen.

I fought the urge to wrap my arms over my breast to cover them from his hungry gaze. He leaned in and kissed me savagely as if I was the salvation to his life. He didn't wait as he guided me onto the bed with him partially on top of me. His left hand trailed up my thighs, and I opened for him. He took the invitation, his fingers skimming up my center, circling my clit to tease me. The moan that escaped my lips was real, surprising me, but I encouraged him to continue.

Gideon peppered kisses down my jaw and neck to my collarbone. Slowly, he eased himself off the bed. His kisses lingering on my breasts, giving equal attention as he sucked on each nipple, all the while his fingers continued to tease and play with my clit. I had forgotten how skilled of a lover he was, his kisses continuing lower over my stomach and hips. When he was on his knees before me, he paused to inhale my scent.

He didn't wait as he looped his arms under my thighs and jerked me to the edge of the bed toward him. My legs rested over his shoulders. He looked up at me, silently asking for permission, and I nodded. His head lowered, and I felt the warmth of his breath against my clit before he sucked it into his mouth. His fingers followed, pushing into me as he worked on a rhythm of swirling his tongue around my clit as he pumped his fingers in and out. I moaned, grounding my hips against his mouth to chase the pleasure I felt.

I raked my right hand through his hair, trying to guide him on speed, when another moan erupted from me. Gideon's pace picked up as he worked my clit until I couldn't contain it anymore. My orgasm crashed within me, and I reminded myself to moan his name instead of the one I was used to.

Gideon didn't need any more encouragement as his fingers withdrew from me. Pulling himself up and grabbing one of my legs, he hiked it up until my calf was firmly flushed against his neck. He leaned over me, testing my flexibility limit as I felt the stretch in my muscles. The tip of his cock pressed against my entrance, and he wasn't gentle as he slammed into me. Closing my eyes, I moaned, breathing in the smell of our sex, allowing myself to enjoy this moment.

I cracked my eyes open when I felt the gentle caress of his long black hair swaying along my body while he fucked me. His hair almost tickled in the way it lightly skimmed me. Gideon's face filled with pleasure as he continued to thrust into me. It didn't take long until he was moaning my name and collapsed on top of me. His heart thundered against my chest as he breathed heavily. Rolling off, he pulled me close to him.

I nestled against him, preparing myself for the next part of the plan I needed to implement. I took his silence as an opportunity to guide the conversation how I wanted it to go. "What are you thinking about, Gideon?" I quietly asked.

"I am thinking about how I never thought I would have an opportunity like this again, Serenity." He squeezed me tightly, and I tried to push the feeling of guilt away. This would never have occurred if Regalius had not been watching him intently. This wouldn't have even been a thought in my mind, yet here we were because I needed something from him.

"Well, there could be more opportunities . . ." I let my words trail off, letting his curiosity grow.

"How?" The confusion entered his voice, but it hadn't taken long for him to bite.

"Well." I trailed my finger along his muscular chest, trying to distract the logical part of him. "If our children married, we could see each other more often." It was a bold move to lay my intentions out like this. It was a risky assumption that Gideon still wore his heart on his sleeve. If he hadn't changed, I wouldn't need to strategize too hard. I was gambling on many things by showing all my cards at once for a man who could be practically a stranger to me now.

"Marrying your eldest would certainly help my kingdom," he replied slowly. There hadn't been an awkward shift in energy. I would take that as a good sign as he continued to hold me.

"I was thinking, my youngest, there would still be a dowry involved on our part," I offered, attempting to sweeten the temptation. If money was where his mind was going, I would maneuver with that.

"But that would only be if Mina became queen?" He asked hesitantly. I felt him stiffening against me. My mind raced. Had he truly never considered his daughter to rule after him? This may be more work than either Regalius or I had thought initially.

"Theorines could become a Queendom. . . Your grandmother ruled. Besides, who would take over if Mina married a first-in-line heir?" I tried to put concern in my voice while maintaining my pacing of words. I almost rushed them out in appalled accusation.

"The next in line is my cousin since we still have not heard a word of my brother's whereabouts. . ." Sorrow laced Gideon. I often wondered how much Finch's disappearance had affected him. Had it affected him enough to become addled in thoughts about his daughter becoming queen, though?

"I am sorry, Gideon. If I had known when he came here that, that was the last we would have seen of him, I would never have let him go." Sorrow filled me, and I realized this conversation was not going as intended. He gave me a slight squeeze.

"It is okay, Serenity. It is not your fault; none of us knew." Gideon paused in his thoughts. "Some days I wonder if he is still even alive. . . It has been twenty-five years since he left without a trace." I pulled myself up to lean over him, my breasts grazing against his chest.

"Gideon, I am sure he is still alive and out there somewhere; please have faith." I leaned down and kissed him gently, trying to redirect his focus back to me.

"Thank you, I will try." I watched as the painful emotions slowly ebbed from his face. "Back to the topic at hand, your youngest matched to my daughter?" He raised an eyebrow.

"Well, I was just thinking if they were wedded, we would have more excuses to be able to see one another. Maybe we did not have a true chance the first time around, but we could have a second one through our children?" I knew I was walking on very thin ice with what I was imposing, considering it was my fault we weren't currently together. This part of the arrangement had never been planned, but I was running with anything that would enchant Gideon to the idea. I was aware of what I would be agreeing to and only hoped Regalius would understand. If his daughter married Killien, I would become Gideon's mistress and him my lover for the rest of our lives if he wished it. This could become complicated and messy, and the only flipside I could see from this is if we were caught, there would be nothing Lydia could do about it. If it became public knowledge, I would need to heavily rely on my Grewt'en roots.

"I will see if I can persuade Mina into it if you can talk to your youngest son. However, Mina has had little to no training on ruling," Gideon commented.

"That is okay, I can train her in the ways of ruling female to female. With my knowledge of history, it could be very beneficial," I paused, trying to contain my excitement. If he accepted my offer to train his daughter, I could guide her even further to my plans with the trade routes. I didn't desire control of them, but I did want my Kingdom to prosper even more. I took a deep breath to prepare myself for the next question I wanted to ask more out of mere curiosity of his thoughts than anything else. "Will Lydia be okay with this arrangement?"

"Lydia will not have a say in the matter. . . I am the King after all," he challenged me. I thought to myself, if only he had exercised that title a lot sooner in life, but kept the comment to myself. The only reason I believed he would pull his authority over his wife now was to have future rendezvous with me.

"That is true, I only wanted to make certain, is all. Are you happy with her?" I did not mean to ask the question, but Gideon had been my friend before everything went sour. Distaste crossed his face.

"The second biggest regret in my life was marrying her," he replied with disdain, his lips twisting in disgust.

"What was your first?" The question slipped out before I could stop it.

"Letting you go."

My heart skipped a beat. "Gideon," I replied softly.

"I should have never agreed for us to attend the courting season. If I had not, you would be my wife, and I would have been a very happy man. Instead, I have a hateful shrew of a wife and a cold bed each night." My heart lurched out for my dear friend. His face blanched, realizing he had uttered the words out loud, most likely not having meant to do that.

"I do not even know how to respond." My voice barely audible.

"You do not have to say anything, Serenity, it was my fault. . . But let me have a chance to make up for some of the past." He rolled us over until he was on top of me and guided his already hardened cock back in. "I want to make up for lost time." He promised with a kiss me.

I sat in front of the mirror, brushing my hair. I had once again done another wardrobe change. The golden dress had become too wrinkled, and while I rarely ever swapped for more than two different dresses, here I was wearing a blue one. It was not as seductive as the earlier one, but still lightweight to combat against the warm summer weather.

I had chosen the dress for my walk with Lydia and Mina through the rose garden. At breakfast this morning, I offered for them to skip needlework in favor of a stroll. When I directed my invitation to Mina, her mother chose to answer instead. I had to bite my tongue in frustration from the disrespect. However, I silently reminded myself at the time I would be meeting Gideon shortly. My nerves had been on hiatus for the entire morning meal.

From breakfast to tea and even through the walk in the rose gardens, it came little surprise when Lydia soured my mood with her dismissal ways to Mina. Whatever nonsense she was filling her daughter's head with, it had become apparent, and it wasn't good. Neither of them having the faintest idea about my prior engagement with the King of Theorines. I only hoped my knowing smile wasn't peculiar during my time with them while I thought of Lydia's scheming coming to a crumpling end.

I was mid-brush stroke when Regalius breezed through the door. He gave me a questioning look through the reflection of the mirror. I looked him over, and he still appeared completely unruffled despite knowing what had occurred hours before.

"Well, you were not wrong; he still loves me." My voice remained light as I kept my hands busy with the task at hand.

"Is our plan going to work?" He didn't bat an eye, treating the conversation as if it were any other plan we made in the past.

"Yes." I inhaled deeply, knowing what I would need to tell Regalius next.

"Excellent." He replied before I could continue. "Anything else interesting come from your meeting?"

I found it quite comical that he was referring to my rendezvous as a meeting, as if it was simply business. I suppose it could be considered that, after all, that was what it was for me. "To convince him to move forward with the union of our children, he is under the impression it will give him more opportunities to see me privately." I steeled myself for his reaction.

"Why would he think that, Serenity?" His voice became guarded.

"Because I did not know how else to sell the reasoning to create a union of marriage between our children." I had been grasping for straws and choosing to go with what the moment presented me with.

My husband stared at me through the mirror while he mulled over the information I had dropped between us. He remained quiet for quite some time, and the nagging sense of fear and nervousness started to fill me. I worried about what his response would be.

"Well," he drawled out, "I will not stop you if that is what you wish to have happen. We need those trading routes." He replied briskly.

I nodded. We weren't accustomed to being at odds with one another. I felt as if I had done something wrong despite him being the one to suggest it in the first place. This whole situation wasn't something I could have ever fathom foreseeing, let alone figuring out how to prepare for it. Things could have been different if I had chosen to not marry Regalius. I never regretted that one bit, but I also didn't think the entire continent wouldn't be in danger because one monarchy was ruining trade with the others.

"I do not like us like this," he stated calmly, breaking the tension.

I turned, wanting to face him. "I do not either." I sighed, feeling defeated. My shoulders slumped as I felt the heaviness way down on me. Prior to all this, I worried about what it would do to our relationship and already on day one it appeared to be straining it.

Regalius crossed the room and wrapped me in his arms. I had taken a bath after my time with Gideon, scrubbing every inch; not wanting to dirty Regalius along with myself. "I am sorry for making you do this," he murmured into my hair. I wrapped my arms around him, pulling him closer to me as I buried my face into his chest. I breathed him deeply, needing to ground myself and feel at peace again.

"You did not make me do anything. . . if we pull this off, it is what we needed to have done to help our Kingdom out and the other monarchies. . . we are just fortunate Gideon still is infatuated with me." I tried to soften the guilt Regalius was now feeling.

"For our Kingdom," he agreed. He began pulling me up off the settee.

"Regalius?" I questioned.

"Come, I do not want him to still linger on your skin and mind." Regalius pulled me to our bed, kissing me slowly and tenderly. Taking his time to emphasize the love and care he had for me, worshipping my body, reminding me that I am his and he is mine.

Chapter Thirty-One

I took a sip of my strawberry lemonade while sitting on the balcony that overlooked the rose gardens. None of the guests below had taken notice of me, and I secretly enjoyed the reprieve. I found the irony in my drink, one of the few strawberry-flavored themes that had stuck with me. Like so many of the guests, I had not the faintest idea of what I was walking into when I arrived here twenty-six years ago. At the time, I believed I would reluctantly participate, knowing at the end of it all I would be married to an heir. Curiosity sparked in me on whether any of the current guests were in a similar predicament as I had been. After tonight, I knew of at least one pair that I would witness history repeat itself. In only a few short hours, I would be sealing my youngest son's fate, something I had never wanted to rob him of.

Somedays, I wish I could go back and live in the memories I had taken for granted. Maybe it was the summer heat that reminded me of home or the strawberry lemonade that made me think about the day we had spent at the beach while visiting my dear friend, Fairness.

I'd forgotten how warm Grewt'en could become the further south we traveled. Even with the breeze and ocean mist, it didn't keep the heat at bay. Fairness and I lounged beneath the beach umbrellas while Regalius swam in the ocean. I had barely made it a day before I stripped out of the daily dresses I wore in T'Lovoness castle in favor of the traditional light-weight silk fabrics of Grewt'en.

I had more skin on display than I had exposed in a long time. A yellow silk wrap that shifted to burnt-orange depending on the lighting weaved around my bosom, leaving some of my mid-drift exposed. The long burnt orange skirt sat high enough to cover my naval and the insecurities I still felt over my pregnancy stretch marks. The skirt had slits running up both sides of it, allowing for my long legs to enjoy the summer sun. My hair was styled up in a bun, all of us royals having discarded our crowns for the day.

I picked up a strawberry from the tray between us and admired my dear friend. Fairness was very petite, and no one would suspect she already had three children, the youngest being a year old. Her red hair was styled in two buns on her head, giving her a more youthful appearance. Her bright green eyes watched our children play together in front of us. Her pouty pink lips smiled.

Turning my attention from her, I looked to see what she found humorous, a smile instantly forming on my lips. Fairness's eldest child, Regina, was a spitting image of her mother, had stolen the flag off the top of the sandcastle Rafael had been building. Despite Regina being two years younger, she was running faster than him, squealing in delight. Killien joined in on the chase, followed by Fairness's second oldest, Montgomery toddling after them on short, stubby baby legs. The only child not present was her youngest, Percival. At only a year old, he had remained at the castle in the care of his nursemaid.

"I wish I could be young and carefree like our children," Fairness said with melancholy. "To not know the pressures that royalty will bring them just yet."

"Their innocence is a thing of envy, although Rafael is already grasping onto his future," I sighed, leaning back.

"Regina is still unaware. Maybe within the next two years, she will *begin to catch on." Fairness pulled her knees up to her chest and rested her chin on them, continuing to watch the children.*

I often wondered how much Fairness had been denied a childhood. From the last seven years of knowing her, little bits and pieces had come out about her mother. If not from Fairness's lips, then by the late Queen Spite's actions. I shuddered from the thought of that cold, cruel woman; she was someone who should've never been granted power. According to the royal family tree, Spite was never meant to be the heir. An unfortunate sickness had taken out all of her older siblings before she was conceived. She had been born years later, most likely in a desperate attempt to produce a new heir to the throne. I believed the closest form of a sibling Spite ever felt was to my late mother-in-law.

We watched as Rafael finally captured Regina, the two of them somersaulting into the sand. Rafael attempted to make Regina let go of the flag without any avail. Only when Killien started tickling her did she lose her grip on the flag. In a triumphant defeat, Rafael removed himself from the tangle of limbs and proudly returned to his sandcastle. Montgomery had barely gotten halfway to the group when he turned back around to toddle after Rafael.

Fairness and I both smiled, enjoying the simplicity of life. Regina shrieked from laughter as she attempted to tickle Killien back. Rafael ignored it all as he knelt down, placing the flag on top of the castle again. Unfortunately, it didn't last long, as Montgomery lost his balance and knocked the entire thing down.

"Someday, we are going to miss this," murmured Fairness.

I silently nodded in agreement.

"Mother," Rafael's annoyed voice broke me from the memory.

"Yes?" I turned to find him striding angrily towards me. Had he found out about Gideon and me? Fear dropped in my stomach from the thought of disappointing my child like that. If he had heard, then who else would know as well? More importantly, how had he already found out? I would need to talk to Regalius immediately, or maybe it would be best if I sent for Regalius to be present. If Rafael saw his father being okay with the matter as we explained it, maybe it would soften his thoughts.

"You will never believe what I had just overheard," he seethed, glaring at me.

I gave a faint smile as I looked past him for a servant of some sort to go fetch Regalius. None were in sight. I had sent everyone away to enjoy some peace alone. I'd need to calm Rafael down until we found Regalius, and then we could all talk like adults.

"Were you aware that *The Tower Princess* is here under orders by her mother to marry me by any means possible?" He spat.

I faltered. *What?* That is not what I had anticipated for him to spew at me. I blinked, shaking my head to gather my thoughts. I had been preparing to defend myself to him, but instead, I was now trying to get caught up to speed on the conversation.

"What do you mean?" I asked cautiously. Nervousness still coursed through me that I was not in the clear.

"After you left, I had conveniently stayed nearby when her mother started drilling her about why she was here. Apparently, if I choose someone else, *Mina* is supposed to end them by any means possible." He glared down at the people below the balcony who were still unaware of our presence.

"You do not need to be concerned; your father and I will handle it." Inhaling sharply through my nose, I finished with, "I suggest you do not attend the evening meal tonight." With his emotions running this high, I couldn't have him somehow ruining our plans.

"Are you not angered by this news, Mother?" He asked in surprise at my lack of reaction.

"While it is a shock, it is nothing your father and I cannot take care of." I smiled, wishing I could tell Rafael that the wheels were already set in motion. No matter what Lydia had planned, it was all going to be thwarted in a few hours.

Tonight's meal would be amusing for more than a few reasons. Rafael listened to my instructions by staying away. Apparently, so did his brother. While Killien did not need to be present for what was about to happen, he would need to be told rather quickly. Granted, with how much he remained out of sight, I doubted the news would reach him before I found him. Then again, this would be the one time it would.

In a bold move, I had chosen to invite the Grewt'en children to dine with us at the head of the table. I needed reliable witnesses to the conversation, and I trusted no one else. Regina would easily spread the gossip in delight, Montgomery would fan the flames, and Percival would only tell the rightful truth. With them present, if Lydia attempted to deny the union of her daughter with my youngest son, I had an arsenal of royal, reliable witnesses. However, my niece and nephews were unaware of my intentions; it was better that way. I needed everyone to act natural and have genuine reactions to the conversation.

The Theorines's princess was once again the last to arrive at the meal. With Killien not present, Regina sat beside his empty seat, followed by Montgomery and Percival. Even with her parents present, she had an awful concept of time, always running late. I'm surprised her mother wasn't chiding her about it. Then again, earlier in the rose maze, I had scolded Lydia about how she's been scrutinizing her daughter non-stop since their arrival.

Not many things surprised me, but the friendliness Lydia showed Regina was one of them. It was to the point that The Theorines's Queen was referring to my niece as 'Gina'. Something didn't sit right with me at their casual ease of conversation. And when Mina had taken her seat, it almost felt as if Lydia was rubbing her fondness for the Grewt'en heir in her daughter's face. I couldn't make sense of it. Lydia was the one who had chosen to keep her daughter locked away, but yet had spent time with Regina at the Theorines's balls that were hosted. Balls that we rarely had received invites to, I didn't take offense to her slight.

"Serenity, do you have a free moment for us to catch up in a more private setting?" Lydia requested, smiling sweetly at me.

I took a sip of tea, watching her over the lip of the cup. I was being petty as I made her wait for my response. Tonight, I would make her suffer and world turn upside down. Maybe I was delighting in making her wait for my response. Setting my teacup back on its saucer, I finally replied, "I am sure I can find some time in my schedule, Lydia."

"Oh, splendid!" She squealed and clapped her hands together obnoxiously loud. "It will be just like old times."

"I will send a servant with a note when I am available." She had an opportunity to talk with me earlier but instead chose to dismiss me. It was during that time I had walked away that Rafael overheard their conversation. Rafael was not prone to eavesdropping, but I had caught him more often than not being found in places he shouldn't be. In the past, when I questioned him, he had answered that it was best he heard the information with his own ears than someone else relaying it.

I ignored Lydia's reply and tuned out from the prattling of the dinner conversation. My eyes landed on Gideon as I mulled over when the best time would be to begin the discussion of our plans. Regalius cleared his throat, his hand coming down to squeeze my leg. I must have given my tell-tale sign that I was becoming anxious about the next few minutes. Taking deep breaths, I tried to calm my heart. Regalius and I communicated silently as he silently soothed me that everything would be okay. I nodded slightly, and then Gideon's voice captured our attention; we had missed a part of the conversation.

"—between kingdom and queendom so often in history, it should not be that difficult for the people to accept a switch considering it was a Queendom for a time when I was a child."

"That is true," I joined in, trying to catch up and steer the conversation the way I wanted it to go before Lydia could interject. "Your grandmother had a difficult time giving up her power to your father, did she not?" Only in the old books tucked away on the shelves of Theorines's library had that information been written down. Outsiders of Theorines's castle were unaware of the power hold Gideon's grandmother had.

"Yes, she did." Gideon chuckled. While his father had to be patient on receiving the title of king, Gideon barely had to wait for the crown.

"Then," Regalius interjected. "Why did you not originally choose for Mina to be heir instead of coming here to potentially give up her claim to your throne?" I offered Lydia an innocent smile in response to my husband's bold question. This was not what we had practiced. Why was he going off-script like this? Was it because I had informed him of what Rafael had overheard earlier?

"Because we would rather see her marry a prince heir, next in line to rule their own country, than someone wanting to use her for the crown." Gideon leveled a gaze at me as he said it. I had never used him for his crown nor for Regalius's.

If he wanted to be like that, then I would momentarily take away the opportunity of our deal. Instead, I offered the thought of his daughter marrying Montgomery instead. My nephew, having attention brought back to him, straightened from the suggestion. Gideon paled slightly, realizing he wouldn't have access to me if that arrangement occurred. Mina sat in silence, slightly paling as we discussed her future marriage prospects. I wondered if an unknown future and ruling her country made her more nervous or if she wouldn't have her mother instructing every detail of her life.

Gideon stared at me as he attempted to play it cool by claiming they had considered the royal Grewt'en males as possible candidates but wanted to offer freedom in the courting seasons. Maybe I had opened up too many wounds by sleeping with Gideon. The conversation was becoming a bit off-topic from where I wanted it to be.

"What about someone like my son, Prince Killien Knox?" Regalius spoke up.

Gideon broke his stare on me and blinked at my husband. "Yes, he would also be a suitable candidate to marry our daughter as well."

Regalius did not back down from Gideon's attention. He waited a beat before proposing to begin preparing arrangements between our children. I did not have the heart to look at Mina's reaction. By this point, Gideon must have known I was talking to Regalius about everything. There were too many coincidental details being talked about.

"Why don't we wait until the end of the season? We did promise Persamina to try on her own," Lydia quickly jumped in. It was her last attempt to salvage everything she had been planning. She continued prattling on with her argument.

"We all did have our own chance, did we not, Serenity?" Gideon stated, pinning me with a look.

I quickly gave Regalius a side-ways glance. Our silent agreement passed between us, and we nodded once. Both of us plastering a smile on our faces, attempting not to respond to Gideon's statement. While Lydia sat there stewing, details were quickly exchanged, and the deal was done that Killien would marry their daughter. The only thing left to do was for me to track the groom down and tell him of his arrangement.

Chapter Thirty-Two

"Serenity, many guests are falling ill," Maxwell's voice interrupted my thoughts three mornings later while Regalius and I relaxed in our rooms.

After our meal, when we sealed our children's fate, I wasn't able to locate Killien first. It had actually been Gideon who informed him of the arrangement. When I finally caught up to Killien, he was not the least bit displeased. Actually, it was the direct opposite. Delight radiated from my son. Well, at least I didn't ruin his life with my planning.

On the other hand, Rafael has remained in a foul mood ever since. Despite his rage from overhearing the conversation with Mina and her mother, the feelings he held for the princess were evident. Killien was completely oblivious to the fact, only focused on the fact he would be marrying The Theorines's heir.

"Falling ill in which regards?" Regalius asked, leaning forward.

"Princess Persamina Rowena was the first to collapse in the hallway last night. It was believed to be a fluke, but now it has been reported another five followed suite," Maxwell supplied.

I glanced nervously at Regalius and found concern filling his face.

Gideon and Lydia had departed earlier yesterday morning. I had been under the impression the following days of the courting season would remain relatively un-eventful. However, if we had an outbreak of ill guests, that would cause nothing but disaster.

"What are their symptoms?" Regalius asked.

"It starts as a fever, dizzying vision, and then they collapse, blacking out and become unresponsive from what we gathered."

My mind raced, trying to pinpoint similar symptoms. It could be mimicking poison; did Lydia do something before she left. If our guests were poisoned, this could cause an outright war if heirs died while under our care. My eyes widened and Regalius must have been thinking the same thing as we looked at each other.

Another servant came rushing in and announced another three guests had collapsed. I swallowed, my mind racing to what precautions I would need to put into effect to minimize backlash. Regalius called for the royal physicians to look into every possible illness that could be causing this many people to collapse within such a short time span.

"I hope it is nothing serious," I whispered, my mouth drying as I tried to swallow. Worry consumed me. If this wasn't an ill-intent poison, what if this was a new plague?

"No worries, Serenity-Dear, like everything else, this too will pass." Regalius took my hand, giving mw a light squeeze.

Almost a week had passed as numerous guests fell ill in those first couple of days. It had taken only two days to deduce it down to being a bad barrel of wine that had been served. Depending on the severity of their consumption correlated with how long their systems lingered. Mina had been the worst of them all, with many eyewitnesses claiming she had drunk quite a few glasses.

Through the chaos, many of the events had been paused due to staffing being allotted to care for the ill. Silently, I was grateful it had not been poisoning. It was a form of poison, but not intentional. Letters had been pouring in from parents demanding to know the welfare of their children. I had round-the-clock staff penning them back with answers.

Both of my sons were a complete wreck over Mina falling ill. Killien never left his betrothed side, and Rafael had become a menace to be around. I was ready to take both of my children by the ear and force them to sit in a time-out. My exhaustion proved that I did not have the physical strength to follow through with it. When news came that Mina had finally awoken three days after falling ill, it caused a worse chain of events. Which is what led to the current meeting I requested to have with Rafael.

"You wanted to see me, Mother?" Rafael's voice came from behind, causing me to jump this time, the tiredness getting the best of me. The words I had been writing became scribbled from how the self-inking quill jumped on the parchment paper. I turned to him, rising from my chair.

"I think it is best you took a seat." I nodded toward the couch. This was a conversation I was not ready to have with my eldest, but it was one that needed to be had before he did something even more stupid and ruined everything.

"Mother?" He questioned, his face becoming guarded.

"Rafael, I need to speak with you," I calmly stated to my eldest child. He gave me a once over and rolled his eyes before listening to me. I sat on the chair next to him. He may be twenty-five, but he still could be a bit juvenile at times. He was always a good son; both my boys were. I glanced at the closed door, verifying it was indeed closed.

"May I ask what the occasion is, Mother?"

I internally sighed; this boy. If we both did not already have silver hair, we would be identical by his mannerisms alone. "We need to speak about your involvement with the Princess Persamina Rowena of Theorines." I did not have time to beat around the bush. A migraine was forming, and this conversation would only add to it.

"What about her?" Rafael became defensive.

"I know you and her are having a bit of a lovers affair—" the rumors from the servants had already come flying back to me. I wanted to massage my temples but maintained my composure for the conversation.

"—we are not," he cut me off. The lie landed between us as the flush crept up his neck and ears.

"Rafael, I am your mother, and I too once was young and foolish before your father, so do not play coy with me, boy." I stated briskly, leveling my gaze at him with a raised eyebrow, questioning if he would really try to lie to me again.

He scoffed, looking away.

"You need to end it, son." There was no time to mince words. His head snapped back to look at me.

"This is the courting season. You have no control over who I marry!" My son shouted at me.

"Unfortunately, son, we need Princess Persamina Rowena to marry your younger brother. It will be a beneficial marriage to our Kingdom," I replied as calmly as I possibly could.

"You cannot be serious, Mother?" Rafael exasperatedly stated, his legs jerked. He was resisting the urge to stand up and disrespect me.

"I am serious. You need to end it with her."

"I will not. I am planning on asking her to marry me!" He dropped the news as if it would be his winning card, but little was he aware I had my deck stacked.

"I know, Rafael, and I am sorry, but you need to end it for the future of the kingdom."

"This is not fair!" He stood up abruptly, raking his fingers through his hair. "I want her, but yet you must think it is mighty *hilarious* to force me to watch my little brother marry my soulmate!" He seethed.

"Rafael, sometimes being royal is not fair." I forced myself to ignore my heart breaking from what I was taking away from him. "I do not think it is hilarious, nor do I like that I am putting you in this situation. You may not like it now, but I promise you will get over her and move on to find love again."

"What do you know about finding love again?" He spat.

"Quite a bit, actually," I countered.

"Oh really? Did Father reject you prior to agreeing to marriage?" He jabbed. I knew he was just trying to get a rise out of me, and I was not going to allow it to get under my skin.

"No, I actually had no intentions of marrying your father. I was in a secret arranged engagement during my courting season." I laid the confession out. We had never told our children the truth of our background, nor did anyone else know about my past engagement. It remained a well-kept secret that had yet to ever circulate.

My son looked at me, completely dumbfounded by this omission.

"Who was he? Did you love him? Did Father steal you from the other guy?" The questions tumbled out of him in an accusatory way.

"Who he is, is no concern. I loved him in the sense of friendship and was quite fond of him. However, he was not who I was in love with. I was actually in love with someone back home when I was only a lady. He broke my heart during the middle of my courting season here. Your father found me crying and offered me a marriage out of convenience and friendship. I agreed to it, and over time, your father and I fell in love. So yes, you will find love again," I answered calmly, the memories of Theo stirring up after years of collecting dust. To this day I have been unable to locate the romance novel with the last pressed flower Theo had gifted me. Even seeing Gideon's daughter did not stir up these feelings as strongly as admitting them out loud to my eldest.

"You and Father did not love each other initially?" His voice dropped to almost a whisper. Over the years, sonnets had been sung of Regalius and my love for each other. To many, we had complimented one another perfectly in a sense. In the beginning, we had put on quite a grand façade to the public, but over time it was no longer an act.

"No, we were friends, but there was no love between us when he asked me."

"Why would Father not choose love for marriage?"

"Because he did not know who truly wanted him or just wanted his crown," I repeated the words Regalius had spoken out loud often in our beginning years. Nervously, at the time, I worried he thought I, too, was using him for his crown. Even though that never had been the case, but it was something that bothered him relentlessly.

"Mina has a crown of her own; she does not want mine," Rafael tried to argue.

I bit my tongue in the matter and moved forward with, "Nevertheless, I do not care what you have to do. You will end it with her, and she will marry your brother, Killien."

"I had to wait my whole life for this stupid courting season, and yet I am still told whom I cannot marry."

"I am sorry it has to be this way, Rafael, but we need Killien to marry her for an alliance between our monarchies to help the trade routes."

Rafael scoffed again.

"End it, Rafael Baylor, I do not care how. But you will end it with Persamina Rowena, and that is the last I will hear of it." I stood up, indicating I would not allow for anymore arguments to unfold. He glared at me, grinding his jaw.

"I wanted to marry her." He growled, stood, and turned on his heel, not waiting for me to say anything. He opened and slammed the door behind him.

Sighing, I returned to my writing desk, staring at the ruined sheet, knowing I would need to re-write it. I hated hurting my eldest like this, but some things were more important than love. It was what I had chanted in the beginning when I spent my days in a loveless marriage. Regalius had been a stranger and I would repeat, *some things are more important than love*. Little did I know that now, my love was more important than some things.

Picking up my self-inking quill, I put the tip on the new sheet of paper. I knew this section would be one of the most difficult ones to write. The story of my life and how I had my hand in making history repeat itself, but with my child. The only bright twist to this story was that Killien was a doting, love-sick, besotted child to his new bride, and in turn, Mina brightened when he entered a room. I, however, could not deny how she looked at Rafael, but I would never be able to write about that as I kept our history clean of all riffraff.

In a month, Killien and Mina would be married, and I would begin her training in the ways of being a Queen. A little something I had agreed upon with Gideon was that I wanted a hand in it. Lydia was to be left out. Gideon had only accepted the offer if he could have additional access to me. I smiled when I agreed to his terms, not allowing myself to reveal my true thoughts on the matter.

What Mina wasn't aware of, is what I had in store for her mother's future. That was another thing that I wouldn't pen in this section. As the author of this book, I could rewrite the section however I wanted. The power I held at my fingertips could destroy many, and in my case, all the dirty details were never recorded. No one would know the true sacrifices the Queen of T'Lovoness, who had risen from status of lady to ruler, had made. Nor would anyone know what I had to accomplish to prevent a war from breaking out from the trade routes. How I soiled my body with another ruler to maintain peace and unbeknownst to him, I now have control of his daughter. As Queen Serenity, I would be known as nothing but the perfect, serene queen to all who read my history book.

Epilogue

(SIX YEARS LATER)

I never believed I would need to prepare my broken heart for this day. The dried tear tracks on my cheeks were covered by new tears. I unwrapped my arm from my granddaughter, Rohanna Myrcella, to wipe my eyes. Glancing down, I checked to see how she was holding up, or if she fully understood why we were all grieving.

Her violet eyes, framed by long silver hair, met mine. I wanted to protect her innocent expression from the devastation she would be facing. I glanced over to her mother. My daughter-in-law, Mina, did not even bother to hide her tears. She held the two youngest children with black hair and green eyes in her arms as they squirmed in her lap. The second eldest child, with black hair and violet eyes, sat on the ground, clinging to the bottom of her dress.

Sobs filled the air as we watched the casket lower into the ground. The crying became deafening. I could not withhold my own strangled cries. The day he passed, a black hole had formed in my heart, and I knew it would never be filled again.

Author's Note

Hello Lovely!

I am so happy you took the time to read my book! I hope you enjoyed the second book in The Courting Seasons series, which followed my beloved Mina's story. Writing Serenity's story has been a complete blast for me. While growing up, I often would write using the name 'Serenity' for a character, but the story never truly became fleshed out. I feel with A Queendom of Heartbreak and Deceit, I am paying homage to my younger self by giving a 'Serenity', a published story.

Many times while writing Serenity's story, I flipped back and forth on whether I wanted it to be two books or one. Eventually, the winner was one book, and I made it two parts. If you're a tandem reader, my website indicates how to read the series in chronological order <3

This is probably one of the shortest author's notes I've written. This past year has been an emotional roller coaster for me as my dad received a terminal cancer diagnosis. He passed away a month before A Queendom of Heartbreak and Deceit was released, and honestly, I am still reeling from it all. To all who have had a loved one pass away from cancer, my sympathy goes out to you.

Thank you once again for reading my book. You will never know how much it means to me to have someone else know about the world and characters I have created!

-N. F. Schmitt

Acknowledgments

Thank you, everyone, for reading Serenity's story in , A Queendom of Heartbreak and Deceit, part of *The Courting Seasons* series. I hope you have loved coming back to the world that gave you Mina's story.

Cody: Thank you for being a wonderful husband and best friend through the years. From being my high school sweetheart to the person I love to spend time with daily, your constant support means everything to me.

My Parents: Thank you both for always supporting me and my dreams. Mom, you will always be the reason I love romance novels, especially with Regency. Dad, I valued every moment we got to spend together this past year after your cancer diagnosis. I know I now have another guardian angel watching over me in life.

Alisha: Thank you for always being my "professional yapper" and pushing me to get out there. You are always there when I need to bounce ideas off of someone, and fan-girl just as hard on my characters as I do. I cannot wait to see what the next adventure brings us!

Amy: Thank you for always supporting me and my writing journey. You're always taking time out of your busy schedule to help me put my train back on its tracks after I derailed it severely, lol. PS. Please forgive me for who the epilogue is about...

Jessica: Thank you for always being there when I bounce my publishing journey off you and listening when I go into detail about where I am considering taking the upcoming stories. Your eagle eye for detail has helped me catch so many little nuances in my stories.

Bookish Sirens: Thank you to my co-founding Admin Team, Dana & Maggie, for always being there to support me while I write my books. These two are family to me, and the book group itself is beyond positive! If you have a moment, please check them out and support Bookish Sirens on Facebook, Instagram, TikTok, and more!

Thank you to all my friends, relatives, and readers who have supported me since I published my first book, and who continuously ask when the next one is coming out. The motivational support has been overwhelming and honestly makes me excited to keep writing the stories in my head.

Social Media

Keep in Touch with N.F. Schmitt

Website: www.NFSchmitt.com
Add me on Facebook: www.facebook.com/n.f.schmitt
Facebook Page: www.facebook.com/NFSchmittAuthor
Instagram: www.instagram.com/n.f.schmitt
E-Mail: NFSchmittAuthor@gmail.com

Want to discuss my books and other fun shenanigans with like-minded readers? Join my reader group:

www.facebook.com/groups/nfschmitt

About the Author

N.F. Schmitt is a born and raised Iowa girl, living in the country with her husband and all their pets. When she doesn't have her nose in a book or head in the clouds, you can find her ATVing most weekends on her dirt bike, video gaming, drawing or planting a new tree in her yard.